I0825392

THE CAVE OF SWORDS

THREADS OF FATE: BOOK ONE

TAYLOR LUST

The Cave of Swords
Threads of Fate: Book One

Cover art by: @dinduarte.jpg
Developmental editing done by: Wendy Higgins of Pink Pen Editing
Formatting and interior design by: @feelinstabbyart
Map done by: Taylor Lust
www.authortaylorlust.com

CONTENT WARNINGS

Please note that The Cave of Swords is an adult fantasy and is not intended for minors. It contains scenes that may be uncomfortable or distressing to some people including strong language, anxiety, panic attacks, blood, violence, death, themes of grief and loss, PTSD, child abuse (referenced as happened in the past), and self-harm (mentioned briefly). This book does not have graphic sexual content but there are some sexually suggestive scenes and language.

PRONUNCIATION GUIDE & TERMS

Nyradonn *(Near-ah-don)* – Undead bone creatures bonded to a chosen human, shifter, witch, or fae (though, they are most commonly bonded to humans). They are often stronger and smarter than in their previous life, and occasionally retain features aside from their bones such as, feathers, claws, wings, and skin.

Eislekest *(Eyes-leh-kest)* – The human kingdom.

Taslae *(Tazz-lay)* – A town in the human kingdom relatively close to the sea and bordering the start of the Lower Tiramunde River.

Tiramunde River *(Tear-ah-mund)* – The main river running through the human kingdom. It is broken up into a lower section and an upper section.

Warille *(War-ill)* – One of the last major towns in the human kingdom before the supposed entrance to the Forbidden Forest. Located close to the Hark River.

Ferrill *(Fare-ill)* – The capital city of Eislekest, the human kingdom, and the home of the human royal family.

Kerimaea *(Care-ah-may-ah)* – The witch queendom.

V'oloth *(Voh-loth)* – A desolate and isolated land located to the south of Kerimaea.

Caelamne *(Kay-lam-nay)* – The fae lands. A massive island containing impressive magic, and located in the northwest.

Rysaram *(Rye-sah-rum)* – A large island in the northeast that is home to the shifter lands and council. It is also the location of the capital, Markael.

Markael *(Marr-kale)* – Capital city of the shifter lands, and home to a legendary library.

Rulanne *(Roo-lawn)* – A smaller island off the coast of Rysaram that is also part of the shifter lands.

Daer e' Mista *(Dare-eye-mist-ah)* – A mythical forest in the northern human lands.

Sela a' Core *(Say-la-ah-core-ay)* – A mythical place mentioned only in legends.

Ilekiir *(Ill-eh-ke-ear)*– A fae word of unknown origin.

Ilphemoura *(Ill-fe-moor-ah)* – The entire realm home to the human, fae, witch, and shifter lands.

Caelamne
T'salae
Sulae
Markael
Mists
of
Sela
Rysaram
Sela a'Core
Daer c'Mista
Laniss Sea
Verre
Sea
Warille
Kingdom of Eislekest
Queendom of Kerimaea
Mara River
Lassa
Laslam
Taslae
Ferrill
Iriad Islands
Thessa Strait
V'oloth
Alphemoura

PROPHECY OF SOULS

One will fail, but all shall succeed.

When five souls journey through the Forbidden Forest, caution must they heed.

A dark ending is waiting – the future written in blood.

The strands of fate are twisting, obscuring divine sight to mud. Tangled truths and long-buried secrets sliced open, the wounds of the past have festered and swollen.

Pain and sorrow, the very foundation of the realm. The Red Threads will call, and those with bonds woven brightest will take the helm.

A cartographer.
A thief.
A witch.
A thread reader.
A weapon's master.

A hidden identity, and a guiding hand. A lost heart, and an agonized soul. The unlikely band held together by a mind wrapped in shadows.

Beware the oily dark, its power lurks deep.
The Lady in Blue's revenge is coming, a devastating power unleashed.

The very fabric of nature was disrupted long ago.
A single death served as punishment, by the name of Kairelo.
Yet things are not always as they seem, and your own reflection may be your undoing. A single battle may be won, but the war will be long and consuming.
The only chance for triumph, a sword the color of sunlit skies, wielded by a –
her light flaring –

For those whose mind screams that they are not enough—I see you.

THE PATH

LAIRA

The world ends when I close my eyes, or at least that's how it always seems. And as I force my eyes open into nothingness, I'm once again swept away into the frighteningly familiar dizzying endlessness around me. While I have some far-off recollection that this is a nightmare, my mind is heavy and full of a dense fog that purges any rational thoughts and plunges them into the abyss. I widen my eyes as far as they can go in a desperate attempt to see something, but this place is so dark that I can't discern up, down, left or right. It's as if I'm floating in empty air, and it's such a disorienting feeling that I close my eyes again, hoping to ease the dizziness. At least, I think I've closed my eyes. Nothing changes, and a rising tide of creeping panic climbs my throat as the darkness closes in, suffocating me. A silent scream builds in my chest, threatening to spill, but I choke it back with haphazard breaths. I don't know if it would make a sound in this complete absence of *anything*.

A voice like scraping stone sounds from every direction, causing a cascade of apprehension to run down my spine.

You must follow the path.

I yell into the void, "What path? I can't *see*!"

Pinpricks of light suddenly appear next to me, and I race toward their protective aura, attempting to use their light to illuminate the empty space and figure out where I am.

Once I am fully engulfed in the glow, it shifts into the wispy outlines of people. They wobble in and out of existence as if they are nothing more than a mirage in an endless desert. I blink, trying to keep them in focus, but I can still only see vague outlines. I think one of them is Willow, but I can't see her face, nor can I see any of the others. I'm not sure how I know it's her, but some intuition whispers that the figure is my friend. A similar feeling overtakes me when I look to the other three figures, though I don't have a name or even a face to put to their forms— only a faint understanding that they are important to me.

It's unnerving and terrifying, but anything is better than the limitless darkness and the voice that accompanied it from before.

I take a tentative step toward the blurry figures, but they race to me instead, taking firm stances on either side of my body. I look down at myself to find I am as semi-translucent as they are, and I shiver at the odd sensation.

Willow's form steps forward, coiling green magic blasting from her and wrapping around a dozen charging bone creatures, crushing them all in one efficient movement before moving on to others. I simultaneously widen my eyes in awe and cringe at the sound of snapping bones like twigs underfoot as the nyradonn are crushed under her relentless power. The creatures continue their unending swarm, and before long, Willow's figure is overtaken. Hundreds of the twisted creatures force her to collapse to the ground even as she throws out whips of green magic, fighting bitterly to the very end. They hold her down until one large nyradonn snaps its head forward to bite through her neck. Bright blood pools, and I flinch as some of the spray hits my face.

I gape in silent horror, feeling down to my very bones that that was *Willow. My best friend, my—*

I don't have time to break down at the sight before my attention is pulled to another gruesome scene. A huge black beast snarls in a swarm of soldiers and more dark nyradonn. Four long muscular legs and paws tipped in razor-sharp claws hold up a partially scaled body with a horned head larger than my entire body. The beast opens its mouth wide, revealing rows of pointed teeth with spittle flying from its muzzle as the nyradonn close in. The bone creatures don't look right—they aren't the gleaming white of my memory but tainted grey with heavy blotches like spilled ink and burdened with a poisonous energy that seeps from their disjointed bodies. They attack the beast relentlessly, and despite its imposing appearance and terrifying presence I have the strangest urge to help it. When a wound opens on its back from a particularly nimble nyradonn, a flash of recognition crosses me and I cry out in alarm, stretching out an arm to help the beast. A tiny ember in my chest pulses, telling me that this is one of the faceless beings from before—someone I know as well as I know myself. I'm utterly desperate to help him as I race across the field, but this battle is being waged too far from me to reach him in time.

When I finally do reach him, I am too late.

The chaos around me continues and the vicious bone creatures find new targets, leaving the heaving beast as he huffs out his final breaths. I fling my body around his head, desperate to save him, but he's dying and there is no saving him now. I stare into his golden yellow eyes as a warm ghostly hand wipes a tear from my face and the life fades from the beast's gaze.

A cacophony of screams sounds from every direction, and it takes me a long time until I realize the screaming is coming from me.

I wilt into a puddle of my own tears, the sobs wracking my body. All I feel is pain. My body is far away, and my mind is breaking into thousands of pieces while the remaining shreds of my heart fall to my feet, useless and limp. I am nothing and no one and the loss I feel is more than I have ever felt before. This unrelenting pain like thousands of tiny needles pressing into my skin and scraping at my bones.

I look up when two bulky figures approach, fighting back-to-back above my hunched position, their swords clanging with each blocked strike. They are fearsome in their power, and I realize they are *protecting* me. The pair hold their own for a long time but eventually even they are overtaken by the horde of vicious bone creatures. They fall together, fighting to the end and I watch them, unable to move but feeling as if my soul has left my body.

I have nothing left.

There is nothing left.

A despair like I've never known pulls me down, down, down into the abyss and I welcome its dark embrace because they are *gone*.

I am utterly lost and broken to the point of no return. Anguish chokes my every breath, but I no longer have the energy to wail. Instead, my arms fall to the side and my head hangs limp, my limbs heavy as stone.

A hollow voice sounds from beside me, as if they are speaking directly into my ear.

Follow the path.

I AM FINE

LAIRA

I wake with a pounding heart. The battle. The blood. The *death*.

No.

Just a nightmare. Sighing, I yank the blanket off in one swoop and move to sit up on the edge of the bed. My room is still, and though it's familiar after many years of living in this small house on the edge of town, I blink into the space as if seeing it anew. The darkness from the nightmare is still heavy in my thoughts and I seek out the single window, the soft dawn light providing reassurance that the darkness outside will soon be dispelled. The bedsheets scratch gently against my skin as I sit up, but I hardly notice the sensation as my eyes rapidly catalogue the room, my mind still primed and searching for danger despite being in a safe space. My mind is addled still from the nightmare and so things that would normally go unnoticed are warped and sinister. Was the wiggling branch outside just the same old tree that's always been there, or a monster clawing its way in? Was that a tower of books or a person huddled in the shadows in the corner of my room?

I squeeze my eyes shut and open them again. The branch outside is clearly just a branch and the pile of books is the same as it's always been—haphazardly stacked against the corner of the room.

I groan aloud. I thought I had mostly stopped having the relentless nightmares that have plagued me since childhood. I thought I was better—fixed. Patched together enough to hide the holes in the fabric and the missing stitches. I place a hand to my chest as if to make sure no such holes persist from where the loss of those unknown figures carved an aching emptiness. Apart from Willow, I didn't know who any of them were, yet I felt their deaths like they were my own, worse in fact. Because the idea of existing without them was the purest form of agony. Tears stream down my face as I sit with the uncomfortable feeling. This nightmare was so unlike the ones I'd had before, and I'm left reeling at the intense emotion of it all.

It's been years since I had regular nightmares. The kind that would have me screaming throughout the night conjuring all sorts of horrific images and waking in a cold sweat in the morning. I wince in shame at their reemergence, sitting forward with my elbows on my knees as I rub my hands gruffly against my face. Nightmares are for children who are afraid of the dark, not for fully grown adults who should have enough common sense to dismiss any irrational fears. It's been over twenty years since the fire that killed my parents and the start of my nightmares; I should be *fine*. I need to be fine, because I cannot go back to the pit of despair I was trapped in before.

Shaking my head in exasperation, I stand and begin pacing in my small bedroom, back and forth in a repetitive rhythm, hands swinging at my sides. A flash of black catches my attention and I freeze in place as I look down at my hand. A thin vein, black as night pulses under my skin and a bolt of alarm swoops over me as I rub at it furiously, hoping it's simply spilled ink or a trick of the light. The vein doesn't budge and the familiar drop in my stomach returns as my fearful mind finds yet another thing to latch onto—the well of emotion threatening to spill over. I feel it bubbling and surging through the doors I've built and the walls I've erected over the years. The heat builds behind my eyes and the threat of frantic sobs has me clutching my chest—but I just *can't*. I can't go back there, I don't want to, and I can't handle this new horror. I attempt to push the swell of anxiety down with the only words I can think of.

I am fine.

I am fine.

I am fine.

I say this mantra out loud until I almost believe it.

I am fine. Fine.

Fine.

Fine.

I am—

And then I crash back to the bed, tears streaming down my face and body crumpling with the weight of everything I wish I didn't have to hold. Of the people I can only carry with me because they no longer exist on this plane. Of the strangers I watched die but feel inexplicably tied to.

The pain and the fear and the sadness pull me into their depths and it's as if I no longer exist. My mind isn't connected to my body, and I am not in control in this moment. This is the part that scares me most—the fear of my past, present, and future gripping me so strongly that my mind becomes trapped in a cage of my own making, never to find my way free again. The loss of careful control rushes away from me like water carrying away branches in a storm, and it's all I can do to stay afloat.

Distantly, like a shout from another room, a lone thought urges me to get a hold of myself before I delve deeper into this panic spiral. I have tasks to do and a bookshop to open, and I must *get up*.

This thought is enough to bring me back to my body momentarily, and I prop myself on the bed, searching the room through watery eyes for clean clothing to wear. I spot the pants I wore yesterday and a shirt crumpled on the floor. Kel hops next to me from the foot of the bed, his feathers brushing against my leg as he does, and I pat his smooth skull, somewhat soothed by his steady presence.

"What am I going to do, Kel?" I mumble under my breath.

He doesn't answer, and so I slowly shift to the edge of the bed, bracing my hands on the frame, creating a cage of flesh on either side of my hips and hoping the pressure is enough to bring me back into my body fully. I sit on the edge for a few moments, waiting for my breathing to return to an even pace and the threat of tears to subside. Feeling slightly more in control, I take a deep inhale and release it before pushing to stand once more.

Stiffly, I pull on a fresh pair of undergarments and slide the pants from yesterday on. The shirt follows, along with a leather vest, which I button slowly before using the two straps on the side to lightly strap over my stomach. A leather pouch with my shop notebook inside is next, resting comfortably on my hip.

The washroom beckons, and I splash water on my face, bringing me a little more into the present and away from the breath-stealing anxious thoughts. I don't bother finding a comb, instead running a few wet fingers through the strands—my hair is straight as an arrow anyway, and it would take too much of my dwindling energy to find the missing comb.

The last thing I do before leaving my bedroom is place my necklace over my head. Its comforting weight rests between my breasts, and I inhale deeply at the feeling. I grip the slender stone with my hand and squeeze. I've had this necklace since before I can properly remember—Mother said I found the pearlescent stone one day and begged her to fashion it into something I could wear. She told me later that I wouldn't let the idea go all night, and so the next day she went into town for some wire and a chain, and here I am now with my necklace. A beautiful reminder of her and the only thing I have from my previous life.

With my morning routine nearly finished, I head into the main room in search of my boots, nearly colliding with Kel as he clatters down from the rafters.

"Hey bud, how are ya?"

I absentmindedly hold my arm out for him to land and pat his skull. He lets out a little screech in appreciation and moves his head more firmly into my hand, brushing his crooked feathers against me in the process.

Laughing, I give in to his demands for more pets. "Spoiled little bird."

Talking to Kel as if he can understand me soothes my fragile nerves, plus it helps to fill the silence in this house. It's entirely possible he can understand me to an extent, but I wasn't the fae to raise him from the dead, so I don't quite have the connection to him that I would if I were his true bone-bonded. I'm not sure why he doesn't have a bonded, or if he does, why he's not with them now. Either way, I am grateful for his companionship. Even if his bones aren't set quite right, causing him to clatter loudly in comparison to other nyradonn—and giving himself away when he attempts to hide in rafters.

It's not his fault he's so poorly put together, but that doesn't stop the criticizing eyes or the disapproving whispers whenever we venture into town.

"I'm running late Kel, so no breakfast I'm afraid. Not that you need to eat anyway, but this also means not as much time for head scratching!"

I grab my bag and place my hand on the door handle to leave. I'm about to push it open when I pause, a heavy weight settling on my wrist. I can't hold the nightmare in my thoughts for the rest of the day or it will drive me to madness, and so, into the caged ocean it goes. I will not let it surface if I can help it. Pinching my brows together and closing my eyes, I take a deep inhale and then exhale while slowly turning the handle and stepping through the doorway into the morning light.

I am not fine. But I need to be.

FOLKTALES, WORN LEATHER, & MAGIC

LAIRA

The path to the shop isn't a long one, but it still takes enough time to allow the sun to fully crest above the horizon. I sling my bag over my shoulder and glance up to Kel flying high above me. It's comforting to know that he has my back, though it's unlikely anything should go wrong simply walking to my shop in broad daylight. The air is crisp, and the slight chill makes me shiver as I trudge along the stone street. The cobblestones are worn from hundreds of years of passersby and despite the town's best efforts, grasses and moss still claw their way through the cracks in the stones—an attempt by nature to reclaim its territory. Taslae has been an established town for many centuries, and while it's not as sizable as the human capital city of Ferrill, it still boasts a wide variety of shops, businesses, and homes.

The smooth stone and wood fronts of buildings gaze blankly back at me in the early morning, and only a few people mill about in the streets. Their cloaks pulled tight to keep out the cool morning and their heads low as they start yet another day. Side streets begin to come into focus as the sun crests the horizon and illuminates each hidden crevice. Unlike Ferrill, we don't boast gifted fae elemental magic to keep streetlamps running, and it's too expensive to constantly fill them with oil, so we are beholden to the rise and fall of the sun.

I pass under a clothesline as I cut through a smaller path and notice a trio of young children sitting on a nearby stoop. I can't help but give them a small smile as I pass. A giant bone creature watches over the children, its slouched back and wide head bringing to mind a bear, though I can't be certain. Either way, it's certainly intimidating enough to protect the children without adult supervision. Its skeletal body is relaxed and ready to jump forward should they need it, but the trio sits happily at its feet, playing in the mud and splattering brown goop on the nyradonn's pristine white bones.

I'm caught in my own memories of frolicking in the mud with my sister, when a flash of red catches my attention, making me double-take and study the group more closely. It takes some focus, but the thin red strand becomes clearer, eventually coalescing into the shape of a single faint thread hovering in the air and connecting the three children. It isn't very bright, like an old red shirt bleached from the sun, but it links the three children in a small circle. The thread pulling from each of their chests, twisting and floating gently as it weaves through them.

The thin thread likely indicates a new bond, one that could potentially grow stronger or fade away with time. Perhaps the children have just met? I study their features as I continue past the trio. They all appear to have different hair colors and face shapes which could mean they're not related and have only recently come into each other's lives. Their nyradonn notices my attention and I feel its energy dip towards me, a warning and a silent demand to keep moving. I nod my head in acquiescence, not wanting to provoke the creature and quickly tear my gaze from the children, increasing my pace down the long road. As I walk down the street, they begin to sing an old children's rhyme. The sound of their voices should be happy and excited, but it sounds haunting and ominous to my ears in the relative silence of the morning.

The Lady in Blue was tall and fair.
With flowers woven in her hair.
Her eyes the color of blackest night,
She always shone with the brightest light.
But then one day, she caused a war.
Causing destruction and lands torn.
Oh, watch out for the Lady in Blue,
Her magic is strong,

Her magic is wrong.

Her magic will bind you by the end of this song.

The children sing it over and over again. Jumping in to correct each other when they get a word wrong and joyously singing the morbid words while playing in the dirt. I shiver and try my best to force the melody from my head. I don't need something like that setting off my already precarious emotions this morning. I have work to do. A new shipment of books should have been delivered, and it will take me all morning, if not most of the afternoon, to unbox and catalog them all, and I do not have time for more childhood fantasies and nightmares to distract me.

Arriving at the front door, I pull out my ring of keys. They clink together as I turn the lock and step into the shop, immediately welcomed by hundreds of books and tall neatly positioned shelves. The early morning light filtering through the front window is just enough to illuminate the space, and I smile as if walking into a room full of friends and family.

I go about my initial morning duties—the tasks so routine at this point that I don't even have to think while doing them.

Light the candle and sconces.

Pull the open sign onto the street.

Survey the notes I left myself from the previous shift and figure out what books I should highlight for the day.

I prefer my lists and careful notes. Having things to cross out gives a greater feeling of accomplishment, and if I write them down, I won't have the gnawing feeling that I am forgetting something. Without my list, I wouldn't even know where to begin, and I'd become aimless in my tasks—getting lost in different projects and skipping to things my mind wants to do instead of what it needs to do in order to keep my shop running smoothly.

Satisfied, I walk around to the back of the shop to where Armas should have delivered the new books. Sure enough, five perfect boxes sit—they would normally be monstrously heavy since they are kept in wooden crates—but Armas knows that I'm not quite capable of lifting so much, nor do I have a nyradonn that could assist in said lifting. When he saw me attempting to carry armloads of books from the massive crates into my shop a few years ago, tripping and dropping books the entire time, I think he felt pity for me and since then has delivered only these smaller and much more manageable boxes.

There is something so incredibly calming and exciting about opening new books and deciding where they should go, and with today likely being a slow day in the shop, I should have plenty of time to sort through them all. Before I know it, a large pile of books surrounds me. Each stack a different category for easy sorting later. I reach back blindly into the last box for my next book to sort, automatically continuing my routine of first examining the cover to determine its condition and then checking the book's contents. But the book in my hands is different than the others in the box; it's much smaller and rather plain.

I frown at it. Plain books are harder to sell—people want flashy titles and intricate designs, not a simple cloth-bound brown tome that could fit in a child's hands. There isn't even a title on it, and as I flip through it, I find that I can't read any of the words scrawled inside. What is this? Perhaps a journal or a simple notebook that was mixed in with the others? I flip again through the pages to be sure. After all, if it doesn't have a title but if I can figure out what book it is, then I could add one myself. Each page is carefully and meticulously handwritten with drawings of landscapes, people, cities, and creatures. From what I can tell, this looks like an old collection of history or someone's field notebook. It must be ancient with how faded the ink is and how derelict the cover is.

I can barely make out what is written on the bulk of the pages. It's in a language that I don't know, though there are some words that stand out and appear to be similar to ones used today. Maybe it's an old fae language? I gape at the small book as I continue to carefully turn each page, astounded at the amount of history that must be contained in this book. If I could get this translated, this could be worth far more than the others if it really is as old as I think it could be.

Kel chirps at me, and I hazard a glance outside to see the light beginning to wane. If I want to make it home before nightfall, I need to leave now. Without a second thought, I place the book carefully in the pouch at my hip and grab my cloak before locking up and returning home.

THE PROPHECY OF SOULS

LAIRA

In the comforting light of my lit sconce, I tuck into bed to flip through the worn book. The bed is small and shoved into the corner of the room; a necessary sacrifice to fit my desk and bookshelves. The shelves overflow with books and various trinkets. Some from my own collection and others from Kel's incessant need to steal anything shiny. It makes for a strange mix of more practical items like candles and bottles, along with broken spoons, bits of metal, and beaded ribbons. But it's impossible to say no to the little creature when he so proudly drops an old scrap of metal at my feet, even if he did steal it.

I pull my blanket higher to cover my thighs and lean against the bed frame, eager to examine the simple book more closely. Kel hops up to nestle at my feet, his body positioned to face the open door as he always does. My precious little guardian. My home is far removed from the center of town and unlikely to face intruders, in an area that is not often trafficked and tucked close to the forest surrounding Taslae. It's a quiet and slow part of town, which is favorable for avoiding the bulk of the nosy townsfolk. Though they have left me alone in recent years, it wasn't always that way. When I first arrived, with an imperfect nyradonn and clear fae heritage, I wasn't necessarily harassed, but I was not welcomed either. I was eyed with careful scrutiny and whispered about in close circles, the busy shops turning just a bit quieter whenever I entered with Kel at my back. The fae have an open invitation to travel through the human kingdom, just as the shifters and witches do, but it is such a rare occurrence that it never fails to draw attention. Even if said "fae" only has enough fae blood for pointed ears and strangely colored hair.

My eyes droop as I turn each page, the unknown words making my vision blurry as I skim over them, until I reach the end. A jolt of recognition floods my mind as I realize there are words on the last page that I can understand. My stomach swoops as I scan the page, my eyes snagging on the scribbled words in the common tongue and frown as I touch the bottom of the page where the paper is roughly torn.

"The Prophecy of Souls?"

I glance at Kel and he cocks his head to the side to look back at me.

"Sounds ominous."

Kel nods his head, and a shiver runs down my spine as I feel my eyes drawn back to the page, even though I have the sudden itch to close the book and never open it again. It's as if I'm hurtling down a hill, unable to stop myself and completely at the mercy of the ground beneath me as I force my hands to still and focus on the first line.

"One will fail, but all shall succeed?"

I squint up at the ceiling at the odd phrase, and a tingle runs down my spine. My necklace flares with sudden heat, and I instinctively drop the book, touching a cautious hand to my chest at the odd sensation.

"What was that?"

I grab the necklace from under my shirt by its chain and stare at it like it's going to bite me, hurriedly taking it off before it can burn me again. Dropping it quickly onto the short table next to me does little to soothe my frayed nerves and I watch it intently for a long moment, deciding if I should continue or not. I glance at the book splayed out on the wooden floor and a well of emotion floods my chest, the rising tide nearly stealing the breath from my lungs at its sudden intensity. The want and urgency to grab the book once more makes my skin prickle, and I shiver from the ferocity of it. A vague awareness tickles the back of my neck, like something is waiting for me to continue as my hand lifts of its own accord, and I find that I can't turn away from the melodic call echoing inside me. There is something so hauntingly familiar about these words and what trepidation I have is quickly replaced by relief as I gingerly pick the book up from the floor and continue to read aloud.

"One will fail, but all shall succeed. When five souls journey through the

Forbidden Forest, caution must they heed. A dark ending is waiting—the future written in blood."

The words sound strangely songlike as they leave my mouth, and my necklace glows as I speak. I stare open-mouthed, utterly at a loss for words. The soft light appears white at first, but as it continues glowing it pulses with not just white but bits of red, blue, green, orange, and yellow. Like the light that reflects off a mirror or a multicolored gem shining just right in the sun. But as quickly as it appeared, the light is gone.

I look to the book again, biting the inside of my cheek and wondering if I'm crazy in thinking these words made my necklace glow or if it's just some wild coincidence. It won't hurt to read it again to be sure, but my heart rebels at the thought of it happening again even as my body is flooded with recognition and the itch to read further. I glance around to make sure I'm alone, paranoid even though I'm at home and well away from any prying eyes.

Satisfied that I am indeed alone, I inhale a deep breath and start from the top of the page again. "One will fail, but all shall succeed."

I glance cautiously at the necklace as I speak the words, and it begins to glow softly again—the same vibrant colors swirling—and as I trail off, the glow dies down.

Ah, so it is tied to these words somehow, I mentally affirm.

Despite being somewhat pleased I discovered the cause for the strange reaction, I still don't want to consider what form of magic may be tied to this book. How is it possible that a hunk of rock I've worn since childhood is reacting to words from a book potentially hundreds of years old, if not older? Acid bubbles in my stomach, but I ignore the warning, convincing myself that this is only an incredibly odd coincidence and nothing more.

"But if it's only making it glow, surely it can't be dangerous. Right?" I ask Kel as he sits at my feet in an attempt to calm my racing heart. He looks at me and tilts his head to the side before bobbing his head once.

Apparently, that is all the confirmation I need, because I don't hesitate before turning back to the book and continuing to read, unable to stop myself. The strange warmth in my chest purrs at my decision and I hungrily devour the words, speaking them aloud once more into the heavy silence of the room.

"One will fail, but all shall succeed. When five souls journey through the Forbidden Forest, caution must they heed. A dark ending is waiting—the future written in blood. The strands of fate are twisting, obscuring divine sight to mud. Tangled truths and long-buried secrets sliced open, the wounds of the past have festered and swollen. Pain and sorrow, the very foundation of the realm. The Red Threads will call, and those with bonds woven brightest will take the helm. A cartographer. A thief. A witch. A thread reader. A weapon's master. A hidden identity, and a guiding hand. A lost heart, and an agonized soul. The unlikely band held together by a mind wrapped in shadows. Beware the oily dark, its power lurks deep. The Lady in Blue's revenge is coming, a devastating power unleashed. The very fabric of nature was disrupted long ago. A single death served as punishment, by the name of Kairelo. Yet things are not always as they seem, and your own reflection may be your undoing. A single battle may be won, but the war will be long and consuming. The only chance for triumph, a sword the color of sunlit skies, wielded by a—her light flaring—"

My voice falters as I try to read the torn bottom of the page, but only a few words of the following passage are visible. Even so, a bright white light flares from the direction of my necklace, and I shield my eyes from the glow. When it dies down, my breath lodges in my throat. It's the same necklace sitting harmlessly on the small table as before, the same chain and old wire carefully wrapped around the long thin stone.

But the stone.

Parts of it have morphed into beautiful bright patterns of red, orange, blue, and green—reflections of the light it was emitting earlier. I peer down at it as the flecks of colors catch the light from the lit sconces along the walls in the most beautiful way, as if a living sunset is caught inside. Parts of the long stone look just as ordinary and plain as before, as if the process is incomplete. I hover my hand over the necklace to make sure it isn't hot before picking it up and holding it in front of my face. Tilting it back and forth causes new colors to emerge and others to disappear—it's utterly fascinating and extraordinarily beautiful, even if only half of it is colorful now.

I hear Kel behind me, his clattering bones breaking me from my examination of the stone.

"What is this? What happened to it?" I ask him, though of course he can't give me an answer.

More questions swirl in my mind, ones I don't have a single answer to. Is this just because of the words I spoke? Why my necklace?

Could it be a spell? Would Willow know something? And what about the odd familiarity that came over me as I read?

My head spins, and I need to figure out some sort of plan before I'm driven mad by the questions cresting like an unstoppable wave. My eyes snag on one line, and I whisper it softly to myself again, the words coming unbidden—bubbling up like water set to boil.

"The Lady in Blue's revenge is coming, a devastating power unleashed."

The Lady in Blue? As in the old children's rhyme? I shiver at the odd coincidence of having just heard that tune earlier today.

And what is this about battles and wars? Are the rumors swirling around town true after all? There are too many questions and not nearly enough answers. I groan aloud in frustration and Kel flutters atop me to rest his head against my arm in comfort.

There have been whispers for some time now of a dark mass growing off the coast of the Kerimaea, emerging from the lost lands of V'oloth to the south. Lands that are desolate and isolated, with nothing and no one capable of living there. The deadly weather and dangerous terrain are simply incompatible with life, and yet, the most outrageous of these rumors claim to have seen a lone figure standing on the coast and nyradonn swimming along the edges of the dark fog surrounding V'oloth and venturing up the coast.

I had thought these fanciful tales I'd heard in the tavern claiming encounters with monsters were entirely that—fairytales and boasting from drunken travelers. Stories originating from so far away along the shores of the witch queendom and V'oloth, that they seemed even further from reality. But what if these stories have some truth to them?

My head feels as if it's about to explode. There are too many questions, too many fears, and too many unknowns. The loss of control and the sinking feeling in my chest has me spiraling at the sudden thought of Taslae being overrun by vicious creatures, even if that is a remote possibility. But once the idea sinks its teeth into me, it takes everything in me not to want to bolt down every door and hide.

I take a deep cleansing breath. *There is no danger here,* I remind myself. If these rumors are more than just creations of the mind, then I'm sure the king's forces will take care of it.

A sudden flash of red fills my vision, and I furiously try to blink it away—not wanting to deal with the threads right now—but am assaulted instead by a scene of buildings torn to rubble and a scent like death filling my nose. A bony claw creeps into my vision, and I jolt back at the sight, jumping from bed and crashing into a bookshelf, knocking several books to the ground. The movement is enough to dispel the terrifying scene, and I shake my head violently to further release it from its hold on my mind.

A lilting voice echoes in the room, soft as a whisper, and speaks three simple words that turn me to stone.

"War is coming."

I whip my head around to find the source of the voice, but the room and the rest of the house are empty, save for myself and Kel.

I tell myself that it was only my imagination and anxiety playing a cruel trick on me once again, stealing my senses and forcing me to watch a worst-case scenario—but a small voice still stalks deep in my mind, cursing me to consider something truly terrible could be on its way. The prophecy's words and what I just experienced race through my head. Of blood and death and the resigned voice whispering of oncoming war—encouraging my already wild thoughts to continue spiraling down an inevitable path of suffering and chaos.

"No. This is just in my mind, it's not real," I say aloud, my hands balled into fists at my side, willing the statement to be true.

But what if it's not? My own insidious voice in my mind comes again, always warning me of potential danger but in the most alarming way possible. This part of me used to be my voice of reason. It was useful and even comforting. It kept me safe when I was alone as a child and in strange houses or unfamiliar cities, but now all it does is caution me against things that haven't even happened and likely never will. It screams at me to be afraid of anything that lurks in the dark and replays every terrible thought I can conjure, working me into a panic-induced frenzy until all I can think is that I won't survive the night. I've been fighting this fearful voice in my head for many years, but despite my best efforts to push it away it still comes through when shadows dance in the waning light or when I'm caught off guard.

It pounces on me again, digging in its talons and forcing me to consider this awful future. If there really is a war coming like the dark rumors circling around town say, then someone else—*anyone else*—needs to make the decisions and defeat this new enemy. Even if lines from this page feel familiar and ring with truths I don't want to acknowledge, the thought of involving myself is utterly ridiculous. I am no hero. This book and this prophecy must be shown to Taslae's council and the king's soldiers stationed around town. If the rumors are true, then surely they would want this information if it could offer even a hint of what is to come.

I look uncertainly at the book sitting on my bed. Its pages are filled with basic, albeit old, history—that much is clear from the drawings, even if I can't read most of the words, but the last few pages have only a broken prophecy and nonsense scribbled in the margins. Would anyone really take that seriously?

The lilting voice whispers through the room again, *"Darkness is coming, and untold destruction will follow."*

The foreboding words filter through my mind, and I whip my head around the room once again to find the source, but the air is still and I sense nothing.

"It's nothing. I am alone and safe. I am simply tired and on edge. There is no voice. It is all in my mind." I speak the words aloud and will them to be true. Even if they aren't, I get enough peace from them to not lose myself—though I do take a moment to check that the window is closed and mentally confirm I locked the front door.

Shakily, I inhale deeply and close my eyes, attempting to ignore the crawling sensation of feeling as if I'm being watched, when another scene of war flashes behind my closed lids once again. I flinch and suck in a breath, flinging my eyes open to dispel the vision, but it plays across my mind anyway. The devastation is severe, the realm as we know it utterly lost in the chaos. As if from a bird's eye view, I look down upon the destruction—at the dead world I once inhabited and feel immeasurable loss. From what I know of history, we haven't had a serious war in over a thousand years and have been in a time of unprecedented peace. The horrible vision recedes, and I'm left standing alone in my room once again. Kel bumps his head against my hand from atop the bed and I kneel to be at his level.

"Kel, what if this prophecy is important? What if it's not some random book? I know my anxiety conjures visions that aren't there, but they are almost always rooted in some truth I haven't yet spotted. And I don't even want to think of that voice…" I shiver and squeeze my eyes shut, as if to block out the memory of the voice and the possibility that it was not simply my imagination.

Kel chirps softly, but when I open my eyes he isn't right in front of me, he's standing behind the discarded open book at the foot of the bed. He lifts a single foot and taps the book once. I lift a curious brow when he nudges it closer to me and stares expectantly.

"You think it's important?" I ask as I hesitantly pick up the book.

Gone is the normal cheerful and somewhat erratic motions of Kel, instead he has a strangely serious demeaner as he slowly walks forward and bows his head ever so slightly. Kel has never been wrong about something before. He's always guided me away from danger and helped keep me calm when I was adrift in my own helpless thoughts. I dart a glance to the book splayed out under my hands—my intuition warring with my want to not have this be my responsibility. But the part of me that strives to do the right thing eventually wins out over my fear and uncertainty. If this book—this *prophecy*—can help prevent bloodshed even just a little, don't I owe it to the realm to say something? Even if it's truly nothing in the end? And what of the note scribbled off to the side?

The bonds of Ilekiir offer strength in the end.

I shake my head. I can't solve every mystery right now. *But perhaps I don't need to solve it and the bloody visions will go away if it's not in my possession any longer,* I think hopefully.

"I'll take it into town tomorrow. Maybe show it to the king's guards and they can take it from there," I say aloud to myself and to Kel, set in my decision even as a feeling deep in my chest writhes at the possibility of being separated from the book.

THE THREAD READER

LAIRA

I wake groggy and scatter-brained the following day, rushing through my morning routine. The book's energy seems to pulse; it sucks the air from my lungs and suffocates my small room. Even as it sits innocently on my bedside table, it pulls my focus. Distracting me enough that I trip over myself, throwing my shirt on backwards before having to fix it and buckling my satchel on with clumsy fingers. I reluctantly place the book into the satchel strung at my hip and recall the spots I'd seen the king's guards stationed around town recently. They had started popping up with more frequency over the last few months—perhaps another indication of trouble brewing—but I hadn't paid them much attention, choosing instead to give them a wide berth and stick to my well-traveled side streets. I pat my shoulder, and Kel lands on me as I race out of the house.

I just need to be rid of this book, and it will be okay. Someone else will deal with this mess – if it's even deemed important enough to look into, I mentally reassure myself.

Something tells me that this book is important though—that it truly does contain a dire warning and a potential dark future. It's either that, or I have gone completely mad hearing voices and seeing bloody visions. And I'm not quite ready to admit that could be a possibility. My mind whirls with questions, but it feels steady enough for now. I just need to hold out hope that the king will know what to do and use the information to fight off whatever darkness appears to be on the horizon. And perhaps the rest of the book is not simple history like I believe, but more information that could be useful—the only way to know is to have it translated.

The walk from my home into town is often a pleasant stroll through cozy wood and stone homes neatly trimmed with bushes and trees that line either side of the cobblestone road. Turning off the side street from my house, I keep to the edge of the main road to stay out of the way of busier traffic. Soft blades of grass sprout between the stones along the edges, the grass muffling my steps as I weave around people meandering down the road. Normally, this part of town is busy but still has an air of practiced everyday calm. Everyone has their set daily tasks, and it teems with the monotony of life. This morning, however, it feels as if there is a fog over the streets, heavy with paranoia and held aloft by rumors, secrets, and fears—or perhaps that is my own restless mind talking.

Neon red eyes peer at me when I close my eyes, and flashes of dark bony creatures stalk innocents in the streets, conjured by my mind. They lurk outside my vision, and when I turn to get a better look, they disappear. There are no official reports of any attacks as far as I've heard, but I'm increasingly paranoid after reading the prophecy and jumpy from the visions that prowl my mind. I keep my steps light and my head on a swivel as I survey the streets and back alleys, ready at a moment's notice to flee.

I cut through a narrow side street to enter the town square, and my gaze catches on a trio of soldiers that stand at attention near the town hall. Their shiny silver adornments on their perfectly pressed uniforms make them difficult to miss in the bright morning light.

The middle of the three soldiers talks to folks as they pass while the other two stand unmoving with expressionless faces, their eyes and most of their cheeks covered in silver metal armor. The chatty one has a warm and pleasant demeanor and manages to snag a few people to listen to what he has to say. I join the group but only hear the end of the conversation, his smooth words causing alarm bells to ring in my head.

"—and that is why we need dedicated folks like you all to join our ranks and protect the great Kingdom of Eislekest. Justice and honor! These are the two promises every Knight makes—to uphold justice in the name of His Majesty, and to honor every being in our kingdom."

A woman adjusts a child on her hip, asking skeptically, "But I thought the rumors of dark creatures and war were false. Isn't that why you lot are here? To assure us of our safety?"

The soldier smiles warmly, giving her his utmost focus. A chill runs down my spine at the mechanical way he switches his attention so swiftly.

"Of course, you are most correct. There is no coming war, and you are all safe here. Any who sign up do so willingly, and we welcome them, though we certainly don't need the extra manpower. Signing up, however, does guarantee stable income and the opportunity to earn a higher title. The King's Army and generosity is grand indeed."

Suddenly, his smile seems far too cheerful, and the way he blocks out the other people gathering around to focus solely on the older woman sets me on edge. This soldier is lying. I know he is. I glance around to see if the others notice his deception, but all I see are nodding heads and relieved smiles. There's even a few young men and women elbowing each other and pointing to the sign next to the soldiers with an already long list of names. Not a single person is skeptical of his honeyed words or notices the tight grip the two soldiers behind him have on the swords gleaming at their sides.

If he is indeed lying, then this situation may be closer to my horrific imaginings than I'd like to think. Which means showing them the book, and the Prophecy of Souls as it was called, is even more important. If they are so desperate for people to join their ranks, then surely they will welcome this book and its knowledge. Though they likely won't talk to me honestly until the crowd has dispersed. I mentally decide to wait them out until I can talk to them freely and alone.

This turns out to take most of the day as more and more people show up to ask curious questions or voice approval over the king's clear dedication to his people. Every question is met with the same fake smile and deceptive words, but no one bats an eye. It's as if only I can see the insincerity of the soldier's words—making me question if maybe I have it wrong and am reading too much into it all.

It's not until late afternoon that the townsfolk seem to grow bored with the soldiers and leave them to attend to their own work. My heart races at the prospect of finally going to talk to them, but I know I will not get a better opportunity anytime soon. The main soldier gives me a wide smile as I approach and begins speaking as soon as I get close.

"Well hello there, Miss! What can the we do for you? Perhaps you are interested in signing up for service to the king as well?" He gestures towards the now long list of names posted beside him.

"Actually..." I unbuckle the satchel at my hip to grab the book. I clench it tightly before motioning for the soldier to take it from me. "I found this old book in a recent shipment for my store, and I noticed that it possibly has important information about..." I discreetly glance around me to ensure no one is listening and lean forward, speaking softly, "About the war that is coming."

The warm smile drops from his face immediately upon mention of the word war, but he catches his mistake and plasters a new one on before I even blink. He doesn't speak, but he does watch me carefully, his eyes darting between mine for a long moment as if to gauge my sincerity before he looks down to examine the book. He flips through the pages roughly, his mouth turning ever so slightly into a sneer.

"Miss, this book is in an entirely different language, and what's more, it appears to only have descriptions of plant life and creatures based on the illustrations." I hear the doubt in his voice, and he raises an eyebrow as he continues, "How exactly is this important information for us to know?"

Nervously wringing my hands, my defense spills from my mouth. "Well if you turn to the last few pages—the very last page to be specific—it changes to the common tongue, and there is what appears to be a prophecy foretelling doom and destruction and chaos and—"

He closes the book in a quick motion that makes me jump and interrupts my tirade. He pushes the book back into my hands and leans close, his calm demeanor and cheerful attitude gone. Replaced instead with a judgmental disdain that says he is done listening to me and has not taken the book—or what I have to say—seriously.

His voice is low and sharp, a hiss that reminds me of an angry snake. "Young Miss. You seem to be confused and misled. As I have said before, there is no war coming, and you and this entire kingdom are *safe*."

"But, this book, it..." I stammer.

He stands straight, his body looming tall over me, and the sight of his hand casually reaching for the sword at his hip makes my knees lock. But I have no choice, I have to convince him. If they don't listen to me then I will be forced to do something about this prophecy out of sheer duty, and it *can't* be me.

It just can't.

I press on, "Look, I know it sounds unlikely, but I really do think you should take a closer look at this book. What if it is important and you are casting it aside? What if..."

A flash of ghostly black catches my attention from the corner of my vision, and I trail off, giving the soldier the opening to speak again.

"Miss, I can assure you that anything the king needs to know, he is told by his advisors. Besides, His Majesty has access to thousands of tomes in the palace library. It is likely this little book is already in his possession. In fact, what you have is almost certainly a copy, and the last pages are random musings written by a past owner."

I open my mouth to protest—I know when a book is original, and this is certainly no copy. However, another flash of darkness coating my vision distracts me, and the soldier decides I have accepted his pacification and will now move on. I squeeze my eyes shut, feeling the intense shame of failure at not being taken seriously and not being able to explain myself in a way that they will understand. My overactive imagination once again holding me back and preventing me from thinking clearly. The familiar fear is insidious and with these new visions, it's all I can do to not panic.

This is all in your head. Ignore the darkness and make them understand, I mentally chastise, having no patience today for a mind that only plays tricks on me.

I continue to stand in front of the soldiers, unwilling to move and not ready to give up on handing off this book to someone more important than myself. But the darkness from moments before is not done with me, and a smoky claw creeps into the edges of my awareness. I nearly jump away in alarm as it reaches for me and gasp as my vision goes completely black.

I've had panic attacks intense enough to cause dizziness and dark spots in my vision before, but this feels heavier. Thick like oil and so dark it's immediately disorienting. I sway on my feet, and the soldier catches me with a firm grip on my elbow before I can fall.

"Are you unwell? Perhaps you should see a physician."

His voice is distant as I battle to keep upright and continue arguing my case, desperate to fulfill this task. A new imagined scenario crashes over me like a wave on the shore, breaking through the oily dark in my mind and materializing as a horrific scene of a large cat-like nyradonn mauling a human soldier. His head is sent rolling, and I immediately feel nauseous as I watch the blood that pools under it.

"Stop!" I shout to the scene in my mind before it dissipates, and I realize I screamed aloud to the soldiers. I press my mouth closed and throw both hands to my head, blinking rapidly to clear my vision. The soldiers look at me with a mix of judgment and disgust, and the small amount of confidence I had in approaching them fizzles out. Words fall from my lips as I realize I never answered their previous question.

I back away slowly, muttering, "No, that is alright. Thank you for your help. I think I just felt a little dizzy for a moment, but I am fine and will go home to rest."

He lets me go easily, returning to his carefree attitude from earlier as he chirps, "Of course! His Majesty's Army is happy to be of assistance. Be sure to get home and rest."

As soon as I turn to walk away, the darkness clears from my vision, as if it was waiting for me to give up on handing the book off and is rewarding me for abandoning the mission. I shiver as the thought crosses my mind, not enjoying the idea that my unconscious mind is fighting me in such a way. I see the long street out of the town square clearly, but I rub my arms and squeeze my eyes shut as the man's head rolls again.

So much blood. And the way his body crumpled—

"No! Stop this." I whisper harshly to myself. "It was nothing, just my imagination again, albeit horrible. I probably just felt dizzy from locking my legs and being nervous. That's. All."

My shoulders relax, and I nod at the simple explanation, because that's all it must be. I was nervous talking to the soldiers, and I wasn't standing properly for correct blood flow, thus causing me to feel faint.

I make it to a nearby alleyway before I question myself again and stop in my tracks to decide if I should try with a different set of soldiers. Because if someone doesn't take this book and use it, then I will feel compelled to. Two words echo in my mind and I grit my teeth as I try to dispel them, but it doesn't work and they flow on repeat.

Thread reader. Thread reader. Thread reader.

The cadence is as steady as beating drums and just as loud—they pound through my head over and over. Drilling into my chest and the rest of my body until my blood pulses with the words, and the knowledge that they could be talking about me. Because I've never met another person who could see threads. Who could see the bonds that connect people through life and through death. Of someone who could determine familial attachments or destined connections, like I can. Not even the few fae books detailing their magical abilities that I've gotten ahold of mentioned anything of the sort. The fae's magic lies only with the elements or with wild creatures. And the witches have no such magic either. Willow explained it to me once after I revealed my secret, informing me that their magic is connected to the natural world. To the plants and the soil, and occasionally—for the most powerful—a connection to the flesh, a magic that can heal wounds and purge illnesses. The shifters don't appear to have this sort of magic either, just the ability to shift into their born creature and the innate power to use the skills that creature possesses. As far as I know, I am the only one with this specific magic. The knowledge that this prophecy mentions the threads and calls for a thread reader is enough to make me sick to my stomach. Even I cannot so easily dismiss that coincidence.

The ocean of anxiety sloshing inside of me roils at the thought of examining the prophecy closer and taking action. At being the thread reader it mentions. Because I'm not built for adventure, and I'm certainly not powerful enough to take on whoever this Lady in Blue person is. This is a job for a trained army, not for five random individuals on the hunt for some ancient sword like the prophecy says. And it's definitely not for someone like me.

With a heavy sigh, I decide I'm not ready to head home quite yet, and so I turn around, avoiding the center square where the guards are still posted to find a quiet bench to sit on. I lean back, suddenly exhausted and full of so many mismatched thoughts that I have no way to know where to begin untangling them. Trimmed bushes tickle my scalp and I have the vague sense that I must have wandered into the gardens on the southern side of town when I hear a gruff voice behind me.

"Sir, I have news to report."

The voice is familiar, and I realize with alarm that it belongs to the soldier I talked to earlier. The person who answers him makes me grit my teeth together in agitation, and I slump low on the bench to make sure they can't see me. I am mostly certain the tall bushes will hide my presence, but there's no reason for me to test that.

High Elder Torghul speaks in a haughty tone, "Yes, yes. Proceed. What do you have to report?"

"There was a young woman who approached. Strange demeanor and was demanding we take a book from her and raving about a supposed 'prophecy.' She mentioned the war as well and didn't seem to believe me when I said not to worry about it. I fear she could spread information that His Majesty is not yet ready to disclose. She must be silenced before others begin to believe her."

"Yes, of course. There is no need to spread panic through my streets by unregulated speech and raving about prophecies. I understand the gravity of this situation." He pauses for a moment before continuing, "What did this girl look like?"

"She had red-tipped hair and appeared to be at least part fae based on her ears."

"Ahh yes—*Laira*."

He says my name with such utter contempt that it makes my blood boil, and I nearly jump to my feet in a blind rage despite my well-placed caution at staying hidden. I once again wonder at what I did to attract the ire of that old man. He's hated me since I arrived in Taslae for no reason that I could decipher other than my not immediately falling to his shriveled feet like the rest of the town does. He's less an elected official and more a minor god in their eyes.

"She has caused trouble from the very moment she set foot in my town. She doesn't belong here, and with this final transgression, I will finally have grounds to act. Discreetly of course. We don't want to cause a scene," Torghul drawls.

"Thank you, High Elder. The king appreciates your cooperation in these delicate matters of safety and security."

Their footsteps recede, and once I'm sure they're far away, I rise to sit properly on the bench, groaning softly as I do. "Great, now I've drawn the attention of that terrible man. Again."

I drag a hand over my face in exasperation, and Kel jumps beside me to peck at my knee. "Should've known those lying soldiers would be corrupt and working with him. They *know* what's going on and have orders not to tell anyone. What in the stars is going on Kel?" He cocks his head up at me, but once again he has no answers to give.

So much for justice and honor. I snort.

There likely isn't anyone who would take this book and its information seriously. There isn't anyone to pass this off to and no one to take this burden from me, and clearly there is something big going on here. But really, me?

Me? Part of a group in charge of saving the realm and recovering a magic sword? I scoff aloud at the ridiculous thought. It's laughable at best, completely and utterly delusional at worst. I need to talk to Willow—she'll know what to do and she always listens to me.

Slowly, I get up to leave for home, consumed with my thoughts and entirely uncertain of what the right choice is.

The soft voice from before filters through the tall bushes, held aloft on a gentle breeze. It has the same melodic lilting quality as the voice from my room that warned me of oncoming war, and I'm certain that it must be the same one. A stone sinks in my stomach as I finally admit to myself that this voice was not imagined.

"Thread reader..."

I freeze, straining to hear the sound and peering down the path to find the source, though I'm beginning to think I won't ever find it.

"Thread reader, why do you doubt yourself so?" the voice whispers.

The question is a punch straight to my gut—doubt is at the very core of my being. I doubt *everything*. Whether I am enough. Whether I'm a successful shop owner. Whether I'm a good friend, a good partner, or whether I have any ability to do anything at all. Doubt about if this prophecy is true or if I am losing my mind and seeing things that aren't there. Sometimes it feels as if I'm treading through mud, the doubts sticking to my body and pulling at me until I want to simply give up and retreat into their depths.

I respond aloud before I can think twice about how I am answering a question from a voice that has no discernible source. "I am not enough for this. I am not brave, nor am I a hero. I'm just…me."

There is no physical presence other than the soft voice, yet it sounds as if whoever is speaking is smiling softly. *"You hold far more power than you realize. Hold tight to the threads and you will see."*

The beautiful voice drifts away, and a spark of red takes its place like an ember alighting in the dark. I blink slowly and look down to see four perfect red threads flowing from my chest. They're bright as the midday sun and sparkle ruby red like the most precious of stones. They stretch far past me, three to other parts of town and one out to the forest beyond. Hesitantly, I draw my hand to one of the strands. It feels feather-light against my skin, and touching it brings a slight buzz to my palm that echoes through my whole body. Wiggling my fingers and tilting my wrist causes the thread to gently tangle in my grasp before floating up again on a phantom breeze. I attempt to hold onto one, twisting it lightly through my palm, but it's like trying to hold onto water, and it flows right out of my hand. I stare at each of them in awe and step forward from the bench without thinking. I've seen threads close to this bright before, with family and close friends, but I've never had them stay in place long enough for me to study them closely, much less touch them.

"They're beautiful."

As soon as I utter the words, the threads fall away and the world comes back into view. It's dull in comparison to the brilliance of the four threads and my mood falls at their disappearance. I glance down at my chest again to see if they are still there, but I only see the clothes I hauled on this morning in the dark.

Kel pokes at my palm and I look down at him as he cocks his head to the side. "What just happened, bud?"

I should feel disturbed by the voice and what it implied, but I only feel a strange sense of calm. I haven't seen that many bright red threads connecting me to others since my parents were still alive, and certainly none with that amount of intensity in color. That level of brightness points to a stronger connection—a best friend, a family member, or a lover. I study the buildings as if I can see through them to the people whom the threads connect to, a strong ache in my chest pulling me to discover who they are.

NIGHTMARES & SHADOWS

LAIRA

I wandered aimlessly through the streets for the rest of the day, not bothering to open my shop, and returning home once the sun began to wane. Kel nudged me a few times throughout the day, clearly worried for me, but I didn't have the words to reassure him. I tossed and turned all night, plagued by nightmares similar to the vision I had when talking to the king's soldiers. Dark scenes choking me with blood and death. Of distorted nyradonn with red glowing eyes and menacing, violent presences I felt emanating from their bones. They tore through body after body—not distinguishing between human, fae, witch, shifter, or even other nyradonn. They had no qualms about slaughtering innocents sleeping in their beds or those walking home after a long day. They tore through bedroom walls as if they were made of paper, and they toppled entire buildings. They attacked with cold fury and a senselessness that left me in utter shock despite knowing these were just horrid dreams and the work of my too vivid imagination after reading the prophecy and hearing the scattered rumors. Nyradonn could be violent, yes, but only in defense of their bonded or other loved ones. They would never raise a claw, hoof, wing, foot or otherwise against someone for no reason.

I had to remember that, though horrible, these were just nightmares and nothing more. My necklace gives a foreboding pulse across the room under the clothes I threw over it last night, like it knows what I'm thinking and doesn't agree with the answer. Nausea turns in my stomach as I stare at the muffled light on the floor.

Don't listen to a stupid rock, Laira, you have better sense than that, I admonish myself.

Exhausted, I pull myself from bed and ready myself for the day ahead. I dress in my normal clothes, reluctantly securing the prophecy book to my hip, unwilling to let it out of my grasp for long despite the discomfort it causes me.

All the while, I attempt to ease my roiling thoughts by reminding myself over and over that these nightmares are *not real*. But the insidious thoughts needle into my mind anyway, echoing what if?

What if it's real? What if one of those dark creatures is on its way here? What if it is hiding behind the door waiting to slash me to pieces?

I know these thoughts aren't true, that there isn't a blood thirsty bone creature here to kill me, but the long-suffering part of myself that has done everything it could to keep me alive for this long races through my blood, readying me for a fight. Like a snake coiling and flicking out its tongue, testing for danger, it hisses at me to be cautious, to watch my back—it screams at me that there is something here that is going to harm me. I reach for the dagger on my bedside table despite my better judgment and sigh in disappointment at myself as my heart races and my ears strain to pick up any sound to indicate there is, in fact, danger waiting for me on the other side of the door.

Nothing.

Of course there's nothing, this is all in your mind, I remind myself once again.

I huff in irritation as I stand poised with my dagger and ready to attack. It becomes more and more difficult to listen to my more practical thoughts insisting nothing is wrong and eventually I give in, creeping silently toward the door and reaching for the knob. Better to get this out of the way, prove there is no blood thirsty nyradonn waiting for me, and then I can go about my day. I whip the door open and look around the open space of the living room and adjoining kitchen. It is as uneventful as it always is, and I relax a little, the snake in my chest leaning back and settling at the absence of danger.

A prickle runs down my neck, and despite having relaxed, I crane my neck to the far wall again. A flicker of black smoke dissipates so quickly I almost miss it—a trick of the light? I stare intently for another moment, the snake coiled in my chest perking up and looking for another fight. I force it back down, grab my bag, and hustle out the door. I don't spare another backward glance before signaling to Kel that we are heading to Willow's shop. It wouldn't be a good idea to open my shop today, lest I start brandishing my daggers in front of customers. Not to mention, this all feels far too big for me to handle alone and I can't keep going in circles with this. I need to talk to someone and get another opinion because Goddess knows I can't always trust mine.

Willow will know what to do. She knows far more about magic than I do and should have some insight into the strange reaction reading the prophecy had on my necklace and of the dark spot on my hand I've been determined not to look at. A quiet voice singsongs in my mind, *and besides, the prophecy called for a witch, did it not?*

I growl at the voice, my own wretched voice, and shoo it away. That part of myself is too optimistic and enjoys getting me into trouble by conjuring ideas of grandeur and importance. I hate listening to it more than the doubtful, anxious side of myself because it always gives far too much hope and excitement and rarely has that ended well for me. The only time it succeeded was when it convinced me to open my bookshop, a lofty endeavor that I somehow managed to pull off despite every obstacle that presented itself along the way.

This timid part of myself whispers softly, wondering at the prospect that this could be *real* – that it could be *important*.

That *I* could be important.

And this is the thought that scares me most.

"Enough of these roundabout thoughts. They are getting me nowhere." I groan to myself.

Kel dashes after me and lands on my shoulder, his talons digging lightly into the fabric. He tucks his bony wings into his body, his feathers tickling my cheek, and faces toward the stone path, urging me to hurry up.

I chuckle in amusement. Willow's shop is always his favorite place to visit because of the myriad of hiding spots, trinkets to steal, and enough greenery to make a new nest each time he's there. I'm sure he has dozens scattered around her shop that she hasn't yet found and disposed of.

I increase my pace.

"Off to Willow's, then."

Aconite Apothecary

Laira

A cheerful bell jingles when I open the sturdy wooden door. The sign above her shop, the words Aconite Apothecary printed boldly across it, flaps in the breeze as we enter. Kel leaps from my shoulder, darting through the latticework of dried herbs hanging from the ceiling and no doubt getting started on his trinket stealing and nest weaving. Willow spots him out of the corner of her eye while putting together a customer's order, waving her hand halfheartedly and cursing him out in a rather colorful string of words that makes me giggle. Her customer is much less amused, and the older woman's face pinches in disapproval. Willow pays her no mind, pulling her golden-brown tresses out of her face, and wraps the herbs and tonics in her order. I wait patiently off to the side of the counter, admiring the many shelves lining the walls and running my hand over the bottles. Different dried herbs and flowers are stuffed into each cubical slot with jars haphazardly sprinkled throughout—it truly is the most organized of chaotic messes I've ever seen. I once offered to help her straighten things up and catalogue her inventory, but she simply stated she knew where everything was already and to move anything was to put her back hours or even days.

It would drive me to near insanity to have her shelves packed full the way she does with no apparent order. But she is correct, she does know where each and every plant, herb, and specimen is—and she's a wonder to watch when she puts them all together in a complicated order, dashing around the shop in a frenzy and throwing things into a pile before, somehow, wrapping it all up in a beautiful package. Truly, there is no better apothecarist in Taslae, or perhaps even all of Ilphemoura. Though

I haven't ventured out of the human kingdom, so I could be wrong.

Once the old woman leaves the shop, Willow gives me her full attention, pulling up a stool and plopping down. Her eyes dart to my fingers tapping on my leg and, as always, she wastes no time getting to what is obviously bothering me.

"What's wrong?" she presses.

"Nothing is wrong per se… but something could be wrong? I don't know."

She doesn't bat an eye at my non-answer, only frowns a bit at my response.

"Alright then." She grabs her cloak and motions outside her shop. "Come on and I'll close up shop for the day. This calls for a round of sparring."

A relieved *whoosh* of air leaves my lungs. Yeah, sparring is probably a good idea to release some of this tension squeezing my limbs like a vice. Kel suddenly makes his presence known by squawking loudly in displeasure that we are leaving already. He drops a small golden stopper in front of us, and Willow screeches at him to leave her instruments alone or she will string his bones up above her mantle and warm her feet underneath him at the fire. He squawks at her again in a way that sounds suspiciously like laughter and follows us out of her shop. She closes the door, narrowly giving her cat, Din, the chance to slink through the small opening. It's a good thing he knows her habits and is still as agile as he was in his first life, or he'd get squished with how often she slams doors with no regard for anything that might be in her way. Din's bony tail whips angrily at Kel who flies above us in lazy circles, clearly enjoying his height advantage over the cat.

I smile halfheartedly at their predictable antics, but my silence persists as we walk, and even I can notice the strain of it weighing heavily between us.

Willow's grip on my elbow tightens, and she quickly steers us off the stone path onto a worn dirt trail in the direction of the outskirts of town. We continue through a small group of trees to reach our favorite meadow, splitting up to walk to the trees we picked out long ago to store extra weapons and training equipment for the times when we didn't want to haul it all out here from home. I pull a slightly dented wooden sword from the hidden opening in the tree as well as two homemade knee pads, knowing Willow is a little deviant who has a nasty habit of going for the knees. The sun trickles into the meadow through the branches of trees that reach across it and I drink in the golden light, feeling for the first time in the last couple of days that I finally have room to breathe.

I square my shoulders and hold out my wooden sword in a well-practiced grip, smiling at her and silently inviting her to charge. She brandishes her staff, a wooden replica of her usual weapon of choice, and beckons me forward with a finger. I purposefully avoid voicing any of my current fears, instead choosing to go straight to our familiar combat. We parry and block each other and more than once cause the other to fall to the ground in a heap, but each time we jump right back up and continue with increased fervor. Before I know it, my mind is clearer than it's been in days, and we are both shrieking in delight, shouting taunts at each other as we attempt to catch the other off guard.

She calls a sneaky root to the surface which snags on my ankle when I take a step back from a particularly well-aimed slash, and I fall to the forest floor.

"Hey! I know that root was you, you little cheat!"

She dissolves into a fit of giggles before collapsing next to me. "I win! Which means that this is now a fantastic time to turn in for the night. And for you to finally fess up about what is bothering you."

She grins at me, and I elbow her in the ribs, firing back, "Yeah, yeah fine. I could tell you were getting tired anyway."

She scoffs. "As if!"

I get up slowly, groaning at my newly sore muscles, and walk to my hollow tree. I quickly remove the guards on my legs, peeling them off and tossing them unceremoniously back into the hole in the tree. I make a mental note to wash them in the nearby stream tomorrow to rid them of the rather ripe smell they've accumulated.

The explanation I've been avoiding for over an hour now sits heavily in my chest, and I feel an uneasy prickle run across my skin at the knowledge that I can't put it off any longer. I came to her intending to get her help, but that doesn't mean there isn't a large part of me that doesn't rage against sharing my inner turmoil, even to someone as close to me as Willow. I have to swallow down the fear of judgment and trust that she will believe me when I explain the prophecy to her and the strange occurrences I've had lately.

Willow makes an exasperated noise, and I turn to watch as she removes her own braces. "Ugh! Why are my knees always so Goddess-damned sweaty after we train?"

Despite my souring thoughts, I bark out a laugh as she continues to bemoan her sweaty knees once again. She does this every time, and it never fails to make me laugh. Perhaps that's why she keeps complaining about it.

I chuckle, still hesitant but ready to get this conversation over with. Because to hold it in any longer would only serve to make things worse. Kel squawks loudly from a stump beside me as if agreeing with my unspoken thoughts, and I sigh before letting the words fall from my mouth in a rush. "I need your help, Willow."

She gathers her things before plopping in front of me in the soft grass. We sit knee to knee, and she lays both hands across her lap, a single brow raised expectantly.

Din and Kel take their respective places in each of our laps, and Kel's slight weight is enough to bring me some comfort as I decide where to begin. I take a deep breath, reaching behind me to grab the prophecy book and explain everything. From finding the book, reading it aloud, and discovering the reaction my necklace has to it, attempting to get the help of the soldiers and being shut down, to the conversation I overheard with Torghul, and even the visions and nightmares that have been plaguing me.

She's thoughtful for a long time, and I can see the gears slowly churning in her mind before she finally asks, "Can you show me the prophecy?"

I open the book to the partially torn page and hand it to her. She fingers the edge of it, a question in her eyes, but I just shrug. I have no idea why it's torn, who did it, or what the rest of the page even says. Only two words are visible where it was sheared off, and the words "light flaring" hardly give any indication of what the following lines may have said.

She hums as she reads, and I notice a spark in her brown eyes as she gets partway through the prophecy. Was it the part about the thread reader and the witch who are in the chosen group it describes?

"And what is this scribbled note on the side? 'The bonds of Ilekiir offer strength in the end'? What does that mean?"

I shrug again. "I wish I knew, but I—"

My eyes catch on a snippet of red, and I stop speaking to examine it. Like a stone rippling in a pond, the thread connecting us surges as it comes into focus.

Willow senses my curiosity but speaks quietly, as if afraid to disrupt my concentration. "What is it?"

"Our thread…" I reach out a tentative hand but don't touch it. "It's glowing. Just like the threads I saw yesterday."

I glance at the book, an idea hitting me. "Try saying that line again." I prod.

She repeats the same words as before, and my earlier suspicion is confirmed. The thread flares again before dimming slightly back to its normal persistent—but still bright—red glow.

"Interesting."

Her tone is teasing as she asks, "Care to explain, thread reader?"

She smiles mischievously at the name, and I frown, narrowing my eyes but choosing to ignore it and speak. "When you spoke that line, our thread flared for a moment."

"What could that mean? Does that not happen often?"

"No, I rarely see the threads to begin with, but when I do they always stay the same brightness and hue. The threads can change over time as relationships become stronger, but I've never seen them flare in response to something like that."

She scrutinizes the book, and the note scribbled on the side of the prophecy. "I wonder what 'Ilekiir' means. A fae word maybe?" She glances at me, an eyebrow raised.

I roll my eyes. "Just because I have *some* fae blood, doesn't mean I know all fae words."

"No. But you do read a lot, so it's not a terrible assumption."

I huff out a laugh. "I guess. But I don't know this one."

"Hmm. And these nightmares? They seem different than the ones you've explained to me before, the ones with your family."

I nod.

"And you didn't come to me sooner?" She frowns at me in disapproval.

"Yes, yes. I know, I should've come to you. But this just seemed…so big. I didn't know what to do and I was—" I tap my fingers on my leg again, squirming under her scrutiny. "—well I may have spiraled a bit."

She reaches across our legs to place a gentle hand on my shoulder. "It's okay, Lair. I understand. But you don't need to do this alone. I am glad you came to me and didn't let this fester any longer."

"Yes, well, do you have any insight into the strange occurrences and the magic I saw?"

She leans back and twirls a long stray lock of golden-brown hair around her pale finger, the hue vibrant even in the waning sunlight.

"Yes, and no. Magic is wild and difficult to control, even for someone born with an affinity like myself. It takes years to master the magic of this world. And it often will act on its own—either for balance, or possibly the will of the Goddess, I'm not sure, but I've never known magic to not have a purpose." She eyes me intently for a few silent moments, brushing a hand absentmindedly through the grass surrounding us, the blades seeming to reach for her like a loving pet. I'd always marveled at the way plants reacted to her, appearing to stretch toward her even when she wasn't purposely calling to her magic.

"And if it's reaching out to you this strongly… showing you visions and shadows, causing such an intense reaction to your necklace and literally *speaking* to you while showing you threads? It has to be for a reason. I don't think it is something to be ignored." Her tone grows more and more serious as she speaks, her eyes heavy and grim. I don't think I've ever heard her quite this somber before.

"So, the Goddess is trying to tell me something?" I ask hesitantly.

Kel lifts his head and coos to us, jumping from my lap and hopping excitedly. I raise an brow at his odd response to my question, but Willow speaks before I can ponder it too long.

"Yes, or the magic of the universe is trying to tell you something. Or both. They are intricately intertwined, but also separate entities. The magic swirling in this realm has just as much sentience as the Goddess, and I'd argue, even more power and ability to act."

I pull my attention from Kel, "But what is it trying to tell me?"

She nods her head in the direction of the open prophecy, pointing a finger at the words. "A thread reader, Lair? Since when have you met another person that can see what you can?"

"It's not like I see them all the time! I have to really concentrate."

My excuse sounds weak even to my own ears, and she doesn't buy it, scoffing and reaching for the book to point at the specific line before reading it aloud to illustrate her point. "The red threads will call, and those with bonds woven brightest will take the helm."

My necklace grows warm in my pocket as she speaks the words from the prophecy. I pull it out so she can see the effects for herself, and she eyes it with mesmerized curiosity when it glows a bright white.

She shakes her head, as if telling herself that studying the stone can come later. "Lair—I don't know what else to tell you, but I think this 'Prophecy of Souls' is about *you.* And likely me since it referenced a witch and I'm your best friend."

She winks at her last statement, and I roll my eyes at her attempt to lighten the mood. But I'm past the points for jokes now, this is all too frustrating and difficult to accept, and I just don't know what to do anymore. Between the awful visions, horrifying nightmares, my own paranoid anxiety, and a prophecy that rings of so much truth—I'm not sure I'm ready for what it's all pushing me toward.

"But how can that be? We are just two regular people in some random town!" I groan.

She counters quickly, always ready to challenge my self-deprecating thoughts. "Can't you feel the magic pooling and drawing you in? There's a weight to the air even as we speak."

I breathe in deeply and spread out my senses to understand what she means. What little fae blood I possess does give me some stronger senses than regular humans, and while there's nothing that my ears or eyes can pick up, there is a slight heaviness to the air and a small spark of energy that curls around the book, stretching out to encompass Willow and me. The meadow hums as if agreeing with her, and a lazy breeze winds between us as she speaks.

She's right. There is something magical here that isn't normal, alluding to something greater being orchestrated. My mind rages at the thought that she may be right, and that if she is right about this, then she may also be correct about my place within the prophecy.

I squeeze my eyes shut firmly to block out all of the unknowns I don't want to look at and the truth I don't wish to focus on.

"What's that shadow on your hand?" she asks me suddenly, the concern in her voice enough to snap me from my frustration.

A stone drops in my stomach as I realize what she's talking about. The thin black vein on my hand seems to pulse angrily as she snatches my hand to stare at it. She rubs at it just as I did, but it doesn't fade at the contact. Her eyes drill holes into me, but I am just as baffled as she is.

"I was hoping you might have an explanation for that too. It appeared after my first nightmare and before I even found the book."

She nods once, determination in her every movement as she places my hand between both of her open palms and chants in the witch's spell-casting tongue. A green glow encompasses my hand, and I marvel once again at her incredible healing magic—something I have long since wished I also possessed. The talent a long sought-after ability of the witches, who normally only have power over the plants and soil instead of blood, organs, and flesh. Willow is special in that she possesses both, a fact which has contributed to her being in a human city instead of serving the witch queen in her courts. She's mentioned briefly of her choice to leave her home, though not the details on why. Based on her innate power and skill, I imagine it has something to do with being used for her abilities.

Thin green tendrils poke and prod at my hand, but as they get closer to the purplish black vein, my hand burns. I cry out, and Willow opens her eyes, staring at me with such intensity that the shout fizzles from my throat. She drops my hand, and the glow fades from it, the warm tendrils receding back into her skin.

I soothe the fading burning sensation on my hand and stare at her expectantly.

"You're infected, Laira." The words drop from her mouth, and I gape at her.

"What?"

"Infected." She points to the dark vein. "That is the start of it. It burned away my healing abilities, and when I touched it with my magic it felt… I don't know. Wrong."

"But—how can I be infected? I don't feel ill."

"This is a different type of sickness, one borne of dark magic."

We are both silent for a moment as we stare at my hand.

She broaches the silence, "Those nightmares and visions you've been having, and now this, it can't be a coincidence. The infection may have been cast on you somehow as a dark spell and is now feeding into your visions, making them worse than just the warnings they were meant to be, making you feel them more intensely instead. But I've never seen that sort of magic ever used before; only mentioned in ancient texts kept carefully locked away. I think… I think eventually it could get so strong that you could start to lose yourself."

"Lose myself how?"

She bites her lip, avoiding my eyes. "Madness, or maybe try to harm yourself, I'm not sure. Either way it's not good. Though, judging by how small that black vein is, you likely have a good amount of time before anything like that happens, and I can stave off the worst of the effects for a time."

I fiddle with my shirt sleeve. "There has to be some sort of actual fix, right?"

"Can I see the prophecy again?"

I hand her the book and watch as she skims the page again.

"The sword…" she mumbles. Her head jerks up, a spark of understanding in her eyes.

"You know the sword it's talking about?" I ask.

"A little. There are texts in Lassa's libraries that mention a sword, mainly its ability to break curses and heal using light. Something witches have long since sought after, though the sword was considered lost to time… If this is the same sword then it could be what you need." She looks back at the book. "The part about the color of the sword being like that of sunlight is too close to what I have read, so it very well could be the same sword referenced here."

She looks pointedly at the spot on my hand. "It was said to be incredibly powerful and capable of many great acts of healing and power. All the more reason to go."

"Whoa, whoa." I hold my hands up, alarm creeping into my voice. "Since when did we say we were going to follow this wild prophecy?"

"Since you showed signs of a magical infection, started having disturbing nightmares, and found this *wild* prophecy that foretells doom to the world and specifically names something only you can do!"

"Exactly! Even better reason to *not* go. Who wants to follow something that sounds like the end of the world? Plus we have our shops, and our lives are here and I'm sure we can find some way to stop this infection; it's only a tiny vein, and I'm sure I'm not the *only* thread—"

She sighs gently, pointedly interrupting me as I run my list of excuses to stay. The prospect of leaving is suddenly too much, and I feel my already shaky foundation crumbling. It feels too daunting, too sudden, and too big compared to the comfortable monotony of my current life. It feels as if I am on the edge of a cliff and told to jump, not seeing the bottom but knowing there is no other option.

"These rumors have only been going on for a few weeks, right? So that probably means there is time to figure all this out. At least a day or two, and then we can talk more." She stands up, holding out a hand to me. I take it, and she immediately loops her arm in mine, pulling me back to the worn dirt path and pausing for only a moment to snag our bags.

"Let's head home and sleep on it, okay?" Her tone is soft and reassuring, and I grasp onto it like a lifeline. She must see my desperation because she gives me a sad, knowing smile. She digs around in her bag, the tinkle of glassware erupting from it as she searches for something. A clear bottle quickly appears in her grasp and she wiggles the small jar in my face. "This is a tonic to help you sleep. Take *all* of it, got it? And I don't want to hear any complaining about it tasting bad! There is no way to make these things taste palatable, I've tried."

I chuckle and snatch the bottle from her hand, shaking it and eyeing it suspiciously as the green color of it intensifies. "You sure it's supposed to glow like this?"

She rolls her eyes, her voice deadpan. "Yes, it's supposed to glow like that."

"Alright if you say so." I laugh but give her a grateful smile, relieved that I might get a decent night of sleep now. "Thanks."

She bumps her hip against mine and grins. "Of course! That's what friends are for."

THE RIGHT PATH

WILLOW

"Do you remember when we first met?" I ask, our feet trudging down the familiar worn path back into town, Din close on my heels.

The low branches of the trees on either side bend and sway in the soft evening breeze and I hold out my hand to them in greeting as we pass. Ferns reach toward my feet, but don't impede my progress, and it takes more energy than I'd like to admit to stop my magic from reaching to them in answer. The power sits relatively dormant inside my chest, its once brilliant emerald hue dim from years of careful suppression.

"Of course I do." Laira laughs softly at the memory, causing me to internally turn from my magic and smile warmly.

"And do you remember when you first told me about the threads?" I prod.

"Yes, but I don't see what—"

I interrupt her before she can continue to deny what I'm trying to get through to her. Sometimes she can be so damn stubborn.

"You said you initially came up to me because you saw a thread connecting us, one that was brighter than others you had seen. You trusted me immediately, you said, and in that moment didn't hesitate to aid me. You told me later that you only remembered seeing a thread so bright with your family." I tilt my head to look at her from the corner of my eyes as hers go misty, her face softening into a gentle smile.

"And you called me your sister." I squeeze her arm, knowing she doesn't want to accept what she's told me about this prophecy. A shiver runs down my spine, and roots shift deep under my feet as we leave the forest, as if sensing my emotions. I know she felt the magic in the air just as I did earlier, and though she doesn't have a witch's abilities, she does have some affinity with magic that she has yet to discover. This prophecy is dire, but if there's one thing I've learned from my travels, it's that the magic of this world has a mind of its own and it's always in your best interest to follow it.

"Five people, Lair. *Five.* And not only that, but they must be strongly connected in some way, and I don't know about you, but I've never even heard of another person being able to see connections the way you do. Don't you see? Your gift is what needs to be used to find the people necessary for this journey."

Din bumps against Laira's leg, purring softly before looping back around to curl around my legs. Not to be outdone, Kel swoops down to hover next to Laira's face and chirps brightly. He bobs his head before disappearing once more, creaking loudly as he does and flying high above us until I can't hear him any longer. I chuckle at them both and grin at Laira, "See? Even the little beasts agree! You can't argue with that."

She smiles, but it doesn't reach her eyes, and the doubt is still written plainly across her face. I know the uncertainty of this decision is eating her alive, and I can't imagine what she must see every night in her nightmares. She's spoken of her anxiety a few times over the years, and I'm certain something this important and daunting would trigger the well of fear and self-doubt in her heart.

I stop our pace before we reach the stone path of town, placing a gentle hand over her heart, and then place her hand over my own. I know the beat is steady, and I hope it's reassuring for her to feel. I hope it shows that I believe in her and believe that this is something we must do. This prophecy feels too important and too critical to the realm to ignore, and I just know she is the core to all of this. I can't explain the calm certainty that floods my body. It reacts with the warm magic curling inside me as it sings a soft melody that echoes through my blood, as if it's been ready and waiting. Knowing all along this was where my path was headed and is pleased that I have finally found the start of it.

A thread reader?

There's no one who can see what she does. I'm certain there's even more to what she could do if she gave herself the freedom to do so. That thought strikes a chord in me as well, my magic beginning to pool in my hands in response, but I pull it back—stifling the green light that emerges before Laira can ask about it. I chose what freedom I could get when I came to Taslae, and it has been enough. But I can't deny the thrill this potential new journey gives me. I know this is the right path, and she will see that too in time, but for now, I need to convince her in this moment that I am with her.

Glancing down at our hands, I say, "Five souls, Lair." I pause. "One." I gently press her hand more firmly on my chest in emphasis and raise my eyebrows in encouragement.

She lets out a huge sigh, pouting a bit before reluctantly saying, "Two."

I see a peek of a small smile, likely in exasperation, before she squeezes my hand resting against her chest. I know she is playing along to appease me, but there is also a spark in her eyes that speaks to her experiencing a similar tug toward this quest and wanting to believe that she can handle this.

"We are the start, and now we only need three more. And with your abilities, my magic, and the skills of whoever comes later—we will get that damn sword and we *will* race to the pits of darkness *together*. And we'll defeat that evil blue lady in no time," I add.

"Evil blue lady?" She laughs, her hand falling from my chest as she pulls us forward to continue home.

"Yes, evil blue lady! With a long dark cape, red eyes, a menacing voice, and… blue. *obviously*," I shout.

"You're ridiculous. I don't think that is how all evil ladies look."

"Ah, know many evil ladies, do you?"

She snorts and then rubs her face with her other hand. "No, I suppose I don't." Her voice shifts, turning solemn. "This is going to be dangerous, Lo. Very, very impossibly dangerous. The Forbidden Forest has never been spoken of as if it's crossed. As far as I know, it might not even truly be *real*. And that's just the first part. What makes you think we can do it?"

I rest my head against her shoulder as we walk, considering and wanting to give her question the time it deserves.

Because she's right.

This will likely be the most dangerous thing we've ever done, and it may not end well. I smirk, an idea coming to mind. "Well, we know that you have terrible direction."

"Hey! Not fair!" She is affronted at first but trails off as she no doubt remembers all the times she has gotten us lost. "I'm not… that bad."

I lean away from her to look her fully in the face so she can see my dubious expression.

"Ok, fine!" She throws up a hand in defeat, but chuckles. "I'm not the best with directions. But you're not an amazing navigator either."

I twirl a finger, my magic attempting to release its confines in a burst of emerald green that I quickly halt before it can escape my body, as I picture this journey actually happening. I had been restless for years before coming to Taslae, but unable to do anything about it. All I knew was that I could no longer stay in Lassa—that suffocating and stifling city full of a queen who only wanted to use me and a family who expected too much of me. I've hidden from them for a long time, keeping my magic below my potential so as not to draw attention. Knowing that using too much of it would draw unwanted attention, even as far from the witch lands as I am. It's a wonder she hasn't found me already and turned me back into her perfect soldier—maiming those she found unworthy and claiming the lives of supposed traitors. The blood that coats my hands is deeply stained and I've spent the last five years healing instead of destroying to make up for it. A stone drops in my stomach as I recall the more insidious and dangerous side to my particular brand of magic—it can heal, yes, but it can also do the opposite. I yank myself from my memories and focus on the quiet trees around us instead. I made the decision to live my own life, to make my own decisions and live however I wish. I was never going to be a puppet again, and if I was going to harm someone, it would be in defense of those I hold dear. No amount of protocol or expectation will hold me down ever again.

But a secret part of me is pleased at the idea of going somewhere forbidden and at the possibility of using my magic to its fullest potential without fear. When was the last time I truly set myself free? It was what I always wanted, and my goal when leaving Lassa, but the shackles of my old life have persisted, leaving me unfulfilled and restless once again. My heart dips for a moment when I think of leaving my apothecary. It has been a sanctuary for me. A place to discover a different side of myself away from the destructive force of my magic, and I've fallen in love with the quiet healing that occurred there—both for me and the patrons I've served.

I push the feeling away. It doesn't have to be forever. I can close the shop for a time and open when we return. There's nothing that says I can't pause my life here and explore elsewhere.

I smile, focusing back on our conversation. "Exactly. Which is why we need a cartographer."

"A cartographer." She sounds unconvinced, and I don't blame her. But this prophecy called for five people with specific skills, and so five people we shall procure.

"Yes, and I hear the best cartographers are schooled at the academy here in Taslae, with the headmaster having his personal shop in town—it's a stopping point apparently for travelers and offers thousands of maps and tools."

I can hear the surprise in her voice. "And how do you know all of this?"

"I may have had… relations with one or two or three cartographers from this academy. They're not bad in bed but terribly boring out of it. All they talk about is mapmaking and magic used in navigation." I pout, remembering the monotonous conversations and patronizing tones of each of them.

Giggling, she shakes her head. "By the stars, well you better give me a list of names to avoid then, because I am not asking a previous lover of yours to join us."

"Yes, that's probably a good idea. Things didn't end super well with those three." I trail off before pounding my fist against my hand. "Ok, it's decided then! I will gather supplies—and a list of names to avoid—and you will go to the mapmaker shop in town to find someone to be our navigator. And if that doesn't work, we will go to the academy."

"I suppose I have no choice in the matter?" She arches an eyebrow at me, and I grin.

"Absolutely none."

She rolls her eyes but doesn't argue. We're silent for the remainder of the walk to our cluster of homes, each lost in our own turbulent thoughts. My eyes drift to the dark vein on her hand and the magic in my chest arches away in response. I've never experienced anything like it. Normally, my magic grasps onto anything living and I can manipulate it to fit my will, but this was like trying to grab onto death itself—with no firm substance and oily like congealed blood. I shudder silently and hope Laira doesn't notice the slight shift of my shoulders as I recall the sensation and the way the darkness inside her *burned*. Like it was angry I was attempting to overpower it, but certain in its ability to ward me off. It was disconcerting how sentient it appeared to be and it made me wonder once again how this could have happened. Was it really connected to a dark spell, or something destined? Why not both? As much as I disliked the thought of Laira being infected with that darkness, I was not about to question the will of the Goddess quite yet. Not with what I know of this realm's magic. There is a purpose to everything, even great pain, and while some of it may be avoided, there is a great deal that cannot. I close my eyes and inhale deeply. *There has to be a purpose to the pain, otherwise I suffered at the hands of my queen for nothing*, I mentally reassure myself.

I don't know where this path will lead, but I do know that the magic surrounding Laira is strong, and I'm certain this sword will be what she needs. In the meantime, I will do what I can to stave off the worst of the infection until we can get there.

DECISIONS

LAIRA

Utterly exhausted, I crash down on my bed once I return home. Willow always goads me into sparring until I can barely move. Though I suppose that's one of the reasons why she's my best friend—she's constantly pushing me to be my best self.

Despite her best efforts to ease my fears and take my mind off things though, I still feel the creeping anxiety whenever I think too much about the prophecy and what Willow said about the implications of my visions and the shadowy infection in my blood. She really believes it's about us—about me—but there's so much fear swimming in my mind that I can't think straight.

Breathing a heavy sigh, I pull the covers over my shoulders. Desperately seeking their warmth and the invincible feeling hiding under them gave me as a child. Kel chirps halfheartedly from across the room, and I blink into the darkness of my quiet bedroom.

"I know Kel. I know. Ugh!" I slap both hands on my face, as if covering it will keep the monsters at bay, even if I know that's never stopped them before.

"What if she's right?" My voice is small as it echoes in the room, with only Kel to hear.

"What if we need to do this? Find that sword and… I don't know, stop a war?"

I scoff and roll over until I'm curled in a protective ball, pulling the blanket sharply over my head. The idea is utter nonsense, and saying it aloud only makes me feel more ridiculous.

"*Of course not.* I can't prevent a war!" I grumble into my pillow, "This is madness."

I look in the direction where Kel normally sits, though I can hardly see him in the darkness. I pelt him with questions, just needing to say them out loud and drown in my misery.

"What am I going to do? How can this possibly be my existence? And fate? That bitch has never been on my side! Why should I trust her now?"

I'm about to spiral into an ocean of never-ending questions, interrogating and arguing with myself as if I have any answers, when I feel Kel settle gently against my hip. He's not warm, but his slight weight is familiar all the same, and it grounds me enough to remind myself to take a deep breath and pause my relentless tirade. And with his steadfast support, the exhaustion weighing down my limbs, and Willow's tonic, it isn't long before I finally drift into a deep sleep.

THE BATTLEFIELD IS deserted and empty when I look up. It's a stark difference from before when dead bodies littered the ground, weapons lay discarded, and patches of grass were left smoking. The dry grass is now a serene scene that shifts in the brisk wind and appears nearly endless. My eyes struggle to open, and my awareness is fuzzy—my mind distantly cognizant that this is a nightmare once more. It takes a long time for my sluggish mind to register that the bloodshed is gone, and what that means for me.

That I am alone.

I nearly cry out at the loss of my friends' limp bodies. They've long since passed, but at least their physical forms were still here. And all I wish now is to fall into them and follow—a fate which has now been taken from me. I am a single drop in a wide ocean. No one was going to find me, and no one was going to help me. I could scream forever, and I'd still be wretchedly alone, the utter emptiness of the world around me every bit the gaping hole in my chest carved from their absence.

A black spot appears at the far end of the field, interrupting my pitiful wails. It swallows the field I sit slumped in and the ruined city that crumbles in the distance.

It grows until I can no longer see beyond it. Engulfing the sky and the ground—

everything in its path succumbing to its pulsing force as it races for me. I stare at it numbly, the horrific deaths of my friends circling in my mind and destroying all sense of self-preservation I might've had before.

Because they are all gone. And why should I exist if they are not here with me?

The blackness surrounds me, and I welcome it. I watch as the last of my body is consumed, until only the tips of my fingers are visible outside of it. It's when my final finger is about to be engulfed by the darkness that a sharp snap of anger rushes through my body. It breaks through the despair eating me alive and gives me a new purpose as I remember my friend's deaths and how they should never have happened. The blinding rage causes a hoarse roar to bubble up from my chest, and I howl into the widening void to pull myself forward with all my strength. Yanking the rest of my arm free until I can pull the rest of my body from its enticing embrace.

I seethe with the unfairness of it all. How dare they be taken from me? If anyone should have gone, it should have been me. Pain blooms in my mouth as I bite down hard, slicing through my tongue and tasting the metallic tang of my blood. It dribbles down my chin and I furiously swipe it away as I turn to face the dark hole which has paused its relentless attack. Its massive bulk hovers in front of me and blocks out most of the field and grey sky—it could continue and there is very little I could do about it. But it stays put, as if afraid of the rage consuming me. I smile widely at the realization.

They are gone, and I will make this world that took them pay for it.

My body vibrates with the wrath coursing through me, and it feels as foreign as it does inevitable. I was once whole, but my soul died with them, and now all that is left are broken shards of glass reflecting a version of the person I once was. The darkness in front of me wavers when a heavy weapon suddenly appears in my hands, as if flinching. My revenge is all-consuming, and as the hatred blooms in my chest, I know the world will not survive the chaos and death I will unleash upon it.

I WAKE TO sweat-drenched blankets and a roaring in my ears like crashing waves on the shore. A tendril of darkness coils at the foot of my bed as early morning light filters into the room, and a bolt of fear shoots through me at the sight. I back away from it quickly, kicking my blanket off me and blindly searching for the dagger on my bedside table. Anger roils in my gut as I remember what happened in my nightmare and now with this twisting tendril of darkness on my bed, I've had enough.

Enough of these awful dreams and tricks of the light, enough of this Goddess-damned near constant state of panic. Enough of death and suffocating darkness. Enough of this heavy despair I'm forced to feel.

And that grating voice from my nightmares—still, it screams at me. Yelling the same words over and over.

Follow the path.

Follow the path.

Follow the path.

I slap my hands to my ears to block out the words echoing in my mind and scream until my voice is hoarse. But still, it persists. Relentless in its pursuit even outside of my dream state.

"ENOUGH!" I yell into my room, not sure where the voice is coming from.

I stare at the inky black curling like a sleeping cat on my bed, narrowing my eyes accusingly and deciding that it will be the target for my ire.

"GO AWAY!"

It unfurls and hovers in the air just in front of my face, and I swear it's looking at me. That it's asking an unspoken question, one I don't want to answer and one I don't want to face. I know what 'path' it's referring to. I feel it down to my bones and the blood racing through my body. I've been hiding from this truth since I found the worn leather book in my shop, but it seems I have no choice, and fate will have her way.

"Fine. I will do it. I will 'follow the path'. *Happy*?" My voice comes out desperate and strained, my nightmare still haunting me. My anger and exhaustion create more bravado than I feel, and I'm surprised by the underlying venomous bite to my words and the hateful stare I give the darkness looking back at me.

It hovers for another moment before slinking around my neck to slither through my hair. Its embrace feels as oily as it looks, and I shudder, holding still but desperately wishing it leaves soon. Kel screeches from across the bed, and I jump at the sound, but quickly relax as the darkness finally floats away. It dissolves into nothing, and I gape in horror as I feel it sink into my skin and curl around my hand. The black vein pulses once and I have the sinking truth that it's not done with me. That this is not goodbye.

Its presence lingers just under the surface of my skin, and I fear it will come out again if I don't get moving and put this prophecy into motion. I don't allow myself to ponder too long on the knowledge that there is something hiding under my skin, because to do so would only lead to spiraling into my panic and I cannot allow that to happen. Willow said that the sword is likely my only chance to rid myself of this dark magic, and likely the nightmares and visions if I had to guess. I need to focus on what is in front of me.

Five people, a forest, and a sword.

"Maybe if I only think of it as those three things it won't sound as terrifying?" I pose the question to myself, but Kel only tilts his head in response. He jumps from the edge of the bed to land on my outstretched legs.

"Oh yeah? And where were you? Did you not see that horrifying dark thing curled at the foot of my bed?"

He pecks at my knee in answer.

"Yeah, that's what I thought. You were scared shitless too."

Sighing heavily, I get out of bed and head into the washroom to start my day. Despite being more exhausted than I've felt in ages, I need to get myself together and figure out a plan.

Turning on the faucet, I splash water on my face. It cascades down my cheeks and drips from my elbows onto the tile floor. I rub my face roughly before finally looking into the small mirror to see how bad the damage is from having such horrid sleep, but it's not dark bags under my eyes that greet me; it's splatters of blood covering my face and arms.

I scream in alarm, falling back from the mirror and checking myself for injuries, though I know I have none. I look to the mirror again but only see my frightened reflection and no blood in sight.

Slumping to the floor, I rest my head in my hands, asking into the pre-dawn light, "What is happening to me? I'm hallucinating blood now?"

I groan. All of this is simply too much for me. Yet another reason why I'm not fit for a journey such as this or to save anything, much less the entire damned realm from war.

I stay on the ground until my joints grow stiff and my ass is numb, but it's only when Kel brushes against my arm that I find the strength to stand. Hesitantly, I approach the wash basin and mirror, searching for any sign that the blood will reappear. Nothing happens, but I still wash my face and finish getting ready as quickly as I can to avoid looking into the mirror for too long. I'm just about to head out when I notice footprints of blood on the floor from where I walked previously. I freeze, my breathing becoming erratic and my blood running cold as I stare at the red prints.

Was that me?

I whip my head around, studying every corner of the room and checking the windows. *Is someone else here?* My pulse spikes as I consider being caught unaware.

The voice from my nightmare sounds again. ***Follow the path,*** it reminds me in a deep cadence.

I find myself nodding before I can think better of the action, wanting to do anything to make it all *go away*.

"Yes. Yes. I will. I will do it. Just please go away."

My voice cracks as the footprints fade and so does the voice, but a heaviness persists in the room, and it's all I can do not to race out of the house. I force myself to inhale deeply, grab my bag slowly, and make a quick but controlled exit from my bedroom. I don't admit to the emptiness around me or myself how scared I actually am, as if the voice would know and judge my actions. Distantly, I feel Kel settle on my shoulder. He taps out a one, two, three rhythm on my arm, and it takes every last bit of focus I have to concentrate on his calming distraction. I count each tap.

One, two, three.

One, two, three.

One, two, three.

And eventually, my racing heart slows and my breathing returns to a more manageable intake. But the visions of blood threaten to pull me under at any moment if I stop my intense focus on blocking them out. I need to lock them away, or I won't be able to leave this house.

I picture a thick stone wall with a large heavy wooden door, and I fling each painful nightmare scenario into it with all my strength, slamming the door behind them and locking it shut with a key that I hide in a dark corner of my mind. I don't have the ability to deal with this now. I don't know when or if I ever will, but I will keep the horrid scenes locked down no matter the cost.

THE HIGH ELDER

LAIRA

I'm preparing to leave the house when a knock from the front door startles me. I freeze for an instant, staring hard at the door and wondering if I imagined the noise or if someone is actually at my house.

I slowly approach, bracing myself to be spooked again, when a voice sounds from the other side. One full of authority and entitlement. I know exactly who it is from that alone: High Elder Torghul. A sinister old man—his face constantly twisted into a frown and his hands held at fists at his sides. He believes he alone controls Taslae. And the worst part is, he's not exactly wrong. He is the High Elder, and thus his word is second only to the King of Eislekest, at least as far as Taslae is concerned.

"*Girl*—I know you are in there. And I advise you to open this door."

His use of the word *girl* instead of my name makes me grind my teeth and clench my fists tightly to keep from grabbing the dagger from my boot and showing him what I truly think of his foul presence.

He knows very well what my name is—he couldn't run this town without knowing it, and I heard him say it to the soldier—yet he takes pleasure in keeping everyone far below him. And so, I am simply a foolish girl to him.

Despite the anger coursing through my body, it's probably in my best interest to open the door and get whatever conversation he came to have out of the way. I take a deep breath, unclench my jaw, and plaster the biggest, fakest smile I can.

In a sickly-sweet voice, I open the door and chirp, "High Elder Torghul! How nice of you to stop by. What can I do for you?"

"Laira Silvane—" He stops to unfurl a short scroll, reading from it with ill-suppressed twisted glee. "You have hereby been accused of conspiracy to engage in dangerous and outlawed magics, spreading misinformation, fearmongering, and defying a military officer. These accusations are not taken lightly. We applaud our diligent soldiers for bringing your concerning actions to the council and always striving for peace in our kingdom. In light of these new accusations, coupled with suspicious instances that have occurred during your years in this town—you are hereby *exiled* from Taslae. You have two days to leave, or you will be forcibly removed and taken to the capital to be relocated elsewhere. We advise you to leave on time and peacefully, otherwise more drastic measures will be taken. We give this sentence with a heavy heart. However, we must ultimately think of the safety of Taslae and *all* of its inhabitants."

He rolls the parchment and tucks it into his pocket before lightly interlocking his knobby hands in front of his torso. The arrogant look on his face indicates he believes he's won, and with a sinking feeling, I fear he's right. Two days. I will have only two days left here. Where was I going to go? What was I going to do? What about my bookshop? The shock of his words stills my body as I stare at him. He surveys my frozen form and his smile broadens. He's enjoying my suffering and my inability to speak only feeds his own superiority.

I mentally shake myself from my stupor. This sad excuse for a decent human has wanted me out of Taslae ever since I arrived as a naive young adult. Even then, he saw something he didn't like, and since he couldn't evict me right away, he had to bide his time and gather just enough "evidence" to convince the council to unanimously vote to exile me. Because it does require a completely unanimous vote. And until now, there have been a few on my side, despite the strange occurrences he claimed in the scroll—times where I saw visions of red threads and told others or claimed I felt a pull in my chest. I was labeled as unwell, but I was young, so they left me alone. Now though, I must have finally pushed too far with my questioning of the guards. Old crotchety men and corrupt soldiers stick together, I suppose.

My hands shake as I ball them into fists, and I am barely able to contain the undiluted rage that slips into my voice as I ask, "Do I get a chance to defend myself, or am I exiled without that basic human right?"

His smile is sinister and his eyes dark as he replies, "Unfortunately, that *'basic human right'* as you put it, is not being offered at this time. The council has decided your fate. And you have until the full moon to leave Taslae."

The anger is temporarily replaced by a swirling vortex of anxiety. This is too close to the times I've felt misunderstood by others or cast aside by those I respected. Of the times where I spoke too loudly and was told to shush, or shared a vulnerable thought only to be told I shouldn't think that way. My tongue feels thick and useless in my mouth as my mind desperately attempts to reach for anything that could explain this away. Something—anything—to convince him that I am not a threat, that I have done nothing wrong.

I blink, my eyes wide. "But… my shop."

I gesture helplessly behind him and down the street in the direction of the beautiful book shop I saved from being torn down and put months of work into restoring. I've had this shop running for years now. It is my life and my livelihood. And the books—*where would all of the books go?*

This might have been a silly question to ask myself, but at the moment it was the only thing that I could think about. All of my preciously curated books, where could I send them where they would be loved just as much? How could I possibly move all of them before my time was up? I suppose I could ask Armas if he knows someone with a book shop or library that could take my inventory in another town.

Or perhaps a private collector? I do have some rather old tomes they may want, I mentally question.

Torghul's sharp voice pulls me from my potential plans. "Your shop is not the council's concern. The safety and well-being of Taslae is. We have let your wild imaginings run too far, not to mention the absolute drivel you sell there. I am shocked the council has not seen wisdom before this to shut you down."

Shut you down. The words sizzle as they hit the air and all at once, the anger is back—a wild, vicious creature rearing in my chest and snapping to be let free.

My gaze turns hard, my voice a deadly calm as I say, "Let me get this straight: I am being told to leave Taslae because I asked a soldier a few questions, had a few odd occurrences happen years ago, and have been accused of spreading misinformation?

Information that I'm certain is not incorrect at all based on what I've overheard you say." I raise a pointed brow and Torghul's smug smile falters just long enough for me to know the answer.

He quickly masters his features though, returning to his haughty tone and replying, "Yes."

I savor the small admission that I am correct, but don't waste any time before continuing, not wanting to give him any time to speak first. "And I do not get a chance to explain or defend myself against these accusations? I just have to accept the sentencing, pick up my entire life here and go somewhere else?"

"Precisely."

"Well then—if I am to be kicked out, then I guess I have nothing to lose." I clear my throat and smile for real this time at finally being given the opportunity to speak my mind. "You, Torghul—" I grin as I purposely leave out his honorific title, knowing it will ruffle him, "—are a sorry excuse for a man. You are painful to be around, surprisingly whiny, and I am shocked anyone listens to you at all. Your views on women, sexuality, and magic are backwards and abhorrent. I am pleased to know that you never married at least, saving whatever poor person would have been your partner. You are horribly ignorant for one so old—completely blinded by hate and disgust that you cannot see that it is in fact *you* who is the problem in every scenario."

I spit at his feet and his nostrils flare with anger, his eyes bulging from their sockets as he prepares to reprimand me. My mouth turns up into a sneer and I don't give him a second to speak before I say, "I wish you the life you deserve."

I savor the furious look on his drooping face as I slam the door. He screeches fowl words through the door, attempting to get the final word, but I don't give in to his taunts. He eventually huffs indignantly, and I sense his retreat. I'm still positively seething as he leaves and I take a few laps around the living room, walking in circles around the furniture, to calm myself. It is the people who believe they are better than everyone around them that boil my blood the most. Those who hold moral superiority over those they deem "unworthy" for no reason other than that they are different and do not conform to their ideals. It makes me sick.

I am sad I must say goodbye to my shop and drop everything that I've worked so hard these past years to build. But if there's one positive thing I can hold onto, it's that I am glad to be rid of this town and its people. There are those who are pleasant, sure, but there are more who would wish someone like me gone. Someone who, even though it's incredibly small, is still part fae, and they fear anything *other*. While the fae occupy their own lands to the north and are treated as respected neighbors, they are still spoken about in hushed whispers by most humans. Some fae are more nature than person and their closeness to the elements or wild beasts of the world gives more power to an already powerful race—something humans have long felt inferior to.

I am reminded once again that I am someone unnatural and strange. *Unwanted.* I feel a tear slip down my cheek despite my greatest efforts to pull it back. I will *not* cry because of these ignorant, hateful individuals.

I furiously wipe it away.

There has to be a better use for this energy instead of pacing and trying not to scream and cry. I decide to make a list of tasks to calm my mind and work out my next steps, methodically moving through each one. I only have two days after all and while I cannot change the minds of the council, and certainly not Torghul, I can lose myself in my shop and figure out my next steps for closing it with dignity and respect. There may even be a way to save part of it, or at least my collection of books, if I play my cards right. And while this is not the way I would have wanted to go, it certainly makes it that much easier to commit to leaving for the prophecy.

My first course of action is to repack the boxes of books that were recently delivered, since I will need to box the whole shop up anyway to move or sell. Next, I'll need to gather more boxes and supplies and talk with Armas to see if he has any contacts to sell or give these books to. After that will be storing or getting rid of shelves, furniture, and anything not worth saving. The odds are not in my favor for being able to box up my precious shop and move it to a new town after this ridiculous adventure, but if I don't keep this ember of hope in my chest, I will collapse in a useless heap on the floor.

I wipe my runny nose and pat the tears from my cheeks as I mentally check my last-ditch effort plan to save the shop I worked so hard to build.

"I can do this. It won't be the same, but I'll at least have something to come back to, and I can move to a new town." I tell myself, willing the words to be true.

I think of my shop. Of the beautiful painted shelves and the rows and rows of books, and I smile. I let myself bask in the safety and wonder I created there, and then I get to work.

THE CARTOGRAPHER

LAIRA

With my plan of action for closing my shop and selling my home complete, I turn to the thoughts nagging at me. The whispers that say the prophecy is in motion and that I must follow it, and with the voices and nightmares I heard and saw over the last few hours, I have little energy to fight against them. Besides, with my exile, I have nowhere to go, and if this prophecy truly does call to me, then perhaps Willow is right and it's best to follow the magic of the realm. My fears echo loudly in my mind, reminding me of the dark infection in my hand and how it was able to somehow coalesce in front of me. Truly my exile is the least of my worries when I have dark magic that I must find a way to purge from my body.

I make my way quickly through town, deciding to start with the mapmaking shop instead of the academy, like Willow suggested. The four bright threads that appeared from my chest the day before come to mind and I'm certain they must be pointing me to the four companions needed for this journey. Three were here in Taslae—with one clearly connected to Willow—so it stands to reason that one could belong to someone residing in this shop or the academy since we need a cartographer.

"If I'm going to commit to this, I might as well go all in." I say to myself, testing the words and my resolve. I find that they don't feel as frightening as I thought they would. In fact, there's a sort of release from giving in and accepting what has happened instead of fighting it.

With newfound purpose, I come upon the shop in the middle of the main square. The gold inlaid on the door, coupled with the frighteningly bright shade of red painted across it, is entirely out of place among the grey, brown, and black accents on the buildings that line this street. Like a puddle of blood in old snow, it stands heavy and imposing, and my stomach twists at the thought of entering and asking for help. I take a fortifying breath and close my eyes, turning the handle before I can second-guess myself, and then I step into the mapmaker's shop.

The shop is large and much grander than I thought it would be even with its ostentatious exterior. More gold filigree sweeps across the walls and along the meticulously catalogued shelves. Everything is neat and orderly without a smidge of dust or loose labels. I assume the owner was going for luxury and decadence, but it feels stifling and lifeless, lacking the character I would expect from a place promising adventure and discovery. I'd seen the outside many times, walking to and from the town center or the market, but I never went inside and never paid it much heed. After all, I never planned to leave this town, so why would I need a map?

How quickly things change.

I most certainly needed a map *now*. In fact, I needed much more than a map—I needed a cartographer, adventurer, and journey member all wrapped in one. I wondered if I would ever find someone who would be all those things. I was hopeful I could find a student here, or a professor, or maybe even the owner of the shop would offer his aid. I'd never met the legendary mapmaking genius who owned it, but I knew of him. He was said to be poised, calculating, and direct. He was also old, likely crabby, and probably a pain to travel with. As old, calculating men often are.

I sigh.

Maybe I didn't want him to join us after all. But perhaps I was being presumptuous and judging him too quickly based on hearsay. I decided before coming in that I would give him a chance. And really, I didn't know who else to ask.

I poke around the various shelves lining the far wall and notice that each is stuffed full of rolled pieces of parchment. I pull a few down to examine and find beautifully detailed maps of distant towns and cities I haven't even heard of located deep in the heart of the witch lands of Kerimaea, the shifter isles Rysaram and Rulanne, and the legendary fae lands of Caelamne. The fae homeland I've heard that has forests that glitter like pearlescent stone, cities that float in the sky, and more beautifully bizarre creatures than you can possibly imagine. My fingers suddenly itch to pull another down and discover more as my mind imagines all the new and beautiful places.

"Can I help you, Miss?"

A strong, demanding voice booms behind me, startling me, and I quickly drop my hand before I can reach for another map. I fumble with the one's I've already opened, but eventually leave them on the small desk I'd been examining them on and turn around to face the owner of the imposing voice. My smile is sheepish, as if I've been caught doing something bad, like a child who knows they are about to be scolded. I internally shake myself from the image. I am not a child, and I have every right to pick up a map and browse it. This is a map shop after all. But one look at the man—who I assume is the owner and the man I've come to petition—has me rethinking my internal debate. He's stern looking, with a sallow cheeks, thin lips, and razor-sharp eyes that foretell misery should I step out of line.

He is downright terrifying.

I was right—there's no way we can travel with this man, but I can't just leave, I need to ask *someone* for help. Willow is counting on me to find our crew for this wild adventure, and I will not let her down. Not to mention I cannot invite that grating voice back in or the oily dark thing that accompanied it should I abandon this mission. I realize he's waiting for an answer to his question as I continue to stare blankly at him.

Right. An answer, what can he help me with?

I step forward, eyeing the space around him in search of a potential red thread, and speak in the calmest and most authoritative voice I have. "My name is Laira, and I am in need of a map, as well as someone to read it and guide a group on a journey."

He cocks an eyebrow as he says dryly, "Miss, this is a serious endeavor and having the right cartographer could mean the difference between life and death. Though it also takes hardy individuals who can handle long days of travel and arduous conditions. Where could you possibly wish to go?"

His tone is patronizing, but he didn't immediately turn me down, so perhaps that is a good sign.

"Yes, of course. And I assure you I am not playing games, and I do wish to leave this town and can handle the difficulties that come with travel. As for where I'm going, I need a map that shows the way through the Forbidden Forest and a person to guide us through it."

"Forbidden Forest?" His stare burrows deeper, and the disapproval rolls off him in waves. He seems almost angry, "You dare come into my shop and waste my time with children's fairytales and lies?"

The way his lips pinch into a frown, and the narrowing of his eyes morphs his face from general annoyance to downright disdain.

Oh, he's definitely angry.

"It's not fairytales. I have a book that says it's real, a prophecy, and—" I wince at my awkward delivery and the fact I brought up the prophecy. It didn't exactly go well when I told the soldier about it, and I mentally remind myself to be more careful about who I tell.

But he doesn't seem to notice my mention of the prophecy. Instead, he cuts me off and spits, "Listen here, girl—" He says "girl" like it's a disgusting word, nothing better than something he scraped off his shoe. "There is no such thing as the Forbidden Forest. I am the most esteemed mapmaker and cartographer in recent memory. I have been to every corner of this land and the next, I have seen far more than you ever have and ever will, and I can assure you I have never seen this supposed entrance to the Forbidden Forest. That is a simple forest up north just like any other. In fact, you shouldn't even be asking about this. It is not proper, nor is it allowed by the academy to spout such lunacy. It is an insult to every mapmaker."

He steps forward threateningly and continues, "Maybe you could use some time in the mental wards and be looked after by a physician. I would gladly escort you there and insist on proper treatment for your... delusions."

My blood begins to boil. *Delusions? I will not be suffering through those allegations again.*

One look in his hateful eyes is enough to know I won't get anything further from this conversation. I'm not about to let him bully me out of the store, however, so I make a point to simply nod and walk away before taking my time perusing the various selections of the shop. He huffs and stands watching me for a few moments longer—likely hoping I will leave—before he shuffles to the back of the shop and behind a large curtain when he sees it's clear I plan to stay.

With his stifling presence finally gone, I find myself relaxing and able to enjoy opening maps and observing various tools of the trade throughout the shop as I try to brush off the terrible encounter. I've never seen so many detailed maps of Ilphemoura, and they are all breathtaking.

My mind wanders as I peruse the aisles, thinking back to what the mapmaker said about the Forbidden Forest. He sounded so certain that it didn't exist—that I was insane for even mentioning it. The prophecy spoke of it, but what if it was only a folktale, or what if the knowledge of it was so lost that it might as well not exist at all? I blow out a long breath. I may be able to use my thread-reading ability to find the people necessary for this journey, but that doesn't mean everything else is true. Or that I'm interpreting it correctly. What if this forest is in the fae or shifter lands, and not the same one I only vaguely remembered from childhood stories told by my father? Both of their lands have plenty of dense forests that could contain a magic forest.

I'm so lost in my increasingly dour thoughts that I don't hear someone approach until a soft clearing of a throat sounds from behind me.

"Hey!"

The voice is soft but insistent, and I turn to find a young man, likely around my age, his gaze not quite meeting mine as he motions for me to follow him behind a large shelf.

"Over here!"

A flurry of paper flits into the air as he waves a hand, nearly tipping a stack of old maps off the shelf, which he quickly restacks. His eyes dart nervously, intently watching the door the shopkeeper disappeared into for any sign of movement.

I eye the young man, confused and a bit suspicious after the lovely chat I had with the mapmaker. Even if this stranger's charmingly disheveled appearance is somewhat amusing and innocent, completely unlike the old man. His blond hair flops into his eyes as he fixes the stack of rolled maps, and the glasses he wears sit crooked on his nose because of his jerky movements. Judging by the pale hue of his skin, I'd guess he doesn't get out much. And with the standard blue, red, and white uniform he wears, it's clear he belongs at the academy. He continues stacking the rolls of parchment, turning to the side and exposing sewn on pockets bursting to the seams with writing utensils, ink, and crinkled paper. I smile despite myself and hold back an amused laugh at his demeanor.

He doesn't look threatening, though it is odd to suddenly be approached by a stranger and told to follow them behind a shelf. Curiosity—and the fact that his movements are getting more desperate—gets the better of me, and I make my way over to him. The shelf is positioned in such a way that it effectively hides us from view from the back of the shop and the prying eyes of the owner.

I don't say anything, but he shushes me anyway, causing a soft involuntary giggle to leave me, which he definitely shushes.

"We need to be quiet. That old man has surprisingly good hearing."

"And what, pray tell, do we need to be quiet about?"

He checks one more time that the back curtain hasn't moved before saying, "You know… the forest. Err—I can…well you see…" He leans down slightly and whispers, "The forest—I know where to go. I can get you to the entrance."

His words cause a jolt to run through my body, my voice rising a few octaves.

"You can? But how?" I ask excitedly.

"Shhhh!" He whips his head around again.

This man is really paranoid, I think to myself as I follow his gaze toward the empty back door. *But I suppose on a good day, I'm not much better.*

"Be quiet—he'll hear you." The serious tone of his voice brings mine down to a soft hush.

"Ok. How do you know how to navigate the forest? How do you know that you can take us?"

"Not here! Meet me outside and I'll explain more."

He dashes off suddenly, snaking behind the shelf before I have a moment to question him further. Bewildered, I stare after him for a moment as I process what he said. Could the old mapmaker be wrong about the forest not existing? And how does this man know about it? The questions pile on top of each other and I have no choice but to follow after him to have any hope of answering them.

The door chimes cheerfully at my retreat, and I look both ways on the street, searching for the strange young man. He didn't say where to meet him exactly, but he couldn't have gotten far. That's when I notice a man in an oversized coat and hood—a very obvious man who is clearly checking behind him before slipping into a nearby alley. Not to mention the fact that it is midday and much too warm for a full coat and hood.

I raise a brow as he disappears. "Subtlety is not his strong suit." I chuckle and walk in the direction of the alley.

A bright red strand floats into my vision, and I gasp, faltering for a moment before pursuing the thread with renewed determination. It sparkles with the same intensity as the threads from the day before and my heart beats quickly in anticipation as I come upon the alley.

I'm grabbed by the shoulders and pulled quickly to the side, a cry falling from my lips in surprise, "Hey! No need to grab me!"

The thread twines around the hooded figure as he glances up and down the street until he's positive no one is there and removes his hood. The alleyway is darker than the main street, but it is still mid-afternoon, so it's not exactly great cover for sneaking around. The soft light illuminates his golden locks of hair, and his blue eyes are bright with excitement.

He really is not subtle – even his hair shouts at you, I mentally chuckle.

"Were you followed?"

I gesture to the empty alley. "Does it look like I was followed?"

"No. Good job. Can't be too careful when it comes to talking about..." He leans in conspiratorially, "The Forbidden Forest."

"Right... so you know where the entrance is and how to navigate the forest?" I ask skeptically.

"I have been secretly studying that mystical forest for years. No one will talk about it—in fact it seems to be borderline illegal to mention. At least that is the impression that Master Hannon gave me. He hates any mention of that forest."

I wince, remembering the ire of the old man. "Yeah, I noticed."

"Yeah, well not much you can do when he goes on a tirade like that. But honestly, I would be careful who you go talking to about the forest. Hannon knows some powerful people, and he's made it his goal in life to erase that forest from memory. But it's not just him, this forest has been purposefully hidden away for over a millennium by every ruler that I've researched."

"But why? Isn't it just a forest—one only talked about in legend? Is it even truly real? How would something like that be threatening?"

"Oh, it's most certainly real, though I'm not sure why the information would be hidden. The texts I've managed to get hold of only briefly speak of a war that occurred thousands of years ago, which seems to be the start of when the forest was regarded as something to fear and avoid instead of something to explore. Before that, I think it was inhabited or at least touched by the fae, which is why it has the magical energy and properties that it does."

"Magical properties?"

"Well… yeah! Haven't you wondered why there's only one entrance that ever gets talked about and how if you can't find it, then you are just walking through a normal forest? Albeit still very spooky for a forest, and still very much forbidden, but a normal forest nonetheless."

"No, I haven't, nor was I aware there was only one entrance. I've really only just started to consider that it's even real."

His eyes alight, and the red thread swirling around his body curls from his chest and delicately between his hands as he waves them excitedly. I try not to focus too much on it—not wanting to have to explain why I'm staring at his hands and the air around his body—but it's difficult not to follow the brilliant red hue. I can tell by the speed at which he talks and the excited tone in his voice that he truly loves talking about this forest. Makes me wonder if he had anyone to share his excitement and knowledge with, especially if just talking about this mysterious forest could get someone in trouble, or if he had to stifle his enthusiasm and keep it hidden from everyone.

"I can tell you the long version later, but basically the magic creates a pocket of sorts or another layer, one in which the Forbidden Forest resides. So, if you don't find the entrance to this pocket within the normal forest, you will essentially walk right by Daer e' Mista and never know it."

"Daer e' Mista. That's the name of the forest?"

"That's what the fae called it, though that particular name is one you definitely won't hear spoken by anyone because it's ancient."

"So, it's fae in origin? Why is it located in the human lands then?" I ask, curiosity clinging to my words.

He shrugs, his eyes wandering to other parts of the alley. "Yes and no. I think it was originally created with fae magic but was inhabited by humans and fae alike at one point. As to why it's in the human lands and not the fae, I do not know."

I pause, considering his answers for a moment. "So, I suppose you aren't simply telling me this to answer my questions from the shop, you want to go to the Forbidden Forest?"

The earnestness in his posture and face brings an unbidden smile to my face as he enthusiastically says, "Yes! I do; I want to go with you. But um… why are we going there?"

Now it's my turn to look around suspiciously for any eavesdroppers. "I found something important. The rumors and whispers about a war and a strange darkness off the witch lands? I think this is connected to it. I'll explain more later. Come to my bookshop tonight and I'll tell you everything."

"Right, of course." He glances around again before winking at me. "Best to find a safer spot from prying eyes. I'll make sure I'm not followed!" He whirls around toward the street in a rush, his cloak flying behind him.

"Wait! Do you know where my shop is? And what's your name?"

He turns slightly and puts the hood back up over his head to partially cover his face. But I can still see his broad smile as he says, "Yes, I know your shop, Laira. And my name is Thelas."

"Wait!" I call after him. "How do you know *my* name?"

I let out a confused laugh at his retreating form, but he slips away in the direction of the mapmaker's shop once again, the bright red thread dissipating into the air, and I am left alone in the alley to ponder the strange encounter I just had. I can't help but smile. His enthusiasm is infectious, and his awkward charm endearing.

And the thread.

The weight of what I just saw finally hits me. It was one thing to see Willow's thread, but to see such a strong connection to a stranger? Even seeing the four threads didn't quite hit me, the way seeing his just now did. I shiver despite the warm weather and wrap my arms around my body.

"Tell-us." I test the name aloud. It's not the most unusual name I've ever heard, but it is strange for a human.

It rolls off the tongue well at least. And even better, it's not one of the names on Willow's list, I think wryly to myself.

PURSUING CHAOS

SEBASTIAN

I toss the coin up in the air again. Flipping it mindlessly and catching it over and over, while I wander the streets of this dreary town. After arriving just a few days prior, I'm sure I've traversed every street and back-alley corridor. And yet, I can't find a single damn piece of evidence to support the rumors that the creatures are heading this way. I sigh heavily, kicking at a loose stone, and it skitters across the cobblestones before coming to an abrupt halt against the opposite wall. I need to find something to make this trip worthwhile, or the risky choice I made in coming here will only prove my father correct.

He didn't put any stock into my suggestions, insisting that we needed our focus to be elsewhere. And he's not exactly wrong, Taslae is in the farther reaches of Eislekest, and not known for major events. With grey shopfronts, grey clothes, and a generally all-around bland atmosphere—it's as if the townspeople have given up what it feels like to be alive in a bustling city of color and excitement. I suppose the one thing Taslae has going for it is the proximity to the coast, the famed academy, and the Lower Tiramunde River which provides ample opportunity for our traders and merchants to access ferries up the river or ships to sail the seas. But that only makes this town a stopping point at best—a brief step off the boat to gather supplies and continue on to more exciting endeavors.

I flip the coin again, shake my head, and let out a long sigh.

Those bastards had the right idea.

That river and proximity to the coast is exactly why I had the hunch to come here. If those creatures are truly utilizing waterways, then this town could be a good place to gather intel. I lean against a nearby building in the shade as the sun dips momentarily behind a cloud and plan my next move. Perhaps I should take a cue from the merchants and move on from Taslae and finally admit to myself and my father that I was wrong.

The idea sours my stomach and I grimace. I'm not ready to give up yet—there has to be something here for me. I'm pondering my current sorry state when shuffling across the street and the sound of someone muttering to themselves catches my attention. I stand up from my hunched position against the wall and glance around to find the source. I spot the mutterer a few feet up the road; she seems to be entirely engrossed in whatever conversation she is having with herself. She passes others, but never once pauses her tirade and doesn't pay a single person any attention—even if they glance at her, confused by her rambling.

She's followed by a nyradonn, which looks to be a sort of bird. It creaks and wobbles as it flies just above her—yes, definitely a nyradonn, and one that has clearly seen better days. It swoops down to lift a lock of hair gently from her head, almost as if it's reminding her to pay attention and watch her step.

She swats the bird away. "Yes, yes, Kel. I know."

Her straight hair brushes the top of her shoulders as she moves, the dark brown color a normal shade for a human, but the tips of her hair tell a different story. They are red, as if someone dipped them in wine, and along with her pointed ears, a clear indication of fae ancestry. The fae are known for their beautiful otherworldly appearances: blue skin, speckled hair, glowing eyes, and the like. And while they are in good standing with the human kingdom, they hardly travel outside of their homeland for long, making it increasingly rare to see someone with partial fae blood. So where did she come from? And why is she in a town like Taslae? It's not the worst town to be in, but there are certainly more accepting cities in Eislekest. The main one being the capital of Ferrill where the royal family presides, and trade is the strongest. Anyone can be anything there, and folks are often too busy to take notice of anyone different.

I take a few steps forward, intrigued by her appearance and wanting to get a closer look. I don't usually make it a habit of mine to approach women on the street, but I find my feet moving anyway.

The bird caws loudly in her face, startling her. It likely is trying to warn her that someone is following her and to pay attention. But she doesn't seem to notice my presence and only grows increasingly aggravated with the bird.

"I swear Kel, if you don't stop messing with me, I will not share my breakfast with you anymore!" She jabs a finger toward the creature, not actually angry as far as I can tell. Just mildly annoyed, and apparently willing to threaten breakfast privileges. It makes me chuckle softly. Nyradonn don't even need to eat—they are dead after all—but this doesn't seem to matter to this strange woman.

The bone creature squawks somewhat dejectedly at her outburst and lands on her shoulder. It hunches over and makes another small noise. Is it… *pouting*? She scratches the top of its bony head, "Oh Kel, I'm sorry. I'm still just a little upset is all. That mapmaker—" She spits the name like it's poison in her mouth, "—is a real ass and you know how hard it is for me to ask for help. I'm just a little rattled still is all."

The bird emits a soft cry in acknowledgment, and she moves him from her shoulder to her forearm, the other hand pointing a firm finger at his beak. "But seriously, startle me again and I will not share my muffins in the morning for at *least* three days."

She holds up three fingers and stops in her tracks to stare into the eye sockets of her little beast. This stare down happens for another few seconds until the creature notices me again and squawks loudly in her face. She jumps a bit from the sudden noise, and I can see her gearing up for another tirade.

Not wanting to be the reason this poor bird is denied muffins for three days, I decide to have a little fun. Increasing my pace, I move to bump into her. I could stand to have something interesting happen, and perhaps this will be my reason to stay in Taslae a bit longer.

A GAME OF CHANCE

LAIRA

"Oof," a deep voice says beside me as someone collides with my shoulder, knocking me off balance.

"Ah, sorry about that, Miss. I wasn't looking where I was going." The voice says again.

I collect myself and look up to see who bumped into me, my own apology on my lips, "Oh, no my ba— "

I stop mid-sentence when I meet the stranger's eyes.

They are clear and green, flecked with golden brown bursts that start from the center to meld with the forest color of the rest of his eyes. I peruse his face, to his strong nose, tanned skin, and full lips. He has silver piercings in his ears, his eyebrow and a small hoop on his nose. They catch my attention, and I feel my gaze bouncing to each silver flash. It's when I get to his lips that I realize they are currently pulled into a knowing smirk, and that is also when I realize I've stopped speaking and am openly ogling the stranger's handsome face. By the look in his eyes and that Goddess-damned smirk, he knows it too.

"You know Miss, some would think it rude to stare." He flips a coin in the air and catches it as he says so, his eyes flicking to it, before flipping it again.

I am not sure if it's the leftover anger from speaking with the ornery shop owner, being slightly aggravated by Kel, or perhaps a combination of the two, but his comment makes my hackles rise.

"You know, *sir*," The last word spits out of my mouth like a curse, "it is quite rude to follow, aggravate, and accost a random woman you don't know who is simply walking down the street."

I count off each offense on my hand, voice growing louder with each one. I can feel my anger rising and my blood beginning to boil. I have had a terrible day, and I still need to find the other group members for this ridiculous quest, get supplies together, and not fall apart at the seams. This *barbarian* of a man is the last thing I need. The rage builds deep in my stomach, and I point a finger right at his annoyingly beautiful face.

"I don't have time for you, whatever strange games you enjoy playing with women, or to continue this conversation."

I turn to leave, because if he will not leave me alone, then I will make it very clear I do not want his company. It seems I caught him off guard with my outburst because he immediately steps in front of me and reaches his hands out to stop me, though he stops short of touching my shoulders.

"I'm terribly sorry, Miss! You are right, I shouldn't have interrupted your stroll. Please accept my apology." His voice sounds apologetic, but something about his eyes makes me think he's messing with me. I don't respond and stare blankly at him, hoping he will be on his way.

"Ah yes, well, it seems you don't believe me." He reaches a hand to self-consciously rub the back of his neck, exposing black lines from a tattoo that reaches up his neck like curling vines grasping for higher ground. I'm briefly distracted by the sight and so don't register what he said. My continued silence doesn't seem to bother him though, as he quickly moves to walk back the way he came. As he passes, he lightly bumps against my arm, which is still propped against my hip from my rant. I follow him with my gaze, but with his quick stride, I barely have time to notice the fleeting smile on his face before he's gone.

That asshole! Who does he think he is?

I pinch the bridge of my nose, inhaling and then exhaling deeply. "I just need to continue on my way and forget about him. I have more important things to think about, and getting angry at a complete stranger is not worth what little energy I have left today." I sound utterly exasperated, even to myself.

I take a few steps, still lost in my anger and frustration when I realize my bag is no longer securely gripped in my hand. I pat both of my hips looking for it and turn to see if I dropped it somewhere—only to find that the stranger has not left after all. Instead, he waits down the street looking smug and satisfied, like a cat who's just caught a mouse. He holds my bag up by the short strap, and the tilt of his head beckons me to come and attempt to take it from him.

Oh, he's really going to get a piece of my mind now.

Marching back up to him, I bypass the outstretched arm with my bag and get right up in his face.

Pointing a finger at him, I say with deadly calm, "By the Goddess, if you don't give me my bag back and leave me alone, I will find where you lay your cocky head at night, cut off your balls, and have Kel feed them to you." I feel and hear Kel land on my shoulder right as I mention his name.

Good boy, there will be extra muffins for you in your future. I smile to myself.

The thief lifts his eyebrows at the mention of his unmentionables, but instead of giving my bag back, he shifts his upper body towards me and purrs, "Goddess save me, you are a *wildcat*, aren't you?"

His eyes turn molten, and that insufferable smirk on his face morphs into a feral grin. And then he is sprinting away from me, my bag slung over his back.

He yells over his shoulder, "Catch me if you can, wildcat!"

I chase after him before I properly think through my actions. He could be a predatory man in search of young maidens, stealing purses to lead them through dark alleys to eventually grab them and steal them away after all.

Nothing in my bag is important enough for me to be potentially led into a dangerous situation, I reprimand myself.

But I find myself continuing to race after him down the main road and careening around sharp corners to cut him off, yelling breathlessly, "Get back here, you little thief!"

"Little, huh?" He slows, jogging backwards so that he can look at me fully, "Wildcat, you wound me."

He holds both hands up dramatically to his chest, as if I have pierced him with a sword. His eyes are alight with mischief, and his grin is wide and surprisingly genuine.

"Stop. Calling. Me. Wildcat." I huff out as we come to a stop, slightly winded from our chase.

"Make. Me." He wags a finger at me and puts a hand on his hip as he emphasizes each word. The act is so ridiculous I almost laugh.

Almost.

He stares at me and waits for me to make the next move, clearly enjoying this game. And though he stole my bag and made me chase him through town, I find my anxiety about the prophecy has dwindled to a quiet buzz in my head, and the anger towards the mapmaker and the frustration at his demeaning behavior is gone. A wild recklessness races through my blood instead, and for the first time in a long time, I feel *alive*. This thief stole from me, yet I don't feel any true ill intent or danger from him. In fact, it seems as if he is needing this distraction too.

"Alright, thief, since it appears you won't stop running and I no longer wish to chase you, let's settle this with a new game."

"Oh, and what would you have in mind?" he asks while swinging my stolen bag absentmindedly.

"A game of chance." A devilish smile crests my face at the immediate surprise and curiosity on his. He clearly didn't know what to expect from me.

His brows draw together in suspicion as he replies in a deadpan, "Chance."

"Yes, chance. I happen to have a set of dice for this particular game. But they are in my bag, so you will have to hand it over." I hold out my hand expectantly.

"Not going to happen. The only way you get this bag is if you win whatever game of chance you're proposing."

I scoff and cross my arms. "Worth a shot. Well they really are in my bag, so you're going to have to find them if you won't hand it over." I raise a single eyebrow, "Can you handle looking through a lady's things, or is that too despicable even for you, thief?"

He throws his head back in a laugh that echoes in the tight space of the alley. The sight causes a strange sensation in my stomach, like fluttering wings preparing to take flight.

"Oh wildcat, if you were a Lady, perhaps I would feel bad."

I roll my eyes and pretend to look offended, but he does have a point. I am certainly no Lady.

He drops the bag to the ground and begins rifling through it. Surprisingly, he doesn't dump everything out, nor does he jostle the items. He carefully searches through it before finding a small leather pouch, which he shakes gently to determine if it holds dice. At the tell-tell rattle it emits, his eyes dart to mine in silent question. I nod that these are in fact the correct ones, and he tosses the pouch to me.

Opening the drawstring, I dump the three dice into my waiting palm. They are simple in construction, made of chiseled and polished stone carefully painted with three red sides and three blue. There's no trick to them, and it truly is a game of chance. They aren't weighted or tampered with, and the ratio of blue to red is even; unlike some sets I've seen. I always loved this game as a kid. Some call it Beggar's Chance, others say Fool's Chance, but I always called it Fate's Chance. A bit of an oxymoron, true, but also a fantastic way to describe it if you ask me. Fate is often set in stone and rigid—at least by the standards of most who believe it—but chance is wild and unpredictable. Putting the two together always made me chuckle like I was in on some secret discovery or loophole of the realm. Was it fate that tossed the dice a certain way? Did fate look the other way to allow chance to prevail? Or perhaps it was an age-old struggle between the two sisters, each vying for a place in the world. Whatever it was, there is one thing I know for certain: a true game of chance is freeing in a way.

The decision to throw the dice and let them make my choice or answer a question should cause my anxiety to flare, but it has always done the opposite. I often have many choices—too many to count—and they collide in my mind like rough seas on a rocky shore. To finally not have to think and have the decision out of my hands is one of the reasons this game has appealed to me since I was young. Though I did keep this particular game to lower stakes decisions. I'm not about to let the three dice decide my entire existence, just take the edge off smaller decisions… or challenge handsome strangers to get my bag back.

There's also something about the red and blue alternating sides that itches a part of my brain just right.

Fidgeting with the three cubes in my hand, I ask the thief, "You know, what a person calls this game says a lot about them. What do you call it?"

I try to tamp down the curiosity in my voice, but it comes through anyway, and I internally wince, hoping he doesn't take too much notice of it.

The wickedly playful glint in his eyes tells me he did, in fact, notice my curiosity, and I'm about to pay for it with a sarcastic comment. "Fishing for information about me, are we? I at least like to be wined and dined before spilling everything about me."

Rolling my eyes, I hold the dice out for him to properly see. "Do you know this game or not?"

"I do. I call it Fool's Chance."

I snort. "Figures."

"Well, what do you call it?"

I feel a thrilling spark at the tips of my fingers, and my eyes alight with excitement. "Fate's Chance."

He raises a single brow but doesn't comment on my lesser-known title for the game.

"A little simple for what's at stake, don't you think?" He holds my bag up in emphasis.

"Perhaps." I shrug. "But it gets to the point."

"And how do I know your dice aren't rigged in some way?"

A purely feline grin crosses my face. "You don't."

He eyes me for a moment, considering my words. "Fine. But I pick the sides then."

I roll the dice in my hand, wondering which color he's going to claim. It doesn't really matter, because despite what he assumes, these dice are not rigged or unbalanced in any way. They are a true set of chance dice.

"Blue for me giving back your bag and red for I keep it." His smile grows as he talks. He's very clearly pleased with the idea of winning and keeping my bag.

I don't like the idea of losing it, but the important thing is that the book isn't in there. Worst I'd lose is some money and a few random items.

"Deal?"

"Deal."

His voice is deep, and it scratches down my spine in a pleasant way that I wish I could ignore as he says, "Then roll the dice, wildcat."

I toss the cubes to the ground. He wasn't wrong, this game really is simple. Call the sides, throw the dice, and whichever color has majority wins. Of course there are other rules that you can employ, like what happens if only two sides are the same color, but we don't need to complicate things.

The dice rattle on the cobblestones before coming to a stop. Three blue dice sit perfectly on the stones, and I smirk up at the stranger while thrusting my hand out for my bag.

He hesitates a moment, but in the next instant is in front of me—only a hands-width separating us. I inhale sharply as he places the strap of my bag in my hand and leans in, brushing nimble fingers over my palm in the process.

He whispers in a gravely voice, "Thanks for the game, wildcat. I will keep my word. There is honor amongst thieves, you know."

I shiver involuntarily at his breath on my neck and immediately yank myself from his orbit. This man may have been fun to play with, but he is still a stranger, and I can't even guess at his motives for choosing to tangle with me in the first place. I eye him warily and take another step back. He appears neither surprised nor offended at my obvious wariness of him, and the next thing I know he pulls that same coin from earlier out of his pocket, flicking it once high in the air before spinning on his heel and exiting the side street.

"What in the Goddess-damned hells was that?" I stare after him until he disappears and even a few moments after that. This day just keeps getting more and more strange. What's next, creatures falling from the sky to steal me away?

The brush of something slightly sharp on my shoulder makes me jump, but a moment later I realize it's just Kel coming to land. I glance up at the sky surreptitiously to ensure that nothing else is suddenly going to come down before patting his bony head. He squawks loudly in my ear, and I bat him away before he can do it again.

"Hey! No need to be so loud. I've already had to deal with so much, not to mention outsmart a thief—"

A thief.

I glance behind me to where the stranger disappeared. "No, no, no, no." Dread and something else I don't want to name curls in my stomach at the prospect of that scoundrel being the thief we need.

Kel chirps loudly again and I point a finger at him. "Absolutely not. He is not going to be our thief, understand?"

Kel's wings flap as he carries himself high above me, his bones creaking in the process, and chitters in a way that sounds suspiciously like laughter.

THE BOOKSHOP

THELAS

Master Hannon made me dust every inch of the shop and sort extra boxes of old maps before he let me leave. It would seem that Laira's visit this afternoon set him in a tyrannical mood.

I smile at the memory.

Most don't have the courage to even attempt going toe-to-toe with Hannon much less demand he find her a map and a guide through the Forbidden Forest, one of the most—if not *the* most—taboo topics for a cartographer to speak on.

She has spirit, I'll give her that.

The path to the bookshop is mostly deserted at this time of day. Late enough in the afternoon, but still early enough in the evening that most folks have made their way home or have finished their shopping for the day. It's a good time to walk about when there's no worry of bumping into anyone or being surrounded by people—which is taxing even on a good day—but it does little to hide the two figures casually walking a good distance behind me. I'm once again reminded of my father's distrust and shame. Despite the fact that I've never hurt anyone or even touched my beast since childhood, he still insists on guards wherever I go. He claims it's to protect the town, but I think it's more likely he wants to keep me in line and ensure I don't show our family's shame to others. It's not my fault he was unfaithful to my stepmother, but no one would know that based on the way I've been treated my whole life. They blame me for the ghastly form my beast takes—a stain on an otherwise pristine and prideful household—but of everything I have read, there is nothing that suggests that is the case. It's simply luck and some amount of family history. Not for the first time, I wonder at who my mother could be, and if I would be an abomination in her eyes too.

The light on the horizon dims, and dusk approaches with its creeping fingers. I shiver as the sun dips lower. If my guards think it odd that I am not going straight home as I normally do after my shift with Master Hannon, they don't show it. Though, I have no doubt they will report the deviation to my father as soon as I return home, and I will likely receive a stern note under my door tonight to not do it again. My mouth quirks up at the side as I let my plan for leaving them behind wash over me. Laira seemed like this journey was to happen quickly, and so I assume we will be leaving within the next few of days—or even as early as tomorrow. If that's the case, I'll pack my bags tonight, and slip away with my antelope, Hael, in the predawn hours before anyone notices I'm gone. No more guards. No more harsh words or cold, unfeeling notes left at my door reminding me to be better.

I turn my face to the sky and smile fully, letting the cool evening breeze rustle my hair and allow myself a moment of peace as I imagine it all. The relief at disappearing is something I never thought I'd feel, and even if I wasn't so keen on getting to the Forbidden Forest, I would most certainly want to take this chance for the sole purpose of leaving my family behind for good. I increase my pace, eager to get to Laira's shop and hear about her plan.

The door to her shop groans softly as I push it open, the smell of books and ink filling my senses. I inhale deeply; while it's not as pleasant as the academy library, it still has that old book smell I love so much. Her shop is neatly organized, with large and ornately decorated shelves—most of which appear half empty. I frown and get a closer look. The shelves are delicately painted with all sorts of magical scenes and designs. Castles and dragons, flowers and swords, golden wispy lines and prickly vines crawling up the sides. The hand painted designs make the empty shelves look that much more abandoned, but I suppose if we are to leave soon then it makes sense for her to pack up her shop. I assumed she would get someone to watch it for her in her absence, but perhaps that isn't an option.

I poke around until I find Laira scribbling furiously on a piece of paper, her words indistinguishable as she mutters to herself in between two of the towering bookshelves. I knock carefully on one shelf. Not wanting to scare her but also wanting to get her attention.

Her voice is far away as she says, "Oh. Sorry. We're closed for today." She blinks a few times, and her eyes widen when she recognizes me. "Oh, you're here! Yes, hi again. Thelas, right?"

I nod, fiddling with my glasses and darting my eyes around the shop. "So, I—um… is now an okay time to talk more?" I ask, wincing at my awkward delivery.

She pulls a small brown book from the pouch on her hip and rubs the cover absentmindedly. There's nothing on the cover or the spine, simply old scratched leather. "Yes. Best to just get right to it and not waste time."

She speaks as if trying to convince herself that this is the best option, but she still hesitates, and her words come slowly as she continues. "I found this the other day. It details a prophecy on the last page and says that a group will need to travel through the Forbidden Forest." She sighs heavily and her head droops, like the entire world rests on her shoulders. "And there's more but…well I prefer not to read it aloud."

She fiddles with something else in her pocket, nervously tapping it, as if assuring herself that it is still there. I almost question the movement and her evasiveness, but think better of it, after all, who am I to call someone out for harboring secrets?

I reach out a hand for the book. "That's fine. I'm capable of reading."

She passes the book silently, opening it to a page at the end. Her nervous energy bleeds into mine, and despite wanting to learn more about this journey she mentioned and go to the forest that has captured my attention since adolescence, I can't shake the feeling that I should approach this with more caution.

Some instinct flares to life inside me, warning me of something that I can't detect but know is there, and I take a deep breath before reading the page to calm myself.

The words fly by as I read them. When I spot Forbidden Forest in the second line my heart begins to race for an entirely different reason. I had never felt the pull like other cartographers to travel and explore, except for when I thought of discovering the entrance to that forest. Something deep within me rumbles that the years I spent learning in the shadows and uncovering every secret I could pertaining to the forest were not in vain.

I quickly read through the rest of the lines, my eyes snagging on the word cartographer before looking back up to Laira's expectant gaze.

"It's torn off at the bottom. Do you have the rest of it?"

She visibly slumps, her shoulders falling and her lips turning down in an annoyed frown. "No. It was like that when I found it."

"Hmmm. And this note scribbled on the side?"

She shrugs. "Also don't know that one. Was hoping you could tell me since you seemed to know about the forest."

Scrutinizing the note, I bring it closer to my face, as if that will suddenly make the word's definition clear in my mind. *Ilekiir* could be broken down into any number of potential meanings if we are going off of expected rules, but this is likely the language of the ancient fae, and they followed no such strict guidelines. And since the note was likely written after the prophecy was recorded—judging by the different ink—I can't gather any clues from it.

"It has a nice ring to it, and it's possible I could deduce its meaning with time, but unfortunately I do not know what it means."

"Forbidden forests and prophecies, huh?" The gruff voice sounds from above, and I stiffen at both the sudden intrusion and the sarcasm, carefully craning my head to look up and behind me to find the source.

Laira has no such reservations, however, and immediately bursts into a tirade I would not wish to be on the receiving end of. I get the idea that she's familiar with whoever strange person is hiding in her shop because she waves her fists in the air, shouting, "Thought I was done with your smart mouth, *thief*! Get out of my ceiling!"

He hops down from the sturdy wooden rafters, landing perfectly and standing to his full height in a move that would impress anyone. He clearly has strength and speed on his side, along with a heavy dose of confidence and an air of superiority.

He flips a coin in the air, giving Laira a feline grin, and my brows raise as she stomps her way over to him, throwing an accusing finger right in his face and knocking the coin from the air. The stranger manages to catch it before it hits the ground, and his eyes light up with glee at her obvious aggravation.

She keeps her eyes pinned on him as she points her finger in the direction of a desk in the corner, yelling, "And don't think I'm not mad at you too Kel! I know you knew he was up there, you terrible excuse for a shop guard!"

The nyradonn hops excitedly, bobbing its head, and I could swear it's laughing at her. She growls at either the bird or the stranger's continued smirk, it's hard to tell, though I suspect it could be both.

"What are you doing here? Did you follow me?" She spits out the words, demanding answers, but he simply slouches back against a nearby bookshelf and lazily flicks his coin into the air again.

Before she can gear up for another shouting session, I step behind her to hand the prophecy book back. "Um. Well I did read it, and while I have many questions, as I'm sure you do, I am still willing to join you."

She relaxes for a moment and nods at me while taking the book and securing it in the small pouch at her hip.

I stand there awkwardly for another long beat, unsure if I should leave her alone with this stranger, even if she does seem to know him and is clearly not afraid of him. I flick my eyes to him and he does the same to me, giving me a slow perusal like a wolf surveying prey before returning his attention to Laira when he finds I am not a threat.

I bristle at the unspoken assessment. I could show him how threatening I can really be—the beast coiling in my mind purrs at the idea, and I swipe it from my thoughts before it can take hold. It stalks back into its hole, and I breathe a small sigh of relief.

Turning my attention back to Laira, I ignore the stranger completely and ask, "Do you want me to stay?"

Flicking a strand of hair from her eyes, she faces me, turning her back on the man in what I imagine is a ploy to irritate him. It appears to work because his smirk drops a fraction as her focus shifts from him.

"Thank you, Thelas, but it's alright. This thief is nothing but an annoying thorn in my side, and I will be kicking him out shortly."

"Funny, I didn't get the impression you'd want to kick me out after eyeing me up and down so thoroughly this afternoon. Don't think I didn't notice that wicked look in your eyes, wildcat."

"Ugh! You are such an ass! I'll—"

"What will you do, love?" He steps forward, tilting his face down toward her, a cocky grin on his face.

"You'll make me leave? Kick my ass?" He looks her up and down slowly as if savoring every part of her. "I've got to say I think I'd enjoy that."

She bristles at his perusal and innuendo.

His demeanor is most certainly a bluff to get under Laira's skin, and I can't imagine what she might have done to garner his attention, but he clearly enjoys inflaming her. I step forward again to put myself between her and the stranger, but she halts me with a swift hand and a bright gleam in her eyes like a lioness about to pounce. It gives me enough pause to step back and bow my head in acquiescence. I have no intention of angering a huntress today.

Her voice dips lower as she practically growls, "Find someone else to bother, and more importantly. Get. Out. Of. My. Shop."

The stranger completely ignores her. Choosing instead to leaf through the tidy line of books to his left. "You know what I find strange?" he asks casually.

"What?" she grits out through her clenched teeth.

"That you haven't asked for my name yet."

"Ugh!" She throws her hands up yet again in aggravation, pinching the bridge of her nose. "And since when would I care to know that information?"

"Wildcat…" he purrs.

"Nope! Enough with that Goddess-damned name! It is not my name, nor do I even like it."

His grin could devour worlds. "Oh well that's definitely a lie."

She gives in, rubbing a hand against her temple. "Fine then. If you are so insisting, how about some introductions?"

He stops his perusal of her shelves, looking at us both and reaching into the pack slung at his hip for three small sacks, weighing them in each hand appraisingly as he says, "I'm Sebastian. Your favorite handsome thief, finest procurer of things that cannot be found, and…" He begins tossing each of the sacks into the air, passing them to each hand in a circular rhythm. "Master juggler."

He continues his act for another few rounds, and we both watch in mild amusement. Juggling may be somewhat impressive, but it's not like I believe him on the rest of his lofty attributes.

I study his face again. Perhaps there is something there on the handsome front. His piercings and mischievous eyes certainly play into that category.

"Things that can't be found?" she quips.

"Why of course! It's my specialty."

"Hmm." She wanders over to her desk, lost in thought, and pulls the prophecy book out to lay open on its surface while absentmindedly patting her nyradonn on the head.

The thief and I stare at each other in mild confusion, but I just shrug. I don't know her much more than I'm sure he does.

We watch as she reads the prophecy again, as if reminding herself of the words I'm almost certain she must have memorized by now. The pensive look on her face is one I've worn many times and am quite familiar with, as well as the look of pain as she comes to the same spark of an idea that I had when the stranger mentioned being a talented thief.

She buries her head in her hands, and I grimace, side eyeing the man who will likely now be joining our group should he agree. I suppose he isn't the worst company—he could even be entertaining with his sarcasm and unserious attitude, and, if he really is as good as he claims, then procuring the sword from the prophecy should be an easier endeavor.

Laira is still lamenting, a small groan falling from her lips, and so I decide to broach the subject in case she can't bring herself to say the words. "If this prophecy is truly to be believed…" I flick my eyes to the stranger, Sebastian, "We will need a thief, and you literally just fell from the sky."

"Because he was eavesdropping in my ceiling!"

I shrug. "He's a thief, seems to me like that's part of the job description. It's not just items that can be stolen. Information is often far more important."

Sebastian's mouth curves into a large open smile, exposing his canine teeth. They are the more blunted ends of human teeth, but canine teeth regardless. I wonder for a moment if he has any idea that in shifter culture, this showing of teeth would be a sign of aggressive pride. I suppose it doesn't matter, as there are no shifters here.

I shiver as the beast roars in anger in the back of my mind, but I won't give in to it today.

"Ah yes, he would be correct, I do happen to have a wealth of information to go with my exceptional climbing and eavesdropping skills as you put it."

Laira throws her hands up in exasperation at us both. "Ugh."

He gives her an appraising look, crossing his arms as he goads, "Said invaluable information may pertain to certain rumors that have been floating around. You know, the ones pointing towards war and darkness for the realm?"

His cocky grin is replaced with gritted teeth and stiff shoulders as he speaks, and though he tries to keep the relaxed, teasing quality in his voice I sense the strain behind the words and the hidden truth that lies beneath them.

Laira scowls at his pointed look as he searches her face for a reaction to this new bit of information. I haven't heard mention of any war, though I'm perhaps a bad person to ask since I am holed up in a library and deep in the archives more often than I'm in a pub and able to overhear such gossip. Not to mention Hannon shuts down any unnecessary talking quickly. Something in Laira's gaze tells me she knows what he is referencing, though, and has heard these rumors herself.

He continues talking, seemingly sensing Laira's renewed interest in what he has to say. "I have it on good authority that the king is planning a mandatory draft to prepare."

Shock rolls through my body at the words, and a sharp tingle runs down my spine.

A draft?

There hasn't even been a war in over a thousand years and even longer since a draft was necessary. I look sharply to Sebastian as they volley back and forth, my attention piqued.

Laira's eyes narrow, and she crosses her arms in front of her chest. "How could you possibly know that?"

"A thief has his ways."

Laira looks to the ceiling and closes her eyes. She doesn't move except to pinch the bridge of her nose and whisper softly to herself.

He opens his mouth to speak, but before he can she throws out a hand, shouting, "Shush! Let me think for a second."

I let out an unexpected chuckle at the chastised look on his face. He doesn't look upset, just shocked he was told to shush—something I doubt happens to him often.

"Wait—the soldiers in town were dispelling any rumors of war and openly told me there was nothing to worry about."

His jaw cocks to the side and a click sounds from his mouth. "That's the thing… these are new orders as the situation has gotten worse off the Kerimaea's coast. These rumors are about to get a whole lot more real."

She blows out a breath, her hair falling into her face. She glances at me, and I nod my head, trying to convince her that this is the right decision. She stares hard at Sebastian, and he matches her intensity, though she doesn't seem to be looking into his eyes. Instead she appears to eye the space around him. Whatever she finds there softens her face into barely restrained shock. Sebastian's brows pinch together as she tilts her face to the ceiling, another silent curse falling from her lips.

She blows out a breath. "Of course." Then she snatches the book and roughly shoves it into Sebastian's hands. "Read," she says gruffly.

He takes the book, scanning it quickly before handing it back to her. "And?" he asks, utterly unimpressed after quietly reading the words on the page and tossing the book back to her..

She volleys back at him, "What do you mean 'and?' Did you not read it?"

He rolls his eyes. "I read a 'prophecy' containing nothing but fairytales and flowery words. What are you expecting me to do with that?"

"Look—I don't care what kind of tough-guy bullshit you have going on here, but there is something serious going on in this kingdom and beyond, and this 'fairytale prophecy' has something to do with it." She begins pacing and a haunted look fills her eyes as she says, "Trust me, I didn't want to believe in it at first either, but I have had too many things happen to me in the last few days to not believe in it now."

He stares at her intently, considering her words and no doubt noting her anxious, almost desperate, energy.

She must have been through a lot recently, and I wonder at what had to happen to convince her the truth of this prophecy and all that surrounds it. I'm not sure I necessarily believe it myself, but I'm not about to turn down the opportunity to finally discover the forest I've spent so long secretly researching.

"Say I believe you. What then?" he asks.

I'm surprised when her shoulders slouch in relief. Was she really so concerned about not being believed?

"We travel as a group to find the entrance to the Forbidden Forest, traverse it, find the sword that is mentioned and… well, after that I'm not exactly sure but one step at a time, right?"

"Who is we?" Sebastian asks.

She gestures toward me. "Thelas, he'll be our cartographer and navigator. He has knowledge of the forest. My friend Willow will also come. She owns the apothecary down the road and is a skilled witch. Then there would be me, and you would make four."

"And what do you do?"

"What?" she asks, bewildered by his question.

"The prophecy—Willow is the witch, Thelas the cartographer, I'm the thief. What's your role?" He eyes her with no small amount of curiosity. "Are you the weapon's master?"

She huffs. "While I can wield a sword just fine, I am no master."

"*Ahh.* So, thread reader then? Care to share what that means exactly?"

Her face pinches together in a frown before lifting back up into a self-satisfied smile. "Not even a little bit."

They stare at each other in a fight for dominance and I purposefully cough to break them from their ridiculous game, even if I'm curious to hear the answer myself.

Sebastian breaks the silence. "I'll join you. On one condition."

"And what would that be?" Laira fires back, crossing her arms over her chest.

His eyes grow dark, and he leans in close to Laira. She stands her ground, unwilling to give him even an inch, her eyes carefully tracking his movements.

His voice is husky as he says, "Tell me your name."

"Tired of wildcat already?"

"Never. Though I am curious anyway."

She grumbles softly, hesitating for a moment before finally giving him her name. "Laira."

"*Laira.*" He says her name in a silky voice, as if tasting it on his tongue like fine wine. A blush rises to her cheeks, and I notice a stiffness in her back at her name on his lips, though I think he is too close for her to notice.

He definitely notices her blush though, and she quickly turns away, backing up a few steps and darting her eyes around her shop to avoid his knowing smirk.

"Nice to meet you, Laira." He nods to me. "And Thelas."

I nod back at him. "So, when do we leave?" I ask her.

"Tomorrow at sunrise. We plan to meet at the clearing outside of town. Bring your own supplies and get your own horse for the trip. We'll pick up some things at our first stop in Laslam, but make sure you have enough to last until then as most of our supplies starting out won't be communal."

"Got it. And where can I find a lust-filled romp to fill my time until then?" Sebastian teases, his eyes growing dark.

"I believe there is a brothel in town that provides those particular services." She provides the statement in a deadpan tone, her hands gesturing outside the shop.

"Well, I was actually thinking of a book, but I am intrigued to know how you are aware of the various services offered there."

Her smile widens, showing her slightly pointed canine teeth—a tribute from her fae blood no doubt—and runs an idle hand over a stack of nearby books. "That is for me to know and for you to never find out."

"Oh, now I really need to know. Don't worry, love, I'm sure I'll get it out one way or another. Perhaps you could even show me." He winks at the last words.

She rolls her eyes. "So, you want a book? Do you even know how to read?" she quips.

"I read the prophecy, didn't I?"

"I'm still not convinced you actually read it."

"What? A man can't want a salacious book?"

"Of course they can, anyone can. I just didn't peg you for the romance type."

He rolls his eyes. "No need to label me so soon, love."

Their banter continues as I say a quick goodbye and leave the bookshop. I chuckle softly at the prospect of seeing those two in continued close quarters while on our journey—they'll no doubt make the long days on the road very entertaining.

THE JOURNEY BEGINS

LAIRA

I gather my things and take one last look at the place I called home the last seven years. The larger furniture items and the various knick-knacks Kel and I've collected can't come with me, but I managed to make arrangements with my neighbor to sell most of them and hold onto the more important ones in the hopes I can sneak back into town and retrieve them when I have a place to move. My only ask of her was to make sure that awful High Elder Torghul didn't receive a single thing—not that he would want something touched by me anyway.

Probably thinks it would be cursed. The thought makes me scoff aloud, the sound echoing in the dim space.

At least I have the comforting knowledge that my desperate plan to save my shop was partially successful and I was able to get some money from selling the shop space and my home. While I couldn't hold onto many of the shelves, I was able to find someone to store my books for me until I can retrieve them, so at least my inventory is safe. I was shocked when the old woman who had become a regular at the shop offered to hold my books and my personal collection for me. And even more surprised when Armas showed up to help move them. I'm not even sure how either of them knew of my predicament, or why they cared, but after assurances from the woman that I could have everything when I returned, I figured there was nothing to lose.

Kel squawks from outside and I know it's time to leave. Willow and the others will be waiting.

Without looking back, I trudge out to the meeting point: a simple field outside of town bordering the forest. The air is cool and mist hangs low over the large grass field, leaking into the forest beyond. It would be eery in the dark, but there is just enough light to see clearly and cast away any suspicious shadows. Our initial plan will be to follow the river to the next largest town where we will get more supplies for our journey and hopefully scout for our final member. I approach the field slowly, apprehension and nerves weighing down my every step when I see my three new traveling companions waiting for me. They all stand apart from each other, and there is an uncertain tension weighing between them. Sebastian sees me approaching and waves a hand in my direction.

"Nice of our sleepy princess to finally join us!"

I roll my eyes and ignore his comment, choosing instead to offer a friendly wave to Thelas and escape in Willow's direction opposite them. She offered to secure my mount for the journey since I was busy with closing my shop, though I wasn't sure where she was going to get one on such short notice.

I recognize her beautiful chestnut mare immediately and see another horse, black as night, standing next to her. The two large beasts stand peacefully, their heads to the ground and happily munching on the fresh grass. Willow waves excitedly upon seeing my approach and thrusts the reins of the black horse into my hands when I get close.

"Here ya go! One mighty steed for our thread reader!" Her smile could light up the world, and I can't help but return it. There's nothing Willow can't cure with her enthusiasm and heart.

"By the Goddess, where did you find such a nice horse on short notice?" I say as I survey the black horse, running a hand down its back and legs. "You didn't rob someone, did you?"

She smacks my arm, causing the horse to jump slightly. I bump her away with my hip and rub a soothing hand down my new horse's rump as I admonish, "Hey! Your horrific violence is scaring my horse!"

She gives me a flat stare before saying, "I did not *steal* her. I bought her. From a very lovely traveling merchant, I might add."

She turns and busies herself with adjusting the saddle of her horse, Star. "And he gave me quite a good price as well. Hopefully that means there isn't something wrong with her..." She sounds sheepish for a moment before continuing, "But it doesn't matter much anyway—beggars can't be choosers! And she was the only available horse I could find that wasn't as old as dirt itself."

I snort but reassure her, "I'm sure she's a fine steed, and you did a great job procuring her in a *legal* and *honest* way. What's her name?"

She's quiet for a moment before slowly rotating to look at me. If she sounded sheepish before, now she looks as if she is trying not to burst into laughter. "Right well... turns out the merchant's daughter named her."

I raise an eyebrow at her. "...and?"

There's a moment of silence before she blurts out, "Your horse's name is Skipperoony."

Thelas and Sebastian snicker a few paces behind her, and I force my attention to stay on Willow as I stare at her dumbfounded. My mouth hangs open uselessly as I search her face for any sign that she is messing with me and playing a cruel joke, but she is very serious.

"Oh, I am not calling her that!" I slap an exasperated hand to my temple and mumble, "Children are such wild creatures."

Willow chuckles, and I pat my poor beast on her thick neck as I think through a nickname that isn't so ridiculous.

"How about just Skip?" The horse nudges me with her large head, almost knocking me over completely, and I smile broadly. "I'll take that as a yes!"

I shift nervously as Willow pats a hand on Skip's neck, and force myself to ask, "Do you want me to introduce you to the others?"

Her eyes track my hands fidgeting with Skip's reins, and her eyes soften before a beaming smile lights up her face once more. "No need. I am very capable of introducing myself."

She winks, walking away to finish loading her gear and then making her way to Thelas and Sebastian, a bright hello on her lips.

I hoist my saddle onto Skip's back and smile. The leather of the saddle slips through my fingers as I finish the final straps and pull down the stirrup. I throw my small bag over the horn of the saddle and secure my other items, checking everything over to be sure it has what I may need on short notice.

Sword? Check.

Coins? Check.

Relaxing tincture when Sebastian's antics drive me to insanity? Check.

I tuck my necklace into the pouch as well, not yet ready to wear it after its strange change in appearance and ominous glowing from days prior.

Throwing my larger bag behind my saddle with my change of clothes, necessities, and food, and firmly tightening it down leaves me finished with my task, and nothing else to do. Which means I have to face the group and get everyone moving. I feel nervous suddenly. Sick to my stomach in a way that is strange, causing my stomach to swoop and a buzz that starts at my fingertips before cascading down my whole body.

I shake my head gently to dispel the nerves when I hear Sebastian yell loudly, "*In theory*? As in, you've never done this? What kind of cartographer are you?"

I turn in the direction of his voice to see him speaking to Thelas, and his sheepish look along with Sebastian's icy tone makes my hackles raise. Thelas' hands are clenched at his sides, and he can't seem to maintain eye contact with Sebastian; instead, he's fixated on a point in the dirt, as if he wishes he could crawl into the soil and disappear.

I don't stop to think, and before I know it, I am stepping in front of Sebastian and pushing him a short distance away from Thelas. "And what, pray tell, are you all wound up about?" My hand is still resting on his chest from when I pushed him back and his eyes dart down to where it sits, and I pull it away as if burned.

Sebastian's gaze travels from my hand to my eyes, and despite being a head shorter than him, I do my best to show my displeasure. What he said is no way to talk to anyone, much less to someone in our group—someone who is important to this cause and the prophecy we are chasing. I tell Sebastian as much, though he seems unaffected and points behind me in the direction of Thelas' mount.

"Isn't that a cartographer's creature? The type that is supposed to take you anywhere without difficulty for the sole purpose of creating maps?" He waits pointedly for a response, and Thelas surprises me by giving one.

He pets the creature's nose, and it leans into his touch. "Oh, right, yes. I mean, yes, they are… but Hael hasn't left Taslae until now, and well, umm... neither have I?" He keeps his eyes focused on the same point on the ground, but his voice sounds surprisingly firm, if a little uncertain.

Sebastian looks back down at me in a huff. "*This* is the one you brought to lead us through that deadly forest?" The incredulity in his voice irritates me, but I decide on diplomacy.

I attempt to calm his fears by saying quietly under my breath, "I know he may seem a little odd, and has no experience and…"

"You do know I am standing right next to you, right?" Thelas asks in a deadpan.

Ah—I guess I wasn't so quiet after all. I tilt my head towards him and grimace slightly, "Sorry Thelas."

Sebastian rolls his eyes in the corner of my vision, and I focus my attention back on him. "I will say this one more time. Thelas is important and vital to this quest—and to this prophecy."

I glance over again at Thelas and see a flash of red thread connecting us as if in answer, the brilliant strand winding delicately from my chest to his. "I know he is." The certainty and authority in my voice surprises me.

Apparently, it surprises Sebastian as well because he gives no further argument and instead replies with doubt heavy in his voice, "Well, I hope you know what you're doing."

Sebastian moves to swing into the saddle perched atop his beast of a horse. I take another long look at its heaving form—how did he find such an odd creature? It appears as a normal horse at first, but upon closer examination, I spot the fur mixed with patches of interlocking brown and white scales on its neck, legs, and back. Spiraled horns protrude from between its ears similar to an antelope, but they are black as night and wickedly sharp. The horse's eyes glow a pulsating orange, like hot coals under a fire.

And it's massive. Even Sebastian has to jump to get a foot in the stirrup and swing himself over. I gape at the animal, certain this is not an easy horse to obtain.

He must have had to steal it from someone very wealthy and important. I eye him atop his saddle, considering for the first time that he may actually be a good thief to pull something like that off. Which could be good or bad for our group. I suppose only time will tell.

Truthfully, it doesn't matter if his presence is good or bad because a bright thread swirls around him, once again reminding me that he is necessary. It twines around him like a lover as I continue to follow its movements—morbidly fascinated that I can see them with increasing clarity. I block out the sight and shift my eyes elsewhere on him to avoid the thread snaking from his chest. I'm certain he can feel my stare, though he refuses to look over at me.

Stubborn man.

I'm about to open my mouth to continue the argument and assert again that Thelas is important when Willow steps in front of me, her arms wide.

"Alright, alright! Break it up, no need to start flirting on day one of this expedition." She crosses her arms and cocks her hip out to the side. "I mean it, at least wait until day four."

I know she is messing with me, that playful glint in her eyes is always the giveaway, but I still feel heat rise to my face, and my mind locks up at the mention of flirting with him. If there's one thing Willow knows how to do, it's diffuse tension, make inappropriate jokes, and push all my buttons. I love her dearly for it.

I throw both hands up in surrender, my voice an octave higher than it should be. "Flirting? Hah, no." I glance at Sebastian, and I scowl at the self-assured smirk on his face.

"Day four, you say? I suppose I'll have to wait to see what our little wildcat is truly capable of." He has a mischievous look in his eyes, one I'm sure I will eventually feel inclined to smack off him on our trip.

Willow snorts and walks to her own mount, her horse's shiny chestnut coat glimmering in the early morning light. She is a rather strange horse that will walk straight into a ditch if you're not paying attention and one who prefers to keep her nose buried in a barrel of oats. Why Willow hasn't gotten rid of her, I cannot fathom. I reach down to pick up her cranky house cat, Din, and place him in her waiting arms. His bones are clean and perfectly intact, unlike Kel's, and I smile at the memory of when we successfully completed the bonding ceremony. Willow had been heartbroken at the death of her beloved feline, and with the little fae blood I possessed, I wasn't sure the ceremony would work. Why the Goddess blessed only the fae with the ability to perform the ritual was beyond me, but by some miracle, I pulled it off, and Din is the perfect shining example of the nyradonn. His bones are pristine, with none missing or incorrectly placed from the hours we spent meticulously assembling them. He can jump higher, run farther, and has a heightened ability to understand speech even though he cannot speak himself. He's also just as feisty with me in his second life, but loves Willow unconditionally, so I put up with it.

He nudges his skull under her palm, and she gives in to his prodding for attention, scratching him under his jaw. Doing so exposes the bonding tattoo on her forearm. Its silvery hue starts from her wrist and winds up her inner forearm almost to her elbow. Delicate strands woven with vines and flowers intertwine with the skull of a cat—*her* cat—representing the bond she holds with Din and the reason he felt compelled to return to this second existence. No creature will awaken without a strong bond to return to—a tether to this world and a reminder of their life. The tattoo is a symbol of the newly bonded souls and carries the magic of their life forces. I've long thought the tattoos to be beautiful and wished for a bonded of my own, not just for the life partner and ally, but also the breathtaking art that would adorn my body forever.

It is said that the stronger the bond in the first life, the more powerful the nyradonn is in their second one, but Din is just as spoiled and lazy as ever, so I'm not sure if that holds true for every bone creature brought back into the world.

"Let's go Star! Time to get this joyful crew on the road!" Willow places Din on the back of her horse, and he settles down, careful to keep his claws off the horse. After gently patting Star's neck and grabbing her reins, she looks to me to get moving.

I glance quickly to the forest, my gut once again beginning to churn. Is this really the right decision? A new winding thread in my periphery catches my eye, and I see the ruby strand curling in the air straight into the forest. I feel a pull and an indescribable knowing that someone, or something, is waiting for us.

I turn to Skip and haul myself into the saddle while Kel settles on my shoulder, his weight as reassuring as ever. I take a breath and look behind me to see everyone on their mounts and ready to go. And with nothing else to tighten down or double-check, the only thing to do is move forward into the forest.

A LONG THREE DAYS

SEBASTIAN

The early morning sun blasts through the thin canopy of trees overhead, assaulting my vision and forcing me to shift my body under my thin blanket to avoid the shaft of light. The last few nights have not exactly been cold, but they also haven't been comfortable. Sleeping on hard packed dirt and awakening at the first hint of dawn under an increasingly thinning forest canopy was not what I had in mind when I decided to join the others on this ridiculous quest. But I'm not about to let them know that.

I sit up, rubbing a rough hand through my hair and tying it back loosely behind my neck as I survey the other three waking as well. We are all in various states of disarray, even though we should be getting used to the uncomfortable sleeping conditions, but it seems as if we are all relatively unprepared for a journey such as this.

Thelas adjusts his glasses and stares blankly off into the trees behind me. I can never tell what is going through that man's head, and he doesn't talk unless he's asked a question about maps, so it's not like I've been able to learn anything about him. Willow stretches her arms to the sky above and hums happily. She has woken in a perfect state of positivity for the three days we have been on this trek, and I have been quietly horrified every time. No one wakes up that chipper and upbeat, and I'm convinced something must be wrong with her, though I'm not keen to ask further. It's not my problem if she's so energetic, and I could do without the barrage of questions or observations of the forest and plants around her as she tries to fill the silence of our long hours in the saddle. I applaud her for attempting to cure the silence, truly, but after a certain point it becomes obvious and only further exposes the fact that none of us know each other and have just embarked on a long quest across the human kingdom. A journey that will—supposedly—lead us to a magic sword and what? A way to defeat the darkness I know to be building off the coast of the witch lands?

I once again doubt why I decided to join them in the first place. I may have wanted to escape my circumstances and find a different way to fight the dangers building across the continent, and I won't lie and say there isn't a part of me that enjoys the adventure of it all, but the Forbidden Forest? My father would burst a blood vessel in his thick skull if he knew what I was doing. I push him from my thoughts. I left for a reason, and despite how utterly wild this fairytale prophecy is, I can't help but wonder at its origin and its potential. Because if I am already running away, what's another month or two of potentially exciting adventure before I return? Especially if there's even the smallest chance this sword is as important as the prophecy claims. It's certainly better than sitting around in Taslae, or any of the small coastal cities where the rumors circulate strongest, and waiting for something to happen.

Laira catches my attention as she stands and stretches, her face upturned toward the sun, seeming to be in a slightly better mood this morning. Yesterday she was grumpy and waves of annoyance rolled off her, permeating every glance and coloring every clipped sentence. Even Willow couldn't seem to break through, and eventually she smiled as if she knew exactly what was wrong and was incredibly amused by it. I wondered what she knew about Laira that I obviously didn't and had to hold myself back from asking about it when Willow had wandered to the front of the group.

What does it matter that you don't know things about her? She's just some random girl, I remind myself.

There's nothing I *need* to know about her. We can continue this journey in awkward silence for all I care, and it can be a simple transaction of skills. Nothing more need come from any of this.

Still, I can't help myself as my gaze returns to Laira's form as she rolls up her sleeping mat and blanket. Her hair is slightly mussed from sleep, and I have the strangest urge to run my fingers through it to smooth it out. She beats me to it, running quick hands over her head and roughly pulling through the tangles. The strange red at the tips of her hair shines in the morning light, a stark contrast to her fair skin, and glows more of a blood red than the deep wine color it normally is. As she finishes with her hair, she looks over at me. The bright green of her eyes captures me from across the dying fire, and I see the realization that I was unabashedly watching her. I smirk, knowing it will set her on edge, and nearly laugh aloud when I see the tick in her jaw signaling I am most likely being cursed out in her mind.

She has gotten under my skin for reasons I can't even fathom. She's beautiful, of course, in a way that immediately caught my eye in Taslae and made me approach—her curves and tempting smile irresistible. But she's fiercer than I expected and genuine in a way I hadn't anticipated. She has a grudge against me that I enjoy poking at, but she has never once used it against me when we needed something as a group. She's fair and always tries to keep the peace when relentless travel and restless sleep leads to useless bickering over where to camp, which path to follow, and what rations we should eat for the night.

She didn't make a fuss when Thelas didn't know how to start a fire or how to collect firewood that's not completely soaked through. She didn't appear frustrated when I asked for a sip of her water because mine was empty, and she never once berated Willow for her constant chatter, even when I was bursting at the seams to yell at her to stop so we could travel in peace.

There's something so oddly calm about her when she is solving our problems but a simmering anxiousness in her when she is left on her own. The tossing and turning before bed, as if she's afraid to go to sleep. Not to mention the times I've caught her staring off into the distance, a look of weary despair on her face. Each time I've wondered what truly brought her on this trek. She found the prophecy I suppose, but was that all it took to launch her into this new destiny? She seemed to have a good life before—a bookshop she clearly loved and a comfortable existence that served her well.

She breaks eye contact, and I take the cue to gather up my bedroll as well. I stamp on the remains of the fire with a heavy boot, and smoke billows up as the fire is put out. Through the haze, I see Laira pouting at the dead fire, a small cup of water in her hands. She sips it absentmindedly before grimacing and glancing down into the cup, a strange look of longing in her eyes. I cock my head to the side, confused at the action. Is she hoping there was something different in the cup? I wouldn't say no to a refreshing ale, but it's a bit early for alcohol. Tea? Or does she prefer coffee?

I mentally strangle my thoughts so they don't dissolve into curiosity toward her yet again. I don't need to know if she likes coffee over tea. I don't even need to know why she was grumpy yesterday or why she isn't so easily rankled. I don't need to know anything about her or anyone else here.

But the itch in my chest speaks otherwise.

AN ENCOUNTER AT A TREE

LAIRA

Rolling up my sleeves, I retrieve the small axe from my pack and walk into the woods in search of firewood. I signal to Willow as I leave so that she doesn't worry at my being gone, gesturing with my axe. She nods in understanding, and I take that as permission to leave the small open area we found for camp tonight. The forest bordering the river that we've been following has been slowly getting less dense, with patches of grass and meadow appearing with more frequency. It's made it easier for finding suitable camping spots for the night, and offers plenty of food for our animals, but it does mean we are more exposed. While it's not exactly dangerous to be traveling as we are, there are certainly things that could go wrong. Large animals or severe weather, and of course the occasional band of mercenaries that enjoys stalking people for sport or steal coin in their free time. We decided we would all rather deal with a creature than potentially blood thirsty men, and so we've stuck to smaller animal paths and far away from the main dirt roads.

The forest is quiet and a light breeze winds its way through my hair as I spot a fallen log not much larger than my calf. Upon further inspection it doesn't appear too damp, and I decide it would be easier than hunting for a perfectly dry one to hack into pieces.

I get to work, chopping into the wood and creating pieces we can use for a fire tonight. The repetitive movement and the way my muscles burn are soothing, and I soon find myself lost in the task. I'm so deeply concentrated that I nearly jump when

I hear Sebastian's teasing voice behind me.

"You know, it's day four, wildcat, and I haven't felt even slightly seduced."

Sebastian's voice is playful as he saunters up behind me. I hear the tell-tell *fwiing* of that damn coin he's always throwing in the air, and I peek from the corner of my vision to see him lazily leaning against a tree.

Can the man not stand up straight? *Perhaps he believes having proper posture is beneath him.*

I scoff and don't bother turning around before saying, "I wouldn't dream of seducing you." I continue speaking in a deadpan, swinging the axe down to punctuate each statement, "In fact, my only dreams of you consist of you being conveniently left behind."

Thump.

I continue, "Swallowed by a lava pit."

Thump.

"Eaten by monsters in the forest or being carried away by a dragon."

Thump. Thump.

I hear him push off the tree and shuffle closer. He comes close enough behind me that I can almost feel the warmth radiating from his body.

"Ah, so you have dreamt of me then?" he replies in a pleased tone, a smug grin no doubt on his face. "You know, wildcat, not everyone is cut out for seducing. If you can't flirt, just say so."

That makes me pause. A wicked smile curves on my face, and against my better judgement, I throw the axe down on the stump, taking the bait he's conveniently thrown in front of me. Turning to face him fully, I look him up and down.

Slowly.

Methodically.

My perusal seems to surprise him at first, which then morphs into delight as he realizes I am engaging in this little game of his.

I've been too focused lately on the road ahead, the prophecy, and keeping everyone together to even think about flirting, seduction, or whatever idiotic frivolous things occupy his mind on a daily basis.

But, oh he is wrong about my abilities of seduction.

I slowly take a step forward, and then another. I bring one hand up to loosen the short leather cord holding my hair up, and when I feel the strands brush my shoulders, I run a hand through the top to mess it up a bit.

If he wants to play, let's play.

"Oh, look what we have here—a big, brave man!"

I make a large show of twirling my hair, swinging my hips, and acting as if I'm about to swoon just at the sight of his muscled chest. I untie the strings at the top of my tunic, exposing the tops of my breasts to the air as I continue with my dramatic display.

My tone is suggestive, and I pout, "Are you here to save me? I am but a damsel and need saving..."

He rolls his eyes and chuckles at my clear attempt to poke fun at him. He looks away for the tiniest of moments, opening his mouth—no doubt to say something sarcastic—and dropping a relaxed hand to his belt. I don't give him time to respond, taking the instant he is distracted to push my body—and my breasts—right up against him, gripping the hand at his belt and using the other to slowly caress the tattoo peeking beneath the collar of his shirt. The bulk of it appears to be on his shoulder, and perhaps his chest as well, but what I can see of it reaches to the top of his collarbone visible at the edges of his shirt. My fingertips graze across the shadowy lines, and I feel a slight shiver from him.

Ah, yes, thief. Not what you were expecting, hm?

My voice is heavier, and silky smooth as a petal as I hum, "This is not a bone-bonded tattoo. In fact, I've never seen a design quite like this one."

I trail a finger down to where the lines dip into the slight opening at the top of his shirt while firmly gripping his hand over his belt to remind him just how close I am.

"What are you hiding, thief?"

I tilt my head to look up at him through my lashes. There is little to no space between our bodies, and as I stare up at his annoyingly handsome face, I part my mouth slightly and let out a soft breath, inviting him in closer. Being pressed against him is unexpectedly intoxicating, and I find that the heat in my gaze is not as fake as

I had planned. I feel pressure near where my other hand is grasping his belt, and it takes everything in me not to shiver at the realization of what my presence is truly doing to him.

Satisfied at the widening of his eyes and the way his throat bobs, and believing I had proven my point enough, I pull away. He quickly grabs my wrist before I can depart and holds my hand firmly against his chest, leaning forward until his mouth is just inches from mine—his warm breath cascading across my lips. My heart races, and the image of him kissing me flashes into my mind. Of the way his mouth would feel, his tongue, his teeth.

"I'll admit, I'm impressed, wildcat. I was beginning to think you didn't have it in you." The hand holding mine squeezes slightly while his other arm snakes around to curl against my waist. "But it appears there is something there after all."

The green of his eyes seems to grow darker as he stares down at my mouth. He's gaining control of the situation, but I am determined to win this battle.

"Perhaps it is because I have had oh so many teachers to show me." My voice is breathy and sounds as warm as honey, even to my ears. His mouth frowns slightly at the innuendo, but he also seems… curious.

I don't think about the consequences when I curl my fingers into his shirt with the hand he is still holding tightly to his chest. "Would you like me to show you what I have learned, *thief*?"

I pull him down ever so slightly, still giving him the chance to turn me down if he wishes. The arm around my waist pulls me even closer, his large hand firmly gripping my hip.

"Yes," he growls before pushing me against the trunk of a large tree.

I smile at the clear intent and want burning in his eyes and at the knowledge that I did that. The triumphant part of me wants to croon at the desire in his eyes—he wants me in this moment, and it doesn't matter that my body is currently screaming for him too because I *won*.

I am the one in control here.

I brush my lips against his in the lightest of touches. His breath is warm and his lips are as soft as I imagined they'd be—but I'm not planning on giving him any more than this. I was simply proving a point, and I will not complicate things further by truly kissing him. And so I pull away just as he leans in further for another taste.

I put a finger to his lips and smirk, "Ah ah ah, that's enough for now, don't you think, thief?"

He clenches his fists against the bark of the tree, causing the muscles in his arms to flex, making me flick my eyes to the spine-tingling sight before I get a hold of myself and jerk my gaze away.

His voice is low as he says into my ear, "Yes, of course." He grits his teeth, pushing the words roughly out of his mouth as if they are the last things he wishes to say.

I stare pointedly at him and lift an eyebrow. "So, are you going to move so I can go back to chopping wood for our fire?"

He drops his arms and turns to leave, grabbing the coin out of his pocket again and flipping it into the air as he goes. I pick up my axe and set a new piece of wood on the stump when I hear him say, "I believe you, you know. You really do have some moves."

His smile is mischievous as he leaves the clearing to return to our camp, and I wonder if perhaps I didn't win after all. If maybe I just started something that I will not be able to finish, cracked open some door that now he will do anything to open again.

Maybe flirting with him like that was a bad idea.

"Nothing I can do about it now, I suppose."

I let out a frustrated breath and set myself on finishing my task of chopping firewood. It's probably more than we need, but we can always tie a few pieces to each of our mounts so that we don't need to collect as much later. I call Kel over, instructing him to get Willow to help me bring over the bundles of wood as I'm not about to ask Sebastian for help.

She doesn't say anything as she approaches, but the look in her eyes and the way she lifts her brows tells me she knows Sebastian came to talk to me alone, and she has some inkling as to what happened. I shake my head, not wanting to talk about it when he could overhear and still feeling a bit flustered by the encounter and my own sheer stupidity at engaging with him. Willow huffs in amusement and begins picking up the firewood, traipsing back to camp and unceremoniously dumping it on the ground as she shouts to Thelas and Sebastian, "Alright, you *big strong men*! Let's get this fire going!"

She looks back at me, winking at her use of my words from earlier, and I decide I would like nothing more than to crawl into the earth and stay there for eternity. Especially when Sebastian's snicker echoes through the small clearing.

"Yes, ma'am! We will get right on it." He salutes her and immediately begins stacking the pieces into a sturdy structure.

I begrudgingly join them but refuse to make eye contact with Sebastian, not wanting to see the smug grin on his face. I feel his eyes on me anyway, and it takes far too much effort to avoid him.

This is going to be a long trip, I groan to myself.

THE STRANGER

THELAS

The forest had begun to thin, and the variety of trees shifted slightly, as we got away from the lake city of Laslam and began to head further north. The air growing colder, but still mostly pleasant, and the dirt firmer under our feet. Hael was a bit restless in these more open conditions, but steadfast as always. Just like her species was bred to be—the perfect cartographer's steed. Nimble and fast, but stout enough to carry supplies and travel long distances as is necessary for this profession. Their long protruding horns were also said to be helpful in clearing debris, though I'd never tested it with her. I pat her neck lovingly—she's a clever beast and one of my best friends. My only companion for many years as I grew up since none my half-siblings nor my stepmother were interested in me. And my father was absent far too often to reprimand them for their negligence. Or reprimand himself for that matter.

And while I wasn't exactly sure what to expect on this journey after leaving home so suddenly, being in the company of Willow, Laira, and Sebastian the last few days has been pleasant. It's been nice to chat with new people and escape, but I don't feel like I should get too close to them. I don't need to be cast aside again, so it's best if this is a surface level relationship and nothing more.

Hael snorts loudly as if sensing my turbulent thoughts, and I lean forward to give her a scratch between her ears to let her know all is well when I feel a warning deep inside my mind. From the dark depths I intentionally closed off years ago, the dark voice slithers through my head—a fierce warning slashing through my thoughts and forcing me to *listen*.

I whip my head around but don't see anything besides silent trees and long flowing grasses, nothing that would cause the beast such panic.

Go away – there is no danger. I don't need you.

I feel his hulking form recede into the hole in my mind like water being sucked into a pipe.

Right before it settles in, I hear his deep rumbling voice say, "***The grass hides them.***"

I'm not fast enough for what happens next. Laira's nyradonn, Kel, swoops down just as three assailants pop up from the tall grass far to our right and two more burst from the tree line on horses and charge our group. The men are massive. Broad shouldered and carrying wicked sharp blades held high as they race toward us. They appear human and wear various mismatched articles of clothing and furs that speak to a life on the road. With their faces twisted in maniacal grins and the feral whoops and hollers echoing through the glade, it's almost as if they are hunting game instead of people. The thought makes me grimace, my lip curling in disgust and fear as the men continue their frenzied advance.

Hael rears her head back in alarm, and I grab the reins to reel her back in. Out of the corner of my eye, I notice Sebastian racing to engage the three assailants on foot—his massive horse thundering across the field, its horns angled forward. He manages to swipe at one man with his blades before I turn Hael in the direction that Willow and Laira hurried off to.

The two men on horseback split off from the group to attack the fleeing pair, and my heart lurches at the sight as they quickly catch up. The men have terrifying swords, with jagged blades ending in a sickening curve to yank flesh away and cause as much damage as possible. Quickly glancing at Sebastian, I see he is managing to hold himself well against the three remaining men. Though even someone as well-trained as he appears to be will struggle under those circumstances eventually.

My indecision weighs on me until I hear Sebastian yell over the chaos, "Go to them Thelas!"

That's all I need to hear before I send Hael into a run and we charge across the field to the opposite side where Willow and Laira have now engaged the bandits. Their horses wait behind them in the line of trees edging the field with roots and branches creating a small makeshift corral to keep them from running off in a panic. I'm momentarily surprised by the sight until I'm distracted by Willow calling out spells and clutching a bottle of something in her hand as roots explode from the ground from the few trees around us and whip toward the two men. They jump from their horses in alarm to avoid the strike, but quickly realize that the roots can be chopped down with a swift blade. Their horses run off into the woods, and I'm glad at least that we no longer have to deal with them potentially running us over. Kel and Din join the fray as well. With Kel swooping down to claw one man's eyes and Din lunging for the other man's throat. The cat scratches a deep claw mark into his soft flesh, but it's not enough to hinder the man completely, so he continues to hack at the roots and advance. That's when Laira draws her sword and steps a few paces in front of Willow, determination in every step.

I make it to them and jump from Hael's back, unsure of what to do, but grabbing the only weapon I have anyway and leaving Hael with the other two horses, haphazardly tying her reins to the outside of the corral. The sharp point of the two arms of my drafting compass pricks my palm, and I angle it to hold it like a short dagger. Only slightly longer than my hand, the point it creates at the end is the only thing close to a weapon in my bag, and it will have to do. I refuse to engage the possibility of inviting *that thing* in my mind out into the open.

I move to stand next to Willow, my arm outstretched and brandishing the drafting compass like a dagger. We watch as Din and Kel continue to repel the men, but it's clear they won't hold them for long. Willow doesn't take her eyes from the men approaching, a pair of disgusting smiles on their lips as if they are enjoying this ambush.

She whispers to me, her lips barely moving. "Stay next to me, Thelas. When Laira says 'now' I need you to get behind me. Do you hear me? This is important."

I don't hesitate before saying, "Yes, got it."

I could ask her why I need to get behind her, but now is clearly not the time, and I imagine I will find out soon enough. I trust her to an extent, despite only spending a handful of days together, and I know she and Laira are capable and have a plan to keep us safe.

The two men grab the two nyradonn and toss them to the side, seeming to gain confidence from the action, and decide to charge forward despite the roots still waving in the air—a loud cry of victory leaving their lips as they do so. Their swords are held high over their heads, ready to swing down with incredible force. Yet Laira nor Willow moves a muscle. I feel the tension in the air as the men get closer.

What are they doing?

The beast chuckles in the back of my mind, "***Waiting.***"

His words send a chill down my spine, and I shout in alarm as the men get almost close enough to Laira to reach out and grab her when she yells, "Now Willow!"

Laira drops to the ground, slashing out at the men's shins as she does. She doesn't slash deep, but she does enough damage to cause them to stumble in pain and seethe in fury.

I remember my cue and jump behind Willow just as she throws the bottle she had clutched in her hands. Laira moves swiftly, twisting herself up and out of the crouch she had been in and cuts to the side of the men, slashing up with her sword as she does. Her blade collides with the bottle, causing it to shatter and the contents to spill directly on top of the two men. Laira races back to us to stand behind Willow as the men gasp and scream in confusion and then terror. The places where the liquid touched their skin are smoking and glowing red. And soon bubbling masses appear on their faces and hands, causing them to drop their swords and roll on the ground in agony.

"Did any spray back on you?" Willow turns from the sight just long enough to survey Laira for any sign of the dangerous liquid.

She grimaces and presents her palm to Willow. "Yeah, there was some spray when the bottle broke, and it got on my palm and wrist."

Willow closes her eyes and holds Laira's wrist tight as bright green tendrils snake from her body and spear directly into the small wounds beginning to fester on Laira's skin. She winces and lets out a short grunt as Willow says a quick spell under her breath. I'm fascinated as Laira's skin lights up green and gold for an instant before abruptly fading—the sores dissolving quickly like water in a receding tide. I have never seen the special healing magic that is incredibly rare among witches and have only read about it in the vast libraries of the academy. It's truly a feat and it takes me a long moment to pull my attention from Laira's healed wrist. Just how far can her healing go?

Laira lets out a relieved sigh and rubs the spot gently. "Thanks."

"Not your best attempt at that little trick," Willow quips.

"Hey! I was working with what I had! I knew you could fix me should I get any of that acid on me."

Laira wipes the blood off her blade on the grass beside us and I stare openly at both of them. How are they so Goddess-damned *calm*?

"Since when do you have a bottle of skin dissolving acid in your belt?" I ask Willow incredulously before they can continue with their banter.

She shrugs. "Since… always?"

I gape at her, my eyes wide.

"Oh, lighten up, Thelas, I would never use it on you!"

Willow steps forward to the now unmoving bodies. Some of their flesh sloughs off as she does and I shudder. I peek over her shoulder at their dissolving forms, not wanting to linger, but also wanting to be sure they are dealt with. "Are they dead?"

"Yep, super dead!" She gives a thumbs up and smiles. She actually *smiles.*

Remind me to never get on her bad side.

The voice in my mind answers, "***Noted.***"

I choose to ignore the comment and attempt to shove the creature deeper into its hole.

Laira's panicked voice sounds next, "Where's Sebastian?"

The three of us spot him across the wide meadow still fighting the three men, though one of them seems a little worse for wear. Sebastian is clearly starting to tire, his steps slower and his body focused on defense instead of attacking. We don't need to speak before we all run towards him.

Laira yells, "You got another one, Lo?"

"No, this is going to have to be done the old-fashioned way!" Willow shouts back.

"Kel! Stop them!" Laira yells at the bird, and I see him flying swiftly to stop the man coming up behind Sebastian—clawing scratches into his face and pausing his assault on Sebastian. One man lies slumped on the ground, and I assume Sebastian was able to deal with him, but the third man seems angrier and more skilled than the rest. We don't get more than a few paces away before Sebastian is knocked to the ground, his sword flung from him.

"No!" Laira screams.

The man who knocked Sebastian to the ground relaxes a bit and grins widely as his buddy flings Kel from his face and into the dirt.

The man sneers, "You killed my best mate, you bastard. Should I break you into pieces?" He points his weapon at Laira as she approaches—her sword held high and murderous intent in her green eyes. "Or should I cut up your pretty lady first?"

Sebastian stands quickly and holds his fists out in front of him. His face is slashed on one side, though it appears to be shallow, and his knuckles are already bloody and bruised.

"Why cut up the lady when I'm so much fun? I killed that sloppy swordsman of yours, remember?" His voice is malicious and taunting, but there is a current of strain beneath his words, like it's taking all his strength just to stay standing. But his taunt works, and the man yells in anger and charges towards him.

He's not going to be able to fight off these men any longer, and Laira and Willow may be able to team up again, but it will be bloody.

The voice whispers from its dark hole, the sound of it seeming to come from right beside me and directly into my ear. "***We can stop them.***"

No! There is no "we!"

Panic wells up in my chest, and suddenly I cannot breathe. I gasp for air as Sebastian throws a punch and Laira jumps forward to slash at the second man, Kel at her back and Willow calling up another set of roots to the surface behind her. I could help. There is something I could do.

But I just can't.

I grip my arm to the point of slicing pain, but the memories are an onslaught of suffering and misery battering my mind like a ship lost at sea. A dark room. A cold collar. A *cage*.

I can't.

I can't.

I can't.

I—

And then both assailants are on the ground. I blink in surprise, momentarily surfacing from my memories to stare dumbfounded at the two men writhing in the dirt—their arms cut clean off. Blood spurts from the stumps, and their screams are deafening in the sudden quiet of the meadow. A figure materializes seemingly from nowhere and stabs both men in the chest in two quick, succinct strokes. The figure looks up at us from under his dark hood as the bandits take their final breaths.

His voice is light and smooth as he says, "I will clean this up. Gather your horses and belongings and meet me on the other side of the meadow."

Shocked, I take a moment to rest and steady my breathing on the ground while the others relax their arms and reluctantly sheath their swords. Laira, Willow, and Sebastian eye the stranger, but he simply turns away and begins dealing with the corpses. We all look at each other in confusion, but eventually Laira shrugs and leaves to grab her horse, presumably to follow the stranger's instructions. I'm not sure if we should do as the figure says, but I also don't think we could fight him, so I don't see a different option. I pointedly ignore the sight of the hooded stranger pulling the bodies into a nearby grouping of dense shrubs as I follow Laira to retrieve Hael.

Laira dips her head as Sebastian and Willow approach us, her voice hushed and urgent. "I know this stranger saved our lives, but be on alert anyway. There is something strange about him. I-I need to talk with him."

She gives Willow a knowing look, and some understanding passes between them that I don't follow.

Sebastian notices their look as well, waving a hand to get their attention. "Talk to him? We should leave while he's busy. No point in sticking around—and what was that look you two had? Keeping secrets already?"

Laira and Willow glare in unison, not bothering to respond and instead choose to unload their horses. I shrug and turn to do the same.

"Might as well let them do what they want. Here's a fine enough place to camp for a while anyway," I tell him.

The stranger returns, approaching us with a calm and steady gait, an enormous copper stag following him. Where was that thing during the battle? Would've been helpful in knocking a few of the men around.

We instinctively gather in a close circle, each of us preparing for another fight, but he stops a comfortable distance away and I eye him warily as he slowly removes his hood. His hair is shorn close to the sides of his head, but longer on top and dark as night, exposing sharply pointed ears. Though, upon further inspection, his hair is not entirely black. The shifting sun reveals hints of colors like blue, purple, and green. Reminding me of the time I spilled oil in Hannon's shop. His face is angular, with intense grey eyes that appear that much more intimidating because of the silvery markings adorning his tanned face. He stares at us intently with an unreadable expression, and I try not to appear intimidated.

His voice is like velvet as he breaks the deafening silence. "My name is Faldorn. I wanted to ensure no one was gravely injured before being on my way."

Sebastian's awed voice sounds to my left, "Is that a Kalleian Elk?"

The fae glances at Sebastian, with only the briefest amount of hesitation as he replies, "Indeed."

"What is a Kalleian Elk?" Laira asks.

"They're a mythical beast from deep in the heart of the fae lands of Caelamne. They're said to only be ridden by the most decorated of fae war generals..." Sebastian trails off, and we stare at the fae again with newfound interest.

The stranger sighs. "Yes."

He doesn't elaborate further, and I get the sense that he wouldn't even if we asked him.

Willow speaks up, probably sensing the need to change the subject. "Hello, Faldorn. Thank you for helping us out there and for cleaning up the mess."

Her eyes dart to Laira, who is staring intently at the stranger as if she is trying to solve a complicated puzzle. Willow nods, seemingly making a decision. "We are not severely injured, and I thank you for your concern. Might you rest with us for a bit? We were just about to make camp."

Sebastian mutters, "We were not—and we do not need to invite strangers into our camp even if we were."

Willow smiles and bats her eyelashes, her tone sickly sweet. "Ah, but weren't you a stranger just days ago? We invited you in, didn't we?"

Sebastian closes his mouth and walks away to unpack, though his jerky movements say he is clearly frustrated with the decision.

The stranger considers her proposal for a moment and then nods his head once, replying simply with, "I will get firewood."

I unsaddle Hael before grabbing my drafting tools and the map I've been working on as we've traveled. I need some peace and quiet after that fight, and there is a smooth stump out there calling my name.

Sebastian snags my arm as I walk away and speaks quietly under his breath, "Don't go too far from camp."

The look in his eyes is serious but also tinged with worry, and my chest unexpectedly warms at the idea of someone worried about my safety.

"I'll stay within eyesight." I reassure him.

He relaxes at my words and lets go of my arm. As he turns to unsaddle his own horse, I say, "Hey—make sure you get Willow to look at your injuries. There's no use in letting anything fester."

He holds a hand up in acknowledgment and angles his head back to me to reply, "I will if you do."

His gaze snags on my arm, and I pull down my sleeve, knowing what is there and not wishing to acknowledge it—the shallow divots in my skin created by claws and the dried blood that surrounds them. I don't look at his face as I turn around, walking silently into the thin tree line.

SMOOTHING OUT THE corners of my map, I survey the lines again. Perhaps I should change the edge of the Lower Tiramunde River and add less trees. Since we have been sticking close to the river's edge, I had noticed the river was wider in some sections and more curved in others, both of which are not quite present on my map. I make a mental note to alter it later so it's more accurate before grabbing the same old book I've practically had glued to my hands since finding it six years ago.

It's a short book. Though calling it a "book" is perhaps too generous; with only twenty pages, it's more of a short notebook than a true tome. But it is bound well and contains some of the most vital information I've come across in relation to the Forbidden Forest. Making it not only an invaluable treasure, but also something that could get me in serious trouble.

Just having this book in my possession is enough to get me thrown out of the Cartographer's Guild. Even worse than that, it's enough to garner the wrath of Master Hannon—which is a fate that many would consider worse than death. The old man is a master cartographer, sure, but he has the most corrupt and darkest spirit I've ever seen. And his power within the Guild is absolute. He even has sway with the King of Eislekest, according to rumors swirling around the academy.

The binding is worn smooth from my years of handling it, and I turn to a familiarly baffling page. To this day I am unsure what it says exactly, despite years spent attempting to decipher it with every language book I could find. The closest I could get is narrowing it down to one of the fae languages—which still leaves an incredibly daunting pool of candidates to choose from. With hundreds of thousands of years to come up with different dialects and thousands of fae species, it's nearly impossible to narrow down without more information.

"Sela a' Core... Sela a' Core." I repeat the words as if doing so will suddenly reveal their meanings and sigh. "What does it mean?"

My quiet frustration is interrupted by a soft shuffling behind me, and I turn to see the strange fae, Faldorn, making his way over to me. The fact that I could hear him approach means he's either terrible at sneaking around or is purposely alerting me to his presence so as not to frighten me. My money is on the latter. Based on his skill in combat, the fae could probably walk through a valley full of sleeping dragons and not wake a single one.

"I have an idea about that," he says abruptly.

I stare slightly dumbfounded at him. "An idea about what?"

"Sela a' Core." He cocks his head slightly at me, studying me in a way that reminds me of a bird listening to the trunk of a tree, readying to snatch an insect from its depths.

"You heard me? From way over there?" I shift my gaze from him to where I had last seen him sitting. And sure enough, his pack and sword still rest comfortably under a tree on the edge of the meadow we decided to haphazardly make camp in.

He cocks an eyebrow, clearly confused at my question. "Yes. I am fae. Now, you said Sela a' Core? Correct?"

"Um yes, I did. Why?"

"Is this a term you know, or do you have a spelling for it?"

I grip the book tightly in my hands before I think better of it, and he sees my reaction, eyes shifting to the pages in my grasp. I'm not sure yet if we can completely trust this fae, but I suppose he did save our lives. And if he knows anything about the words in this book, wouldn't it be better to show him so he can tell me? I've spent so long wanting to understand, and this could be my chance. I look down at the open book in my lap, knowing these pages have taunted me for so long.

I nod once to myself and show him the book. "Sela a' Core is referenced multiple times throughout this book. Best I can deduce is that the term is an important location, though I have yet to discover the meaning or even the language it's from. I believe it to be fae in origin though."

He takes the book gently and studies it for a moment. His eyes grow wide as he says, "The Cave of Swords."

His reaction is surprising, coupled with the slight awe in his voice and the fact that he can read the words, has me jumping to my feet in excitement.

"You—you can read it? You know what it means?"

I move in close to him to read the page myself, as if now that he has read something from it, I suddenly will be able to as well. But of course, the words are just as mysterious as before.

"Sela a' Core as you have it here, means 'The Cave of Swords.' I wanted to read the spelling first to be sure, but it is as I thought."

He hands the book to me and begins to walk back toward his things.

"Wait! What else does it say? What is The Cave of Swords?" I yell to his back, already starting to jog to follow him.

The fae is exceptionally fast and is already digging through his pack before I even get close. The others quickly notice the exchange and rush over to see what the noise is all about. Laira opens her mouth to say something when Faldorn speaks instead.

"I must go. Sela is nothing I need to be involved in, and I have already stayed too long. I must be moving on." He slings his pack over his shoulder as he speaks, and a sharp *shwiing* sounds as he sheathes his sword at his back.

I step in front of him, which is perhaps the bravest thing I've ever done, seeing as how he is at least a head taller than me and as broad as a tree trunk. He effortlessly sidesteps me, so I end up talking to his back as I shout, "You can't go!"

He doesn't respond, but he does slow slightly. Enough that I can walk up behind him and grab his shoulder in an attempt to turn him around. He doesn't budge, but he also doesn't continue on his way.

He is unnaturally still, but I don't take the time to study him for too long before I blurt out, "You know what this book says, and you know something about why it's important. Please, at least just stay and tell us what you know. You saved our lives before. And I don't know what it all means, but I have a gut feeling that knowing this information will help us in the future."

I visibly deflate when he still doesn't respond, but then I notice a strange flash in the distance. Directly in front of us, at least twenty paces away, a single beam of sunlight is disrupted as it filters through the trees. As if something solid has passed in front of it and blocked its path for a moment. I squint to try and get a better look at what it might be, but all I can see is the disruption of light as whatever it is moves.

Suddenly, Faldorn whirls around and marches back to his tree—setting his pack on the ground and removing his sword and sheathe to rest against the rough bark. We all stare in confusion, exchanging glances with each other as his back is turned to us.

He doesn't look at any of us, but his voice is firm as he says, "I will stay."

I'm struck speechless for a moment before I exclaim, "That's great! We can—"

He holds up a rough hand, interrupting the beginning of my excited rambling.

"I will stay, *for now*. I will tell you what I know of the words in the book and the tales they connect to. And I will hear you out, as you all are clearly here for a reason I can't fathom. But I will not promise to stay and join you after that."

Laira speaks up then, her gaze contemplative and focused. "Understood." She eyes him a moment longer before turning to meet my gaze. "Thelas, do you mind sharing whatever is going on right now? What book? And what cave?"

A self-conscious smile forms on my face, and I rub the back of my neck nervously. "Right, well, I was going to share it with you all eventually, but I was hoping to try and figure it out first."

She nods gently, as if encouraging me to continue and sits down on a fallen log.

I exhale and dart my eyes around the group, not sure who I should look at first. "I found the book six years ago when I was cleaning the archives in Ferrill. It had clearly been forgotten, and when I opened it to see where it should be shelved, I saw the map inside. And though I couldn't read the words and I wasn't at all certain of what I found, I suspected immediately the map was detailing parts of the Forbidden Forest…something that has been taboo to talk about for years. The Cartographer's Guild refuses to speak of it, and it's not an unknown secret that they punish those who do."

Laira's eyes light up in realization. "That's why that old mangy cartographer reported me and was in such a fit when I brought it up."

I nod grimly. "Yes, it is. You're lucky he didn't take you seriously and only reported you to the Elders. I've hidden this book for years. Secretly spending all the time I could spare attempting to decipher the words and the map."

Sebastian steps forward and says, "That's why you believe you can navigate this forest that most believe doesn't even exist. Because of that book."

"Exactly. I've found other things over the years as well, but only snippets and scribbled notes. Nothing as big as this book. This forest is shrouded in not only the magic of its creation but also in its purposeful exclusion from our collective history. Even in the sacred libraries of Markael there is no mention of the forest existing."

"That is because it doesn't."

We all whip our heads in Faldorn's direction and Willow, Laira, and I say in alarm, "*What?*"

He crosses his arms and smiles like he's the only one in on an amusing joke. "Well, it does and it doesn't."

Sebastian casually leans against a tree before saying, "Spit it out, old man."

Faldorn frowns but ultimately answers our question. "The forest is magic. Made of magic, infused with magic—and so it has strange properties because of this. I'm not certain exactly how it works, but it somehow exists in our realm *and* another. One of deeper, more ancient magic that is rarely tapped into anymore. Similar to how parts of the fae lands exist in a space separate from the physical land. A sort of parallel plane of existence that can be accessed only at certain points in this one."

Laira crosses her legs and asks, "But I thought you said something about a cave?"

"Well yes, that's what young Thelas was repeating to himself. Sela a' Core means 'The Cave of Swords' in an ancient fae language, of tree sprite origin, I believe."

"So where does this magical forest come in?" Willow counters.

"It guards the cave." Faldorn rumbles.

Sebastian laughs. "Guards the cave? You make it sound as if this forest is some beast guarding treasure."

Faldorn's smile turns sharp as he looks over at Sebastian. "It *is* a beast, worse than any you can imagine and twice as smart. It supposedly harbors all manner of traps and magical forces to stop anyone from successfully navigating it. Without a competent navigator, you would become lost in mere hours and wander aimlessly until you died. And it is believed to be guarding treasure, though I don't know what."

Sebastian scoffs. "Magic forests that don't exist but also sentient enough to guard a treasure. I'll believe it when I see it."

Laira gives Sebastian a scathing look at his refusal to take Faldorn seriously, before throwing a question of her own. "That cave must be where the sword from the prophecy is being held. Do you know anything about a sword made of light or one with incredible power?"

Faldorn scratches his chin in thought. "Can't say that I do. What prophecy?"

It's Laira's turn to look a bit sheepish at having accidentally revealed information but she doesn't hesitate for long before pulling the small book from the pouch at her hip and passing it to Faldorn.

"The last few pages have something called 'The Prophecy of Souls' written on them as well as a few scribbled notes that we haven't been able to interpret yet." She shifts uncomfortably as he reads the page. "I found this not long ago and it sort of… started this quest that we are on."

Faldorn finishes reading, an indecipherable look on his face as he stares at each of us, before he simply hands the book to Laira and leans back against his pack. He doesn't speak for a long time, but we all continue to stare at him, waiting for his reaction and any information he can give us.

He sighs, swiping a scarred hand through his hair, before reluctantly meeting my gaze. "That prophecy is in the common tongue, but many of its words—as well as the rest of the book—are written in the ancient language of the fae. One not used ubiquitously in thousands of years. I don't know much of the language, but I could attempt to tell you what I can of both books in your possession."

My eyes widen and I nearly fall forward on my face despite being firmly sat on the ground. "You can help translate this book? And Laira's?" I look over at her, and she gives a mystified smile to match my broad grin.

"I will help you, but I will take no further part in your quest." He dips his head to me. "After all, what you said before is true. This information could save your life, and I would not be an honorable fae if I didn't at least offer you this."

"Thank you!" Laira and I echo at the same time.

She gestures toward the book in my hands, "You first—you've waited far longer than I to uncover the truth of your book."

I clutch the worn book in my hands, an unspoken gratitude shining in my eyes, and move to sit next to Faldorn.

Soon, we are lost in scribbling notes, going back and forth on pronunciations and potential meanings of words and passages. The rest of the world fades away, and I hardly register the others as I focus on finally revealing the secrets this simple book has hidden from me all these years.

A NEW THREAD

LAIRA

Thelas and Faldorn spend many hours translating what they can of Thelas' book. The rest of us took that time to properly set up camp: stoking a fire, cleaning up the area for bedrolls, feeding and watering the horses, and dividing up rations for the evening. The sun slowly dips and before long it is nearing sunset. The temperature in the meadow drops as the sun does, and soon I'm reaching for my cloak to throw over my shoulders. Kel and Din sit wrapped up in each other near the fire, carefully intertwined in a ball of bones and white feathers and I decide to take their lead to get comfortable for the evening. Kel lets out a soft trill when he realizes I decided to sit next to them and I smile warmly at them both, giving Kel a little pat on the head while absentmindedly surveying our surroundings. The air has a slight chill that prickles my skin, but it smells divine. Like soil, evergreen, and a cool early summer's evening. The meadow is surrounded by a large circle of trees, and the upper branches of the forest to our backs sway in the breeze—the sound utterly melodic. I close my eyes and inhale deeply. There is something so alive about this place, and as we've traveled further from town I've enjoyed stretching my fae senses. When in a populated city, the advanced hearing and sense of smell can be overwhelming and stifling, but out here it is peaceful.

Willow plops down on her own bedroll beside mine and I smile. She takes my lead—leaning back and stretching her arms as she no-doubt savors the same sensations I do. Early on in our friendship, we bonded over our shared love of the natural world. We both have a connection to it, what with her witch magic and my innate fae instincts, and it was easy to spend our days in the small forests surrounding

Taslae. All witches have some ability to wield nature, whether that be simply having a knack for growing plants or by bluntly controlling them. And I always enjoyed when Willow would explain her magic and the different forms it can take. Over the years, I learned that the witches were said to have been granted skill over the natural world by the Goddess, with male and female wielders being practitioners—though it was much more rare to see a male witch. While I had been able to glean a lot from Willow's stories and from my books, I knew little of Willow's other magical abilities. Of the all too coveted magic to not just manipulate plants, but manipulate bodies. It wasn't something she talked about much, and the few times she did open up it was to insinuate that her gifted power was something that went too far—progressed beyond the bounds of what anyone should be allowed to do. I know it haunts her still. Her past, her magic, and the knowledge of just how far she can go.

My mind drifts to the fight and the men Willow and I took down. I never expected to need to use the skills we've honed over the years to that extent, but I'm thankful we didn't hesitate. Already, I feel a blooming affection for Thelas—and even Sebastian. In the face of danger I'm proud I could protect them and myself. Perhaps I should feel guilty for killing two men, but I don't. Their lives were forfeit the second they made it clear they had no intentions to leave us alive.

Thelas' voice rises, breaking through my morose thoughts as he talks excitedly with Faldorn, and I can't help but smile at his unbridled enthusiasm. It's nice to see someone's true passion come out, and I'm glad Faldorn agreed to help us, even if it's just to help us translate part of these books. I take the opportunity of distraction to study the fae more closely. He's exceptionally beautiful and entirely inhuman. His black hair is not simply one color in the waning light—it shines in hues of blue, purple, and green as he moves, and his eyes are the palest shade of grey I've ever seen. Almost translucent and full of a calm energy that radiates from his whole body. Sharp canine teeth flash as he speaks, showcasing deadly fangs that could easily tear skin and harken back to the predators the fae used to be. Scars crisscross his arms and hands, a history of violence scrawled across them. But perhaps the most interesting thing about his features are the swirling lines on his face and arms. They form points around his nose and on his forehead and branch out in sweeping arcs across his cheeks and under his eyes before continuing down his body and ending on his hands. They have the appearance of scars, but their silvery hue makes me think they are markings of some kind, whether that be from natural forces or not, I'm unsure. Either way, they are striking.

One look and you know he is not human—but there is also something familiar as well, something I can only describe as my own fae blood recognizing his. I'd seen a few fae in the towns I lived in over the years, and they all gave me a similar feeling, as if there was a part of us that called to each other.

Thelas stretches his legs, and when he begins gathering his notes, I get up to join them.

"How'd it go?"

He beams at me. "Great! We didn't get everything, but what we did manage to translate is fascinating."

"That's good news." I smile at Thelas as he absentmindedly waves to me and walks away to find his pack before devolving into a new mess of paper, ink, and muttering.

I giggle. "He's very good at that, focusing wholeheartedly on a single thing."

Faldorn's voice is smooth, but he can't hide his own underlying amusement as he nods toward Thelas. "Indeed."

"So… any chance you want to take a look at this book too? Or would you like to rest first?"

He nods once. "Now is fine."

I plop down next to Faldorn, handing him the book and watching intently as he opens it and flips through the pages. There is still just enough light to see by, though I suppose for a full-blooded fae like himself he shouldn't have any problem reading in the dark anyway.

"Tell me, do you recognize any of these words?" He eyes the tips of my ears visible through my hair.

"Not really, though a few do seem strangely familiar." I take a deep, steadying breath before continuing carefully, "Ma always said that when that happened, it was our fae blood calling to us."

Faldorn returns his eyes to the pages. "Even if you knew some of our language, it likely still would've been difficult to read. This is old. Far older even than I am, though I can understand most of what it says. Of what I can tell from this book, it was likely someone's field notes from their travels and details various creatures and plants. Sorry to say not as helpful as Thelas' book, but interesting all the same."

My shoulders droop a bit that there weren't any secret notes that would help us, but I suspected as much from the drawings scattered throughout the pages. At least the prophecy is useful to us.

He smiles, noting the drop in my shoulders and adding lightly, "And your Ma was right."

I whip my head to look at him. "She was?"

"Yes, many of those who are part fae talk of the feeling of being drawn to other fae. And even if they have no knowledge of the fae dialects, are able to pick them up quickly and often instinctively know the meanings of some words. Our fae blood will always call us home in that way, among others." His face grows somber at his last words, and I wonder at his reasoning for being in the mortal lands if that is truly the case.

"I haven't seen many fae in the past, is there a reason why?"

"The fae keep to their lands for the most part, but some do venture out. Our magic and connection to Caelamne is strong, but many enjoy visiting other lands from time to time. To do something new with their long lives, to trade, or to simply explore."

I ponder his explanation for a moment, thinking back to the few times I had actually seen fae. They weren't ostracized, but they were definitely treated with a heavy respect and generally only the boldest of humans would approach. From what I noticed, humans often had a tendency to shy away from what was different. And the fae were different. Their magic was ancient and powerful, and their appearance was always striking.

"If that's the case, then what are you here for?"

Faldorn immediately stills at my question, and I want to take it back as pain flashes in his silver eyes. He doesn't move, doesn't even appear to breathe and I quickly jump to cover my probing with a different subject. "My necklace also had an odd reaction when I read the prophecy at the end of this book aloud for the first time. It started to glow."

He chuckles softly. "I have seen many strange magics in my lifetime, a glowing necklace is the least of them."

I shift nervously and smooth out a lock of my hair. "Right."

"Shall we try it? I'm interested to see this reaction," he suggests.

"Of course!"

I get up to snag my bag from across the camp and dig through it for my necklace before making my way back to Faldorn. Gingerly, I hold it out to him on an open palm, and he takes the cue to begin reading.

He reads a few clipped sentences from a random page in the beginning of the book, and we eye my necklace waiting to see if it will glow, but nothing happens.

He's contemplative as he remarks, "Not the rest of the book then. Interesting."

He flips to the last page and reads the first line of the prophecy, causing my necklace to emit a soft glow. He watches the stone for a moment but otherwise doesn't appear impressed by the display.

He points toward the few lines written to the side of the page. "And what of this?"

"It activates my necklace, same as the prophecy."

"Hmm… Could it be part of the missing passages from the section torn from the bottom?"

I shrug, unsure. "I hadn't considered that, but it is possible I suppose."

His eyes are apologetic as he hands me back the book. "It's only speculation at this point without that missing section unfortunately."

"Yeah, I know. I don't like the idea of following this prophecy when we don't even know the whole thing, but I didn't really have much choice." I trail off as the dark vein on my hand pulses once and the nightmares threaten to bubble to the surface again. I move my hand behind my back in what I hope is a nonchalant manner, but Faldorn's eyes miss nothing, and I know he saw my strange movements. He doesn't say anything about it though and I'm relieved I won't be forced to explain myself.

"Thank you for your help," I tell him, truly grateful for his expertise and willingness to stay longer.

He studies me, likely noticing my sudden stiffness and voice laced with an undercurrent of fear, but he doesn't ask any questions.

A spark of a thread briefly ignites in my vision as we sit together, and I blink, unsure if I really saw it at all. Squinting my eyes, I attempt to focus my attention to will the thread to return, needing to see if my instinct is correct or if the connection I feel to him is simply fae in nature. The thread flares to life again, and I watch as it swirls between us, a vibrant strand that is too bright for only having just met. The knowledge settles over my skin, and I relax, pleased with the fact that my instinct about him when he first appeared was correct.

You should trust yourself more, a small voice echoes in my mind, but I turn away from it, not wishing to encourage that thought any further.

Faldorn's curious voice startles me, and my cheeks heat as I realize I've been staring at him. I was focused on the thread, but he doesn't know that and likely thinks I am a brainless fool.

"You have an intriguing magic about you."

Not expecting that response, I sputter, "What?"

He gestures with a hand around me. "The magic around you. It glows like fire and has an ancient quality that speaks of something timeless and knowing."

I examine my hands and body as if I will suddenly see what he is talking about, but I see nothing of the sort.

"What kind of magic do you have?" he asks, tilting his head to study me.

Threads from the corner of my eye snap into place, and I bask in their comforting energy. I know the threads present here and the ones I've seen in the past signify important relationships, but apart from that, I am unsure what they actually are or what it means that I can see them.

"I don't know."

My answer is honest, but I know there is more I could tell him. In the end, I decide to hold the rest of the information back unless he joins us, afraid that if I tell him of the threads, he may further retreat into himself. I suspect he's been alone a long time, and it's entirely possible that hinting at a deep connection between all of us could push him away.

He nods, accepting my response without argument, and gets up to move closer to his pack and chosen spot around the fire. His face is illuminated in the now dark evening, the firelight having a fascinating effect on his silver markings. Like coins glinting in the sun or scales on a fish in a swift river, they sparkle and seem to shift across his skin. I watch him settle, sending a prayer up to the Goddess that she will change his mind and convince him to join us.

I look down at the words of the prophecy again, counting off the different people in our group and knowing we still need a weapon's master. I eye Faldorn's assortment of swords and knives and his fluid movements. A pang of sadness for him pulses in my chest—he may not want to join us, but I wonder if, like us, he has any choice in the matter.

LIKE CALLS TO LIKE

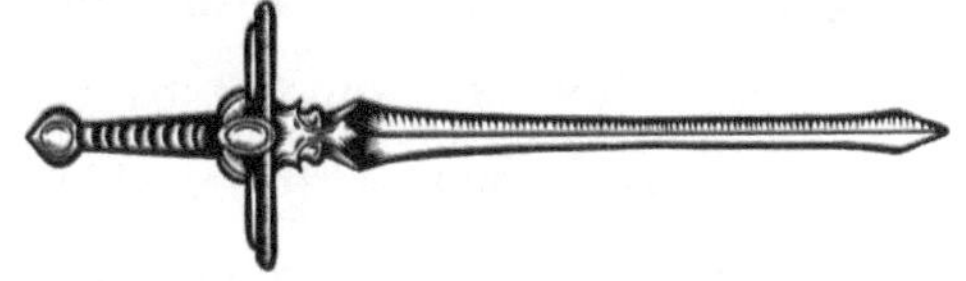

LAIRA

I stare into the small campfire, my mind drifting. I'm not entirely sure what I was expecting from this quest, but it wasn't complete silence among my fellow group members. Or getting attacked by bandits. Or being so cold my bones rattle as loudly as Kel's. I suppose I grew used to the ease of living in a town, in a house with all the amenities needed to live comfortably. It's been quite some time since I've felt so uncomfortable, though I know I should get used to it. Who knows how long it will take us to reach our destination?

Who knows if our destination actually exists? A gloomy voice interjects in my mind.

Maybe this is some elaborate goose chase for a treasure that is truly just a myth. I cease staring into the fire to glance at the others as they, too, seem to be in their own worlds. Either blankly gazing into the fire as well, or on alert studying the forest beyond for more threats. Faldorn being the one to stare the longest into the darkness.

The threads suddenly spark into my vision, each bright red strand delicately connecting us. I glance down to see four threads spreading from my chest to each person, but upon further examination, there are also the beginnings of faint threads connecting the others as well.

We are each intricately connected, then, not just myself.

Willow may believe that I am the catalyst for all of this, but I simply see the strands. I can't actually do anything with them. She also believes I am the center and leader of all of this, but the threads clearly show I am not the only pin holding this group in place. Squinting my eyes, I study them more closely. They vary in thickness and intensity, with the thread between Willow and me woven with multiple strands like a thin braid and shining a brilliant shade of scarlet. The thread with Faldorn, however, is thinner but still strong and bright like a glittering ruby.

To my annoyance, I see the thread between Sebastian and me is even brighter and stronger than it was when we first met. I suppose that is to be expected when you spend day after day with someone and are connected by a prophecy. Even if they annoy you the entire time. I silently huff and lean back against a tree, staring openly in his direction.

That thief is too flirtatious for his own good and far too playful with that constant smirk and teasing attitude. I grumble internally as I have to admit to myself that it has been at least partially entertaining trading barbs and teasing him right back. Though I'd never tell him that.

The tree's bark digs into my back, and my hands fidget with the soft grass at my sides. I breathe in deeply, inhaling the scent of pine and moss. There is something calming about a steady tree—the stillness and serenity contained in their tall trunks is something I am often grasping for in my mind when it's a maelstrom of difficult thoughts and near constant self-doubt. But being near them allows me to practice the stillness they do so well, and for a time my mind is clearer.

Even so, the relative silence in the meadow begins to grate on me, though I keep quiet in the hopes someone else will fill it. Soon, the need to say anything overcomes my anxiety of speaking first, and I open my mouth, "Alright, enough of this silence."

I look over at Sebastian and Faldorn. "You both have been studying the tree line for long enough. Is anyone or anything going to bother us?"

Sebastian opens his mouth to answer, but Faldorn beats him to it. "I do not believe so. I have not heard a presence other than small game for some time now. We should be safe for the night." He eyes me curiously as he speaks, as if he is trying to figure out what I am going to say that would require I first make sure we won't be disturbed.

"Good, now we can stop being so silent." I gently clap my hands together. "Anyone want a story?"

Willow immediately perks up from across the fire. "Oh! Yes! She has the best stories."

"A story?" I turn from her as Sebastian crosses his arms, his voice dubious. "What are we, babes in our mother's arms?"

Always so grumpy.

I cover my laugh at my internal assessment with a snort, and roll my eyes, choosing to ignore his comment. He will change his mind after this particular story, I'm sure. It's one my father would often tell my sister and me, and he knew all the best stories.

I find a small stick next to my thigh, thin enough that I will have an easy time breaking it up and peeling the layers off it. I always remember the tales best when I have an object to fiddle with while I tell it.

I take a deep inhale, picking the words from my memory and speaking slowly. Soon, though, the words come faster and flow easily as I speak into the dark night.

"A very, very long time ago, when the lands were new and the realm young, there was a Goddess. She was incredibly beautiful. With hair the color of an evening sky—black as night and twinkling with spots of light and swirling colors of purple, blue, and white. Some say, there were entire other worlds contained in her long tresses of midnight locks. Her beauty did not end with her hair though; her skin shone with shades of pearl dipped in sunlight, and her eyes sparkled like expensive jewels—changing from blue, to green, to red or yellow, purple or simply clear as ice. Like light that is filtered through prisms of glass."

I pause my fidgeting of the stick, its bark now part of the way stripped, to see four sets of eyes watching me intently. I sip from my canteen before continuing. The words a steady cadence, an easy dance I know well.

"But her beauty was not what made her great. No. She was strong, and she was kind. This new land she found herself in was a dangerous place for all who dwelled in it. And she took it upon herself to come to their aid. From the smallest creature to the largest, she helped them all. Because it is not just the weak that require aid, it is also often the strong that need a helping hand. The Goddess came across one such creature one day, the giant beast groaning in fits of despair, stuck pitifully in a small valley it could not climb out of. The walls were steep, the ground soft and moist from relentless rain days prior. She watched the beast for a time to determine in what way it needed assistance," I pause, taking a moment for the scene to settle and to gather my next words. "The creature appeared to have two wings, both wilting uselessly on each side of its back. It was clearly much too weak to climb the steep walls of the valley and fly away."

I focus on my small stick as I continue, "She tried many times to get close to the beast, yet every time she got within a few paces—it roared in fury and thrashed about. So, she had to bide her time until the beast was too exhausted to protest her healing." I pause long enough to share a meaningful glance with Willow, the understanding flowing between us with my next words. "The Goddess knew the creature was only acting out of fear and anger at the circumstances, not at her. She could see it was hurt that pooled behind the great beast's eyes. Not fury."

Willow's eyes glisten slightly as our contact holds—that fight many years ago glimmers between us. One of misunderstanding, fear, and utter helplessness. It nearly ended our friendship, that fight, but like the Goddess, we learned the other was not acting out of malice, only extreme hurt and pain.

I nod ever so slightly to her, acknowledging the past, and smile softly for the continued friendship and understanding of the future. She returns the simple gesture, and I lift my gaze from hers to stare into the dark forest before continuing in a lighter tone.

"The Goddess was patient, and eventually the poor beast became too tired to lift even an eye to her, and she knew she had little time to waste. She used everything she had learned of healing and magic, crafting braces for the wings to hold them in place so they might heal properly, and placing bandages packed with herbs to mend the various scrapes and cuts on the beast's dark green hide. She marveled at the creature as she worked, finally able to get a close look at the intricate scales, long serpentine body, and great branching antlers. The wings were especially impressive, taking up a large portion of the small valley floor and speckled with pinpricks of golden scales against the dark hide."

I smile at the image I've painted of the creature. I've always wondered what such a beast would be like and just how grand it would be to witness in person. Such creatures were rare these days, having mostly been lost to time.

A chill breeze curls through my hair, causing the fire to pulse wildly before calming once more. The effect is somewhat eerie, and my gaze is drawn to the fire for a moment before I remember myself and continue with my story.

"The beast never moved, nor appeared to acknowledge the Goddess's presence, except for the occasional breath and twitch. Despite this, she talked to the creature—partly to elicit at the very least an ear twitch or claw flex, to determine if the beast still fought for life. But also, to cure the ache of her own loneliness. For she was truly alone. There were many creatures in this world, but none that shared her ability to speak. And none that stayed long enough to form a bond. She spoke of her adventures with the creatures she'd helped, the things she liked and things she didn't. She eventually even told the great beast about her place in this world, and how she didn't know how she came to be or what her purpose was. She spoke of her longing for beings like herself. For companionship and understanding. But the beast continued its silence, and so the Goddess continued speaking to fill the quiet."

I again glance at Willow, knowing from previous iterations of this story that this part usually makes tears glisten in her eyes. She wipes her eyes quickly to hide the evidence of her sorrow and I smile grimly. Faldorn appears moved by my words as well, his face haunted, but mouth turned in a frown as if surprised he is feeling such strong emotions. I watch him for a brief moment, intrigued, as the various emotions flit across his face: pain, sadness, surprise, and frustration. They each curve across his face in quick succession, but ultimately he settles on a blank expression—casting aside all emotion from his features.

My eyes soften as I watch him. Some tales have a way of breaking through every defense we thought we had and end up striking clear into our hearts in a way that can be shocking and frightening. To see yourself in someone else's story is both magical and bewildering, and I don't blame him for shying away from it.

I take a deep breath to clear my mind, opening my mouth slowly to speak and return to my earlier easy cadence. "After many weeks, the beast was fully healed. She watched in joy as the creature unfurled its wings and stretched them carefully beneath the quickly rising sun. But the pit in her stomach also grew at the sight—she was pleased the beast was healed, but she knew this meant that it would leave. What little comfort she received being in its presence would be snuffed away, like a candle on a windy night. But to her surprise, the beast dropped its large head—its wide antlers settling on either side of the Goddess to rest in the soft dirt. It bowed over one clawed foot and finally spoke. In a deep rumbling voice, felt even in the soil beneath the Goddess's feet, it said, 'Dear Goddess. I do not comprehend this loneliness you have often spoken of, for I am a solitary creature and know my place in this world. I am content soaring the skies alone, catching my own prey, and solitarily sleeping under the stars.' The Goddess, at first so excited to hear words from another being, returned to her crestfallen state. This great beast, despite its ability to speak with her, would not stay to keep her company or help her find what she was seeking."

I pause to briefly dart a glance to Thelas, wondering at his reaction so far to my story. His hands are still and while he stares in my direction, he has a far-off look that tells me he's lost in the tale. My mouth quirks up to the side, pleased that he is listening so closely to it.

I pick up a new stick to fiddle with and pick up where I left off, "The beast noticed her dismay, reading the question on her face as easily as if it read her mind. Its lip curled slightly to reveal sharp fangs, in what the beast meant to be a comforting smile. 'No, I will not stay,' it said. 'But that does not mean your place in this world is not still out there. It is simply not with me.' The beast stood from its bow, its claws digging firmly into the ground. She watched in awe as it stretched its wings to the bright sky and reveled in the feeling of healed wings and strong limbs once more. The Goddess smiled warmly, truly happy to see the creature restored to its former glory."

I lift my eyes to the fire as my voice dips and I shiver as the next part of the story coalesces in my mind. The words wash over me, and I feel their weight just as I did as a child when my father told me the tale.

"The beast turned to her once more, 'Goddess, there is much out there for you to discover and learn. But for now, I offer this wisdom.' The beast craned its neck down so that its large head was level with her, so that it could look properly into her iridescent eyes. The deep rumble of the beast sounded again, though this time the words were softer, as if the beast was telling her a great secret. 'I have found throughout my travels, there is one singular, intangible thing that connects certain beings together. This is something that is felt, not seen, and appears when you least expect it. It is warm like a fire, soft as fur, and as comforting as a moonlit night.' The Goddess opened her mouth to inquire further, but the beast stopped her. 'The realm provides those we need when we need them most. Continue your path, and you will find what you are searching for.' And before the great beast flapped its shining wings, it whispered softly to her, 'Like calls to like after all.'"

I trail off for a moment as the last phrase pulses through my body and sizzles down my spine. The words settle over my skin like a warm blanket—soothing and exhilarating all at once. I feel an easy smile slide onto my face before I finish the final part of the story.

"The Goddess, you see, was left slightly confused by the beast's words, and she pondered over them long after the flaps of great wings were unable to be heard. She felt a buzzing in her chest as she replayed the words 'like calls to like' and felt a renewed sense of purpose. She vowed to follow the great beast's advice, to continue on her path and await the day when the realm would provide her what she'd been searching for."

I sit forward slightly and let my eyes wander to the others, allowing for another dramatic pause, just for fun. My lip quirks to the side as they each eye me with anticipation and I can't help but let the silence linger for another long moment before speaking once more.

"And so, she does. She helps everyone she comes across, she grows her magic, and travels far. She sees a wide ocean with islands sparkling in glittering coves. She sees dark forests and tall mountains. She traverses open plains full of rolling grasses nearly as tall as she is. The buzzing in her chest never ceases, filling her with hope that the beast's words ring true and that she will find what she's searching for. The Goddess often repeats 'like calls to like' to herself, as a way to fill the silence but also to keep her steps moving forward." I let the stick I was tinkering with fall to the ground, its bark now completely stripped, and lean back against my tree. Crossing my arms against my chest, I stare down the rest of the group—knowing there is still one last line to this story, and those who have heard it have one of three reactions. I smile wickedly in anticipation.

"And to this day, it is said that the Goddess is still searching…for her purpose, for her people, and for her place in this world." My smile broadens at the simple finality of my words. I watch Faldorn, Thelas, and Sebastian carefully, gauging their reactions to the end of the tale. Willow has heard this story many times and is thus not surprised at the lackluster ending.

I chuckle when I see the moment Thelas realizes there is no more to the story and that there is not necessarily a happy ending for our Goddess. He stares at me as if believing that if he simply waits long enough, I will take back the final line and continue until she has a warm, happy family.

Faldorn wears a look of soft confusion, his brows pinched ever so slightly, and his hand hovering near his blade, as if he wishes to fight something. I watch the movement carefully, my easy smile falling slightly, but only feel sadness for the fae. He must have gone a long time without feeling strong emotions, if his first reaction to experiencing them is to reach for his sword.

I glance at Sebastian to gauge his reaction to the tale as well. I shouldn't care what he thought of it, but sharing that story is always surprisingly vulnerable for me. I make eye contact, only to find that he is already staring at me. A deep, curious expression on his face—as if he's trying to decipher a puzzle he has no answer to yet. He doesn't speak, but it does appear as if he is pondering the story and its many interpretations. A small part of me hopes he finds it as quietly hopeful as I do, but a much larger part reminds me he is practically a stranger still, and a thief, and I should not care what he thinks of me or my campfire tales.

Determined not to let him get to me, I focus my attention on the dark forest as I hear Willow attempt to placate Thelas as he peppers her with accusations.

"You knew she would tell this story, and you still asked for it? You knew how it would end?" Thelas' voice is high, clearly baffled by her deviousness. She cackles and Faldorn huffs.

Thelas continues his tirade, unable to keep the laughter from his words as he says, "You despicable woman!"

He points an accusatory finger at me that I notice from the corner of my eye, but I don't turn toward him. Instead I hold in my laugh knowing that if I do look at him, I will lose it.

"There has to be a different ending! There is a different ending, right?" he prods one more time.

I swallow the laugh threatening to bubble up my throat and finally turn to Thelas, offering only a simple shrug. He throws a hand to his forehead, massaging his temples. He's exasperated, but truthfully, I don't know if the story has a different ending.

I always enjoyed this particular tale. It was by far my favorite of the ones my father would tell us before bed, but I never asked if there was another ending. I didn't think there needed to *be* a different ending. There was something about the Goddess's loneliness and search for belonging that pulled at me. And that phrase, 'like calls to like'—I often spoke it to myself as a young child. Said in hushed tones as I drifted carefully through the forests, hiding behind trees, and pretending I was in another world searching for adventure. Each time, it felt like a secret. Like an answer to a question that I didn't even know to ask. The simple phrase, when uttered, felt like warm liquid metal in my veins—a calming mantra and a promise all in one. And that feeling was enough for me, just like it was for the Goddess in the story. I didn't need to know exactly where I belonged because I knew I would get there someday when I truly needed to.

Of course, that was before the fire that took my parents and my childhood. So perhaps I should have been more concerned with what was to come.

Faldorn surprises me by offering a question in the following silence. "I have not heard this tale, though the phrase 'like calls to like' sounds familiar. Perhaps it originated as a fae saying?"

I shrug. "Perhaps, but I don't know the origin. I only know the story at all because my father told it to me as a child. I'm not even sure where he learned it."

After a few more beats of silence, Willow speaks up. "Well, since Laira shared something, how about we all share something? You know, as a way to get to know each other?"

No one says a word, so she continues in a singsong voice, "Might be helpful since we are going to be walking into certain death and dismemberment when we enter that Goddess-forsaken forest, you know?" She smiles broadly, blinking rapidly at each of us, silently urging the others to say something.

Faldorn takes the bait first. "Yes, well I will not be joining you. We may share this fire for tonight, but come first light I will be on my way."

His words land heavy in front of us, a declaration that sounds firm and sure, but his thread flits into my vision again. As if reminding me not to worry, that he is the last piece of this puzzle, and he will join us one way or another. I decide not to say anything and instead will trust that he will change his mind somehow.

Willow stares hard at him, narrowing her eyes before saying, "Be that as it may, could you not share one small truth? I'm sure with your incredibly long lifespan, you have seen and done so many things. Perhaps share something with us poor mortals?"

He stares at her, considering, and then cracks a small smile. "I have a friend who owns a tavern back in T'salae who often said I was too competitive for my own good, but also not very good at the tavern games."

He picks up a blade and begins absentmindedly polishing it—a faraway look in his eyes as he's seemingly momentarily lost in his memories. "He would say I was a sore loser, but I would always tell him that he gave me the drunkest fae as a partner on purpose." He laughs softly again. "He never did play fair." He looks over at Willow then. "But I swear I did still manage to beat him from time to time."

"Fae tavern games, huh? What does that even entail?" Sebastian leans forward, his elbows resting gently against his knees, clearly interested in learning more.

"Not much different than I imagine your human games to be. The one we often played involved two angled boards on the floor with a small hole near the top on each. They're placed a good distance apart to have a challenge when throwing small sacks into the hole on the board."

He leans back slightly, picking up his sword and resuming his polishing with more intensity. And perhaps he saw our slightly baffled expressions because he quickly adds, "It makes more sense when you actually play it."

I stare at Faldorn in shock. He hasn't spoken much since we met him just a few hours ago, and I'm surprised he shared as much as he did just now with only slight prompting from Willow to do so. He must really enjoy his fae drinking games.

Willow claps her hands together before excitedly saying, "Yes! You will have to show us sometime."

He shakes his head, back to his relative silence.

I know what she is attempting, though I'm not sure it will work. I pulled her aside after speaking with Faldorn to tell her our savior of the day had, surprisingly, a bright thread connected to each of us. I told her of my suspicions that he may be the final member of our group, and it seems she is trying her best to convince him to join us. But despite the connection I can see between all of us, it doesn't mean he will come with us. I get the feeling he's used to being alone, and possibly quite content that way—adding on two young humans, a part-fae human, and a witch is likely not something he ever had in mind.

TALKING WITH THE WIND

FALDORN

I hadn't planned to stick around long enough to share a campfire with these young mortals, but when I saw the condensed mist twisting through the trees earlier, something made me pause. Thelas had noticed something strange as well, but without fae blood he would not have been able to see what I did, only the disruption of light as it moved through the trees. Laira had not shown any sign that she had seen the mist, but I had no plans to ask her, and so I was left to ponder the phenomenon on my own. Something about it was familiar, and the stone weighing down my heart suddenly felt a little lighter upon seeing it. So, I decided to stay and tell them what I knew. Translating the book for the enthusiastic blond was easier than I initially thought, and working alongside him was effortless. We worked in similar ways, and I was surprised at how quickly he caught on to the ancient language.

I pause again to listen intently to the trees to the side of us, but nothing stirs beyond the occasional small animal skittering in the brush. The mortals sleep surprisingly soundly based on their deep and steady breathing. It makes me wonder if perhaps they hadn't had a decent night's sleep in some time—and that having someone such as myself on watch was enough to allow them to finally sleep through the night.

I shake my head. I can't think like that. I cannot get attached to these mortals, and I need to remember I am leaving in the morning. It doesn't matter that they feel safe enough to sleep or that they have a strange camaraderie—I must not get involved. I cannot repeat the mistakes of my past.

The familiar ache returns, and once again I feel the heaviness of loss like an ocean in my chest. It's been centuries, and yet it feels as if no time has passed at all. That's the price of near immortality it seems: having enough time to make every mistake imaginable and a mind capable of remembering it all in vivid detail. I came to the mortal lands to escape from it, and to punish myself. I did not deserve to be with my own kind, nor bask in the magic of the fae lands. It took many years, but eventually the nearly irresistible call to the ancestral lands that every fae hears was lost to me. I don't feel connected to it anymore—I don't feel a connection to most things anymore. It's better this way, though, and I'm not sure I could care and be in the presence of others even if I wanted to.

Still, these mortals are amusing and charming in their own way. The chatty one, Willow, shines like a bright beam of sunlight. Her demeanor like the sharp chime of a bell—vivid and lively. And the female, Laira, her partial fae blood sings and echoes to my own with a single word: *kin*. She has a quiet strength and a kind heart, and the others gravitate toward her though they don't know it. The suspicious one, Sebastian, puts up a tall front of humor and an indifferent attitude, yet I see the uncertainty and care beneath. He feels everything far more deeply than he lets on. The cartographer, Thelas, has a similar feel to him—of someone hiding who they truly are, stemming from fear. I sense he has a great internal battle ahead of him though he does not let this stop him from expressing enthusiasm for his craft and bravery in the face of danger. I saw him with his simple tool during the fight today. Of the way he held it out, ready to defend himself and his friends despite it not being a weapon at all. He used what he had available and stood tall—an admirable feat.

Faces echo in my mind, those of fae who had similar traits. I push them to the side, not allowing myself to remember and I tilt my face to the side to focus back on the meadow. Mist hangs heavy over the tall grass and coalesces in a dense pocket just in front of my face. My brows pull together as I focus on it, and I ready myself to grab my sword should I need it. There's something otherworldly about the mist, yet I sense no ill-intent coming from it. In fact, it projects a feeling of warmth and comfort. I'm momentarily mesmerized as it flips and twirls, undulating like waves crashing on a shore until it's dense enough to fit in my hands. Something in my body loosens, and I relax involuntarily, though I don't make any move toward the ball of grey mist. A faraway voice whispers in the back of my mind that this could be a fae's spirit finding me—something that happens on occasion in the fae lands, but should be impossible in the mortal ones. I quickly toss the thought from my mind, uncomfortable with the idea and the hope that blooms unbidden in my chest.

I turn from the mist, determined to put it from my mind, when I hear a lovely sound. My breathe catches and I immediately still, listening closely for the sound to appear again.

"My darling, I've missed you."

The words are spoken in a whisper heard close against my ear, with the faintest brush of something like a breath.

"You—how? Is it really you, my love?" I ask in awe as I reach out to cup the mist in my palms, my previous hesitation and disbelief forgotten.

Fae magic works in strange ways, and I long ago resigned myself to expecting the unexpected. But this—it shouldn't happen this far from Caelamne. The mortal lands have little magic to speak of compared to our ancestral home, and a spirit returning from the Eternal Realm would find it nearly impossible to appear. Yet, she is here. It's her and she's here and I haven't heard her voice in many centuries. A tear slips down my cheek before I can stop it. She's *here*.

"Is it my time to join you?" I ask, hopeful for the first time in ages.

I feel a touch on my face, and my single tear is wiped carefully away. "No, darling, it is not your time. But these young ones—you see the souls behind their eyes, don't you? You see the similarities to the ones you lost."

I return my gaze to their sleeping forms as she continues. "It is never too late to live again."

A flicker of warmth begins in my chest at the suggestion in her words, but I shake my head, a refusal already on my lips. A soft hand caresses my face, and I sink into the feeling—the feeling of her. I quietly voice my fear, something I haven't spoken aloud before.

"My love, I cannot. I failed them, long ago. I failed you, and I can't do it again."

"You did not fail us then, and you will not fail now. Live for me, my darling. They need you." Her voice sends a shiver down my spine, and I close my eyes, picturing her beautiful, golden eyes as she speaks.

"Do it for me, Faldorn. Help them, travel with them, and then your soul may be ready."

The idea of holding her in my arms once more brings a soft smile to my face and I nod. "Yes, my love, I will aid them if that is what gets me to you once more. I will go with them, and once they complete their journey, I will come straight to you. My soul will be ready and it will be my time to cross to the Eternal Realm. I know it."

I see a knowing smile appear in my mind. Her lips lifted to one side, her eyes bright, and brows lifted in amusement—and I know that this is how she looks in this moment on the other side.

"We'll see. Perhaps these mortals will grow on you and you'll want to stay a bit longer." Her melodic voice drifts off, and the wisp melts away into the air. One last soft breeze flits across the grass, causing it to bend and sway as it does, and I know she is gone. Back to the Eternal Realm and resting with the only family I've ever known.

I turn back to the fire, only to see Laira's piercing gaze staring at me. She has a curious expression on her face with her brows pinched in silent concentration and her lips pursed in a thin line. I wonder what she heard of what just occurred. Or perhaps what she saw—she has the blood of the fae, after all, and she likely has some ability to see beyond the veil. If she did hear or see anything, she doesn't say it, instead choosing to lie back down on her bedroll and sleep.

Hours pass, and before long the early morning sun shines into the meadow. Orange and pink hues dance on the horizon, and bright beams light up the brightly colored flowers peppered throughout field. I inhale deeply and continue to watch as the sun slowly rises.

For the first time in a long time, I feel a quiet sense of peace and a hope that flows through my body like a river through a dry canyon. It lights up dormant parts of myself that I haven't touched since I lost my family.

One more adventure.

One more mission.

And then I rest.

The mortals begin to stir, and I take that as my cue to put out the fire. We have a long way to go, and we had best get moving.

A WITCH'S CURIOSITY

WILLOW

The next few days after meeting the mysterious Faldorn pass in tired monotony. The simple dirt path lined with overgrown bushes we follow always looks the same as the day before, and I find myself growing weary of the familiar scenery. We are still surrounded on all sides by tall trees, but they grow thinner in number each day. It's enough to provide us cover though, and we are all grateful for the relative safety they provide. I use our travel time to reach out to the trees as we pass, flexing my magic and recalling their language. It's been far too long since I allowed my magic to stretch this far, and I quietly revel in the freedom and joy it brings me. I've spent so long simply crafting potions and working with dried herbs, and not enough time basking in the vibrant life around me. The forest sings with it—calling to the dormant part of myself that I locked away for my own safety. To fully release my magic, is to alert the queen to where I am; and no matter where I go, she would find me eventually. But with this journey, we are on the move so often and will likely enter a forest that even she can't traverse before her elite soldiers would ever locate me. Still, I'm hesitant to let my magic completely free. For fear she will be faster than I expect, but also because it unlocks the dark side of my magic that I have long loathed.

I was blessed with the incredibly rare ability to manipulate flesh and cure all manner of illnesses, and because of this, I was gifted to the witch queen before I could even walk. Witches are known for their healing abilities, but that is through potions and plants grown by magic. To force skin to close, blood to flow through the body, and plagues to leave the system, that is the calling of the Sancaro. They are revered and treasured above all other witches—an entirely different sect of magic that only appears every few generations, and never more than one at a time. I was treated with the same respect as the witch queen herself, and grew up believing I was born to save people. But there is a darkness to my abilities too—something she made sure to take advantage of. It started small, causing small tears and breaking small bones only to heal them immediately, but soon I was tormenting prisoners and leading executions. Each one bloodier and more theatrical than the last. The queen enjoys suffering and because I was drowning in it, and knew no other alternative, I stayed. For ten long years she had me under her thumb, and I took more lives than I can remember—their faces blurring together over time.

I was no longer primarily a healer. I was her personal assassin and executioner. A mockery of the healing I was supposed to give and of the sacred duty all Sancaro witches undertake to bestow new life.

I squeeze Star's reins tight in my hands until my knuckles are white and reel my magic back inside my chest. As nice as it feels to use it properly again, perhaps it's too soon to do so. Din purrs reassuringly at my back and I smile softly. It may be too soon now to fully dive into my power, but once we reach the Forbidden Forest, I will be truly out of her grasp and will only have to worry about my memories.

I crane my neck to look behind me, looking for a distraction and spot Thelas atop his mount, Hael. His hands move over parchment even as he plods along on the path. I raise a brow. It is rather impressive that he can keep such a steady hand on the back of a moving creature. I slow Star to pull beside him, and she leans her head to nudge Hael in what I'm pretty sure is a gesture of "hello," but it could easily be a passive aggressive show of dominance, knowing the old mare. I reach forward, tapping her on the head to remind her to behave before turning to Thelas.

"So, Thelas. When did you know you wanted to be a cartographer?"

He is certainly studious and has an extreme eye for detail, but he doesn't strike me as the adventurous type—which seems to me like a very important aspect of being a cartographer who quite literally catalogs and explores faraway locations. I assume there must be positions he could hold where he stays in one place: making copies of maps, book-keeping, or perhaps teaching. But he is far too young for those positions. Every time I would visit the academy, I only ever saw old men and women shelving items or painstakingly recreating maps by hand. People who were too old to travel—to go on an adventure—and were thus relegated to simpler tasks. Thelas didn't seem incapable. So why did he choose this profession and how has he never left his home until now?

"Well…" he begins, his hands stilling on his map across his lap. "I think I chose being a cartographer because I had the artistic skills, but also the analytical mind for the more technical aspects of the job. I also have a rather strong memory and can easily replicate what I see in person onto a map."

"So, then what have you been doing before this? If this is the first time you've left home?"

He rubs the back of his neck, glancing away from me to focus ahead. "Ah, right. Well, I um…had a rather sheltered, I guess you could say, upbringing. I wasn't paid attention to much, unless of course, I was leaving the manor—in which case I needed a chaperone at all times."

I look him up and down and quirk an eyebrow. "Are you some sort of bigshot in town?"

He shrugs, a slight blush to his cheeks as if embarrassed to talk of his family and status. "I wouldn't say that. However, my father is a successful merchant and so I did grow up with money."

"So, you needed a bodyguard to go into town? Were your parents afraid of kidnapping and ransom notes or something?"

He looks away, and his voice takes on a strange, haunted quality. "The guard wasn't to protect me from others."

I pick up on what he doesn't say. That the guard was there to protect *others* from *him*. I reassess him with new eyes. From his gleaming blond hair, glasses, and slender frame, he doesn't strike me as someone capable of violence, or even someone I would find intimidating. It makes me wonder what he's hiding that instills such a carefully controlled demeanor. It's not my business to ask further, though, especially when I have my own past to be weary of. I know all too well what it is like to be in control of something that is far more dangerous than you ever wanted it to be. Something that could harm others in an instant.

He clears his throat and looks at me out of the corner of his eye, like he has to force himself to make eye contact. "What about you? I know witches are born with magic, but how did you come to Taslae and open your apothecary? What was its name again?"

I smile at the mention of my pride and joy. "Aconite Apothecary—named after a favorite plant of mine, Wolf's Bane."

His expression turns teasing. "Another poison?"

"Actually, yes. It's a vibrantly purple flower that can cause all sorts of terrible things to happen to the human and witch body. Not quite sure what effects it has on shifter or fae bodies though… I haven't gotten hold of many books about their anatomy, unfortunately."

"It's a little unsettling how cheerfully you say the words 'all sorts of terrible things'."

I shrug. "Perhaps. But poisons are not all I know. In fact, I know many remedies for all sorts of illnesses. That's one of the reasons I opened my apothecary—to heal people." *And to atone for my sins.* I move Star closer to his mount so that I can throw a teasing arm across his shoulders. "Besides! Poisons can be used to heal just as much as they can harm. It's all in how you use it."

His cheek is squished against mine, making his words come out garbled as he grunts, "Is that so?"

Faldorn interrupts us with a firm hand held high in the air, informing us all to stop. I let Thelas go and peer around Laira and Sebastian in front of me to see a field of brilliantly white flowers. My mouth drops and I silently motion Star forward to approach the gleaming sight. It's utterly breathtaking. Each tiny flower is nestled among wispy green leaves that ripple in the afternoon air like a tiny ocean of pearlescent gems. Sebastian and Laira approach on their mounts behind me, a similar exhale of astonishment from Laira, and I know she is thinking the same thing I am. This is nothing like we've ever seen before, and these flowers sparkle in the sun in a way that speaks to magic being hidden in their delicate petals. My mind wanders immediately to what the properties of the flower could be, and if we have the time for a quick stop so I can collect some. It's not often I get a chance to encounter a plant

I've never seen before. Especially one like this with clear magical properties in the human lands where wild magic is limited.

I shout at Faldorn, who is nearly to the edge of the field, and gesture toward it. I smile broadly, hoping to get on the strict fae's good side and sidle up beside his giant beast of an elk. Ever since he joined us, he's been a bit tyrannical with our movements—waking us up at dawn and keeping us moving until we collapse, only stopping for absolute necessities. We've made a great deal of progress, but I don't enjoy the regimented schedule.

"Do you mind if we stop here so I can take some samples? I don't think I've ever seen this species of flower before!"

Faldorn surveys the meadow quietly for a moment before motioning his mount forward.

"Well, I guess that's a no," I say, annoyed, signaling to Star to move forward as well.

Before he can get more than a few steps on his elk, however, Laira's voice sounds from behind me. "Wait!" She glances at me, a conspiratorial smile on her face. "Could we rest here a minute?"

Faldorn sighs and looks behind him. "We really should keep moving."

"But I'm not feeling well and could use a short rest."

"You look fine."

"Ah—" She glances down, abashed, and I have to hold back a snort at her poor acting skills. "But you see, I'm feeling a bit sick to my stomach and light-headed. The heat doesn't always sit well with me and it would be helpful to stop and rest."

She winks at me and even though her acting could use some work, I could kiss her for trying. She knows how much I love discovering and cataloging new plant species, and she created the perfect reason for us to dismount for just long enough for me to collect some samples.

Faldorn sees our interaction and rolls his eyes. "Fine. We can stay for a very short time." He stares at me knowingly. "You have until Laira miraculously recovers to forage as many of these flowers as you want."

I squeal and hop down from Star, tossing the reins to Thelas and bounding toward the edge of the field. Din lets out a squeak of irritation at being ousted from his spot behind me, but he quickly recovers as he races to catch up with me.

I grin back at him, and warmth floods my body at his devotion. My precious little shadow. If there's one thing that I can count on, it's that he will always be at my side.

The field stands calm and innocuous, but I approach with caution before spearing my magic into the earth to probe the flowers for potential defense mechanisms. Many of the most dangerous plants appear simple and harmless at first but can easily surprise you with a myriad of secrets. I grab a long wooden probe from my pack and prod the nearest flower with it, testing the elasticity of the petals and checking the leaves for signs of thorns or tiny barbs. The petals gleam like pearlescent shells on closer inspection and are covered with a sort of shimmer, or perhaps a coating of dust, creating the strange metallic appearance. A perfect yellow circle sits in the middle of the flower, and the stem and leaves are devoid of any noticeable physical harm, but that doesn't mean they still couldn't secrete something damaging to my skin. My magic flares as it comes in contact with the root system below the field, and I jolt in surprise at the criss-crossing roots forming a dense layer deep beneath the soil. I use a smaller tendril of magic to expose the roots of the nearest flower and find they are the color of darkest night—a smattering of silver dots like diamonds shining on the bumpy surface.

I continue to dig, but it quickly becomes clear that I will not be able to find where one root system ends and the other begins. I scan the field and the closely packed flowers and ponder this oddity. If the roots are this jumbled, then perhaps these flowers are connected? But are they individuals that happen to be connected, or are they more like a single organism with many heads?

I grumble at the many unanswered questions. I may not be able to answer them all yet, but I can at least catalog what I see and attempt to solve the puzzle later. I safely collect a few stems, being careful to avoid touching any part of the plant to my skin. I may be a powerful witch with the ability to manipulate most plants with practice and time, but I can still be harmed by their innate defenses—just as a sword master can be harmed by their blade if not careful.

I rotate on my heels and stand, satisfied with what I was able to procure and am about to tell Laira that she can stop her fake illness, when I find four bodies collapsed to the ground a few paces behind me. Racing to them, I call their names, darting to each to check their eyes and attempt to wake them, but whatever is wrong is keeping them from answering me. I examine Laira more closely and notice a thin sheen of yellow dust around her face and in her hair. Closing my mouth immediately, I step back, not wanting to inhale the dust. My gaze lands on the pale-yellow centers of the otherwise white flowers, and dread sinks in my stomach at the possibility that they were not as careful with the flowers as me, and the plant is indeed as toxic as I feared.

"Shit!" I groan.

I scramble for the pack at my hip and pull a bundle of dried leaves the color of mud. Placing a leaf under my tongue, I race to the others and pry their mouths open, shoving a leaf under each of their tongues as well. The effect is immediate, and their shaking subsides temporarily. Another moment passes, and they each stare dumbfounded at me—relatively fine, but it won't last for long. Sebastian reaches towards his mouth, a look of pure disgust on his face, as he feels for the leaf under his tongue.

I throw out my hands to get his attention before he removes it and ends up thrashing around again. Glancing nervously at our mounts, I see them snort in agitation, and I know we are running out of time before they fall prey to the dust now rippling in the air as well. The leaves won't work on them, nor do I have enough for all of them, so we will have to be quick and get away from these flowers before they collapse on us.

"Do not remove the leaves from your mouths. Do you hear me? Do. Not. Remove. Them." I turn toward Star and pull myself into her saddle.

"But it tastes awful," Sebastian responds.

I throw up my hands in exasperation. "A bad taste in your mouth is better than being dead!"

The others continue to stare at me in confusion, even Faldorn appears dazed. They are likely still suffering minor effects from the dust and did more than just inhale the substance, like I did. I notice the yellow shimmer on their hands and arms as well, and my panic flares again. We need to get out of here *and* find a water source to wash that off, or there may be very little I can do. My healing does have its limits once things progress too far.

My voice is urgent as I shout, "Well? Come on! The leaves will only protect you for a short time from losing consciousness—just a simple stimulant that is keeping you on your feet and nothing more. The fastest way out of here will be across the meadow, and hopefully we can find a water source not far away so we can wash the dust off. If we are all going to survive this, we need to run *now*."

This gets them moving, and before I know it, we are all mounted and ready to go. I make sure my staff is securely fastened against Star's opposite side—I definitely do not want to fish it out of the meadow should it fall off as we run.

"What about the horses?" Laira chimes as she pulls herself into Skip's saddle.

"They'll be fine for a short while as long as we run through this field. They are large enough to be able to withstand more of the dust than we can—just keep a firm hold on the reins and go as fast as you can!" I shout and then click Star into a gallop across the field. Time is of the essence now, and I glance beside me to make sure everyone else is following my lead and running at breakneck speed.

Faldorn's elk seems to be handling itself fine enough. I'd imagine a legendary fae creature like itself would have a more robust internal defense against such dangers. Still—it's best not to tempt fate. Sebastian's mountain of a horse also seems to be faring okay. Its strong legs and large hooves carve a path into the soft dirt of the meadow. Sebastian sits hunched over on his horse's back, but his grip looks firm enough, so I turn my frenzied attention to Thelas and Laira, who are both a few strides behind me and lagging.

They appeared to have had the most exposure to the flower's dust, and I fear they transferred that to their horse and antelope when they got on. There's a wildness to Skip's eyes, and the normally sure-footed antelope is stumbling and getting its delicate hooves tangled in the now exposed black roots, causing it to slow further.

I reach behind me where I feel Din holding onto the back of my saddle and pull him to the front with one arm. Anchoring back on the reins slightly, I signal to Star to slow her pace in order for Thelas and Laira to catch up.

Once they are directly on either side of me, I yell to Din, "You know what to do! Make them speed up!"

I still haven't figured out exactly how much of what I say is understood by Din. After all, when he was alive he couldn't comprehend speech, but there was a sort of silent communication that we shared. But now, in death, it's almost as if he can understand what I say and comprehend my feelings on a deeper level. So as I toss him onto Laira's horse, he knows exactly what I intend for him to do, and he digs his claws into the horse's backside. Skip lets out an alarmed bellow but renews her pace and passes Star and me in a rush. Din jumps from her back at the last second, and I turn toward Thelas.

"Alright, Din, one more!"

He leaps from me, but the antelope must sense his approach because she jolts to the side suddenly. Din plummets to the ground, and I almost pull back on Star's reins to retrieve him when Kel swoops down to snatch him from the air, claws catching on Din's ribcage, and drops him onto Hael's back. It's enough to cause the antelope to jump forward in panic—though Din digs his claws in anyway. Likely as a measure to simply keep himself on the antelope's back as she hops wildly and sprints toward the tree line.

I don't have time to sigh in relief at the sight of the end of the meadow because I feel the creeping effects of the toxin. Blackness edges into my vision, and I blink it back while a burning begins in my chest. It feels as if I've swallowed glass and then someone took the contents of my stomach and lit them on fire. No wonder they looked at me so blankly at first when I found them—the pain is immense, and I didn't have half the exposure they did.

"Kel!" I hear his answering screech above me and know that he is listening. He's not my bonded or Laira's, but he is more intelligent than any other nyradonn I've met. While I am still wary he won't understand me, we unfortunately have no other options, and so I send a prayer up to the Goddess that the little bone bird senses our need for running water.

"We need a source of water to clear off the dust! Find one!" I'm desperate and mentally calculating the chances that we are close to a stream or pond. We left the main river long ago, so we must now hope for something smaller within close enough distance that we can reach before we're too exhausted, fall unconscious, or both.

We run in a small pack, following Kel as his shadow passes above us, and we don't stop once we pass the border of the meadow. Kel leads us far into the trees, forcing us to continue until our mounts are foaming at the mouth from exhaustion and we have well and truly left the toxic field behind. Kel swoops down and I see his target—a small creek winding through large tree roots and boulders. I nearly collapse from relief at the sight, jumping down as Star slows and running the last few steps to the water. I shout orders even as I hurriedly splash water on my arms, face, neck, and anywhere else the dust may have settled as we ran.

"Sebastian and Faldorn—wash your arms and face! Laira and Thelas—dunk as much of yourself as you can into the water! Even your clothes!"

I hear stumbling and then loud splashing as I finish washing every trace of the toxin off my body and turn to where the others follow my instructions. The water is no deeper than calf-height, but Thelas and Laira already have a surprising amount of water soaking their clothes and streaking down their faces—good. Once assured of their progress, I jump up to examine the animals.

Faldorn appears behind me, and I waste no time in passing his elk and Sebastian's horse to him. "Make sure they don't have any on their legs or hindquarters. When in doubt, splash them again. They should be able to recover after that, and I can take care of our side effects once we are cleared of the dust as well."

He nods and leads them toward an unoccupied spot in the creek, quickly soaking their legs and cupping his hands to wash the rest. I grab Star and instruct her to lie down in the running water—one of her few tricks—to wash off any dust before grabbing Thelas and Laira's mounts to do the same.

Sebastian stands soaking wet at the creek's edge. "I can take Skip."

I nod, quietly handing him the reins, and we lead them into the water, following Faldorn's lead by using our feet to splash their legs before cupping water in our hands for the rest of their bodies.

My breath is still ragged when we finish washing everyone, and after I triple check that no trace of the dust remains, I fall to my feet, my limbs suddenly too wobbly to hold me up. The others join me, and we catch our breaths in a wet and sagging heap on the forest floor. The horses, stag, and antelope move closer together as they recover from the sprint we just did, huddling in a warm patch of sunlight that filters through the trees.

Pine needles and broken twigs dig into my legs and hands as I brace myself in the dirt. The midday sun peaks through the tops of the trees, warming parts of my body where the rays hit, but the water in the creek was cold, and I shiver as my heaving breaths finally slow. Once I am able to breathe normally, I throw my arms out in exasperation, eyeing each of them with ire that only immense fear can create. "What were you guys doing? Snorting the random mysterious flowers we found? Honestly, you'd think you'd have a little more common sense than that."

"We were not *snorting* them!" Laira huffs, indignant. "Thelas and I were curious about the flowers, and we didn't have any of your fancy equipment or magic! I tried not to touch them directly, but Skip got spooked by something and kicked up a handful of petals at us when she stomped on the ground." She gives me a mournful look. "I'm sorry we scared you. Thank you for saving us."

Kel lands on her shoulder, and she gives him a pat. "And thank you, Kel, for leading us to water." Din gives an angry yowl as he pads into my lap. She gives him a beaming smile. "And thank you, Din, for attacking my horse and making her run so fast I nearly flew off!"

The others chuckle softly, and I relax at her words, realizing for the first time since I spotted the yellow dust on their arms and faces that they are safe. Prickles run down my spine at my release of tension, and tears pool behind my eyes. What would I have done if I had lost my best friend? If I had lost any of the others I'm starting to care so much about?

I swipe at an escaping tear, giving her a watery smile. "Of course."

Sebastian's face is quizzical as he asks, "What was that nasty thing you put into our mouths? Tasted like musty forest floor and..." He pauses, clearly at a loss for words on how to properly describe the Talis Leaf I gave them.

"Ass?" Thelas supplies.

"Yes, musty *ass*. Thank you, Thelas."

The dried leaf is extremely important and was the only thing keeping us conscious until we could wash off the flower's dust, but he is right, it does taste like musty ass.

I don't bother responding to their complaint, instead I internally catalogue my body, focusing my magic on the symptoms I experienced earlier from the dust. Warmth pools in my limbs, and after a few seconds, the lingering burning sensation and sharpness in my chest is gone. I reach out my awareness to the four bodies in front of me, curling my magic around each and infusing it into their bodies to diffuse the effects of the toxins. In the few moments that my magic inhabits their bodies, I feel their discomfort and pain as if it were my own—an unfortunate drawback to my abilities, but one I'm well practiced at pushing past. My magic doesn't extend to animals, so I make a mental note to monitor the mounts over the next few hours and give them a few tonics that will work for them to ensure they are able to fight off the worst effects of the toxin from our race through the field.

Once satisfied, I slowly get to my feet, brushing off dirt and leaves that stuck to my wet clothes and skin. "Alright, time to get up! It's not cold outside, but let's get a fire going to dry us and our clothes faster."

"Oh, and let me know if anyone starts feeling worse. I imagine the symptoms from the toxin are still present—well, maybe not Faldorn; his fae system had cleared most of it from what I could tell with my magic." I raise an eyebrow at him in question and he nods.

"Right. So, the rest of you—" I whip around to glare at Thelas, Sebastian, and Laira who sit somewhat dazed on the forest floor and point what I hope is a menacing finger at them. My wet hair whips around me in a giant arc as I do, and I make a mental note to braid the annoying heap back while it dries.

"You better tell me if any of you feel more symptoms in the next couple of hours. No hiding anything, okay?"

Laira speaks for the three of them before I can demand an answer again. "Okay! Yes. Okay. We promise."

"Great. Now everyone strip! We need to dry these clothes and get into some fresh ones or the shivering is about to get really intense for *all* of us."

Faldorn doesn't answer, he simply gets to his feet and complies with my demand. The other three grumble, but follow his lead, with Laira walking off a short distance to change behind a wide tree, grabbing her pack as she goes. She has some qualms about changing in front of others—and I suppose I do too—but Star's plump frame should be enough to hide the most important bits from the others.

After we all change into dry clothes and hang our old ones to dry near the fire, we sit in a rough circle hashing out the details of where we should go next. Thelas has multiple maps surrounding him and argues with Sebastian about the best path forward while Faldorn watches with quiet patience. Apparently, his tyrannical behavior only applies when we are actually on the road and not when we are deciding on where to go.

I squeeze water from my hair and interrupt their pointless bickering. "I don't care where we go, but we definitely need to stop at a larger town to restock, especially after I used some of my most important herbs on saving all your lives."

"I second this," Laira says from beside me.

Faldorn points toward one of Thelas' maps, his voice calm. "May I offer a possible path forward?"

Thelas and Sebastian scowl at each other, but hand over the map, and he spreads it out in front of us so we can see as he follows a path with his finger.

"I believe skirting to the west and passing out of this forest, and then north into the town of Warille will be our best solution to everyone's problems. It has a large market with an abundance of herbalist and witch items as well as being a good spot to stop as we search for the secret entrance to Daer e'Mista, since it is the closest major city to the forest's supposed edge."

"Sounds great to me!" I say, excited at the prospect of boosting my herb supply and exploring this new town.

Thelas and Sebastian are reluctant but eventually mutter grunts in agreement, obviously not pleased that neither of their plans were chosen, but giving in to the validity of Faldorn's suggestion.

I turn to Laira. "Maybe you can even use the opportunity to scout locations for your new shop!"

A ghost of a smile crosses her face as she considers my proposition. "Perhaps. I have to actually like the town first though."

"New shop? What happened to the one in Taslae?" Thelas asks.

I wince as Laira's face falls, but her voice is steady as she explains to Thelas what happened. "High Elder Torghul exiled me from Taslae before we left. I had no choice but to abandon my shop and sell most of my belongings. Though a nice older woman offered to hold on to most of my book inventory and personal collection, along with a few other items until I can return to collect them and start fresh somewhere else."

"I'm so sorry. I had no idea he did that." Thelas' face is sorrowful as he reaches a hesitant hand to pat her shoulder. The gesture is a bit awkward, but the intent is there, and she smiles weakly in thanks.

"It's alright. I was able to at least save the books. And Willow is right, I will be able to scout Warille as a potential place to live and set up my new shop, so at least there is that potential to look forward to."

Thelas withdraws his hand from her shoulder, and my eyes drift to Sebastian to find him also watching the touch, his eyes growing stormy, either from Thelas touching Laira or from what happened to her, I am unsure. He catches my watchful gaze, staring intently as if daring me to comment on his obvious irritation. I shrug at him as if I have no idea what is going on, not wanting to start a whole new argument when we have finally decided what to do next and have some relative peace.

I brush off my legs before standing to check on our clothes hanging from nearby branches. "Well, we can rest for a bit and give these some time to dry, but then we should be on our way to Warille if we want to get there before nightfall."

A series of noises follow my statement, which I take as approval and so I decide to use the time to reorganize my herbal stock and determine my list of what I'll need to find once we reach Warille.

I internally groan at the large sum I will be spending to replenish everything, and what I'll need to get extra of, since this group seems determined to run headfirst into trouble.

WARILLE

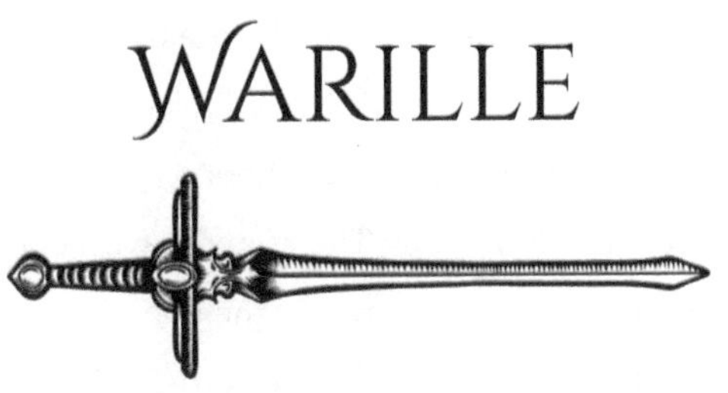

LAIRA

The room the innkeeper leads us to is dingy, but at least it's large enough to house the five of us. Even if one person will need to brave the floor since there are only two beds to cram on. Bright sunlight filters through the single window in the room, illuminating the tightly packed space and the dust coating all of the surfaces. We made better time than we thought, and we were able to make it to Warille a few hours before sundown. Which is apparently necessary, not only to retrieve the supplies we need tonight, but also to clean up this room. This clearly is not an inn that gets much traffic, but perhaps that is why Faldorn and Sebastian steered us toward it.

The woman drops a key in my palm, reciting in a bored tone, "No magic indoors. Dinner starts at the sixth bell, and breakfast is served at first light. Best be on time if you want it hot."

I nod. "Any chance we could wash our clothes?"

"Yes, though it will cost you extra."

Sebastian reaches into his coat pocket and tosses her a few coins. "Will this do?"

She snatches the coins out of the air with surprising speed, holding them in front of her to ensure their validity.

"Leave what you wish to be washed by your door, and I'll return everything by morning," she replies simply before walking away.

I drop my bag unceremoniously on the first bed, claiming it for myself and Willow. "Well, it's not as nice as I hoped for our last inn before the forest, but at least we can have fresh clothes tomorrow."

Sebastian throws his bag on the other bed before turning to Faldorn and Thelas to see who will take the bed with him. Thelas looks at Faldorn before carefully opening his pack to pull out his bedroll for the floor.

"I am a seasoned fae warrior, young Thelas and have slept more nights on cold hard surfaces than you've been alive. I can take the floor."

Thelas continues unrolling his bed. "No, it's alright. I rather enjoy sleeping on the floor; plus I'm a bit of a whirlwind in bed."

Sebastian's smile turns sly and his voice teasing. "Is that so? Don't tempt me with a good time."

Thelas' cheeks turn slightly red, but he only rolls his eyes at Sebastian's teasing. "You know what I meant. I toss and turn in my sleep. I sincerely doubt you want to wake up to me jabbing you in the ribs with my knee."

"Yeah, I think I'll pass." Sebastian pats the bed. "Well, looks like it's you and me, old man."

Faldorn crosses his arms and stares blankly at him. "I am not a man. I am fae."

"*Right.* Old fae? Sounds pretty obvious if you ask me, all fae are ancient. Old man rolls off the tongue much better."

Faldorn grunts softly but doesn't push the subject. We stand awkwardly in a silent circle for a few heartbeats before Willow loudly claps her hands together, gaining all of our attention.

"Alright!" She rummages through her bag for the list of supplies she put together for us to gather in town.

"Thelas and Faldorn." She points to each in turn. "You will go get dried meats, fruits, and any other foods that will keep well for our journey. And then after that, I suppose see if there is anything else that could be useful that isn't too bulky? Thelas, do you have all of the map supplies you need?"

"Well..." Thelas places a hand under his chin in thought. His head slightly cocked to the side and angled up—like if he made eye contact with anyone he would be distracted from picturing his supply needs. "I could use more ink, just in case. As well as more parchment for my own mapping—because it is important that I catalogue as much as possible and I'm sure there will be some amazing discoveries to write down and—"

"OK! Great! Go do that." Willow leans in toward Faldorn, a conspiratorial hand cupped over her mouth. "Keep him in line, would ya? We don't need to bring the entire store with us."

"Hey! I only require a few more—"

Willow crosses her arms and smirks at Thelas, who flounders for words before realizing she's teasing and knows he does not, in fact, mean to buy an entire store's worth of items to take with us.

"Ah, right," he says sheepishly, rubbing the back of his neck.

"Come, young Thelas, let's see what we can find." Faldorn claps a firm hand on Thelas' shoulder, smiling good-naturedly.

Willow turns to me then, her mischievous gaze landing on mine and causing my stomach to drop briefly in anticipation just before she points to Sebastian and then to me. "And you two—you're in charge of the odds and ends. Extra fire starter, extra blankets, necessities for the group." She sidles up next to me to gently push my shoulder with hers. "Oh, and make sure to get more coffee. I sure as shit don't want to see another morning where you don't get your coffee." She shudders in emphasis and looks to the rest of the group. "Seriously, she can be a real terror."

"Willow!" I gently push her away, laughing even as I pretend to be affronted by her accusation. Because she's right. I do need my coffee in the morning, and I *will* attack first and ask questions later. I've had to get up even earlier on this trek to sneak a cup or two in before Faldorn forces us to get on the road as part of his relentless marching, and I'm dangerously close to the end of my stock.

I feel Sebastian's presence suddenly despite knowing he'd been casually leaning against the wall a moment ago. His chest nearly touches my back, and his arm is braced on the edge of the bed next to me so that his head is level with mine. The quick movement causes me to jump slightly.

Quiet sneaky bastard.

"So it's possible for you to be even more of a spitfire? I'll have to remember that." I can hear the obvious smile in his voice as gooseflesh involuntarily shudders down my spine at his whispered question in my ear. I immediately stiffen and take a large step forward before turning around to face him.

"Do you have to have a snappy response to *everything*?"

I intend to come across as unbothered to let him know that his words have no effect on me, but I can hear the underlying agitation in my voice lingering on each word. It seems he can also tell that he did, in fact, ruffle my feathers because he lifts a single brow in amusement at the outburst he elicited. The glint of the piercing in said eyebrow further catches my eye, and I briefly wonder what made him get one in the first place. It is not a common feature of human men—though I have heard it is popular among shifters and the nobility. Something about showing strength and mental fortitude.

I groan internally, *Goddess save me. I should not be caring about what is on his face – this infuriating man is taking up far too much of my mental space.*

I turn to find the other three staring pointedly at us, and I throw my arms out in exasperation. "*What*?"

Thelas looks away as if embarrassed to be caught staring at something he shouldn't, but Faldorn continues to stare—out of slight curiosity or to simply not show weakness, it's unclear. And Willow has an absolute shit-eating grin on her face that tells me I am going to be teased about this little interaction later.

Sebastian pipes up from behind me and looks to Willow. "So then, what are you going to get?"

"I need to replenish my herbs and tonics as well as make sure we are stocked up on bandages and the like. I imagine this little jaunt into the biggest and scariest forest in all of Ilphemoura is going to come with a few scrapes and bruises."

"Hah—likely a great deal more than that," Sebastian says. "Make sure to get something to keep a person awake. We don't need anyone falling asleep on guard duty."

Faldorn takes a small step forward, clearly affronted by the accusation. "I can assure you, I have never fallen asleep whilst on guard."

"It's not you I'm worried about, old man. It's the three who have never left the safety of their little podunk town that worry me."

Thelas, Willow and I call out in unison, "Hey!"

Sebastian throws up both hands in a placating gesture. "I'm just saying."

Willow huffs in indignation. "Yes, I will get a proper stimulant to keep us awake should the need arise." She pauses writing on her list to eye each of us. "We should also keep in mind that the townsfolk here will likely disapprove of us going inside the forest. I've seen more than a few people stare at us openly just in the short time we've been here already, and I have a bad feeling about it." She sighs loudly, massaging her temple. "The innkeeper clearly doesn't ask questions or seem to care about us, but I'm nervous about running into trouble with others who may not be so adept at minding their own business."

I sit on the bed and suggest, "Perhaps we should be extra cautious while getting supplies and have cover stories? As well as not mentioning that we are heading into the forest, of course."

Everyone is silent for a few moments as we ponder the idea. Sebastian surprises me by agreeing first, "That's not a bad idea. I have heard the people in this town are especially suspicious of outsiders, and there have been a few cases of mistaken identity that turned… a little violent. It seems Warille takes pride in living so close to the supposed entrance of the Forbidden Forest but also threatens anyone they think is investigating it too closely, especially outsiders."

"Like when I was exiled from Taslae for asking the mapmaker about it?"

"Yes and no," Sebastian responds. "Taslae is far enough that it shouldn't have aggravated them so much. Plenty of people whisper about the forest in the capital and surrounding cities and aren't punished."

"So, they really just wanted me gone then?" The words come out with more sadness and defeat than I intended.

Sebastian's eyes soften at the obvious hurt in my voice, but he doesn't contradict me.

Willow sits on the bed next to me. "So… cover stories?"

She throws out a dramatic hand in front of her—her voice pitching slightly higher than normal. "I will be Laventi! Just a simple human with no magic whatsoever. Collecting herbs for her teacher and cataloging plants along the Upper Tiramunde River. I'm currently making my way through the connected lakes and rivers to the

Laniss Sea where I will catch a boat back home to the small coastal town of Caper." She beams at her new role, clearly enjoying this turn of events.

In a firm melodic voice, Faldorn voices his cover story next. "Thelas and I will be traveling merchants gathering supplies before re-boarding our river boat. They need not ask our names, and we will not give them."

Sebastian chuckles and slaps a hand on Faldorn's shoulder. "Straight to the point. I like you, old man." Sebastian looks over at me then, a wicked glint in his eye, and I know I am going to hate whatever is about to come out of his perfectly shaped mouth.

"I will be Polvak. A very handsome and extremely charming young man touring various cities throughout Eislekest with my newlywed wife, Halle." He gestures toward me. "Isn't that right, Halle dear?"

I burst to my feet, alarm in my voice and my fists balling at my sides. "Oh no. I will not be your *wife.*"

"Ahh, but wildcat. It's just a cover story, right? And it is a good one. No one will question two young people in love waltzing through their town."

Willow bursts to her feet, clapping her hands together in ill-contained delight. "That's a fantastic idea!" She grins at me and giggles, enjoying the irritation on my face. I have no doubt she thinks this is a good idea because she's hoping for an interesting story from me later.

I grumble and stare daggers at him but eventually give in to the ridiculous story since I can't think of a better one. "Fine. But you are not allowed to touch me without my permission."

He bows theatrically. "I will await the day you give me permission then."

I mutter under my breath and turn away from his annoying face. "I will never give you permission."

He appears to hear me anyway, and I see him from the corner of my eye as his smirk tilts to one side and he lifts his head out of his dramatic bow as if in challenge.

"Well, with that out of the way, let's get going!" Willow claps her hands together again excitedly. She's an actress at heart and appears to be very pleased at her new role.

I huff out a breath, already exasperated with this entire plan. "Yes, yes, let's get this over with."

I pull a few things from my bag that I won't need while in town and shrug the entire thing over my shoulder before a devious idea pops into my mind. I roughly toss the entire bag at Sebastian, hitting him squarely in the chest with a loud *thud*. He manages to catch it, a surprised look on his face as I say sweetly, "A wife should never have to carry her own bag, don't you agree, dear husband?"

His voice is strained, as if the air has been knocked from his lungs as he says, "Of course, my lovely wife."

THE CHARADE CONTINUES

LAIRA

"Anything I can help you folks find today?" the busty owner of the shop asks as Sebastian holds the door open for me to enter.

My attention is pulled to the front counter where the older woman leans over it, a single arm sweeping behind her to indicate the many shelves full of tea bags, coffee, sugar, spices, and more. The red and brown stone shelves stretch from the floor to the ceiling and line the four walls around us with other goods like cups, bowls, and specialty brewing items. The smooth stone is beautiful and matches the exterior of the many shops and homes in this town—there is clearly immense pride taken in the stonework and utilization of the material here. I give her a small smile and approach the counter, eyeing the perfectly organized coffee pouches with poorly contained glee. There was never this large of a variety of selections in Taslae and my fingers itch to open multiple pouches and inhale their wonderful scents.

I'm about to ask the woman to pull a few down when Sebastian steps closer behind me and speaks. "Yes, my wife and I are looking for some of your finest coffee and—" He glances over at me, "and perhaps some of those special sugar-milk cubes. That is what you prefer, right Halle dear?"

I scowl at the way he calls me "wife" until I realize what he said and blink at him in stunned silence, slightly flustered that he knows how I like my coffee.

I face the woman again, doing my best to ignore the grin on Sebastian's face. "Um... yes. Do you happen to have any coffee spices as well?"

"Of course! I'll pull a variety for you to choose from." The shopkeeper smiles broadly before turning around to survey her back counter, and begins pulling various items, starting with the coffee bags I was surveying. I elbow Sebastian in the ribs as soon as she turns, and he grunts softly, but that quickly turns into a snicker at my annoyed face.

That bastard is *enjoying* this.

The shopkeeper whirls around with an armful of items and sets them neatly on the counter. I glance at Sebastian, but he simply waves a hand at the pile as if to say, "pick whatever you like." And so I do. I gently open each pouch and sniff, giving them all a thorough examination as if choosing one will be the most important thing I do all day. They smell heavenly and I can just picture myself smiling happily beside our campfire while enveloped in the calming aroma. Some people prefer tea for that effect, but nothing relaxes me like a steaming cup of coffee. The woman answers my eager questions with a pleasant smile, not batting an eye when I ask where each variety is from and how they get their unique flavors.

I'm so busy focusing on choosing a few that I like and speaking with the shopkeeper that I almost miss Sebastian slowly drawing closer to me. He braces a hand on the counter on my other side, and I feel the warmth of his body as well as the faintest brush of his clothes against my back, yet he is careful not to touch me. It just looks like he is from the shopkeeper's perspective—selling the act of newlyweds without compromising his promise to not touch me. The thought puts me more at ease, and some of the tension I felt at his approach leaves my body, knowing he is respecting my wishes.

The woman claps her hands together excitedly, tucking them under her chin and eyeing us like we are adorable puppies in a shop window. "Oh, aren't you two so cute together! And you both have such lovely features—you will have the most adorable children, I'm sure!"

I freeze.

Only for an instant before I remember myself, my made-up role, and that this is a perfectly normal thing to say to a newlywed couple. I relax my shoulders, mimicking her cheerful tone and force a smile to my lips. "Ah yes! A whole house full of them, I bet."

My smile is fake, and my voice strained, but the shopkeeper is fooled enough by the display, looking pleased at my response and sighing happily. Distantly, I notice Sebastian pull away to pay for the items I picked out, and I slowly pack everything into my bag and sling it over one shoulder. My previous enthusiasm is gone, and I feel dim in comparison. It's not the woman's fault of course, she wouldn't know that line of questioning is frustrating for me. But still, I feel my legs trudge along and my heart sagging in my chest, as if I've been caught doing something I shouldn't.

Before I know it, we are out of the store and into the fresh air—the dull thud of our feet as we walk down the stone street echoing in my ears. We walk a few paces before Sebastian playfully remarks, "I thought a wife shouldn't have to carry her own bag?"

I halfheartedly slip the bag from my shoulder and hand it to him, smiling weakly.

"Hey—are you alright? I felt you freeze for a second in there, is it what the shopkeeper said?"

The silence stretches for a long time as we continue down the cobblestone path and I ponder the idea of what it would be like to tell him the truth. It's not something I speak of often because it's not anyone's business, but also because it goes against what most people want for themselves and so I've felt like the odd one out more than once. You can only go so many times of trying to explain yourself and your decisions before you give up. And while I've tried to fight it before, there's still a part of me that is afraid of the reaction I might receive, even though it shouldn't matter at all. My mind flits through all the scenarios, one by one, like a hand quickly flipping the pages of a book. Would he feel sorry for me? Condemn me? Or worst of all the reactions I've received, try to tell me I will change my mind later?

The questions swirl in my mind and I'm mildly alarmed by the fact that I *want* to tell him. The feeling becomes so strong and it's not long until the words I'd been holding back suddenly burst from my mouth. "I can't have children."

I stop walking and look at him fully to explain further before he can give me a pitying look. "I *chose* not to have children is the better way to put it, actually, so don't feel bad for me."

I point an accusing finger at him, as if he were just about to start feeling pity for me.

He doesn't reply. He just stares at me, a questioning, but surprisingly soft, look in his eyes. His voice is soft too as he replies, "I would never pity something you chose to do."

I can tell he's curious but won't push me if I decide to drop the subject, and for some reason, that gives me the courage to continue.

"I knew from a very young age that I did not want children. That I was not meant to be a mother. There are some things that you just know. And I *knew*. And so, I took every precaution over the years to prevent it. Until I found a witch who could perform a type of surgery infused with herbal magic to make me completely incapable of bearing children. No questions asked."

I motion us forward to indicate we should continue walking, and he keeps pace with me as we meander down the worn stone path.

He angles his head toward me, speaking slowly, as if expecting I won't answer his question. "If that is the case, then why did the woman's comment upset you so? If it was something you feel confident in having chosen?"

I turn my head slightly to look at him, gauging his question. His eyes are surprisingly genuine, with just the corners of his brows turned down, as if he is truly interested in my answer. My hearts swoops at the realization and a surprising tenderness fills my chest. No one has asked about why I can be evasive about this subject, or exactly why it makes me frustrated. The sudden vulnerability of opening up to him is overwhelming, yet I still find my mouth opening to speak.

"I have not met many people who think the way I do. And there are only so many conversations you can have before you start to feel like you are the outsider. That you are the strange one. An oddity who 'goes against her barest instincts' and is therefore 'unnatural'."

My eyes turn watery as I remember the words I've heard spoken before; from someone I thought cared for me no matter what. Someone who accepted all of me. I swipe a single tear before it can fall from my eyes. But I was wrong to assume that.

Sebastian surprises me by stepping in front of me and gently gripping my arms.

"Someone said that to you?" The hard edge to his voice could slice through stone and I blink at him in confusion before realizing he is angry on my behalf. For some reason, this thought is comforting, and I smile weakly despite the awful memory.

"Yes. But that was a long time ago." I reply softly. I glance down at his hands still caressing my arms and raise an eyebrow. He has the good sense to look slightly abashed before quickly dropping his hands.

He doesn't move out of the way for us to continue on the path, and so I simply stare at him—curious at what else he clearly wants to say.

His jaw ticks as if he is still upset, but his voice is devoid of its previous agitation as he says, "Such people cannot be reasoned with." His eyes turn serious, and he leans forward as if he wants to touch me again but stops himself just before doing it. "There is nothing wrong with you. Nothing wrong with the choice you made, and nothing wrong with being upset when people assume incorrectly."

The declaration stills my blood and for a moment I can't breathe. I've been told these things before, by Willow, by trusted family, and even by myself. But it feels different coming from him. Maybe it's because he doesn't know me as well as they do, or perhaps it's because I like the idea of him not judging me.

Not that it matters of course, I am not about to actually be his wife, I think dryly to myself.

I give him a sincere smile. "Thank you. I appreciate that."

Satisfied, he returns my smile and turns around, pausing for me to catch up to his side once more. We amble on in companionable silence until we arrive at another shop, but Sebastian stops me with an arm across the door before I can reach for the handle. "Well you know, I never really wanted children either." His smile is mischievous but also soft in a way that makes me believe he's serious.

I gape at him, utterly at a loss for words until I spit out, "*What*?"

The confusion evident in my voice makes him chuckle as he drops his arm and opens the door for me, motioning for me to head inside. His laugh is like velvet brushing against my skin, and I shiver as the sound rolls down my spine.

"We are married after all, better if we have similar opinions on the subject, no?" He winks, and my cheeks flame at his statement. I duck into the store, the door chime twinkling as I attempt to avoid his heavy gaze.

THE NEXT COUPLE of stores pass by without incident, and we gather the last of our supplies. No one else asks if we're married, and I breathe a sigh of relief that we don't have to pretend to be in love again. One time was enough for me. It's not until we get to the final store—to pick up some small luxuries for our trek, soaps and cooking spices and the like—that I notice Sebastian acting suspicious. The slightest clench to his jaw and a noticeable hard glint in his eyes, not to mention the constant *thwiing* of his coin as he flips it in the air. He sticks close to me as I walk around the store, yet doesn't reach for me to continue our newlywed charade. He's up to something; I just know it.

The shopkeeper is an older gentleman with a gruff voice who tosses my items into a sack and stiffly holds out his hand for payment once I approach the counter. I quickly move to place the coins in his hand, but he roughly grabs my wrist before I can. My body screams in alarm as his fingers dig into me, and I know I have missed something—I wasn't paying attention yet again, and another person is taking advantage of that. An ocean rushes in my ears until Sebastian steps up closer behind me. His warm weight is welcome in this case, and I lean back into him, attempting to pull my arm away from the man, but he yanks me forward again.

"I'd recommend you remove your filthy hands from my wife before I remove them from your body." The icy steel in Sebastian's voice slices through my panicked thoughts, and the strong arm he places around my waist to hold me tightly against him causes an unexpected warmth to bloom in my chest.

The man sneers but lifts his gaze from mine long enough to make eye contact with Sebastian. I see the moment when he realizes that Sebastian has a sword strapped to his side and is noticeably taller than him. The blooming fear is quickly replaced by forced laughter and a nervous smile as the man drops my hand as if burned.

"Right, well it was only a joke." He looks at me then as if I will save him. "Right, sweetheart?"

My blood boils at the endearment on his lips, one I've heard far too many times over the years, said only to mock or belittle me, and I snap at him before I can think better of it.

"It's small, horrible excuses for men like you that give humans a bad name. I see the shriveled heart behind your cowardly eyes, and it brings me pleasure to know you will never truly experience happiness because of it, that you likely have never experienced true happiness. That you live alone in an empty house, and wake surrounded by liquor bottles, covered in your own piss and vomit. Did I get that right, *sweetheart*?" I spit the last word, and it lands like acid on the table. The man stares in bewildered shock before his face scrunches in rage. It reddens his cheeks and creases his forehead in a way that is almost comical.

What a pitiful, angry man.

He opens his mouth to speak until Sebastian steps in front of me, menace radiating off his entire being. "You heard my wife. Fuck off."

The man continues to stare in a barely controlled rage—his eyes bugging out of their sockets and his nostrils flaring, but he makes no move toward us. Sebastian holds his gaze for another moment before turning me around and placing himself at my back as he leads me from the shop. I don't blame him for not trusting the man enough to turn his back on him. I did call him a coward, and I do believe that—but when pressed, you never know what someone is truly capable of until it's too late.

The quiet and empty street greets us, and the cool air weaving through my hair immediately provides a calming sensation. I hadn't realized how stifling the shop felt, or how warm my face had become. We don't speak as we make our way back to the room at our inn, not even when we set our bags in the corner and settle on one of the beds. It isn't until he drops down onto the small bed across from me and tosses a small glass cylinder into my lap that he speaks. "Here—took this from that bastard's shop. You like woodsy scents, right? It's what I always smell on you."

"Um, yeah I do." The cylinder reads 'Tam's Premium Perfumes. Moss & Fir' and I open the small bottle to inhale its earthy scent. I meet his eyes but can't read the stormy emotion there.

"Huh, it does smell like me." I arch a brow at him. "Since when do you know what I smell like? Are you secretly sniffing me?" I can't help but crack a smile as I poke fun at him, hoping to lighten the mood.

"Pff—you wish, wildcat. I just noticed the soaps you grabbed were forest scents and assumed that's what you liked."

"...But you said—never mind." I decide not to push further on the whole "I always smell on you" comment—there's no way I would even want to think about what that indicates and that he's been keeping a closer eye on me than I thought.

"When did you take this? I didn't see you do anything when we walked out."

He absentmindedly scratches his chin and replies, "Oh, I swiped it when I saw him eyeballing you as soon as we walked in. Would've taken something bigger had I known what he was going to do and say to you."

"He was staring at me when we walked in?"

"You didn't notice?" He peers at me closely, as if trying to see if I am lying or not.

"No, I didn't." I sigh and rub a hand over my face. "I often don't notice, actually."

He tilts his head in question, and I begrudgingly continue. "It's one of the reasons Kel is so helpful—though he disappeared before we went shopping, the little bugger—I'm not the best at keeping a sharp eye on my surroundings. I assume people will pay me no mind, or sometimes I don't even notice someone is there at all. It has gotten me in trouble in the past, which is why Kel knows to alert me to pay attention."

"Remind me to thank that bird. Where is he anyway?"

"He's probably on the roof. He likes to keep an eye on things from high above. But it was strange that he didn't accompany me while we were out..."

He grins then. "Well, he probably saw that you were with an honorable thief with considerable muscles, plus a sword *and* a dagger." He holds up two fingers in emphasis, and I can't help but giggle at his exaggerated description of himself.

"Right. I'm sure that's why."

"So you really don't notice people staring or being potentially dangerous?"

"I do have *some* survival instincts, but yes, for the most part, I don't. For one, if I paid attention to every person who stared or made comments at me, I'd never be able to leave the house. Kel isn't exactly a model of the nyradonn, and you know how people assume and judge specimens like him. And for another reason, when I am focused on something—*I am focused*. The world drops away, and it's almost as if I'm in one of my own making."

He considers my words for a moment before saying in a teasing tone, "Yep, it's decided. I'm definitely going to thank that bird. He likes muffins, right?"

I bark out a laugh, unable to contain the bright sound. Sebastian's eyes light up, encouraging him to continue, "Seriously though, since when do nyradonn like muffins? Since when do they even *eat*? What kind of strange bird do you have?"

I shrug. "Kel is special, and yes, he likes muffins. And no, I have no idea if he actually consumes them."

I hear the door creak open and Willow's head of golden brown hair bounces inside the room. "Did someone say muffins?"

"Unfortunately, these are hypothetical muffins, sorry to disappoint," I call across the room to her.

"Ugh! Rude!" She sets her things next to the bags already slumped in the corner. We are getting quite the hoard going and I try to picture just how we're going to get it all loaded on our animals.

Maybe we should get a pack mule, I giggle to myself.

She lets out a frustrated grumble. "Well, at least it looks like you got your end of the supplies. I wasn't able to find a few of the herbs I need. Ones for blood thickening, poison treatment, and allergic episodes. All of which are *absolutely essential* for going into a strange forest where you have no idea what to expect!" She pouts, placing a hand on her hip and rubbing her temples in weary agitation. "We might have to stay a few extra days so I can ask around if anyone has them. I heard there might be a monthly market being set up soon that should hopefully have more variety."

"Okay, well, that should be fine if we stay longer. I'm sure Thelas will need time to figure out where the entrance to the forest is anyway," I assure her.

"Yeah..." she says quietly, a thoughtful expression on her face, and I tilt my head in question. Her eyes dart to me uncertainly and upon seeing the confusion on my face, motions for me to follow her out of the room. I feel Sebastian's presence on the opposite bed and realize she must want to speak in private.

My curiosity is piqued even more as she pulls us further from the room and down the short hallway before finally turning to me, anxiety woven into every shifting movement.

"Spit it out, Lo, what's going on?" I snap, unable to take her nervous avoidance any longer.

She bites her lip before taking a deep breath and rushing through her next words, as if she needs to get them out or she'll burst. "I hate to admit it, but if we're going to keep up this ruse for our cover stories to stay here longer until we figure out the entrance and get my herbs, I think we need to sleep in different rooms so people don't start to think we're all together… otherwise what's the point?"

"Right," I trail off, unsure where she is going with this.

"That means—" Willow grimaces in sympathy. "You'd have to share with Sebastian since you're 'married.'"

"No." The word falls like a boulder, landing with a thud between us.

"Laira, I know it's not ideal, but I know you've seen how secretive and distrustful people can be here, and this quest is too important to jeopardize. We can't afford to be run out of town until Thelas can find the entrance and I can get my herbs." Her voice turns desperate, and her face scrunches in agitation. "Because we need to find that sword, Laira. The darkness—I think it's the only way to save you."

I reach for her, wrapping a comforting arm around her shoulders and leaning my head down to rest on hers. "It'll be okay. You think this is truly the only way to help me?" I look nervously down at the branching black and purple vein on my hand but quickly hide it from her view.

"Maybe? I don't know. Right now I don't know a lot of things, but I just have this sense that the sword is what we need."

I let out a heavy breath, blowing strands of hair out of my eyes and release her shoulders to look at her properly. My words feel like wet sludge coming out of my mouth, but I force them anyway.

"I think your plan for separate rooms is smart."

She swipes a single tear from her eye and gives me a wobbly smile. "It will just be for a little while," she promises weakly.

I sigh, resigned to my fate. "Alright. But I'm not sharing a bed with him."

She smirks, her eyes growing mischievous as she bumps me with a hip. "Not even to recreate a scene from one of those books you love?"

I can't help but laugh. "Yeah, not even then."

"Too bad."

We return to our room, and Willow relays our plans to Sebastian. I try to ignore the smirk that blooms on his face by relaxing on one of the beds and fail miserably, so instead I try thinking of ways to get through the next few days without going completely mad.

Thelas and Faldorn creak into the room, the former clearly exhausted from the trip, but before they have a chance to even sit down, Willow pounces on them to relay the new rooming situation and our reasoning for changing it. Faldorn simply nods, uncaring of the new plan, and Thelas appears too exhausted from whatever shopping adventure the two just came back from to offer up an opinion.

Willow claps her hands together. "So it's been decided!"

Thelas lifts himself from the chair he collapsed on, asking the group, "But wait, don't you think someone has noticed us all together already?"

Sebastian is quick to reassure him, "No, when we arrived there was no one around the inn, and the only person to really take notice of us so far has been the innkeeper, and she didn't seem the type to ask questions. As for anyone who may have seen us as we left our shared room today… well, we'll just have to hope they didn't think it odd or won't cause a fuss until we can leave this town ourselves."

Satisfied, Thelas settles back against the chair and closes his eyes to rest.

Utterly resigned to my fate now, I decide to get the ball rolling to get it all over with so I can rest for the evening as well. "Should we go get more rooms then?"

Sebastian moves from his spot, leaning against the wall to stand next to me. His nearness causes the skin on my arm to tingle, and I mentally chastise my body for behaving like it enjoys his company.

"No need," Sebastian tells me. "I bought the end of this hall of rooms when we got here as a precaution to keep nosy people away. We can each take one."

I whip my head to look up at him, my mouth falling wide open. He has the funds to buy multiple rooms as a precaution? I doubt the innkeeper gave him a good price, so he must've spent a good amount of coin.

I close my mouth quickly, muttering, "Must be some thief to have that much gold lying around."

His eyes glitter and his mouth tilts up in a cat-like smile, exposing his teeth. "Oh, you have no idea, wildcat."

"Stop calling me that."

Thelas pipes up, interrupting our back and forth, "So I won't have to sleep on the floor?"

Willow giggles. "No, you will not. You and Faldorn can fight over whatever bed situation is in one of the rooms Mr. Money Bags here bought for us!"

I chuckle at her nickname for the thief before groaning aloud as the thought of sleeping in the same room as said thief finally settles in my stomach, flipping in a way that makes me avoid his eyes and hide my face with my hair.

Is it too much to hope that we go about our evenings in silence? I mentally grumble.

"I'll let you pick the room, princess." Sebastian's smile is teasing as he crosses the room to grab my bag.

Yeah, silence is definitely too much to hope for.

TAVERN DANCING

LAIRA

The tavern down the road from the inn is surprisingly cozy, and after ordering hot soup and a cold ale, I feel full and satisfied. I sip the brew and watch as a band sets up in the corner and patrons gather in the center of the room, waiting expectantly for them to play. The floors are worn smooth from many patrons, and the walls have a pleasant dark brown wood, shot through with streaks of red that is striking. My gaze wanders and I take in the various people seated around the tavern. They appear to be mostly humans, but a few witches are easily identifiable—their staffs always the giveaway. My eyes dart to Willow, who sits at the bar, chatting with a pretty human girl and twirling a lock of her hair, her intricate silver staff nowhere in sight. Witches are rarely known to go anywhere without them, as they are a symbol of their magic, but also conduits for more difficult spells and for combat. Without it, it's unlikely anyone would even realize she is a witch, especially with how locked down she keeps her magic. It should make her vulnerable too, but anyone that has seen her magic work knows she doesn't need a staff to increase her power—she is a force to be reckoned with all on her own. But I suppose with our made-up identities, it makes sense that she wouldn't carry her staff. Though, I've also noticed her reluctance to use it recently, like when we fought off the bandits.

Reluctantly, I pull my overly concerned thoughts over her decision to not use her staff and continue mildly surveying the tavern. Tables made from old barrels are scattered across the space, along with more private tables set up in the corners. Thelas and Faldorn sit in one such corner, chatting amicably and I smile warmly at their easy conversation before quickly darting my eyes away. We are supposed to be in separate groups to avoid any potential suspicion, and we promised to not interact unless necessary and leave separately.

Sebastian steps into my view, and I frown. He holds out an expectant hand and I cock an eyebrow, peering up at him above the rim of my cup. "You know how to dance?"

He rolls his eyes. "Give me some credit, you little viper. I do know how to do *some* things other than steal, give fantastic advice, and look devilishly handsome."

His smirk grows as he lists each attribute, as if they are actual skills he possesses. I'll give him the handsome thing, but fantastic advice? I don't buy it.

I scoff. "Right…" I stare down into my nearly empty cup when I realize what he called me, and my lightly exasperated voice turns accusing. "Another nickname, really? Since when did you get the right to call me whatever ridiculous thing you can think of?"

He winks and gently reaches for my hand, unfurling it from the handle of my cup and setting the ale on the table. "Since you agreed to dance with me."

Despite my better judgment, I let him do it, and I stand to follow him onto the dance floor. A few other couples have already jumped up to join in on the upbeat tune. Deep drumbeats and a fiddle lift up a rugged voice singing a morbid story of a dark ship coming alive and swallowing his crew after they attempted to command it. *Serves them right for trying to claim what wasn't theirs,* I mentally chastise.

It's a strange tale, but I can't deny it has a thrilling energy that lends perfectly to the fast swinging and stomping Sebastian leads me through. We bob and weave effortlessly through the other couples, and I occasionally have a different partner as we are passed around the floor. The vibrant energy in the room is palpable, and I revel in it. Nothing matters in this moment—it is just me, the pulsing music, and Sebastian.

The song slows suddenly as it builds to its grand finish, a haunting bell sounds, and the band sings a spine-chilling low hum. The effect makes my hair stand on end, and I can almost picture the beastly ship they sing about. Sebastian uses this slinking melody to pull me close, an arm curling around my waist. With the music still flowing through me, I don't fight him. Instead, I lean in closer—the thrill of the dance and music pulsating in my blood and causing me to act much bolder than I normally would.

His breath tickles my ear as he whispers, "See? I know what I'm doing."

Before I can utter a word in response, the song explodes again, and I'm spun out of his grasp. It's jarring enough to make me pause at his absence, but he grabs my hands again and we continue twirling and stomping to the strong drumbeats. They echo through my bones, and I don't realize I'm smiling broadly until I notice Sebastian is as well.

I jolt at the thought that crashes into my mind as I stare up at him. *He looks so handsome when he smiles.*

The song ends too quickly, and I'm surprised at the sadness I feel at the prospect of sitting back down. My racing heart and the pleasant buzzing energy running through my body are exciting and a lovely reprieve from the constant stress of the last few weeks.

He seems to notice my hesitation and feel the same, because he holds out his hand again and grins. "Another?"

I don't hesitate before reaching for him, my answer coming out in a breathless, "Yes."

We dance until I lose track of the number of songs we have heard. I crash back down into a chair, my energy finally spent, and feel satisfied at the slight ache in my feet. I haven't danced in years—not since Willow tried to take me to that awful bar back in Taslae—and it feels so good. My muscles are exhausted and my breathing is heavy, but it was all in the name of a frivolous activity that brings such joy, instead of the hard weeks of travel we've endured. Dancing is a bright spot in this otherwise grey existence.

Sebastian falls into the seat next to me, chuckling softly as he finishes the last of his ale. His mouth quirks up to the side. "Not too bad for 'just a thief', eh?"

I elbow him in the ribs and roll my eyes. "Yeah, yeah. I suppose you're not the worst dance partner I've ever had."

I look up to find he's already staring at me. His gaze is intense and full of an emotion that I can't quite name, but it captivates me all the same. I don't realize we are simply staring at each other until Willow clears her throat and knocks on the table to get our attention.

"Hello? You guys gonna stop ogling each other to listen to what I just said?"

I break his eye contact quickly with a sheepish smile directed at Willow. If I wasn't already flushed from the dancing, I'd surely be red with embarrassment from her comment. I glance around the tavern, uncertain if she should be talking to us so openly, but the place is nearly empty. And the folks who are still here are slumped against chairs and in no position to notice our conversation.

Satisfied that no one will realize we know each other, I ask, "Sorry, Willow. What did you say?"

She crosses her arms and cocks out her hip in a huff, eyeing both of us for a long moment. She has a disapproving look on her face, and her mouth presses into a firm line that is reminiscent of a school teacher frowning at two kids misbehaving in class. My eyes dart to Sebastian's, and the chagrined look on his face forces me to hold a snort of laughter. He notices my effort not to laugh, which then causes a similar muffled sound to bubble up from his throat.

Willow throws out her arms in exasperation, but the amused smile on her face tells me she's not actually upset, just mildly annoyed at our antics.

"You two are ridiculous. I tried to tell you that we are all going back to the inn and to bed."

My feet suddenly feel heavy and my limbs feel as if they are full of sand at her words and the realization that it is well past midnight. It's impossible for me to tell how long we've truly been here, especially when I didn't even notice Thelas and Faldorn leaving.

"What time is it?" I ask.

"Nearly to sunrise now." She yawns. "Best we get at least a few hours of sleep if we are to begin our search tomorrow."

SECOND ONLY TO THE GREAT GODDESS

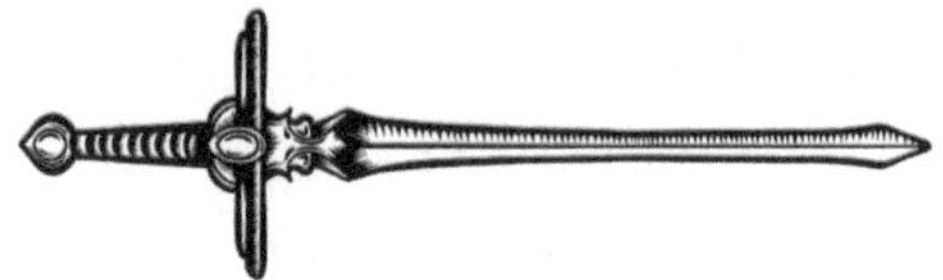

LAIRA

The next morning, I wake to a stiffness in my body and a grogginess in my head that only a night of dancing and a bit of alcohol can achieve. I can't find it in myself to complain though. Last night was fun and a much-needed breather from everything that has been going on, even if I did have to admit by the end of the night that Sebastian is actually a good dancer.

I stretch and roll over on my side. And what made him want to ask me to dance anyway? A warm shiver rolls down my spine at the memory, and I'm loath to admit that I liked it.

Groaning, I pull the covers over my head in belated embarrassment as I remember the awkward encounter when we came back to our room and how I changed in record time before slipping under the covers, too afraid to look at him or speak up about the single bed in the room. Which was a silly thing to do since we had been sleeping in close proximity for weeks now as we traveled. But there was something different and more intimate about the private room, and I was relieved when he took up a spot on the floor without comment.

I pull the covers from my face, gazing up at the ceiling and pondering how in the stars I got here. Sleeping in the same room is one thing, but having to pretend around town that we are married? That is a whole other beast I have no desire to take on for another few days or however long we will be here.

"At least he doesn't snore," I say aloud to the quiet room.

"I may not snore, but you certainly do, wife."

My eyes dart to Sebastian, who wears a sly, self-satisfied smile. The way he leans against the bathroom door frame and angles his body exposes a portion of his chest from the top of his semi-open shirt, and my cheeks immediately redden at the sight. I stare open-mouthed at his sudden appearance, but I try to cover my momentary embarrassment by chucking a pillow at him, which he ducks smoothly to avoid, sending the pillow flying into the tub behind him.

"I do not!" I shout.

He shakes his head and stalks forward, flopping down next to me in the bed. He throws his arms behind his head and leans back, fully relaxed atop the covers even as my heart kicks up into a galloping pulse at his proximity.

I attempt to dispel the nerves by prodding, "And what do you think you're doing in my bed?"

He doesn't even glance at me as he smiles to the ceiling. "Our bed, my dear."

"Our bed? I was not entirely sober last night, but even I remember you sleeping on the floor."

He looks at me then, tilting his head and flashing me what he no doubt thinks is his most smoldering grin. "Yes, and it was incredibly uncomfortable. At my ripe age of twenty-eight, I'm developing back problems, you know?"

I scoff, muttering, "Back problems my ass."

He chuckles and shifts his head to look up at the beams in the ceiling, his tone growing more serious. "Really though, if you want me to continue sleeping on the floor, I will." He's quiet for a long moment before adding, "Though, I can't say it wouldn't be nice to sleep in a bed while we still can."

I let out a long sigh and squeeze my eyes shut. It is comforting to know I could make him sleep on the floor if I wish, but he is right—it would be cruel of me to do so when, in the near future, we will have nothing but cold dirt and leaves to contend with once again. Besides, this bed is large enough for both of us not to touch if we don't want to. And I definitely *don't* want to.

An uncomfortable feeling stirs in my stomach at the small lie, but I push the thought away quickly. Even if I do want to touch him, it doesn't mean I should, nor that it is in any way a good idea.

It's just been too long since the last time I indulged in the touch of another, I tell myself before turning to study his profile.

He is handsome, that much I begrudgingly admit to myself. His dark, nearly black hair falls across the pillow, gathering at his shoulders in haphazard strands. With thick eyebrows, lashes to match, and a strong slightly sloped nose, he is every part the type of man I would have pursued had he not pushed every button possible within me and irritated me so much as a result. Still, he's not turning out to be quite as bad as I initially thought. I think of the way we danced the night before, and how he listened intently to me whenever we spoke. Not to mention when he came to my defense with that brute of a shopkeeper.

So, maybe that's why my next words leave my mouth easily, "You can sleep in the bed."

He turns to stare at me, surprise showing in his eyes that shifts to amusement as I continue. "But, if you touch me before, after, or during sleep you will be back on the floor!"

"Deal, wildcat."

I roll my eyes at the nickname but fail to hold back my smile.

He smirks. "So? What's the plan for today?"

"Well, Willow is going to try and get the herbs she wants at the market. But other than that, I think it will mostly be on Thelas to find the entrance to the forest. Which, now that I think about it, can likely only be done at night to avoid any suspicious eyes."

He's quiet for a long time as we sit in companionable silence while the early morning light filters through the window and casts a beautiful golden glow over us in the bed.

I lift my hand to place it in the sunlight's ray, marveling at the golden hue and slight sparkle it brings to my skin. "This type of sunlight has always been my favorite."

"You have a favorite type of light?"

I snort. "Of course. You don't?"

"Can't say that I do. I'm more of a 'close all of the curtains and live in darkness' type of fellow."

I chuckle. "That explains a great deal about you."

I feel his curious eyes on me as I continue to bask in the glow of the light. "Why is it your favorite?" he asks, cautiously, as if he's hesitant about asking for fear I may not answer.

I shrug, the explanation spilling freely from my mouth. "I suppose a few reasons. For one, it is the light of the morning, and that means my day is just beginning, and there are endless possibilities for what I can do. For another, it's just so bright and lovely, and sometimes I feel as if I'm bathed in honey."

"Can't imagine bathing in honey is actually pleasant. So sticky."

I roll my eyes. "You know what I mean."

"I'm not sure I do all the time, but I'm enjoying learning."

I side eye him and when a flirtatious smile curves its way onto my face, I don't stop it. "That was very smooth, husband."

His answering purr sends a shiver rolling down my spine. "That is only just the beginning, love."

We stare at each other for a heated moment, unspoken desire pulsing between us, before I shake myself free of his gaze and sit up quickly to break the connection.

"Well, I should probably get ready for the day. Willow may need help in the market after all."

"Of course. Though, aren't we supposed to be pretending we all don't know each other? Isn't that the whole point of this ruse? Or did you and Willow come up with this plan just for you to sleep in my bed?"

I whip around to face him, but I keep my spot on the far edge of the bed, not wanting to tempt my precarious self-control. "*My* bed," I snap.

"Ahh. There's my wildcat."

"Ugh! Not your—you are maddening, you know that right?"

He shrugs and gives me a knowing grin. "I've been told that once or twice."

"You are right though—we aren't all supposed to have much contact unless it's where no one can see us."

Sighing loudly, I drop both of my hands to my side and stand from the bed, gathering a fresh set of clothes and making my way to the bathroom. Before I close the door, Sebastian suggests lazily from across the room, "We could go shopping and peruse the town. Maybe look for a spot for your bookshop."

I frown. "We did that yesterday and got our supplies already."

"That's not what I had in mind."

Perhaps the wild smile on his face should scare me, but I'm only intrigued by his proposition.

Lifting an eyebrow, I fire back, "Only if you're paying."

"A good thief always has funds for his lady."

"Not your lady!" I yell behind me as I close the door and turn on the waterspout.

His answering chuckle follows me into the large bathtub, and I spend the entire time bathing trying to dispel his beautiful yet taunting green eyes from my head.

THE LATE MORNING light is blinding as we step from the inn and onto the already incredibly busy street. People hurriedly walk by, pulling carts or hauling large baskets containing all sorts of wares, from fruits to textiles and even magical items that sparkle brightly and glow strange colors. I'm stunned by the chaos and unsure of how to enter the fray, or even where to begin. Sebastian seems to have no qualms and, sensing my hesitation, grabs my wrist, dragging me straight into the hustle and bustle. We slip between rows of people, carts, and large and small nyradonn alike, and I marvel at his ability to effortlessly weave through such a large crowd.

I suppose his profession as a thief could explain why he's able to move like this. I dart my eyes to his other hand, watching for any sign he is about to steal from a passerby so I can reprimand him. We do not need to attract any unnecessary attention because of his sticky fingers, but he doesn't reach for anyone's pockets, so I relax my probing and focus on keeping up with him.

We finally burst into a wide open square. Shops and stands with colorful awnings line the perimeter and form neat rows around a massive fountain that sits perched in the center. People go about their daily shopping, but instead of the light hearted atmosphere I would expect from such a bustling town square, people seem keen to not linger anywhere too long. They move from shop to shop, only speaking when necessary, and more than once I catch someone clutch at a bag and watch others carefully as they walk by. Maybe Sebastian was right when he said this town had some suspicious people in it.

Despite the less than enthusiastic atmosphere, I'm impressed by the sheer size of it all. Based on what I've seen of Warille so far, it must be nearly double the size of Taslae. Not to mention it clearly boasts a larger variety of people and selection of shops. I take in the vibrant colors of the shops and beautifully carved stone buildings, determined to get a closer look later at the artistry I glimpsed yesterday as we hurriedly gathered our supplies.

"This town was founded by artists, wasn't it?" I ask in wonder.

He tilts his head down to look at me, and his hair falls in his face, giving him more of a boyish charm than he normally has. "I believe so. Why do you ask?"

"The buildings." I gesture a hand to the white stone carved figures on the tops of each shop, the swirling designs that line the fronts, and the masterfully harvested bricks of brown and red stone. "They're beautiful. And clearly touched with a creative hand." I tap the side of my head in emphasis. "An artist always recognizes another, you see."

"You're an artist?"

"I dabble." My shrug is punctuated by a secret smile, and I walk forward into the town square to avoid him asking further questions.

His low chuckle at my obvious dismissal of the conversation follows me, and it's not long before I feel his tall presence behind me.

Angling my head over my shoulder, I ask, "So, where should we head to first?"

He catches my gaze and as the light perfectly hits his eyes, I am momentarily struck again by the realization that this man is far too beautiful than I would like to admit. He continues to stare, as if knowing what I am thinking and inviting me to explore that thought further. The silver piercing on his eyebrow and the one on his nose glint in unison as he gives me a flirtatious smile—my stomach flipping at the sight.

Quickly turning my head, I increase my pace and walk straight into the first row of shops, my cheeks flaming red. Piercings are not all that common, and I haven't encountered anyone with similar ones, so it would be just my luck that I find them ridiculously attractive.

I shake the thought from my head. *Yes, he is very attractive, but that doesn't mean I need to act on it.* The thought settles me, and I focus on the shops to further keep my mind from dwelling on the feeling of him behind me for too long.

I jump from stall to stall, unable to choose one to look at properly. They are all so different, and I have to remind myself more than once that I do not have the space in my pack to carry any unnecessary bobbles, even though I desperately want to take some with me.

Perhaps I'm not so different from Kel and his collection of shiny objects after all. I chuckle to myself, only realizing I made the sound out loud when Sebastian asks, "What are you laughing about?"

I freeze, momentarily surprised that he heard me, before I dissolve into full laughter. "No reason!"

He gives me a strange, slightly curious look, but doesn't push further, gesturing instead toward the various shops still ahead of us. I realize belatedly that he hasn't looked at anything himself; he's simply followed me around, silently observing my chaotic jumping from shop to shop.

"Anything catch your eye?" he probes.

I don't want to tell him that nearly everything has caught my attention, so I say, "Perhaps a few things, but nothing I can't live without."

"Hmm," he replies, unconvinced.

I side eye him, unsure what he was hoping I'd say but not willing to dig further to find out.

A small table catches my eye with tidy rows of small boxes and a beautiful fae woman behind it. Her hair is tightly braided down her back, but even so, I can see the shimmer of blue and green, like a glittering ocean on a sunny day. Her eyes find mine, and I'm struck by the ageless depth in them. This fae looks not much older than myself, but my instincts tell me she is far older than even Faldorn.

I walk towards her, a pleasant smile on my face, and she gestures appreciatively toward the collection on the table. Unbridled joy fills me at the sight of rows and rows of glowing stone rings. I left most of my jewelry with the old woman back in Taslae—apart from my necklace in case it was useful later—thinking it would be a waste of space, but I've found myself missing the familiar weight of the rings I would normally wear as we've traveled. It's a silly thing to miss when there is so much going on, but still a pang of regret goes through my chest at the loss.

But here at least, I can try on a few and chat with the fae about her craftsmanship. Because they are all truly stunning. I pick up a thin gold band with a six-sided carved stone in the center. The gold of the band wraps delicately around the gem, encasing it in a protective and fashionable frame. Upon further examination, I realize the stone is nearly translucent and not only crystal clear as I thought, but light green as well. Holding it to the light reveals wispy green filaments trapped inside, which gives it the illusion of a clear stone from afar but green up close.

"It's almost as if moss is trapped inside," I muse aloud.

The fae's voice is light and musical as she says, "Yes, it is indeed moss. This particular stone was gathered from a specific region of the fae lands known for its strange incidents of stone fusing with living materials."

"So, the moss is alive inside the stone still?"

She smiles warmly. "It is. And because of that, it has enhanced properties that a normal ring would not possess."

I look up at her angular face, intrigued, "Like what?"

"It is said to always lead its wearer to the light. Some take that to mean safety, others think it means actual sunlight or moonlight due to the living moss' need for light. Both could be true. It is also possible it offers some slight protection from outside magical forces, though I have not personally seen any examples of this occurring."

I put the ring on the pointer finger of my left hand—carefully avoiding bringing attention to the thin dark veins on my right hand—and smile in appreciation. A ring that leads you to sunlight or safety? I think of my earlier conversation with Sebastian back at the inn and how I admitted to loving the warm hue of the morning sun and am filled with joy at the prospect of a ring that could help me find sources of light all the time. A sudden rush of unexpected tears builds behind my eyes, and I'm flustered at my strong reaction to the comforting idea of always being able to find the light.

Perhaps I am more afraid of the dark than I ever thought.

The ring settles nicely on my hand and I admire it for another moment before deflating as I notice the exorbitantly large number on the small tag hanging from it—there's no way I could afford something like it, even when my bookshop was in its prime and certainly not with the meager funds I brought to contribute to the group's essentials on the quest.

Slowly, and with great reluctance, I pull the ring from my finger and hand it back to the fae. "Thank you for telling me about this ring. It is absolutely beautiful, and you have an amazing eye and an incredible skill to make these yourself. But unfortunately, it just isn't in my budget today."

Despite my disappointment at not getting the ring, my smile is genuine as I thank her. Artists like her should be respected and prized, too often people forget the wonders a mind and creative hands can make and I only feel sorrow for those who cast artists aside.

She dips her head in thanks, placing the ring back in its box and giving me a sweet farewell.

I linger for a moment before pulling myself from her table and continuing my path down the line of shops. I nearly jump from my skin when Sebastian says from behind my shoulder, "A ring that locates sunlight sounds right up your alley."

I huff out an annoyed breath as I am reminded of his presence. "Yes, unfortunately it was not meant to be."

He cocks his head and stares intently at me, and I'm taken aback by the sudden shift in his energy.

"You're right-handed but chose to put the ring on your left. Why is that?"

The question makes my stomach drop and the veins on my hand burn as if exposed. I stare at him, eyes wide, and unsure what to say. I don't want to tell him the truth. Only Willow knows and I don't enjoy the thought of everyone else finding out and adding to my already precarious thoughts on the matter. Not to mention, I don't need them all worrying about me.

His gaze finds my right hand half hidden at my side. "Is it because of the lines on your hand?"

My continued silence must bother him because he quickly adds, "Is there something wrong?"

He begins reaching for me and I step back before reassuring him with the first words that come to mind. "No. Nothing's wrong. Don't worry about it."

He arches a brow, unconvinced.

"Really. It's fine and I'd appreciate if you don't ask about it again."

He watches me carefully but ultimately gives in to my plea with a short nod.

I exhale and look around, wanting to focus on something else. "Maybe we can try some food stalls this time? We never did have breakfast, and it happens to be my favorite meal."

He hesitates, as if still wanting to continue the conversation, but eventually chuckles softly and says, "Of course it is."

I narrow my eyes at him, searching his words for an insult that isn't there.

He holds his hands up in surrender. "Hey! I only meant that you seem to be a morning person is all."

I grumble.

He points a thumb behind us, his arms still raised in placation. "Speaking of which. I believe I smelled some coffee a few paces back, shall we head that way?"

I straighten at the mention of coffee, peeking my head around his large frame to find the stall he's talking about. He holds out his arm, gesturing for me to take it so he can lead us there, but I eye it like it's a snake coiling to attack.

"I won't bite, love." He flashes me a smile, his canine teeth momentarily visible. "Unless you'd like me to, of course."

My blood runs hot, and I suppress the visceral reaction my body has to his suggestion, strangling the part of my mind that attempts to play a rather delectable scene of lips, teeth, and bare skin before it can gain traction.

I swallow the feverish emotion down, determined to show him he has no effect on me. I loop my arm through his, leaning my body into him more than is necessary as I chirp, "I'm going to ignore that. Let's find that coffee!"

COFFEES AND SNACKS in hand, we settle on a bench on the edge of the town center. I sip the hot beverage contentedly as Kel swoops down to land next to me, tilting his head and chittering expectantly.

"Sorry, Kel, I didn't get you any—"

Sebastian thrusts a muffin in the direction of Kel, who happily snatches it from his grasp and tears into the top with reckless abandon, flinging bits of muffin on the bench and my lap.

I brush the crumbs off, laughing affectionately. "Kel, you silly creature! Watch where you're flinging that!"

I glance over at Sebastian, surprised he remembered Kel's favorite snack. "Thank you for thinking of him."

His answering smile is warm, and he laughs alongside me at Kel's enthusiasm. "Of course."

I nibble on my warm pastry, my eyes drifting aimlessly around the bustling square until it snags on the statue in the middle of the oversized fountain. It appears to be a graceful woman, her back turned to us as she lifts her arms to the sky. I squint at her right hand and how it's closed in a fist but has a definite hole in the middle as if there used to be an object there. My feet move of their own accord, quickly bringing me in front of the fountain to examine it more closely.

Sebastian calls after me, but I hardly hear him as I focus on the golden plaque at the base of the statue, trying to read what its faded letters say.

"What are you doing?"

"Getting a closer look."

"Of the goddess statue? Pretty sure there's one in every larger town."

"I don't know, something about this one is different." I shift my stance to get a new angle on the plaque and am finally able to read what it says.

"In memory of our savior and highest lady, second only to the great Goddess herself."

"Huh, so not the Goddess after all."

"No…" I trail off, my mind far away as I ponder the strange dedication. Second only to the Goddess? That is high praise indeed.

I read the words again and stare up at the woman's face. I realize with a bolt of shock that she is fae—her delicately pointed ears and intricate markings on her face reminding me of Faldorn, but the sharp look in her eyes is not at all similar to the quiet calm in his. It's yet another indication that this is not the Goddess. In the old tales, she is spoken as being woven by starlight and shifting easily from one form to another when interacting with the beings of this land. So, she's most often portrayed with a crown of stars and varying features depending on who created the statue. It wouldn't be the strangest thing for a fae artist to have created a piece with fae features here, but it's more likely she would be given more humanlike attributes.

I cock my head to the side, considering the odd feeling swirling in my chest. "She seems familiar." The words are soft as they leave my lips, and I wonder if I even said them aloud.

A crawling feeling drifts over my body, and I shiver at the uncomfortable sensation. Suddenly unable to look at the statue any longer, I step away and return to the bench to finish my coffee and breakfast while pointedly ignoring the fountain. I feel Sebastian's confused stare, but he doesn't ask questions about my odd behavior, which I greatly appreciate.

After a long bout of silence, he offers, "Want to walk back to the inn and see if we can find out what the others are up to?"

I nod, relieved by the suggestion and more than happy to get far away from the fountain and the disconcerting statue.

"Yes, let's do that."

DREAMS & EXPECTATIONS

THELAS

I read my notes again and roughly cross out another line. It's been weeks and I still can't find the anchor point to the entrance. The need to find this hidden forest grows every day, and while we haven't had any outright incidents of townsfolk attempting to follow any of us, we know it's only a matter of time before someone questions our continued presence even with our careful cover stories. The people here are suspicious at best, and I fear what could happen if we aggravate the wrong group or let it slip what we are looking for.

I growl. We don't have time for this endless searching.

My theory was that the entrance was connected to a tree, but there were thousands of trees on this side of the Hark River, and there was no guarantee that it was even on this side or that it stayed in one place for long. I glare at the opposite shore as the sun begins to wane, knowing it would be just my luck to have the entrance be further into the trees and across the river.

Willow and Faldorn approach behind me, their steps muffled by the water, but the beast informs me of their approach. His long body in the back of my mind unfurling and a single ear flicks in their direction.

"Any luck?" Willow asks.

I turn around slowly, not wanting to admit to another dead end. "Not yet. Do you sense anything?"

A small green tendril floats from her upturned palm, the point flicking about like a snake tasting the air. She lets out a frustrated grunt. "Nothing. Who knew it would be so Goddess-damned difficult to find the blasted thing?"

"It has been lost to time for a reason," Faldorn says.

"Yes, yes. Dangerous forest and secret entrance. *Thank you* Faldorn for reminding me." She throws her arms to the side and stalks away, stomping through the dirt but avoiding any wayward plants. Her magic flares from her for a second, and I nearly take a step backward at the blast of green tendrils that snake from her. But they disappear in a blink, and I'm almost certain I imagined them entirely.

Faldorn crosses his arms and stares after her. "She's rather fiery when frustrated."

I huff out a weak laugh. "Yeah."

"What about you? How are you faring?"

"I'm okay, I suppose. I should have been able to find the entrance by now though." I eye the fae male out of the corner of my eye, bracing for his disappointment and agreement.

He assesses me for a long moment, and I squirm under his gaze, unable to meet his eyes. He has a way of looking directly through a person, and it's unnerving to say the least.

"You are very hard on yourself. If this were easy, it would have already been done."

I gape at him, not expecting that answer. When was the last time someone far older reassured me instead of berating me for not doing what I was told? I don't reply, unsure what to even say, but my shoulders feel lighter and my hands loosen their firm grip on my notebook.

He tilts his head, considering, "Perhaps you could use your other senses to seek out the entrance."

"My other senses?"

He nods. "My fae blood gifts me the ability to see at great distances and hear even the quietest of sounds, but it also gives me an innate sense of nature and creatures. Other beings have heightened senses for the physical world as well, like witches and plant life, shifters and the tangible magic of this realm, or humans and their affinity for connecting to the nyradonn."

My blood runs cold, and my skin turns clammy at his words. The beast slithers to the forefront of my mind as if called, and I desperately shove him back before Faldorn can see evidence of him in my eyes. The only things that await me should he escape are pain, suffering, and unending loneliness. I have no desire to drive away the only people I have ever tentatively thought of as friends.

"I—I have no such abilities. I'm sorry."

He watches me before nodding once and turning to walk back the way we came. "Do not be sorry. It is not your fault. But perhaps a new tactic is needed, something to consider, no?"

The beast roars in my mind as Faldorn walks away, and I lash out at him, driving him swiftly back into his hole. There is no place for him here.

I WANDER AIMLESSLY along the riverbank for a long time, grateful for the heavy darkness cocooning around me. Willow returned not long ago and was convinced she felt an odd tremor in this section of forest, but after a thorough search, we found nothing out of the ordinary. She left once the sun began to rise, claiming she needed a few hours of sleep at least and to check on Laira and Sebastian. Something about making sure they didn't kill each other. I snort at the memory, doubting that killing is what we need to worry about with those two.

The river thins, and though it's still moving swiftly, I feel as if I could almost jump across it.

"So why don't you?"

I ignore the beast and trudge onward, scanning the trees as I go and searching for any sign that could indicate they are the anchor point I'm looking for.

"I could get you across, you know."

Cold fear washes over me, a thick suffocating blanket of ice. "Absolutely not," I say aloud.

My back prickles. Phantom slices tearing open the skin and tears well unbidden in my eyes. The pain of those lashes is carved deep into my memory even all these years later. I haven't let the beast out since, and he knows that.

He growls, pacing back and forth, and I feel his confinement as if it were my own. But I will never let him out again. Were he a normal creature, perhaps things would be different—if only he were something palatable, easily understood, or tame. If I wasn't harboring an abomination, maybe things could have been different; maybe I wouldn't have been cast aside.

He settles down, sensing my resolve, and speaks in a rough voice, ***"You may not let me out, but I can help in other ways."***

I push against his advance, but he wins the small battle, stealing my vision as his and I know if anyone saw me, they would see slitted pale golden eyes shining in the darkness.

"Use my abilities—our abilities—and see."

While I could see well enough despite the darkness before, the forest comes into startling focus now, lit up as if it's midday, and I can see every tiny detail. Fish swim with the river's current, and a leaf floats down from an overhanging branch that is quickly swallowed by the water and carried away. The opposite bank shines with wet boulders sparkling under the moonlight, and far into the distance an ember burns. Before I know it, I'm hurtling across the river and racing to the orange dot floating in the air. When I come upon it, I realize it's not an ember but a swirling mass of orange and yellow energy. It hovers above my head for a moment before diving into the massive tree in front of me.

It's ancient. Thick branches stretch from it—each covered in a layer of green moss and tiny ferns. The lowest of the branches is low enough to sit on, but I don't need to rest when the beast's power floods my system.

I place an open palm on the tree and close my eyes, the orange glow reigniting in my mind. The beast purrs and sits back on his haunches, pleased with himself. ***"I will require more than a simple run through the woods the next time you need me."*** I brush him away, and he slinks back to his corner.

The glow intensifies, and when I open my eyes, the entire tree is glowing a bright amber, and a pinprick of light flickers to life in the center.

Disbelief and elation war in my chest as I stare transfixed at the spot on the trunk. Years of research and daydreams coalesce into this one moment, and all I can imagine is how happy everyone will be.

I've finally found the entrance to the Forbidden Forest.

A Kind Gesture

Laira

My eyes peek open to the blissful golden light of early morning, and I smile before snuggling into the warm blankets at my back. The day may be ready for me, but I could use a few more moments of sleep before fully committing to the morning. A contented sigh nearly leaves my lips, but a heavy arm settles over my waist and freezes me in place, halting the sigh before it can escape. It takes my sleep-addled brain far too long to realize I cuddled back into a warm body and not a lump of blankets.

Sebastian.

My pulse ricochets and I attempt to wiggle out of his grasp, but his arm is a dead weight and holds me firmly in place against him. I am all too aware of the way every part of him feels against my back, and a part of me wants to sink into it. His arm is firm and the way it curls around my hips in a slightly possessive way makes my heart flutter and my mind skip to things it shouldn't. His breathe tickles my neck and I shiver before frowning at my body's reaction. *Get ahold of yourself,* I mentally reprimand.

I lift my shoulder and crane my neck behind me to see if he's asleep or if he's doing this on purpose and it's some amusing game he's playing with me. But his eyes are closed, and his breathing is steady, so I assume he is fast asleep. I stare at him for another long moment, enjoying the way the soft light cascades across his face—he looks younger in this moment, less guarded, and softer. The moment is surprisingly intimate, and I feel as if I am doing something I shouldn't; like I'm witnessing something he wouldn't voluntarily give or wouldn't want me to see. I dart my eyes to his arm around my waist and my mouth pulls up at the corner, even as I try to fight it. It's almost a sweet gesture, him reaching for me in his sleep.

Would he ever do it on purpose?

I mentally berate myself for my silly question. *It doesn't matter if he would do it consciously or not because I do not need to get involved with him.* I turn back over and finally am able to angle my body away from his and under his arm. As carefully as I can, I get up from the bed and tiptoe to the washroom. I'm nearly to the door when a floorboard creaks and I freeze in place, darting a glance back at the bed to see if he woke from the noise. The mess of blankets doesn't stir, and I let out a quiet breath of relief. I would like to be fully dressed and ready to go before he gets up, and far away from my sleepy morning thoughts about how good it felt to be that close to him.

"Where are you off to in such a hurry, love?" A gruff voice drawls from under the covers.

Cringing slightly, I slowly turn to face Sebastian. He sits up in bed, his hair mussed from sleep and a pleased smile on his face.

He pats the space next to him. "Come back for a few more minutes. I'll even pretend to be asleep again, so you can stare as long as you want."

His smile is devilish and my cheeks flush immediately at his words. *He was awake the whole time?*

I cross my arms over my chest, sputtering, "You—you were awake?" I look him up and down, trying not to focus too long on the spiraling tattoos winding up his chest from his partially open tunic. "For how long?"

He huffs a low laugh, and the seductive sound trails down my spine. It's intoxicating and I have to remind my body once more to stop reacting so strongly to him. He rises from the bed and makes his way to me. His steps are slow and purposeful, and my heart seizes in my chest when he stops a hands width from me and places his palm on the door frame behind me. His eyes are molten as he stares down at me, and I'm unable to stop the sharp inhale of breath when he gently cups my neck and leans in to whisper in my ear.

"Wouldn't you like to know, wildcat?"

His hand is warm against my neck, and I want to melt into it. The sensation is so intense from that small touch alone that I almost give in entirely. We've been playing this game with each other ever since arriving in Warille, and while it has been somewhat amusing, I haven't given him more than a few innocent touches and wayward glances. Maybe he feels emboldened because of my reckless staring while he was feigning sleep?

He pulls away and I make sure to hold my ground so I don't follow him. He smirks as if he can see my internal fight written across my body, but he doesn't approach me again and I take the opportunity to dart into the washroom. Throwing my back against the door, I still my mind and close my eyes to collect myself, silently urging my racing heart to calm. Once I feel like my mind will behave and not insist I jump back into bed with him, I get ready for the day. The realization that today is finally the day that we are leaving Warille hits me—a mix of apprehension and excitement lighting my veins. As far as we've come, I know this is truly the start of our journey and that is both terrifying and intriguing.

AFTER TAKING A long bath to fully wash and prep for the long weeks of travel ahead, I catch myself staring longingly at the soft bed I've had the last few weeks. I will miss its warm embrace when I'm sleeping on the cold hard ground of the woods once again. Despite sharing with Sebastian, I never slept poorly, and I made sure to tell myself it was because of the bed and not his presence—though a part of me was glad to not sleep alone. There were many nights back in Taslae when I would wake in a cold sweat, absolutely certain someone was stalking my home and about to enter to harm me. When that would occur, I'd had to creep around the entire house with my sword or daggers until I was convinced no one was lurking in the dark corners. But with Sebastian there, the fear of an intruder was not as strong.

I shove a change of clothes in my pack and briefly pause to stare at my necklace before shoving it in as well. It hasn't glowed since Faldorn read the prophecy aloud, but I still feel strange wearing it, and I don't have the heart to get rid of it, so down at the bottom of the pack it goes.

"Don't look so glum, love. We'll still be sleeping next to each other, we just won't have as much privacy as before. But if you can keep quiet, then—*oof*."

I chuck a pillow at his face before he can continue, effectively cutting off whatever raunchy statement he was going to say. I have a wicked idea of making space in my bag for one of the extra pillows to keep for this very reason while we are in the forest but decide it's not worth leaving something else behind.

He tosses the pillow back on the bed, and my smile must be fierce because he eyes me carefully, like I'm a wild animal about to lash out again. "I don't even want to know what idea is running through your head."

I chuckle darkly. "Just imagining ways to shut you up in the future."

He gives me a smoldering grin, tilting an eyebrow.

I roll my eyes. "Yeah, yeah. Suggestive comment and all that, lots of ways to shut you up that you'd enjoy—*I get it*."

He stares at me in amusement, and for a second it's as if his entire facade of sarcasm and flirtation drops away to reveal a genuine smile and soft eyes—momentarily stunning me and causing my heart to flip before he's back and brandishing his green eyes like a weapon once more.

I turn around to avoid his stare and the brief glimpse of something softer in his gaze, buckling my pack shut and busying myself with straightening the leather straps. I'm well aware of his presence behind me as he gets closer, his feet hardly making a sound over the smooth wood floor, but I don't turn around. A large hand comes into my periphery, and I hold back my shudder as his chest nearly touches my back and his arm hovers above my shoulder. Even with my above average height, he stands at least a head taller, and as he shifts ever closer and bends his elbow to place his closed fist in front of me, I feel completely surrounded by his presence. Utterly engulfed in his scent and his warmth—unable to move even if I wanted to.

But I find that I don't want to move.

My mind rebels against the feeling, but my heart jumps as he places the lightest of touches on my hip—so gentle I almost imagine it's not even there. His firm arm curls at my shoulder, and I tilt my eyes down to look at it. When he doesn't move or open his hand, I place my palm underneath, wondering if he's trying to give me something. A tingling sensation brushes my fingertips as he places a small metal object in my palm, and my breath leaves my chest in a rush as I realize what it is. The golden ring with the moss-infused stone from the market rests in my hand, a soft warmth emanating from it as I stare in bewildered wonder. Heat pricks in my chest, and I feel it as it travels to my eyes. My vision grows watery as I stare at the perfect ring, recalling all it had symbolized to me when I first beheld its story—of how with it, I would always be able to find the light. I think of all the times I've been haunted by the darkness both in and outside of my mind and how now, with this ring, a comforting certainty straightens my spine knowing I will never truly be lost again.

I blink away the unshed tears, turning to the right to look at Sebastian. I study his face, taking in every feature. Attempting to puzzle out why he would get this for me, as if I'll find the answer written plainly on his face. Finally, I flick my eyes to focus on his.

"Thank you." The words are not enough for what this gift means to me, but they are all I have.

His eyes shine a soft green, and they crinkle at the corners as he gives me a small smile. "You're welcome."

His breath mingles with mine, our faces inches apart, and I see the moment between us as if I am looking from the outside. The two of us staring deep into each other's eyes as an invisible fire lights between us.

I could kiss him right now.

The thought should startle me more than it does, and the urge grows stronger the longer we stand hovering in front of each other, the tension unbearable. I go as far as to tilt my head slightly closer, my lips a hair's breadth from his. A thrill runs through my blood, and my eyes fall closed as I imagine what it would feel like to be kissed by him. Someone as wild and fierce as him must kiss like the world is ending, and I am the only thing that would save him. It's getting harder and harder to deny that isn't something I would like to get a taste of.

He doesn't move closer to me, waiting to see what I'll do and if I'll close the final bit of distance between us. The idea is far more tempting than I would like to admit, and my body screams out a treacherous roar as I step out of his embrace.

He drops his arms, and we stand facing each other, that roiling tension still present despite the new distance.

I hold the ring out to him, and he shakes his head. "No, that is for you."

I smile. "I know."

He tilts his head to the side, confused, and the movement is so feline that I almost laugh.

"I want you to put it on me." The words leave my mouth with more confidence than I anticipated.

Since when am I someone who demands a handsome man place a ring on my finger? A part of me shies away from the thought, but another part is emboldened by the pleased look in his eyes.

He steps forward, his heat once again in my space as he reaches for my left hand and the ring. He brushes his fingertips against the back of my hand, and I shiver despite myself.

Why is this more sensual than the damn almost-kiss we shared just moments ago?

He lines up the ring with my pointer finger, looking up at me, and I nod in confirmation at the correct placement. He holds my gaze as he slides the ring on, and I can't help but give him a grin as I revel in this unguarded moment.

I pull away, surveying the ring on my hand. It's absolutely beautiful, and I'm once again swept away by this strangely thoughtful gesture. I'm in no way convinced he isn't still a complete scoundrel, but I must admit that there is a side to him that is tolerable, if not pleasant.

A sudden thought occurs to me, curdling my stomach, and while I don't think it true, I need to be sure before I can fully accept this gift. "You didn't steal this did you?"

"I did not," he says, his face open and honest.

I nod, satisfied he is telling the truth and pleased that I will not need to return the ring to the lovely fae at the market.

We share one last heated look before grabbing our things and meeting the others outside with the horses.

THE TREE

LAIRA

Thelas leads us atop Hael away from town and to thinner section of the Hark River, though it's still far too wide and fast for us to cross successfully on horseback. I look downstream to see if there are any potentially easier points for crossing when a *whoosh* of energy flies by me, startling Skip and causing her to sidestep nervously.

"Easy girl, it's alright— " My mouth drops open as roots as thick as my arms and hundreds of vines crawl across the river and stop at our feet. They curl together in a complex latticework of braids and knots, forming a dense bridge just wide enough for us all to cross on horseback.

I whip my head around to Willow who sits innocently atop Star behind me. Her hands are just barely raised in front of her, and she has a pleased smile on her face. A few green tendrils of her magic snake from her, and a fuzzy haze of green and gold tinted energy surrounds her body. It lights up brilliantly with the rising sun behind her, and I find my own grin widening just as far as hers. I knew she was a powerful witch, but that was unlike anything I've ever seen her do before.

Thelas gapes at her. "Since when could you do that?"

She smiles and prods Star forward. "Since always."

Star sniffs the bridge, but it doesn't take long before she's walks carefully across it and prances around on the other side.

"Well come on!" Willow shouts to us over the rushing water. "I may be able to summon the bridge, but I can only hold it for so long before I'll start to get tired!"

Sebastian pulls up beside me on his horse and leans down to whisper, "Creating a bridge strong enough out of roots to hold up under all of our weight will only make her a *bit* tired?"

I shrug, but I can't help but laugh at the incredulity in his voice. "She's strong."

He watches Willow who waves at us across the river, a new understanding and appraisal in his eyes. My stomach swoops uncomfortably as I stare at him, and I motion Skip forward to try and escape the sensation. Who cares if he sees Willow in a different way? It shouldn't matter, but my stomach constricts anyway—my eyes darting in his direction once more before quickly forcing them away. A secret smile curves on my lips when I find him already staring at me and I dip my head down to hide it.

We quickly cross the river and Willow's bridge sinks into the soil. It's slightly unnerving that she has that much power over the trees and plants, but I am happy for her. There's been a shift in her ever since we started on this journey—a looseness to her movements and a willingness to let go. She's been using her magic more freely and the quiet joy that has filled me each time she has is a bright spot in every day. Perhaps this journey will be good for more than just retrieving a mythical sword and freeing me from my shadows—maybe it will allow her to release her magic permanently. The vein on my right hand pulses and a slight burn cascades up my arm, ending at my shoulder. My eyes drop to it and my hearts sinks, my blood running suddenly cold despite the burning sensation. The veins aren't that dark, but they have crept up past my wrist now and branch off in four different directions before disappearing beneath my skin. I pull my hand closer to my body and angle it out of sight, using my left hand to hold Skip's reins, and keep it purposely from my view. Worrying about that darkness is not something I can handle right now.

Thelas takes the lead once more and after a few quiet moments through the trees, we come to an opening that dumps us out into a small clearing. My eyes widen as I take in the ancient looking tree that sits at its center. Sprawling branches stretch in a wide arc around the base of the tree and warm golden sunlight filters through the dense green canopy. The massive tree does the work of ten and as we slowly approach, a slight hum fills the air. The energy of the tree is enticing, and I can't help the thrill of excitement that runs down my spine at taking it all in. Willow is the first to leap from her horse and approach the tree, lifting a confident hand to its trunk and inhaling deeply. Green tendrils spark to life around her and slowly sink into the tree and its branches. She turns around suddenly, a brilliant smile on her face and meets our expectant gazes.

"This is it."

As the words fall from her mouth, I heave a relieved sigh at having finally reached our destination.

But it's not really the end is it? We still have to navigate this forest, I remind myself.

Sebastian's unimpressed voice cuts through my thoughts, "Am I the only one who doesn't see something special about this damn tree?"

The rest of us look at each other as if to confirm, before turning back to him and saying in unison, "Yes."

He sighs dramatically, but a smile curves across his face as he speaks. "Figures. Of course I'm the least interesting of this bunch."

I snort. "Even as a human you should be able to tell this tree is important." I pull Skip forward to stand beside him and his horse, "Follow what I do, and you'll feel it too."

"Feel what?"

"Hush and follow along." I suppress my giggle at his stubbornness and close my eyes. I peek them open to ensure he is doing the same and settle into my saddle once he does.

"Okay, now relax your arms and drop your reins. Take a deep breath and then exhale." I follow my own instructions and hear his intake and exhale. Still with my eyes closed, I continue, "Good. Now, keep breathing and focus your attention on the tree. Keep your eyes closed and cast your senses in front of you. Feel the breeze in the air and hear the rustle of the leaves. There's a weight to the air around us, and an ancient energy that pulls us toward it."

I open my eyes to watch him. His face is scrunched in concentration and his body is tense despite my encouragement to relax. *He's trying too hard.*

I can't help the soft smile that winds its way across my face, or the light hand that I place over his. "Relax, Sebastian."

He tenses at first, but his shoulders drop quickly and soon I'm met with intense green eyes and a buzz echoing through my body for an entirely different reason. But I don't move my hand.

"Do you feel it? The energy from the tree?" I ask, my voice nearly a whisper.

His eyes dart between mine and he leans forward just the barest amount, like he can't help himself. "I do feel something."

"From the tree?" I prod, not quite willing to accept what he's not saying and trying to give him a way out.

He grabs my hand from atop his, squeezing it once. "Do you think I'm talking about the tree?"

My mouth goes dry and I quickly avoid his too heavy gaze, removing my hand and attempting to get some space between us. I feel his eyes on me as I force myself to watch the others as they chat in a circle and pretend they aren't listening to us.

Willow clears her throat and gestures to the tree. "Well then. Should we go?"

She lifts her brows at me expectantly and I scowl at her. She hops atop her horse, smiling broadly, and I gently prod Skip to join her—still wanting to put much needed space between Sebastian and me.

The horses grow slightly agitated as we approach the tree, and Skip throws her head back in alarm when we get within a few paces of it. I rub her neck, attempting to soothe her.

"Is there something wrong that is causing them to act this way, or is it just the tree?" I ask the group.

Faldorn leads his elk to the front and carefully surveys the tree and our surroundings. "I believe it is just the tree itself, there is nothing to cause them alarm in this clearing or beyond."

Thelas leads his antelope forward and places a hand on the rough bark. Nothing happens, but as he pushes harder, his hand is suddenly swallowed and disappears entirely. I gasp and crane my neck to get a better look. Thelas' triumphant grin shines in the morning light, and I can't help but smile broadly back at him—though I can't help the heavy anticipation that weighs me down suddenly, and the churning that begins in my stomach. This is exciting, yes, and

I'm happy for Thelas that he was able to find the entrance, but that doesn't stop my body from screaming at me that I should flee.

No way but forward, I remind myself.

My hand doesn't pulse again, but I'm all too aware of the dark veins and the knowledge that they will continue to spread. I have no choice but to move forward.

Faldorn takes the lead, insisting that he enter first in case there is trouble on the other side, with the rest of us following, and Sebastian at the rear. Faldorn and his massive elk disappear into the tree's trunk, and I'm in awe at the way it swallows him so thoroughly. How does it *do* that? Thelas and Willow follow, and then it's my turn. My hands are slick with sweat and my heart flutters at a rapid pace, the wide trunk looming before me as my mind rebels at the thought of walking through a tree into a place I can't even see. Kel senses my hesitation and fear and lands quickly in my lap, giving me a soft nudge with his beak and trilling quietly. I stare at the rough bark, unable to look away, but also unable to motion Skip forward, until I hear a low voice at my back.

"I'm right behind you."

Sebastian's words, along with the lightest of touches on my shoulder, wrap around me, and for some reason it settles my mind. The nerves are still there, but they are distant like voices on the other side of a door.

I nod once and give him a small, grateful smile. He returns it and gestures toward the tree. "Whenever you're ready."

Inhaling deeply, I kick Skip forward, and after some hesitation on her part, she slowly steps forward when the tree shows no resistance. I blink my eyes into the new space and find it to be significantly darker than the brilliant sunny morning we left behind. The entire forest floor is covered with a thick carpet of blue-green moss, and peppered along the trees and ground are tiny plants that pulse with a soft glow. The canopy hangs low, the branches of trees overhead reaching down to create a dark enclosure, like a cellar chamber. It's surprisingly cozy, if a bit darker than I would prefer; it feels separate and other, like we stepped into an alternate world. And perhaps we did. The odd sensation I felt as I entered the tree—as

if I was in a bubble that was stretched too wide and then popped—finally dissipates and I shudder, shaking my arms to rid myself of the sensation.

I look around at our decently large group, but even with the five of us, our mounts, and Kel & Din, we fit comfortably in this rounded space—almost like the forest knew we were coming and created a perfectly sized welcome area to begin our journey. It's an odd thought but I try not to think too hard on how sentient this forest may actually be and why it would want to come across as welcoming if it's supposed to be guarding treasure. Lure us in perhaps? Like honey left out to trap helpless insects.

I keep a firm grip on Skip's reins in case she gets spooked by the forest and drop to a crouch to inspect what appears to be small mushrooms that are unlike any I've ever seen. Tinged with the slightest blue color, they glow softly, but some groupings appear to be moving, wiggling from side to side as I lean in closer. I jerk back in alarm, causing Skip to fling her head in agitation when one of the mushrooms blinks at me with one eye, that quickly turns into many eyes that cover the entire top of the mushroom. I cross the small space to the others—who are also inspecting various aspects of the strange forest nearby. Deciding that I do not need to look at anything else too closely if they are suddenly going to sprout eyes and blink at me, I keep my gaze up. Ignorance suits me just fine in that case. I'll leave the plant research and dissection to Willow.

"Did we make it?" I ask, even though deep down I know the answer. No one replies, but Willow does pose a question of her own.

"Are we sure this wasn't actually a portal to the fae lands? How can we possibly still be in Eislekest?"

Faldorn steps forward to place his palm on a tree and hums, handing off the reins of his elk to Sebastian as he goes. He's quiet for a moment as we all watch him. Is he communing with the tree? Is that a fae thing? His humming continues and with it, his skin and hair begins to change color. Whirls of blue and silver dance just below his skin, the bright pricks of light causing the markings on his face and body to glow. His hair—though it held hues of blue and purple before—now glimmers brightly, the colors shining vibrantly through the black strands until it nearly eclipses it completely.

I glance around to see if everyone else is as shocked as I am at Faldorn's change in appearance, and it turns out I'm not alone as we all share similar expressions of wonder and awe. He's absolutely beautiful. The kind of beauty that artists spend their whole lives trying to capture. I wonder if all fae are like that or if he is beautiful even among them.

"This is not Caelamne. We are still in Eislekest." He turns and walks the short distance to Thelas and claps a hand to his shoulder. "It appears that our young Thelas did it." He nods to Willow. "And of course the lovely Willow as well."

She beams. "Well, it was mostly Thelas, but I'd say I was a great help!"

Thelas is silent for a moment before murmuring, "I did it."

The self-doubt and disbelief in his voice nearly breaks my heart. He wasn't sure he could find it, wasn't certain of his abilities. But I knew he would find it. Even knowing him less than a month, I can see that Thelas is brilliant and knows far more than he realizes. But I understand the urge to doubt yourself, to believe you are less than. That insipid voice in your head snapping at you that you are not enough for this world—will never be enough. Maybe Thelas and I can learn to quiet that voice in our heads together.

I place my own hand on his shoulder and say, "You did it Thelas. We're here."

He doesn't look at me, nor does he take his eyes from his hands, but I see a ghost of a small smile on his face before I turn to survey our surroundings yet again. We need to figure out how to navigate this forest—and fast. But it's just so… strange, and I'm unsure exactly how we will manage it. It's incredibly dark for one. With the only light seeming to come from the glowing plant life along the forest floor and scattered on the trunks of trees. There's a surprising stillness to the forest as well—an almost absence of sound that is unnerving to hear. Or I suppose *not* hear. The sounds you normally associate with a lively forest of dirt shifting underfoot, small creatures skittering, or the crunch of a branch just aren't here. Instead, there is a hum of buzzing energy felt in the back of my head, a *tick-ticking* coming from who knows where, and a soft chime of twinkling bells.

"Strange indeed." I hum to myself as I take in the small pocket of trees.

Sebastian's voice breaks my curiosity. "So, what now? Which way do we go?"

"Good question." I bounce back.

Thelas seems to emerge from his thoughts at the question, and I'm surprised when he immediately pulls out at least four maps, a compass, writing utensils, and some strange contraption with metal bits that I couldn't begin to guess the purpose of. Faldorn helps him set up a space by clearing a spot on the ground, avoiding the mushrooms I examined earlier, making me wonder if he saw the eyes too.

I raise my eyebrows at the display. *Huh. Maybe it won't be so difficult to get through this forest after all.*

The thought is comforting and even if it isn't true, I feel a renewed confidence and energy because of it. My brows knit together as a new emotion flits across my mind, one completely at odds with my bubbling optimism. I don't have an exact thought to go with it, only a sense that it is open dislike. I turn my head, snagging on Sebastian as he leans down to poke at a vibrant purple slime clinging to the side of a tree and scrunching his nose in disgust as it jiggles. I cock my head to the side, a wild idea coming to mind before I bat it away, certain that it's impossible.

Faldorn gives Thelas enough time to look at his maps to confirm we need more information before we can fully decide on a direction, and then he promptly mounts his elk, walking through the opening into the forest beyond without another word. Thelas packs up quickly and leaps atop his own antelope to follow. The rest of us jump onto our own mounts, entirely used to Faldorn's quick exits by now and knowing we will need to stay close.

The opening into the rest of the forest is only wide enough for us each to walk through on our animals single file, and apart from Faldorn, we each glance around nervously as we pass through. Coiling vines make a sort of doorway between two trees, and they slither together as I bring up the rear, the makeshift doorway closing behind me.

"Well, there goes our exit I suppose." I say uncertainly to no one in particular and watch in morbid fascination as the opening closes, sealing us in this forest.

Faldorn's reassuring voice sounds from the front of the group. "It's no matter.

We knew we would not be leaving the way we came anyway. Nothing to do but press forward."

I nod, but that doesn't stop the uncomfortable itch that crawls over my skin at being trapped in this place. The darkness is already suffocating and while I can see just fine with my fae vision, it is still much darker than my sun-loving soul appreciates.

Willow pulls Star back to walk beside me and gives me an easy smile. "It'll be alright, Lair. We just need to keep moving."

"Your optimism is frightening sometimes." Sebastian chimes from in front of us, gesturing to the close trees and dense foliage. "We are in a forest darker than I've ever seen, I can hardly see shit, and our only escape is gone."

Willow scoffs, rolling her eyes. "And your attitude could use some work. Nothing wrong with wanting to assume the best! Besides, it's not like having that exit would have helped us anyway. Faldorn is right, we have no choice but to push forward."

A soft rumbling in the earth interrupts their squabble and makes us all pause, pulling up our mounts to a swift stop, but nothing else seems to happen. I carefully survey what I can see of the trees, roots, and plant life in our immediate area and realize with no small amount of alarm that some of the roots are *moving*.

Thelas speaks from beside Faldorn in the front of the group, his voice full of alarm, "What was that?"

I'm not sure if the others notice the moving roots or simply felt the vibration, but Faldorn continues forward quickly while keeping a watchful gaze around us. "Let us move from this area."

I click Skip forward uneasily, feeling dread settle in my stomach like a seed hibernating for Winter, ever-present and biding its time until it can bloom. I'm so distracted by the new sounds and appearance of this strange forest that I almost don't notice flashes of red in my periphery. But when I do, I am struck speechless.

If I thought our threads were bright before, that's nothing compared to how spectacular they are now. Each one glows like the brightest of stars and the red hue is so vibrant I almost feel the need to avert my gaze. I watch in awe as they curl from the centers of each of my four traveling companions, twisting

and twining together in a playful dance, as if they are old friends coming together after many years apart. Pleased and surprised at their intense appearance, I'm mesmerized as I watch the scene unfold. Details that were once lost to me now come into focus, showing braided sections of the brightest threads connecting us, and hundreds of smaller threads branching out from each of them in every direction and disappearing into the forest. I've never been able to see more than one thread at a time in a person, and a surprising tenderness sticks in my throat, forcing me to swallow it down so I don't start crying at the impressive display.

"So many threads," I whisper to myself. It truly is a wonder of this world that there can be so many people we are connected to who have an impact on our lives, whether we know it or not.

I smile, the dark forest completely forgotten for a moment as I watch the threads spiral and dance in the air. I sigh in contentment as they fade from my view, certain in the knowledge that they will appear again.

There must be something about the magic of this forest that makes it easier for me to see them, similar to what made Faldorn's appearance more like his actual fae self. I wonder at what else the forest could reveal and feel an almost giddy excitement bubble up until I spot a shadow dart through Sebastian's horse's legs just ahead of me. His horse doesn't pause his steady pace, and Sebastian shows no sign of having noticed the slinking shadow, but it has me immediately on edge. I recall the heavy darkness that seemed to have been watching me after one particularly wretched nightmare back in Taslae, and I feel a growing sense of panic that it may have followed me here.

My eyes dart from tree to tree, checking every crevice that I can see and searching the figures ahead of me for any trace of the dark shadow, but I see no other sign of it. I slump into my saddle, reaching for Kel's comforting presence. He lands on my shoulder, nuzzling my head, and I lean into him, feeling his feathers brush my cheek and his smooth bones press into my neck.

"Kel, keep watch over everyone, okay?"

He lets out a quiet murmur of acknowledgment before jumping from my shoulder and flying into the trees. He can't go too far because of the thick branches that crisscross high above, creating a sort of impenetrable canopy, but it's enough that he can spot any potential danger in our vicinity. I relax a little in my saddle, knowing that with Kel watching, we have nothing to fear.

IT ACTUALLY EXISTS

SEBASTIAN

Faldorn led us through the forest for a time, but soon the small path we had been following was cut off by a wall of trees, and we all turned to Thelas to figure out the direction we should go next. He fumbled for a minute, entirely caught off guard that we needed him so soon, but it wasn't long before he was completely lost in his maps and formulating the path forward. The man had been relentless about creating them as we'd traveled—devising all sorts of alternate routes and potential features of the forest from his newly translated book. Even now, he was constantly tweaking them. Pulling them from his pack as we rode, muttering to himself all the while and scratching notes in the margins of the book he never let out of his possession. I zero in once again on the odd book currently splayed out beside Thelas. How did he manage to find it? And how did the king let something so important get lost? The king of Eislekest is suspicious at best and domineering at worst—I can't imagine he would willingly let a book that detailed such a large portion of his kingdom out of his possession. That leaves two options: he isn't aware of its existence, or he hoped it truly was lost, and that no one could use it. Otherwise, I have no doubt he would be hell-bent on finding it.

Thelas tucks the small book in his pocket and I force the questions from my mind—what the king does and doesn't know is not my problem. I focus my attention back on Thelas, and have to squint in the dusky blue light of the forest to try once again to figure out how he thinks and what exactly he does with his maps and fancy tools. His affinity for his craft is amusing to say the least, and it is becoming clearer by the day that I was wrong to question him at the start of this journey. He may not have traveled anywhere, but he does have immense skill and I have to admit he is essential for this journey.

The rest of us leave him to it, using the time to care for our mounts and explore the area we stopped in. I tie Rei to a low branch and pat his thick neck. He bobs his head and drags his hoof through the dirt in agitation as I leave to walk along a small stream tucked between the trees. The sounds of the others grow quiet and I turn to make sure I can still see them in the distance before kneeling to examine the water.

Tiny fish dart in the shallow water, and thin reeds secured to rounded rocks float in the current. Everything glows with that same strange blue hue as the rest of the forest and a heavy dose of caution weighs down my limbs. It's not often I'm proved wrong, but that blondie actually did it. There's no other explanation for the otherworldly environment, persistent unnatural darkness, and the tense atmosphere—we are most certainly in the Forbidden Forest of legend.

A fairytale come to life.

I scowl. Those stories are nothing but illusions and fantastical dreams that will never be real. I learned a long time ago there was no such thing as a happily ever after—only crushing responsibility and a life I have no choice in.

A small stone catches my eye, its bright green color reminiscent of the ring that now sits on Laira's finger. My turbulent thoughts slow as I hum in satisfaction at knowing she wears something that I got for her. The look on her face as she asked me to place it on her sends a pleasant shiver down my spine once again. I dip my hands into the cool water and splash my face, smirking at the memory.

Shuffling catches my attention, and I'm about to tease whoever it is for following me, but when I turn my head downstream, my body grows still and the words halt in my throat. A fierce creature the same sea-green color of the water sits on the opposite bank, its coat covered in feathers that gleam like gemstones. Great wings sit folded at its sides, and its four long black legs are covered in thick fur. It pauses its drinking to stare at me, and I place my hand on the sword at my hip as I take in its owl-like face, dark eyes, and horns that sprout from its skull like blades. Apprehension runs down my spine as I stare into the eyes of the predator, knowing

this beast is built to kill and undoubtedly faster than I am. It growls as I slowly get to my feet, my body preparing for it to spring forward and attack.

It bares its teeth at me and arches its spine as I teeter between pulling my sword free or walking away slowly and hoping it doesn't follow. It darts its eyes to my sword, and I remove my hand from the hilt, not wanting to agitate it further. I hold my hands up in placation as I take a small step backward; it watches me as I do so, but it ceases its growling. I take that as a good sign and continue my retreat, watching the beast carefully for any indication it will attack. The creature slinks into the trees, but before it disappears from my view, it cocks its head to the side as if intrigued and the innocent movement is so reminiscent of our hounds back home that I stumble. Confused, I shuffle the rest of the way into camp to find all of our bags upturned and emptied, the contents scattered around the forest floor.

I raise my brows, the creature by the river momentarily forgotten. "Damn. What happened?"

Willow huffs as she shoves herbs and potions back into her bag. "Not sure. We weren't paying much attention to our bags, and suddenly they were all like this."

"Hmm." I walk to where my bag sits perfectly untouched next to Rei's hooves.

I double check the contents, but nothing has been disturbed. Laira shoves items into her bag to my right, a flash of white stone and copper flung into the air before she dumps it into the bag as well.

She grumbles, "What could have done this?"

Willow eyes my untouched bag, her voice accusing, "Maybe it's our resident thief."

I scoff, rolling my eyes. "Please. If this were me, you'd never even know something was missing. I would never leave my marks in such disarray."

She watches me intently for another minute, a thin tendril of green light coiling from her palm but seems to ultimately decide I'm telling the truth and lets it dissipate into the air.

I cross my arms, mildly offended she would accuse me of something so childish, especially after the time we've all spent together. "Why would you assume I'd do this?"

Laira speaks before she can, her face a stony mask and her lips pulled in a frown. "Maybe because you stole my bag when we first met and then eavesdropped on me for hours? You reek of suspicious activity." She wrinkles her nose at me.

"You're still upset about that? I gave it back!" I throw my arms wide, offering what little defense I can but inwardly cringe at my previous actions. She's right, I didn't exactly come across as chivalrous but, like Willow, I expected by now that she knew me a little better.

She holds her stony expression for a long moment before dissolving into giggles and my shoulders relax. I shake my head at her, rolling my eyes as she grins triumphantly—that little fox really had me going for a second.

Willow closes her bag and attaches it to Star, saying, "Well if it wasn't our less-than chivalrous thief, who was it?"

We all stare at each other, but it's clear no one here is the culprit, which leaves only one solution: something in this forest has decided to mess with us. A figure darts in the corner of my vision behind a grouping of mushrooms, and I whip my eyes toward it, stepping closer to get a better look. Whatever it is, it's gone in a flash and I can't get more than a short glimpse of tiny legs, a bat-like face, and a round body like that of a mouse. A sound like chittering laughter sounds to my left, and I have the sudden feeling that we may have some mischievous creatures invading our camp.

Thelas comes up beside me, whispering conspiratorially, "You saw that too, right?"

I nod.

"We're going to be fighting those little things the whole time in here, aren't we?" he laments.

I nod again, my jaw tightening. "That would be my guess."

"Great."

I pat his shoulder. "Let me know if they steal your map stuff, and I'll fight them off for you."

He gives a half-hearted smile. "Right. My very shiny, very expensive drawing supplies and instruments…"

We watch as the creatures skitter away and then I pat him

on the shoulder again, turning us around to face the group.

"We've fought off Kel for this long, we should be able to fight these creatures off too. So… Which direction do we go, smart boy?"

"Smart boy?"

"Would you prefer map boy?"

Thelas grumbles, and I don't quite catch what he says, but it sounds suspiciously close to "map man" and I grin.

THE TREES ARE STRANGE HERE

WILLOW

"We are going in circles," Sebastian says dryly.

"Not circles, exactly." Thelas tilts the map he's holding, staring at it intently. "More like wandering and back-tracking."

"So we're lost," Sebastian fires back, his mouth falling into a thin line.

Thelas doesn't speak, and a prickle of worry crawls over my skin, making me think Sebastian could be right. We've been traveling for hours and yet everything still looks the same, and while I don't exactly have the sense that I've seen these particular trees before, I do feel as if we haven't gained much ground. Which seems nearly impossible at the breakneck pace we've set since morning. The horses and Thelas' antelope are all covered in a sheen of sweat and droop their heads in exhaustion; only Faldorn's elk seems unbothered by the trek.

Thelas dismounts, laying his map flat on the forest floor near a cluster of glowing blue mushrooms for light, and pulling out a few golden instruments, spinning them across the parchment and marking points with a pencil he pulls from behind his ear. I giggle softly as Kel lands on an exposed root next to Thelas and eyes his glittering instruments hungrily. I know all too well what it's like to be on the other end of that stare, and I'm happy that it's not me this time who will have to be on guard.

"We should be here." He draws a small circle on the map nearly halfway through the dense forest he has drawn on the paper and swats Kel away when he gets too close to his map.

"But—I think we are actually here."

My smile drops and my bones sag as his hand travels down the parchment and stops just two fingers widths away from the forest's entrance he has marked on the map.

Laira kneels beside him, studying the map. "But how is that possible? It's as if we haven't traveled longer than an hour, instead of nearly all day."

He looks at her helplessly, and I feel sorry for him. He has such a monumental task set before him. Even if he volunteered for the position, he still has to lead us through a magical forest that hasn't been mapped before and that also has no stories of people navigating it successfully. With only what he's been able to draw himself through the help of his mysterious book and what he's been able to visualize so far as we've traveled.

I step forward, intent on studying the map as well to see if there is any help I can offer when a voice whispers against my ear, the sound so soft I almost miss it. I freeze, focusing on the voice, and it comes again, this time much stronger but I still can't quite make out what it's saying. I shift to look behind us, realizing the sound is coming from an even darker section of the forest from where we came. A skittering sensation rolls across my skin, and my magic blooms in my chest. I have to fight the urge to tamp it down, still a little unused to allowing my magic out in the presence of others. But it bubbles to the surface and presses through my hesitation—green tendrils shoot from my palms and dive for the dark trees, seeking the source of the sound. I hear it again, deep beneath the earth—the strange speech only trees possess, though this is much stronger than anything I've heard before. It's more forceful than a normal tree and the sound is less a sluggish, ambling thing like a slow stream and more like a crisp, rushing torrent. It demands to be heard.

"'Guide'?" I whisper softly under my breath, astounded that the trees said something so clear, even if I don't understand what they mean by it. I'm lost in thought when I realize the forest is now deadly silent, the entire place turning eerie as if holding its breath. The others are deep in conversation, huddled over Thelas' map, and they don't seem to notice the sudden stillness. Before I can say anything to get their attention, a root whips out and grabs me by the ankle.

I scream, and the root yanks me back to the darker portion of foliage before suddenly going still once it's pulled me from the others. Brambles scratch my face and arms and I see the blood trickle out in fat droplets more than I feel it.

The others cry out in alarm, but I wave them off. "It's fine! I was more startled than anything else."

Din rushes over and yowls in concern, already gnawing at the root to detach it from my ankle. I pat him on the head and look down to see it's not a root, but a small vine wrapped around my ankle. The thorns dig into my skin, but it doesn't hurt as much as I would expect, even with the small amount of blood trickling down. It feels similar to a firm hand, like someone or something is trying to get my attention. I listen to the magic flowing through me, crouching low to touch the vine and follow its trajectory even as Din finishes releasing it from my body. I feel the eyes of the others as they watch me carefully, waiting to intervene if I'm pulled back again, but nothing happens as I get up and follow the vine back to its source. Din follows, his tail twitching violently and his gaze fixed intently on the vine that grabbed me as it lays limp on the ground.

A wide tree stands slightly apart from the others, its trunk covered in the same vines that wrapped around my leg, and I reach out tentatively with my magic when I get within a few paces. The soft green tendrils stretch toward the tree and sink into its bark, the vines parting along it to allow easier access. It's been years since I allowed myself to connect to a tree like this but even so, the spell rushes back to me and I speak a few hushed words as I sift through the tree's memories. They aren't so different from my own memories, though they lack words or emotion. Instead, they show flashes of scenes and important events that happened to the tree.

Trees are sacred to all witches, but with our capital being located in the eastern grasslands of our queendom, there aren't many opportunities for young witches to study their language. We do have a few ancient trees, but they are jealously guarded by the queen and only those she deems worthy may commune with them. It wasn't always that way though, there are plenty of stories that speak of lush forests as well as sprawling grasslands—a beautiful dichotomy that

highlighted the balance witches were able to achieve with nature through their abilities. But that was before the most recent set of queens we've had, with each one being more corrupt and uncaring of the old ways than the last.

I force the queen's face from my mind and focus on the tree's memories. Nothing stands out to me immediately, but I do notice the trees surrounding it shifting and moving unnaturally. Their roots drag them around like spindly fingers, and they inch across the forest floor at a surprising speed. I retract my magic and gaze around at the trees—these memories could be from a long time ago, but I get the feeling this tree was showing me something recent on purpose.

"Hey Thelas?" I call over my shoulder, still keeping an eye on the dark trees scattered around me. "Any chance the trees can *move*?"

I turn to face him, noticing he and the others have stopped a few paces away, as if wary of approaching the vine-draped tree.

Thelas is frozen in stunned silence, his mouth hanging agape, and I can see the calculations and scenarios running through his brain. He whips around, heading back to the animals and pulls the map he'd been studying in front of him, muttering and scribbling furiously in a notebook beside him.

I raise an eyebrow, turning to Laira. "Didn't know my suggestion would have that kind of effect."

She shrugs. "He really gets lost in his work sometimes."

Thelas looks up at us suddenly, a wide and slightly mad smile growing on his face. "I know how to get through the forest."

Thelas focuses on me, his gaze intent before he lists off a barrage of questions. "What did the tree tell you? How fast do the trees move? Do they only move during a certain period of time? Can small trees move too or only fully mature ones?"

I hold out my hands to stop him. "Whoa! Wait, hold on! Too many questions, I need you to slow down."

He takes a deep breath, his excitement leaking into his voice as he continues to speak at a rapid-fire pace. "Canyoutalktothetreeforme?"

I let out a breath of laughter, his enthusiasm infectious. "Yes, I can do that. Come with me."

SHE'S HERE. SHE WATCHES.

WILLOW

It turned out the giant tree wanted some of my growth magic in exchange for the information, and after Thelas got all of his questions answered, he set a new direction for us. Every hour or so, he'd adjust our position in accordance with his prediction for how the trees moved. Sebastian scoffed at the idea, not fully convinced the trees could actually move the way the guide tree claimed since we hadn't seen one do it in front of us. I didn't blame him. It was a wild idea to imagine trees with the ability to move themselves and the intelligence and desire to roam on top of that. The guide tree made it seem as if the others moved regularly, but especially when creatures were near. I suspected their purpose was what Faldorn had alluded to all those weeks ago, about a forest that acted as a beast to guard the mystical cave holding the sword.

I shared as much with the others, but Thelas seemed convinced he could win this game of strategy. I suppose only time will tell if he's able to fully learn their behavior and outmaneuver them.

The fire Faldorn put together crackles in the quiet space and illuminates the otherwise small and dim clearing we've decided to camp in tonight—the bright yellow and orange hue a stark change to the dusky blues and greens of the plant life in the forest. We sit surrounded by massive trees, their root systems protruding from the soil and creating a sort of cage around us. Faldorn appraised it to be a good form of cover, assuming these trees don't decide to move on us as well. The dense canopy far above our heads creates another cage of sorts—blocking out any sunlight and the outside world—but, surprisingly, I don't feel trapped. Instead, it feels like a pleasant embrace as if I'm snuggled under a comforting blanket. Laira thought I had lost my mind when I explained the feeling to her, and I nearly spit out my dinner when I beheld the rounded eyes of her poorly contained horror. She really doesn't like this darkness and not being able to see the sky.

Laira's voice pulls me from my thoughts, and I focus again on the others sitting around the small fire.

"Have you noticed that nothing has bothered us so far? We've seen plenty of strange creatures but no outright aggressive ones that I can tell," she asks.

Sebastian smirks and crosses his arms. "Perhaps our dear Faldorn has scared them off with his large muscles and obvious fae prowess?"

Faldorn chuckles darkly. "Or perhaps there is something worse waiting for us ahead, and the smaller beasts are leaving us to our fate."

We all stare open mouthed at his morbid explanation. "Well that's reassuring," says Thelas, sarcasm biting in his tone.

"But really, don't you all think it a bit strange?" Laira asks with concern. "We are in this giant mysterious forest, and the worst thing we have run into so far are glowing mushrooms with eyes and tiny creatures that go through our things?"

"I saw an odd creature by a stream our first day in the forest. Didn't seem overly aggressive though, just wary," Sebastian cuts in.

Laira throws her hands wide, saying to the group, "See? That's exactly my point! I'm not complaining, I guess I just thought we would need to fight more things off is all."

Din sits happily in my lap and purrs loudly as I run an idle hand over his head. "What about the trees that are currently trying to cut off our route through the forest?" I ask.

"I guess. But we haven't actually seen that to be true, only assumed it to be the case and they—at least so far—haven't tried to harm us. Unless you count the vine that grabbed you."

I shake my head. "No, that was only a minor inconvenience."

She is right though, there is no possible way that there isn't at least *something* extremely dangerous in this forest. I can't always understand the trees to my normal degree—it's as if they speak a slightly different dialect—but I can sense enough to know that we are most certainly not the scariest beings in this forest. It's not a question of what will pose a problem for us, but when.

Laira gestures toward Din sitting contentedly in my lap. "Or maybe it's because of Din and Kel? I know they aren't the most formidable, but the living generally have a healthy respect for the nyradonns' expanded abilities."

"I'll be honest, I don't know much about the nyradonn apart from the basics of the bonding and that they are… well you know…" Thelas scratches nervously at the back of his neck as he trails off, not wanting to say the obvious word.

I help him out. "Dead?"

Din lifts his head and hisses at Thelas, causing him to jump slightly in alarm.

He holds his hands up to Din in surrender. "Hey—whoa there, sorry Din! I didn't mean it! You're not dead, you're ahhh…"

"Dead!" Laira cheerfully supplies for him.

"Exactly! I mean, no! *No*!" Thelas flails his arms and nervously glances at Din as if he's expecting him to jump down his throat at his accidental agreement. Din grumbles softly before turning in a few circles and plopping down, his legs dangling over my thigh. Laira laughs, and the sound draws a snicker from my own lips. Poor Thelas.

I brush a hand across Din's smooth legs, and he purrs at the contact. Even in death, he still loves a good pat.

"Thelas, calm down. Laira and Din are just messing with you. *Of course* he's dead—he's just bones after all." I roll my eyes in amusement at his obvious discomfort with the word. "And it's not offensive to say so."

"Ah." He settles back against his pack and awkwardly places his hands in his lap. "But um, back to my original statement. I don't know much about them, care to elaborate for me?"

Kel flies down from his perch above us to land next to Laira and she pats him on the head as she says, "Well, they are dead, as we have already covered. And they are made of bones."

Kel lets out an ear-piercing shriek and Laira adds, "Ah yes—bones, and sometimes feathers, hooves, claws, or the occasionally membranous skin for those with wings or other similar appendages."

Thelas waits another moment, expecting Laira to continue, but she just smirks at him, attempting to hold in another laugh.

"Thank you, that is very informative." Thelas rolls his eyes, his voice deadpanned. "I've never noticed the bones before, in fact, so thank you."

"Happy to be of service!" she replies, and Kel squawks his agreement, causing the rest of us to burst out laughing. Even Faldorn joins in with a quiet chuckle.

Faldorn takes pity on Thelas, offering a more in-depth explanation. "The nyradonn, and more importantly the magic that creates them, is of ancient fae descent." He nods at Laira. "It's why you must have at least partial fae blood to conduct the ritual at all."

Laira cocks her head in curiosity. "I thought the Goddess bestowed the knowledge and for some reason chose the fae as the bearers? And how did you know I've performed a ceremony?"

"Yes and no. I don't know for certain, but I believe the Goddess may have been the one to first attain the knowledge, but only the fae are capable of leading it. From there it becomes murky on how the ritual came to be or why only the fae can perform it."

He gestures toward Din in my lap. "As for your second question, there's a sort of faint energy coming from our friend Din here. You and Willow emit a similar energy. And as you are not the one bonded to Din, that must mean that you had some hand in performing the ritual."

She stares in surprise at Din, and I look down at him as well. But I see no faint aura, so it must only be a full-blooded fae ability to visualize it.

Faldorn answers as if reading my thoughts, "I have trained for many years to sense magical signatures. And I have performed many bonding rituals myself, so I am well adept at sensing those specific connections."

Laira nods in understanding. "That makes sense." And then with clear interest, she asks, "What else do you know?"

I notice Faldorn has all of our attention now. Even Sebastian is sitting slightly forward, awaiting his next words.

Faldorn chuckles softly and scratches his chin in thought. "I suppose I know a few other things… you want to know more about nyradonn and their bonds?"

I smile and pat Din's smooth head as I say, "I think I know a few things about that."

"Yes, I'm sure you do. It's clear your bond is strong. Tell me, are you able to speak mind-to-mind yet?"

My jaw drops open as I stare at him, my hand paused mid-pat, making Din grumble in dissatisfaction.

"It's possible to speak to him?" I ask in awe.

"Yes, it is. I've heard of the strongest pairs sharing thoughts and ideas across incredible distances. Actual speech is still difficult, but as you know, once the shift happens into the second life and the nyradonn are bonded to your life-force, they seem to gain some abilities that we possess."

"Like gaining intelligence and the ability to understand what I'm saying." I breathe out in fascination.

He smiles. "Precisely."

Laira beams at me from across the fire. "That's amazing! That means you'll be able to talk to each other in no time!"

I pick Din up and hold him in front of my face. His empty eye sockets should hold no emotion whatsoever, but I swear he is winking at me—as if he's always known this is something we could do, but I was just in the dark about it.

"You sneaky little feline," I tease him. He wiggles out of my grasp and settles back in my lap, walking in a few circles before he deems his spot comfortable enough and plops down.

Sebastian throws a stick into the fire, causing it to flare brighter, and I glance at Laira hesitantly. She has a long and awful history with fire, and it occasionally rears its ugly head to cause her all sorts of panic, but she doesn't look too put off by the flames. Instead, she seems too occupied by scowling at Sebastian's back as he leans forward next to her and throws in yet another small stick, to notice the flames.

I snort, and she flicks her gaze to me. When she realizes I caught her eye-stabbing the thief, she rolls her eyes as if to say, "How can you not find him annoying?"

Shaking my head, I turn my attention back to Faldorn and wonder what else he knows. The history of nyradonn is much more interesting than watching Laira pretend she doesn't desperately want to flirt with the alluring thief.

Sebastian beats me to asking another question though, his tone quizzical as he states, "You said 'nyradonn and their bonds.' I didn't realize they could have more than one."

Faldorn nods. "Yes, a single bone creature can bond to multiple people—whether they be fae, human, witch, or shifter. Though, historically, this hasn't been practiced regularly for some time since having multiple bonds is not necessary with most creatures. A regular non-magical creature, like that of Din, only needs one bond to pull him from true death. But you see, something magical, mythical, or something much stronger, would need many bonds in the ritual because its life-force would be too heavy a thing to bear for one person."

He leans back and sips from his canteen as he considers it more. "Besides, the trend now is to bond only once. With more than one being seen as excessive even for the richest of folks—royalty included."

After a long silence, Laira asks in a serious tone, "Do you know anything about why Kel isn't with his bonded?"

We all stare at the bird as he sits perched on a rock next to Laira. He opens his wings as if reveling in the attention.

"I do not. It is rather strange that he is not with his bonded. I've never known a nyradonn to do that, to even want to do that. The nyradonn bond is strong, and while being separated won't cause physical pain, it can cause mental strain."

Worry punctuates Laira's every word. "I tried a long time ago to get him to leave to find his bonded, but I never could shake him, and so I just accepted his presence. While I am grateful and love him dearly, I worry what could happen if he doesn't ever reunite with his bonded."

Faldorn hesitates, and there is a slight doubt in his eyes, but eventually an answer leaves his mouth, "There is something I could try, if you would like me to. I can't tell where his bonded is, but I can memorize the bond's signature, and if I come across it again or sense it later, then we can reunite him at that point."

Tears shine in her eyes as she clasps her hands together in relief. "Really? Yes, please—whatever you can do!"

He reaches out a hand to Kel, silently waiting for him to hop onto his arm when he is ready. Faldorn must believe Kel has been following our conversation enough to understand what he means to do, and it appears he is right because Kel jumps to Faldorn without a moment of hesitation. He grabs Faldorn's forearm with his talons and tucks his head down, giving Faldorn a clear signal to place his large hand on the bird's skull. He's quiet for a long time, and I glance at Laira to gauge her reaction to the encounter, but she doesn't seem anxious or upset; she's simply waiting in anticipation for whatever Faldorn will discover. It's an incredibly small possibility that we would come across Kel's bonded, even if Faldorn is able to recognize them. What are the chances in a realm this large that we ever find them? But I suppose this small action is enough to give Laira hope. I know she harbors some amount of guilt for Kel following her when she knows that he must have a bonded who misses him somewhere. It's not her fault of course, but that never stopped her bleeding heart before.

Faldorn lifts his hand from Kel's skull and looks up at all of us, but his expression is one of confusion and not the calm self-assurance I expected.

Laira notices immediately. "What's wrong? What did you see?"

She shifts, leaning toward Kel without even thinking, as if there is something she must protect him from. Her hand starts a soft tapping on her thigh, and I know she is being overwhelmed with terrifying possibilities for what he could say next. Sebastian's gaze tracks her tapping hand as well, and his face becomes slightly pained at the sight.

Interesting.

He shifts ever so slightly to be closer to her, leaning a casual arm to rest behind her and providing what comfort he can without actually touching her. Laira's shoulders visibly relax as his body half-encompasses her from behind, and I doubt she even realizes she's doing it. She's too focused on Kel and Faldorn and waiting to see what he says, even though I'm sure she's dying to ask him again, to notice Sebastian's movement.

Very interesting.

Faldorn finally speaks, and the confusion in his tone matches the look still present on his face. "I don't know. It was… different." He looks to Laira, addressing her directly. "His bonded aura was stronger than anything I've seen before. But it was also incredibly bright—like starlight or flickering flames in a blazing fire."

Kel hops back to Laira, and she gathers him in her arms, holding him tightly. "What does that mean?"

"I'm sorry, but I don't know."

"It's not bad, is it?"

"I don't think so. I think it means that whoever his bonded is, is incredibly powerful, and it may be harder to find them than I assumed."

"Why is that?"

He hesitates. "They may not be present in our realm, at least not in the same way that we are."

"And what does *that* mean? They're dead?"

"No. If they were dead, then Kel would not be here. It's something else. I'll need some time to think about it, and it would help to ask someone from Caelamne."

"Well, as long as he's okay, then I suppose we will just have to wait and see."

Sebastian speaks up from his place leaning behind Laira, and I can tell she's finally noticed how close he is to her by the sudden reddening of her cheeks. "We can attempt a more thorough search once we find this sword, if you like," Sebastian offers.

The shock on her face is comical, and I would've shared in her surprise had I not noticed the small ways Sebastian has attempted to be close to her and please her in the last few weeks. If I didn't know better, I'd guess he has a bit of a crush on my delightfully clueless best friend.

I grin. This is going to be very fun to watch unfold.

"Really? And you would help?"

"I happen to have many contacts gathered from my work, I'm sure I could ask around and find Kel's bonded for you."

She cocks her head to the side. "You have such a large network for being a thief?"

His smirk drops for such a short time that I barely notice it before he says, "Well you know what they say… the larger the network…"

She rolls her eyes in disgust, throwing up her hands and exclaiming, "Ugh! Do not finish that."

"What?"

The feral grin that appears on his face is enough to light Laira on fire, and I'm beginning to realize that may be his main goal in life. He relishes in getting a rise out of her, and it makes me wonder when those flames of passion might turn the other way towards something less antagonistic and more… amorous.

"I was going to say 'makes for a better thief,' but now I'm dying to know what you were thinking, *wildcat*. Care to share?"

She growls at him. *Actually* growls, and I bark out a laugh. She whips her head to me, causing me to double over with more laughter, and before I know it, everyone is laughing with me.

"By the stars, Laira, did you actually just make that sound? I didn't know you could sound so menacing!" My shoulders shake uncontrollably as I speak in between heaving breaths.

Her face squishes in annoyance but eventually cracks into a reluctant smile as she too realizes how ridiculous she just sounded.

Why she lets him rile her up so much, I don't understand. She's smart enough to realize he does it on purpose, but maybe she likes playing along with him deep down.

"Alright, alright! Enough laughing at my expense. We should get some rest—we have another long day tomorrow. Who's starting with watch duty tonight?"

"I can start," Faldorn states, leaning back against his pack and crossing his arms against his chest. "I have far too many things to ponder anyway. I'll wake Sebastian in a few hours."

Sebastian nods his head in acknowledgment, throwing one last teasing glance at Laira, which she pointedly ignores, and turns to his bedroll for the night.

I do the same and feel Din resting peacefully on my hip as I close my eyes. We really do have another long day tomorrow, and I only hope that we are able to find our way a little easier than we have been—this forest is strange, and I feel the eyes of what seems like hundreds of creatures on us constantly.

The nearest tree whispers a string of low sounds as I drift off, but I manage to decipher its meaning by digging deep in my mental archives.

"She's here. She watches."

I shiver at a sudden cold breeze, but it's not enough to pull me from my beginnings of sleep, and before I know it, I'm dragged under completely, entering a dreamless sleep with only the ominous words from the tree to envelop me.

"She's here."

"She watches."

THE PAST CAN HURT

FALDORN

The first half of the night passes in silence, and it's not long before I'm rousing Sebastian to take over before getting a few hours of sleep myself. Even so, I sleep fitfully and wake long before the mortals, deciding instead to sit beside Willow, who took over after Sebastian, until the others wake. The ever-present dim light makes it difficult to determine night from day, and I wonder how long it will take for us to get thrown off completely. The low ferns and mosses only cast so much blueish light, and it keeps the forest in a constant state of dusk. While my fae sight can see clearly in any light, Sebastian and Willow have had the most issue so far. Though, Sebastian is the only one to have tripped over low roots as of yet—I assume Willow's magic is to thank for that. Their horses have fared well though, especially now that they have grown accustomed to the darkness, and no longer spook at every sound.

I motion to Willow to wake the others to start our journey for the day and we pack swiftly and are atop our mounts once more. Once Thelas determines the direction we should start, we are on our way—the routine nearly second nature at this point. I'm not certain how far we've gone, or how far we need to go, but now that Thelas can successfully navigate these woods, I'm sure we will begin to make progress. He's deduced from the contents of his book that we will need to cross this forest and exit on the other side before we will be able to start looking for the cave system that houses the sword. So we've all resigned ourselves to a long trek and many days of constant travel. It's an odd feeling, relying on a young mortal such as our enthusiastic cartographer, but he is intelligent and resourceful, and I find I'm

not as opposed to the idea of leaning on someone else as I would have thought. After centuries alone, I never thought I needed company anymore, but even I can admit that it has been a more comfortable journey with these mortals around. With more eyes to watch for danger and more hands to set up camp, my ever-present vigilance has lessened some.

My elk, S'alorr, tenses below me and I draw my attention to him, surveying the forest more intensely and seeking out what caused him to shuffle nervously, but don't see or hear anything out of the ordinary. Still, it's best to be safe, so before we move further, I stop the mortals and instruct them to dismount quietly. Sebastian reaches for his sword and surveys the dense trees around us—but if I couldn't sense anything, then neither will he.

I walk a few paces forward, keeping my stance wide, and catalog the area for sign of the danger S'alorr sensed. The blue-green light of the plants here isn't unlike the forests deep in the high mountains of Caelamne, and I try in vain yet again to block the memories from trickling in. Of a similar trek through a dark forest, on a mission that should have ended with us safely in T'salae. My blood sings in recognition of my homeland, but my body aches as I remember the way I discarded S'alorr's warning and failed to recognize the danger until it was too late.

It is not a mistake I will make again.

We've been traveling for days with no obstacles or danger besides the ever-shifting forest, which Thelas has been careful to map and plan for each day. But that doesn't mean there isn't anything dangerous in this forest, just that we haven't come across it yet.

Dripping sounds from above, but as I open my senses, I realize it is not rain or trickling water as I first suspected, but saliva that drips from a mouth of razor-sharp teeth. I take a few measured steps back, eyeing the tensive aura from the towering beast as it watches us with six careful eyes—three on each side of its broad head, that brim with intensity.

I offer a series of clicks toward S'alorr and he departs from my side to quickly round up the other animals of our group, gathering them to relative safety in the trees behind us.

Most of the creature's body is hidden behind the trees but as it steps into the small section of forest where we stand, massive horns twist into view. They curve upwards from the creature's sloped head into graceful points. They're covered in glowing moss that illuminates the beast's head in a way that is both haunting and beautiful, as if the creature is bathed in a pool of moonlight.

Protruding fangs grace either side of its mouth, and its nostrils flare in agitation. It stares down at our group with a wariness in its intelligent eyes that sets my teeth on edge—we've stumbled into its space, and there's no predicting how it will react. Rearing its head up suddenly and stomping its feet, I know there is very little time to decide what to do. The area we are in is semi-open with mostly flat ground, and ringed on all sides by thick trees. There's not enough room to fight properly, especially when the creature's body is so large. It towers over us as well, yet I notice that even it does not begin to grace the tops of the trees—the broad trunks and branches continuing far above us all.

It stomps an agitated hoof into the dirt again, causing a small crater in the soil and spraying dirt, roots, and rocks into the air. The mortals flinch at the display, and their animals bellow in alarm. I scent their fear, sickly and tainted like food left to rot, and a memory shoves itself to the forefront of my mind, of a gaping hole in the ground and the stench of death.

I'm nearly swallowed whole by the memory when Laira's insistent voice sounds from behind me, "Faldorn?"

A soft voice echoes her question in my mind, *"Faldorn, what is it?"*

And once again, I'm back in those woods, looking down into a dark abyss with no warning for what came next. I forcibly yank myself from the wretched memory and stare hard at the towering beast in front of me. A heavy weight settles over my shoulders as I reach for my weapons—I will not make the same mistake as before.

The promise echoes through my blood, priming my body for a fight, and it's not long before I'm lost to the prospect of battle. This new, single-minded purpose is driving me forward with the intensity of a raging storm. It has me reaching for my sword hilts, despite the deep-seated fae instincts that fight against it—

recognizing another intelligent creature and insisting unsuccessfully against violence. But holding back hasn't helped me before. If I had just listened to what my body ached to do hundreds of years ago, then they would be alive right now.

My mate would be alive.

The natural world is vital to the fae. Every creature, plant, and buried stone has a purpose. In my naivety as a young fae, I assumed this meant every creature could be reasoned with, that they would recognize us as equals and leave us be. My hubris left me with little warning before the worm-like creature attacked our group—its rows of sharp teeth and scaly body unlike anything I'd seen before. It attacked senselessly, growing increasingly agitated as more and more blood was spilled by my loved ones. I killed the beast after many well-aimed strikes, but by then the damage was done. The worm was dead, and so was my family.

All creatures have a purpose, yes, but some are built only for death, and as I watched my mate's life drain from her eyes, I wondered if perhaps my purpose was one only of death too.

My hands twitch at the sensation of sticky blood coating them. I ignore the feeling, familiar with the old trick from my mind, and slowly withdraw my swords. I direct my senses to the mortals and say, "If you can fight, fight. But do not endanger yourself unnecessarily. I will handle this."

The sharp scraping of metal as someone withdraws their sword makes the creature stiffen and focus its attention behind me. I dart forward before the beast can focus too long on the mortals, not allowing the same hesitation that stopped me before to bloom here now.

These mortals will not die on my watch.

It only takes a dozen steps to reach the creature in the small clearing, and with little room for the massive beast to maneuver, it can't charge me so it must resort to close range combat instead of simply trampling us. I slash at its legs with both swords and the creature bellows in pain as deep gashes open, bright blood pouring from the wounds. It dips its head to swipe at me with its horns, and I pull both swords in an arc to block it, the edges of my blades carving shallow divots in the horns from the pressure of holding the beast back.

Vines reach for and wrap around the beast's legs, twisting and writhing until they are nearly at the creature's knee before it thrashes out of them and pushes me back to the edge of the tree line. Sebastian quickly scales a tree behind the creature, placing a well-aimed blow to its hindquarters before jumping to a different branch to avoid a back hoof. Blood pours from the wound, and the beast huffs in pain, but it doesn't stop trying to push me back. With my swords crossed in front of me against the beast's horns, there is little I can do as it forces me to the tree line. Gripping the hilts firmly, I use all my strength to shove the blades forward at the same time, gaining enough momentum to leap to the side before the creature can slam me into a tree.

Regaining my footing, I adjust my swords in front of myself once more but pause when I catch the fathomless brown eyes of the creature. My instincts sing to the creature, begging me to stop, and the thought freezes my body in place before I can attack again. My arms droop as I stare into the beast's eyes, the battle momentarily forgotten, until the mortals dart forward in front of me and the beast swings its head again in defense.

No.

I force my legs forward and step in front of the others before they can be knocked down by the massive horns. A moment of weakness nearly killed them, just as it did before, and I rage against myself for letting my guard down. I force the beast back. Each vicious strike from my sword born of desperation opens new wounds and slows its advancement. The slices echo loudly in the small space until the cutting of flesh is all I hear. The macabre sound a symphony of severed flesh and the whisper of approaching death. Buzzing in my blood screams that this is wrong, quickly replacing the fevered blood lust with an ache in my chest that deepens as I continually push my instincts away until I can scarcely breathe.

Heaving, I stare at the creature. It lays on its side, breathing just as rapidly as I am, its eyes full of pain and its legs limp beneath it. The mortals cautiously approach behind me, and I numbly turn my head, cataloguing each of them for injuries—breathing a sigh of relief when I see nothing wrong. Their

expressions hold something akin to worry and I still as I realize it's directed at me.

Laira steps forward, passing her sword to Sebastian, and gently places her hands over mine to lower my weapons. They drop to the dirt with a cold thud, and she looks at me with such sorrow I wonder if she hears the approaching death of the creature too. Emotion chokes me, causing a hard lump to catch in my throat as I see the understanding and compassion in her eyes, and I want to fall to my knees and weep at the destruction I've caused yet again.

Laira slowly shakes her head, as if sensing where my thoughts had gone and shifts her gaze to look behind me. We turn to the dying beast, and Laira squeezes my hand, gently pulling us toward the creature. Blood soaks the dirt, and its rattling breath is so loud, it feels as if the world is ending. She pulls us down to kneel reverently before the beast, as if her fae instincts are guiding her to the action just as mine are.

Another memory suddenly strikes, one from the deep wells of my long history and from back when I still resided in the fae lands. A large swathe of pristine grass and the scent of sweet warm air washes over my senses as I give myself to the old memory. A creature approaches me, one similar in appearance to the one here now, though it is much smaller. It stands a few steps from me, an expectant look on its intelligent face, and a melodic voice sounds from beside me, gently reminding me to always bow before attempting to make contact. The rest of the vision floods my system, and I remember everything of that day. A lonely pang hits my chest at the happy memory as I recall just how joyful those times were.

Quick twitches of the beast's long furred tail bring me back to the present, and I let out a heavy breath, uncertain if this will work. The beast may be too far gone to be saved, but the pull in my chest says I have to try. Still on my knees, I bow deeply to the creature, pressing my forehead into the dirt before rising to my feet and placing a hand over my heart. The beast stares at me for a long moment and becomes so still I fear it is about to take its final breath, but it ever so slightly dips its large head and closes its eyes briefly. A star illuminates on its forehead, pulsing softly, and I drift toward it. A beacon in the darkness, the light calls to me, and as I press my hand against it, the forest goes still. I close my eyes, feeling the warmth of the beast, and for the first time in a long time, I open my mind to another creature.

A warmth blooms in my chest. A soft call and answer that I haven't heard in centuries. I jerk my eyes up and catch the quiet tenderness in the beast's gaze—realizing the warm feeling in my chest is not mine, but the creature's.

A new flurry of images appears: a small group drifting through glowing moss-covered trees. Foals darting about, chasing small insects and inspecting roots and streams—their curiosity insatiable. Elders watch on in contented peace, the kind that only true family can bring. Warm summer days pass, and the small herd brings in new life. They rejoice at the immediate belonging the little one feels as it recognizes its kind upon the first blink of its many eyes.

The warmth in my chest is comforting and happy, though it also brings sorrowful tears to well in my eyes, for I know what the loss of this sort of family feels like. However it happened that this beast turned out to be the last one remaining, I know it must be a wound that has never closed. My own deep gash festers in my heart still as I ache at the loss reflected in this beast's soul.

My voice is choked and heavy as I say, "I am sorry, dear one, I was lost. Forgive me."

The pain of what I've done here threatens to tear me apart—this beast was not anything like what stole my family, and the regret coursing through me sours my blood. But the beast's tender voice in my mind soothes the ache, *"We are all lost for a time."*

Laira's hand rests on my shoulder, followed by the presence of Willow, Thelas, and Sebastian behind me, and I relax. The beast's thoughts flicker to the mortals, before addressing me again, *"But now you are found."*

Startled, it takes me a long moment to understand the beast's meaning, and I immediately want to turn away from it. So instead, I focus inward and draw my strength to the surface—it pools under my skin, and the others gasp as the swirling lines covering my exposed skin glow brightly. The beast is weak as I offer my life force to it, suffusing its limbs with my strength and resolve. The slashes along its legs and body close, and its eyes flicker open with newfound energy.

My own energy is sapped from my body, and I slump to the forest floor. The others catch me before I can hit the ground, and I'm quickly held up between Sebastian and Thelas. I likely won't feel completely like myself for days, but that is a small price to pay for the renewed life of this creature whom I so senselessly attacked.

The beast slowly gets to its feet, and we share another long look.

It blinks once before flicking its gaze behind me and shows me one final vision in our waning connection. One that is far less comforting as I peer through dense trees, a thick white mist oozing between them, and a small sleepy town perched on open cliffs with an ocean beyond. The mist blankets the forest floor, reaching high before turning wispy and dissipating into the air. A shadow snakes through it—a sharp spine and four long claws parting it and darting forward to its chosen prey. Inky black tendrils stick to the twisted nyradonn, coiling behind at an unnatural angle like bony fingers.

The beast doesn't show me what it's hunting, but the sinking feeling in my gut tells me all I need to know.

"Thank you, dear friend, for the warning and the lesson. You will find your family again in time, just as I will when I pass on," I whisper quietly to it in my mind.

My brows pinch together as I notice the beast shifting its gaze to stare at the mortals. Something stirs in my chest again, and the beast looks to me one final time before turning to leave, a deep knowing in its ancient eyes.

I watch its retreating form with apprehension. It gave me a warning, a remembrance of what we both lost, and a new path to follow—of protecting these mortals and finishing this quest. But this beast is far too intelligent to tell me what I already know. Of course I will protect them, it is what I agreed to do and what will finally set my soul at peace so I may pass on. So why do I feel as if there is something I'm missing? I stare long after it disappears into the trees, knowing there's something much more than simple duty calling me to watch over these four.

Willow pulls gently on my tunic, and I rub a weary hand across my face.

"Are you okay? How did you heal the creature?" Her voice is a mixture of concern and wonder, and when I look at her I see green tendrils of her magic reaching for me. "You are exhausted, but other than that completely fine. And you *saved* it."

My voice sounds far away. "Yes. I am fine."

I shift my shoulders, indicating to Sebastian and Thelas that they can set me down against a nearby tree. S'alorr returns to the group, slipping his soft nose into my hand and sniffing my body to check on me.

"I gave the creature a portion of my life force."

Shock echoes in the silence that follows my statement, and I nearly chuckle at their incredulous expressions.

Willow searches my face, as if she will discover the meaning of my words with what she sees there. "Life force? But how?"

My smile is faint. "It is a gift bestowed upon the fae to give life to creatures they form a connection with. We are stewards of the natural world, and when a life is taken before its time, we have the power to correct it. Don't worry, I will recover what I gave in time."

Willow's eyes dart quickly to Laira, but I don't miss the action or the intensity of her next words. "Does this work on humans or other fae?"

My eyes soften. "Unfortunately no. Our connection is with creatures and to the balance of the world, not with humans, fae, witches, or even the shifters."

Her shoulders droop and I want to comfort her, to ease her worry, to tell her that the strange darkness I have sensed coming from Laira is something that I can fix. But I fear what is happening to her is out of all our control.

I drop my head in renewed shame and sorrow. "We should not have fought the beast. My instincts warned me against it, and I did not listen, but I thank you for taking up arms with me regardless. That sort of bravery and trust is hard to come by." I look at each of them in turn, and not wanting them to bear the burden of this mistake, I add, "Do not regret your actions. I aimed the first strike and allowed the pain of the past to cloud my vision."

They nod, the heavy weight behind their eyes speaking to an understanding I didn't know if I'd ever see again. Perhaps these mortals are more like me than I thought.

I slowly get to my feet and reach for the pack I dropped to the ground, before turning in the direction we had been heading when the creature appeared. I walk a few steps, my feet heavy, but realize no one is following me.

"We shouldn't stay in one place too long," I remind them softly.

This seems to break them from their stunned stupor, and we all collect our things, wipe the blood from our blades, and mount our animals once more.

SHADOWS

LAIRA

We spend the next few days winding through the dark trees in companionable silence—the heaviness of the fight with the beast beginning to fade and Faldorn's strength returning—until an incessant pounding begins in my head in the afternoon on the third day. I grimace at the sudden sharpness building behind my eyes. The burning in my hand had been increasing the further we traveled in the forest, and more than a few times my vision had been briefly coated in darkness. I blamed it initially on adjusting to the dusky light of the forest, but even I couldn't deny that it had something to do with the shadows inside me when it happened again and again. I bring a palm to my forehead in an attempt to stop the pain, but it only intensifies until I am doubled over in my saddle and Willow's concerned voice is behind me.

"You alright, Lair?"

Fire splits my skull in two, and I clutch my head in pain, a low groan escaping me.

"Stop! Something's wrong with Laira!"

Before I know it, I'm pulled to the ground, and a flame is held to my face. I instinctively flinch at the small flame brought so close to me and immediately regret the action as it only makes me dizzier, along with the awful thumping in my head.

"What's wrong?" Willow asks.

Warm hands cup my face and peel my eyes open, checking one and then the other before searching my head for injury.

"She clutched her head before she nearly fell off Skip so

she must have an injury there." Thelas' uncertain voice sounds to my left as I feel Willow's nimble fingers checking my scalp.

"I don't see any cuts or bruises." She says under her breath.

Willow holds up my chin, and I try in vain to focus on her face.

"You have to tell us Lair. What's wrong?"

My voice is feeble and strained as I somehow manage to get out, "Pain. Behind. Eyes." The effort of trying to speak is immense, and I'm out of breath with those simple words.

Faldorn's voice comes from my right and quick hands hold my wrist, checking my pulse. He sounds calm, his assessment direct. "Heart rate is decreasing rapidly. And she has a cold pallor to her skin and mild sweating."

I distantly hear glassware clinking together and Willow's hurried but determined muttering as she sorts through herbs and bottles.

She yells behind her without looking up, "Check the top of her right hand! Are there dark veins spreading up her arm?"

My hands feel unattached from my body, so I don't feel them check, but they report back to Willow, "Yes! Five that arc from her knuckles to just above her wrist and continue up her forearm."

"Shit!"

Thelas sounds very concerned now. "What does that mean?"

"I thought those lines were nothing to worry about?" Sebastian's concerned voice is angled at me, and I wince as I recall the lie I told him in Warille.

"Less talking, more focusing! Just keep her awake." Willow shouts, saving me from having to answer him.

Darkness begins to coat my vision, and a tiny black tendril spirals out from my chest as if testing its limits and ability to leave my body. I stare in horror as the small inky tendril curls away from me, growing larger and denser as it does.

A warm hand rubs circles into my back, and I feel a light puff of breath behind me. It would be soothing in any other circumstance, but right now I'm only focused on the blinding pain cracking my skull in half and the insidious black oil-like snake twisting through the air toward Willow's turned back.

I put all my strength into bringing a weak hand up in the direction of the person behind me, but he must misinterpret my action and not see the menacing substance hovering in the air because he says, "It's alright, we've got you. She'll fix you up in no time."

My head lolls to the side, and Thelas snaps his fingers in front of my face. "Hey! Hey—no sleeping, alright? Witch's orders."

I nod absentmindedly, a strange wild giggle bubbling up my throat and spilling out like a mad woman.

"Shit, shit, shit!" Thelas says. "She's losing it Willow!"

"I know! I'm almost there—"

My body screams at me to move—to do anything—but all I can do is watch in despair as the twisting dark force spears toward Willow's leg, knocking her herbs to the side and carving a purposeful and deep jagged line down her thigh before dissipating into nothing. I shiver violently as I watch the blood stream from her leg, feeling as if the shadow had looked at me before it attacked her—gleeful malice projected in my direction.

She bellows in surprised pain but doesn't drop the bottle of liquid she just made. She passes it to Faldorn and grabs a strip of cloth from her bag, tying it roughly at the top of her thigh while saying to Faldorn through gritted teeth, "Pour that down her throat and make sure she doesn't choke since I couldn't grind the herbs. Ah—" She doubles over in pain, gripping her thigh, but continues, "If her pain doesn't go away in a few minutes then dose her with this—" She hands him another small bottle with an electric blue color. "—and she'll pass out and stay in a sort of temporary stasis until I can properly examine her."

Faldorn wastes no time, hurrying to follow Willow's direction. I barely feel the cold liquid as it travels down my throat, and I must look pitiful indeed because even this battle-worn soldier looks concerned. I swallow it down with little effort and slump against the warm body behind me. They catch me effortlessly and hold me tightly. The world comes into slightly more clarity as the minutes pass, enough that I can hear Willow shout at Thelas.

"Thelas!"

"Yes, what can I do?"

"Thelas, look at me—I'm about to pass out. I need you to tie another bandage around my leg to stop the bleeding. Can you do that?"

He looks down at her bleeding leg, his voice is stronger and more sure than it was a moment before. "Yes."

"Good. I'll also need you to catch me."

"Catch you—*ah*!"

Willow slumps to the ground, and Thelas barely manages to stop her fall, cradling her against him and snagging another strip of cloth from her bag. He's surprisingly adept at tying the bandage tightly around her leg, and once he's done he looks to Faldorn and Sebastian for direction.

"We need shelter." I say weakly, my voice hoarse.

My head flops to the side again, the effects of the shadows still coursing through me, though Willow's mixture is taking effect. It gives me enough strength and clarity to look around for a possible solution. I could've sworn we were in a small patch of open ground surrounded by dense trees—the same ever-present darkness punctuated with only the soft blue-green light of the plants—but when I look to the side, I see a wide open field. It's just as dim as the rest of the forest because of the latticework canopy above, but it's much higher than what we've seen so far. High enough that it nearly feels like open sky, and I realize with no small amount of alarm, that clouds hang heavy overhead—their roiling depths dark as night.

I shake my head, blinking rapidly to adjust to this new environment. Those Goddess-damned trees and their ability to move have caused us far too many problems, and right now it seems they are either being incredibly helpful or setting us up for a trap. Because it seems far too convenient for a cabin to suddenly appear right when we need shelter the most. To further prove this point, thunder *cracks* in the sky above, and rain pours down on us. The horses shift nervously and more than one cries out in a panicked whinny, though thankfully, none of them flee. We all lift our arms to shelter our heads as much as we can. It's a futile attempt, and even though we are at the edge of the tree line, we are all quickly soaked to the bone.

At the far end of the field, the small house sits completely overtaken by vines and looks to be partially devoured by nature. Its thatched roof sits lopsided and like it's about to fall inward—but that doesn't matter right now as long as it can hold until we can properly treat our wounds and get out of the strange storm that appeared.

Tilting my head upward, I am baffled at how a thundering storm can appear *under* the trees. It must have something to do with the fact that this is a magical fucking forest and nothing makes sense or works how it should.

I inhale sharply. Feeling my control slipping and my mind spinning into a faraway place that I cannot afford to go right now. Perhaps the potion is still taking some time to work through my system, and I'm not as fixed as I thought. The ground crumbles beneath my fingers as I push myself slowly to my knees, and then to my feet. I wobble for a moment, but force myself to stay standing—we need to get moving and I can't be the one that holds everyone back, especially when this was my fault to begin with. Even if the shadows have a mind of their own and I didn't mean to cause this.

They still reside inside you. You did this. A cruel voice echoes in my mind, and I feel it like a slap to my face. The desperation to make up for what I did forces my feet to shuffle one in front of the other and make my way toward the horses. Kel chirps in agitation at my movement, but I wave him away and focus my attention on Skip.

A warm, solid hand grips my shoulders, and I jump at the sudden contact, whipping my head toward the source of this new panic, only to relax at the steady face of Sebastian. The look of quiet determination on his face is enough to quell the rising anxiety for the moment. I search his face for any sign he is losing control as much as I am, but all I see is calm.

I breathe in deeply. If he can keep it together in this moment, then so can I.

I don't trust myself to speak yet, so I point in the direction of the dilapidated cabin in the distance, to which he nods once before springing into action. He grabs my horse and holds the reins out to me, but as I try to grab them with shaking, cold fingers I know I won't be able to mount Skip myself. I can already feel the freezing rain and debilitating fear zapping me of my strength and resolve.

Sebastian doesn't hesitate before tying her reins to his horse and making sure everyone else is up and moving. Thelas seems to be in shock, but able to get on Hael and ride with us. Faldorn swings Willow onto S'alorr's back, securing her carefully and keeping a firm grip on her so she doesn't fall. I have enough sense to silently remark at the fact that he's going to run the entire way to the cabin while holding on to Willow.

If only I possessed the true strength and speed of the fae.

My mind is sluggish, and I only have a vague awareness that I should be moving—that I should be getting on my horse and riding as fast as I can to shelter, but the black tendrils continue to grip my head in a fierce embrace. Dragging one clawed hand after the other, they shred the very foundation of my sanity, and I feel a silent scream welling up in my throat. I drop to my knees in agony as their serrated blades dig into my mind.

I'm lost in my misery and so I only distantly feel rough hands lifting me from the ground and swinging me effortlessly into their arms, one muscled arm under my legs and the other encircling my back. I shiver suddenly, realizing how cold I am in the presence of such a warm and steady force. The smell of moss and soil embraces me, and I curl into it, desperate for anything to pull me from the inky dark trying to pull me under. I'm hauled atop a saddle and instinctively reach for the saddle's horn for stability, squeezing my eyes shut in the process to block out the slight dizziness from the quick change in elevation. The comforting heat from before is momentarily lost and I whimper softly at its departure. But it quickly returns when a heavy weight settles at my back and a strong arm loops around my waist, holding me firmly in place.

Thundering hooves permeate through the shadows still coating my mind and I'm dimly aware of the fact that we are racing swiftly to the other end of the large clearing. A warm breath tickles my cheek and a far-away voice softly chants, "I've got you. I've got you. I've got you."

Closing my eyes, I focus my other senses on my surroundings. The dark claws may be buried in my mind, but they are not in the physical world, so I must find a way to anchor myself there instead. Gripping fabric, I lean further into the light forest scent and inhale deeply. Spreading my palm wide, I concentrate on the body engulfing mine. Of the way we bounce because of the horse's movement and the steady heartbeat beneath solid flesh.

It grounds me in the moment, and I feel my own heart slowing to match his. As it does, the world comes into greater detail and the dark tendrils begin to recede. It's only when we come to a full stop that I realize who I've been clinging to. I jolt away from Sebastian, nearly falling off his tall beast of a horse in the process.

"Easy there! No need to break something just to get out of my arms."

He sounds almost pained, as if I hurt his feelings by immediately trying to flee when I came to my senses. I wince in apology, though he doesn't see it, as he eases me from his saddle and quickly dismounts from his horse. It isn't long before I'm forgetting my guilt and racing as quickly as my weakened body will allow to Faldorn, who is cradling Willow. He's already facing the front door of the house as we huddle around him, and we share a collective wary glance.

It is rather convenient—and suspicious—that a source of shelter suddenly appeared when we needed it most, and I know we are all thinking the same thing: this could be a trap.

A low, pained moan sounds from Willow, and I throw caution to the wind. Not thinking of the consequences, I reach for the handle and rip the door open, motioning for Faldorn and the others to follow. Closing the door behind me, I quickly survey the interior of the cabin.

A large open room greets us with cushioned couches, a low table, and a fireplace burning in the corner. Hallways branch off on either side of the main room, presumably leading to bedrooms, and hopefully, a stocked kitchen.

The hearth flickers merrily, filling the space with much needed warmth, and only then does it occur to me this home is most certainly lived in. Though it appears whoever does live here is not present at the moment. I breathe out a relieved sigh at the lucky break. Hopefully, we will be gone long before they return.

Faldorn settles Willow in front of the fire and immediately begins barking orders. He tells Sebastian to find a pot to boil some water, Thelas to find bandages in our packs, and for me to search the house for any sign of company. Though he eyes me up and down thoroughly before he does, no doubt looking for signs I'm on the verge of passing out again. But Willow's potion did the trick of keeping me upright and has suppressed a good deal of the dizziness, so while I don't feel as if I can continue for long, I can at least check the rooms. The fear from before propels me, along with the same guilt and shame at being the source of our current problems, and my heart pounds in my chest—urging me onward and insisting I be useful.

He pats me on the shoulder, pulling a dagger from his belt and handing it to me. "The last thing we need right now is the owner of this home to show up and kick us out... or worse."

I nod, accepting the dagger since my sword is still strapped to my horse's side, and cautiously approach the first hallway to my left. I hold the small blade firmly in front of my body and scan the long hall. My ears strain to pick up any sounds apart from the racket the others are making, but I can't hear anything suspicious. I notice two rooms on either side of the hall and decide to search the left one first. Nothing but a dusty bed, dresser, and accompanying closet greet me. I check the closet to be sure nothing is hiding in there, but all I see are piles of clothes and unused fabrics. A large desk sits next to the door that I ignored when I entered, and I trail a curious hand across a line of worn books. They range from a variety of topics—animals, crafts, and fiction stories. An eclectic taste that fills me with a surprising familiarity. Whoever lives here is getting more interesting by the minute. *Do not get comfortable,* I admonish myself. *You do not want someone to show up here, despite how intriguing their choice of books may be.*

The next room is similarly furnished and equally as empty. I relax slightly before returning to the main room to continue my scouting. I sneak a glance at how Willow is doing and notice Faldorn is nearly finished sewing her leg and packing it with herbs. She is awake and fussing with the mixture, infusing it with her own magic—though it's weakened from the blood loss. I briefly wonder at why she isn't using her magic to simply knit her skin together, when I realize her abilities are likely hindered because she was attacked by the shadow. I remember how she said it burned her magic away when she tried to make contact with it before and I grimace. She smacks Faldorn's hand away, admonishing him to be gentler, and I grin softly despite my guilt at her feisty attitude. A single tear threatens to spill, but I wipe it away quickly before focusing my attention back on the last rooms. The guilt at being the one to do that to her spears into me once again. Even if it was the shadows inside of me that did it, she was still hurt *because* of me. Because I couldn't hold them back.

I take a deep breath, the panic at knowing those shadows are still deep within me threatening to pull me from my task and dissolve my focus. *She's going to be just fine,* I remind myself, *one disaster at a time.*

I pass Sebastian and Thelas as they search cabinets in a surprisingly large kitchen. Sebastian notices my appearance, and my dagger, and grabs his own weapons before silently falling into step behind me. Only slightly annoyed at his presence, I signal him to search one of the last two remaining rooms—at least he will make searching the rest of the house quicker.

A buzzing sensation lights across my skin as I step into the new room, and despite it looking the same as the other two I searched, I feel a sharp tug in my chest telling me to be wary. I search every corner of the room but find nothing to explain the mounting uneasiness I feel. The bed catches my eye, and I have a sudden crawling sensation up my spine at the idea of looking beneath it.

Steeling myself, I glance briefly under the bed, afraid if I do it too slowly a monster will appear and confirm my worst fears. My shoulders fall and I place a hand to cover my face in shame—because there is nothing under the bed.

Of course there isn't. You got worked up over nothing.

A small laugh turns into a groan as I recall how foolish I was to spook at nothing but silly childhood fears of monsters under beds. I'm about to call out to Sebastian that this room is clear when I feel a presence behind me.

Outlined in moonlight from the lone window, a small, hunched form stands. A flash of pale eyes, silver hair, and white teeth shine in the otherwise dark room.

"Looking for monsters, are we?"

I let out an ear-piercing scream.

MIDNIGHT CAKE

LAIRA

We gather around a small low table in the center of the room, each of us shoved onto small couches, and I squirm at being stuck between Willow and Sebastian—their shoulders driving into mine as I sink slightly into the center of the couch. Mismatched sconces are littered around the room, illuminating the space with different colored flames, showcasing large paintings of beautiful landscapes, and knick-knacks I missed when we first entered. Figures of strange creatures, small ornately decorated wooden boxes, and bookshelves are scattered throughout the house—with not an open space to be seen. It reminds me a bit of how my room back in Taslae looked, when Kel would bring home random items and I decided to use them as decor instead of tossing them.

The old woman returns with a tray of refreshments, offering a small cup to each of us. I take mine hesitantly, darting my eyes to Willow and then to Sebastian and Thelas, wondering if I should be concerned at the normality of this situation when minutes ago I was convinced we were about to be devoured by a ghost. The only one who doesn't seem ruffled is Faldorn, who smiles good-naturedly at the woman and offers his thanks as she hands him a cup. It's swallowed by his large hands, and he sniffs it carefully before taking a small sip, grey eyes lifting to mine. I nod and lower my shoulders. If he isn't afraid, then I shouldn't be either.

The tea smells awful and tastes even worse. The woman notices my grimace and lets out an amused chuckle. "It's good for you, dear. A special blend I've made myself. It will help with your cuts and bruises and revitalize your bodies."

Thelas looks cautiously into his own cup. "It looks like dirt."

"Bah! Not all things that are good for you look good too, now drink up! You all need to recoup your strength. Those storms are nothing to mess with and will cause far more harm than just tired bodies."

Willow sips the tea, grimacing before carefully setting it back down. "Really? What else can they do?"

She shows all her teeth as she grins widely. "Well, some storms can cause your skin to fall right off, while others paralyze you, pummeling you into the dirt until you are devoured by the surrounding roots."

Thelas lets out a nervous laugh. "You sound like Willow."

"Hey!" Willow cringes after her outburst, realizing her defense may have been offensive. "Sorry."

The old woman shrugs, returning to her task of setting out the various items she procured from the kitchen. "So, tell me, how did a rowdy group like yourselves end up barging into my home, making a mess of it, and causing me trouble?"

I nearly spit out the foul tea at her admonishment, nervously glancing at the others, unsure of how to respond.

She belts out a loud laugh, cackling at some supposed joke that only she finds amusing. "Well, better make up for it by explaining why you're here."

"Well… I suppose we can start with some introductions. I'm Laira." I point to the others in turn as they each say their name and stare at her expectantly as we finish, hoping she'll share her own without having to prod her.

"You can call me Em."

"Em," I say uncertainly.

She raises an eyebrow, a stern look in her eyes. "Yes, just Em, got a problem with that?"

"No! Of course not. Just Em. Got it."

I mentally berate myself for questioning her. I don't want to incur her wrath and potentially have her kick us out. She seems mildly pleased with my response though, enough at least to snatch one of the snacks from the tray and take a bite as she stares pointedly at me.

Right, explaining how we got here. Where to even start? I mentally groan, attempting to find the best place to begin and also decide on what to hold back from this mysterious woman.

She may have let us stay even after rudely barging in, but that doesn't mean she's safe or trustworthy. I look to the others circled around the room, reclining on various couches and chairs, but they all look to me. Willow squeezes my arm and I take a deep breath, but a cold wave passes through my body anyway and my stomach feels like it's been dropped unceremoniously to my feet.

What if I say too much and it puts us in danger?

I tap my fingers against my thigh as I fret over what I should say, and more importantly, what I should *not* say. The inside of my cheek is going to be raw and bleeding by the time we are finished with this night if I can't get a hold of this roiling anxiety at being in charge and the more insidious fear of being a conduit for that dark coiling substance from earlier.

I close my eyes tightly, trying to block out everything. If I just had one clear second to think without my mind screaming at me, I could finally breathe freely, but unfortunately I have yet to figure out how to quiet a mind such as mine, and so I'm left with swirling thoughts, horrid scenarios, waves of panic, and the three words I've carved deep into my soul over the years: not good enough. It all cascades over me, and despite my outward appearance of relative calm, I am a churning storm.

I take a deep breath and open my eyes to stare at the woman. Perhaps if I could get even just a glimpse of her threads, I could figure out if she holds any extra meaning to us, like when I saw the threads connecting me to everyone here, even though they were complete strangers. But when I try and focus on her, nothing happens. Even with whatever extra magic is present in this forest, the threads don't appear. Could she not be important to us then? A whisper in my heart tells me she is, and I suppose that is all I will have to go on.

I take another breath, steadying myself as I launch into our story of how we got here, choosing to omit some things like the threads, the specifics of the prophecy and the dark magic that plagues me. The old woman watches me as I speak, occasionally letting out little huffs or soft muttering. I get the feeling she knows I'm holding information back, but she doesn't prod me to explain further. I continue talking of our trek through the forest and the beasts we've encountered, as well as the trees that have gotten in our way. She smiles knowingly at the mention of the trees moving, but again doesn't say anything, instead she carefully folds the thin brown parchment that her snack was wrapped in into a tight square before tucking it between her first two fingers as I continue speaking. My words slow slightly as I watch the odd movement, but she just waves the two fingers with the folded wrapper in my direction, as if to tell me to keep going.

What a strange woman.

Finally, I finish the story with a modified version of how Willow got hurt. Carefully leaving out mention of the darkness that seeped from me to attack her and the effect it had on my mind and body. The elixir Willow gave me seemed to have given me enough strength to recover, though there is still a tiredness to my bones and a pressing weight in my temple that reminds me I'm not fully recovered yet. I make a mental note to talk to Willow about it later once she's feeling better. Though, if Em's tea works, perhaps I won't need to.

Em doesn't comment on the story; she simply nods and gets up from her chair, motioning to both hallways on either side of the large room we're in.

"Feel free to claim a bedroom, they are all open since I prefer to sleep out here anyway." She eyes us, a sudden softness relaxing her features. "Get some rest. You have a long road ahead of you still."

WILLOW, FALDORN, AND Sebastian turn in for the evening shortly after Em leaves to bustle about in the kitchen, having chosen their rooms and snagging some fresh linen that Em laid out for us. Not quite ready to go to bed, I settle down across from Thelas in the main room, who sits silently with his face turned toward the fireplace.

"You did a great job with tying that bandage on Willow; pretty sure that is what helped stop most of the bleeding," I say to him.

"I… um… have experience when it comes to that sort of thing." His voice is somber as he speaks, and a lonely pain shines in his eyes even as he shifts them to look at his drink, avoiding my gaze.

I don't know what he's been through or why he would be so good at tying bandages and stopping bleeding, but I do know he is a kind soul that would never deserve any mistreatment and likely has experienced far more than he should.

I reach out my hand, squeezing his forearm gently. "I'm sorry you are burdened with that knowledge, but it did save Willow at least."

He lifts his head up at that, studying me silently, and I suddenly have the feeling of being prey standing before a beast, though, shockingly, I don't feel any fear. I know Thelas would never hurt me, and so it's not fear that I look at him with, but acceptance of whatever demons he carries.

I give him a warm smile that I hope says all that I can't in this moment, wanting to offer him the support he needs. "You know I'm here if you ever wanted to talk about it."

He doesn't speak, taking a long sip of his drink as he turns away from me. But for a split second before his gaze left mine, I could swear I glimpsed a glistening hope and a hint of blazing yellow in his normally cool blue eyes.

Not wanting to bother him too much, I get up to leave and sit closer to the fire. As I pass, Thelas reaches a hand to squeeze my arm once. He doesn't look directly at me or say a word, but I sense the acknowledgment and gratitude in his gesture all the same.

I'm lost in thought for a long time, and so I don't notice Thelas leaving for bed, but when I look up, I realize I am the only one in the main room of the house. Judging by the stillness in the air, I'd guess it's well past midnight and nearing the beginnings of dawn, yet I feel no closer to sleep than I did hours ago.

With a sigh, I stretch my legs and stand, feeling the creaky stiffness from sitting on the hard wood floor. Setting my cup on a nearby side table, I rub my eyes with my palms. As if doing so will force sleep into them, and I can finally rest after this whole ordeal of a day.

I shiver at the thought of the piercing darkness that shot at Willow and hurt her. My best friend could have died if the shadow had been able to do more damage, and I'm almost certain it was my fault. That thing was living inside me, coiling and gaining strength so it could spear out of me and hurt the people around me.

But *why*?

And how did it get into my body at all?

The action to harm Willow seemed purposeful, like it knew that she was our healer, so it would attack her first before moving on to the rest of us. But it dissipated into nothing right after slashing her. Could it be that it didn't have the strength yet to go after the others? Cold fear splashes over my body at the thought of this *thing* hiding inside of me, stealing my strength to fuel its own with the purpose of causing death and destruction. I had no control over it whatsoever—what if it happened again and did more than just injure Willow? The dark veins pulse on my hand and I grimace at it as I try to focus on it. Maybe if I can pinpoint its energy in my body, I can hold it back so at the very least it can't escape me again. My eyes drift out of focus as I stare at the vein that has slowly grown up my hand, and a spark of an idea comes alive in my mind. I feel the dark energy pulling taut from my hand to the center of my chest, not unlike how the red threads feel when connecting to others. The sensation of their similarity sends a chill down my spine, but if that is the case, then perhaps the next time I feel it leaking from me again, I can yank it back. The idea is feeble, and relies on some sort of control over it—something I haven't been able to do even with the red threads—but it's all I have.

I sigh, "It'll have to do." I hang my head back against the back of my chair and glumly close my eyes.

A flash of a memory appears in my head, and I recall the very first nightmare I had months ago, where indistinguishable people battled and died horrifically, and how after I woke up a strange black substance had been hovering around me. Had it somehow fused itself with me at that point? Is that where the black veins on my hands are from? Is its purpose meant to kill my friends or something else? What is its true goal?

"Ugh. This is too much for one day." My shoulders slump in defeat at the questions I have no answers for, and perhaps never will. "I should at least try to get some sleep."

Walking down the hall to one of the remaining empty rooms, I pass the kitchen. A soft warm glow permeates from the space as I near the door, and I hear dishes clanking together and the shuffling of feet. Peeking my head around the doorframe, and see the old woman, Em, stirring something in a large wooden bowl.

She doesn't look up from her task as she asks, "Can't sleep?"

I pause for a moment, deciding if I should tell the truth or not, but what would be the point of lying? It's likely just hours until dawn, and it's obvious what my answer is.

"No."

"Neither can I. I'm something of a night owl."

I watch as she expertly combines ingredients, sifting flour with quick strokes of her hands and adding pinches of other ingredients as she goes.

She notices my attention and asks off-handedly, "Know how to bake?"

I shrug and take a step inside the kitchen. "Somewhat."

"Here." She shoves a wooden bowl into my hands containing a large amount of an odd clear substance. It's goopy and not at all appetizing looking. She must see my hesitancy and slight disgust because she explains.

"Egg whites. Go ahead and whip them together as fast as you can—I'll tell you when to stop." She grins conspiratorially. "Better for a strong young lady like yourself to do it rather than my old bones. Would take me three times as long."

I take the offered whisk and begin whipping the egg whites as requested. It takes a surprising amount of energy, and if I wasn't awake before, I definitely am now. My hand begins to cramp, and my arm grows tired, but I push on. This one small task is comforting in the face of so many things I need to do for the future, and there's also the fact that we did barge in on this woman's home, and I don't want to disappoint her.

She leans over and smiles approvingly at the contents of the bowl. "It's like magic, isn't it? How it completely changes into fluffy white peaks."

I giggle. "Yeah, I suppose you're right."

"This recipe is special. Been in the family a long time. I know it had a different name before, but I like to call it Midnight Cake."

I nod as if this makes complete sense. "And what about the recipe makes it a 'Midnight Cake'? The batter is pale yellow, almost white."

"Well, I make them at midnight, of course!" She huffs, as if this should be obvious.

"Yes, thank you for clearing that up." My wry smile comes surprisingly quickly, and I'm equally fascinated and perturbed that she is so easy to talk to. She could be waiting to turn us into soup for all I know, but instead she is showing me how to bake a cake.

She thrusts a new bowl into my hands, one that contains the yellow batter she was mixing. "Fold it in."

Luckily, I know what she means and immediately begin scooping the whipped egg whites and gently mixing them into the batter. She hums in approval at my technique and busies herself cleaning the rest of the supplies.

A sudden nervous energy takes hold of me as my thoughts drift. There's an odd familiarity with this house that is unnerving, and I can't figure out if it's something I should be concerned with or pleased about. It's as if I've been dropped into the fading remnants of a familiar dream—grasping at the scene but unable to bring it into focus.

I stare into the bowl, unable to look over at her as the words tumble from my mouth in a rush. "Can I ask you something?"

She gives me an amused smile. "Of course."

I trace the rim of the bowl with the spoon, once, twice.

"Why does this house, why do you, feel so familiar?" My voice is soft as I speak and I stare into the bowl as I ask the burning question, too nervous to look at her for fear of what I won't see on her face, or even worse, what I will see on her face.

"That, my dear, is because we have met in many lifetimes."

I stop my fidgeting to look sharply at her.

"Tell me—how well can you see the threads?"

My mouth parts. "You know about the threads?"

She smirks, her eyes dancing in the low light of the kitchen. "I've been around a long time."

I hesitate but decide I have nothing to lose by sharing what little I know, especially if she can tell me more.

"Yes, I can see them, but not all the time. They usually flash into my vision for just long enough for me to see who they connect to." I think back to when the thread wound around Sebastian in a loving embrace at the start of the trip and grimace before adding, "And sometimes I swear they only show up to make my life difficult."

She laughs, the sound a soft chime in the relative silence of the house. "Yes, they can be tricky and occasionally take on a life of their own to show what the thread reader needs to know but might be suppressing…"

She cocks an eyebrow, giving me a pointed look.

I huff, feeling my cheeks growing warm. I do not care if that thread was being touchy-feely with the thief. I have no plans of getting any closer to him than I need to.

"Wait, can you see them too?" I ask as my mind catches up to what else she just said.

She shakes her head, and my chest falls slightly at the admission. She must see my disappointment, because she quickly adds, "I cannot see them as you do, but that doesn't mean I don't know a few things about their existence."

I lift an eyebrow. "Like what?"

"Like how what you described is only the beginning, and your ability to see the threads will grow with time. As for the actual threads themselves, have you ever asked yourself what they truly are?"

I absentmindedly stir the batter again, looking away from her to think. "Well, I guess I haven't. I know they're connections and show how strong different relationships are. A thin, dim strand appears for acquaintances or distant relatives. But a thicker, brightly lit strand signifies a strong bond."

She nods, pulling a square pan from a low cabinet. "That is all true, but there is more to it." A conspiratorial glint lights her eyes and her smile widens.

"You see—the threads are the very essence of a person. The only part that stays the same even as more is added or taken away with each new life experienced. They connect people through entirely different lifetimes, ages, and paths—they are the foundation of this realm and an intricately tied web that can never properly be unwoven, though some have tried."

I look to the empty doorway of the kitchen, and the hallway beyond to where Willow sleeps peacefully. I think of the others in their own rooms on the other side of the house and realize the same familiarity I felt with this house, and this old woman, I have felt with each of them.

She plops the pan next to the bowl. "And all of this is especially true for those fated thread bound couples."

My stomach flips at the knowing look in her eyes, and I quickly glance away to dump the bowl's contents into the pan in an attempt to tamp down this new wave of anxious butterflies.

Not wanting to continue the conversation, I shrug, hoping she believes my nonchalance and will drop the subject. "I wouldn't know."

"Hmph. Yes, well, I just think it's lovely how two people can change drastically between lives, yet still find each other and fall in love in each one. Don't you think so?"

"I suppose…"

"Some may even say they find 'the matching half to their human whole.'"

I nearly choke, and she grabs the bowl so I don't spill the rest of its contents on the floor. My voice is a small squeak as I gape at her. "What?"

She smiles innocently, poking at the hearth to her left and placing the pan in the center, her sharp silver eyes on me the entire time.

"Well—I don't. You see—I'm not fully human, I'm part fae, so I don't think that applies to me." I wince at the way my words come out scrambled and useless.

Her smile is smug and knowing as she chuckles softly. "I never said it did, dear. Besides, that's only one saying. Other beings besides humans can have a fated bond."

"Oh. Right. Of course."

I stand there for a long moment, feeling awkward after

finishing our task, not wanting to be rude and leave but also not wanting to be under her penetrating gaze any longer.

She shoos me away before I can come up with a suitable excuse. "I can take it from here. Besides, it will need a few hours to bake and cool before I can frost it."

I don't move, unconvinced she's letting me go so easily, and she swats me with her wooden spoon.

"Go on to bed! The cake will be ready when you wake."

I yelp, hurrying to my room to avoid another red mark from the spoon.

ON THE ROAD AGAIN

LAIRA

Thelas hovers a pencil over a notebook, his maps spread out around him in a wide arc on the soft ground outside Em's house. I walk to him, about to ask if he needs help packing up when he beats me to it.

"Hold on, I just need to do a few more things to determine the best path through the trees. They've been getting more and more difficult to out-maneuver."

Em comes up from behind me, observing his notes before waving a fist at the trees in the distance. "Ah, don't worry so much about them. I'll tell 'em to quit messin' with ya. Sneaky bastards!"

"I knew they've been messing with me!" Thelas yells, pointing a finger at Sebastian, who grins.

"Oh, come on Thelas, enough of this. Trees don't move!" Sebastian huffs loudly, a smile playing on his face as he saddles his horse. I'm almost confident he believes the trees have been moving on us this entire time, but he has too much fun goading Thelas into believing he doesn't.

"They do in mysterious forbidden forests!" Thelas shouts back.

I chuckle at the playful banter and walk to where Skip and Star stand together to start saddling Skip. The familiar motions of threading leather, tightening straps, and securing my bag helps to settle my nerves. I don't know what it is about this house in the middle of the woods, but I don't want to leave. We are safe here, and the anxieties I've felt over this journey don't feel as heavy.

I sigh.

We have to leave, we need to continue. I know this and feel it in the very core of my being, but that doesn't make it any easier to go.

I give Skip a few light scratches on her forehead, and she rubs her entire giantess head against my torso, nearly knocking me over in her attempts to get more affection.

I laugh as I swat gently at her. "By the stars, Skip! You don't need to knock me down for more pets, I will gladly give you more!"

I hear footsteps come up beside us and a soft chuckle. "Skip, huh?" The old woman approaches and runs a hand down Skip's neck. "She hasn't changed a bit."

I tilt my head. "What do you mean? Have you met her before?"

It would have been nearly impossible for Em to have met Skip before, unless the horse somehow got through this mythical forest on her own.

She smiles at me, replying in an almost wistful tone, "No, not as she is presently at least. Her spirit is the same, though. And it's been tethered to yours for quite some time."

Heat grows behind my eyes, and I feel the threat of tears coming on, though I don't exactly know why. I've grown rather close to my sweet mount, but I'd never considered her to be anything more.

"Animals have threads too?"

She nods, pulling away and staring out into the forest. "Yes. Everyone does. Even the land can have threads, though it is exceedingly rare that they connect to a person." She cocks her head to the side before shifting her gaze back to mine. "You cannot see these threads?"

I frown, feeling suddenly inadequate. "No. I didn't even know that was possible."

She gives me a reassuring smile. "You will learn many things in the coming months. I'm certain you will understand all there is to know when you need to."

I nod somewhat glumly, not entirely convinced of her statement but accepting it anyway.

An unfamiliar emotion wells in my chest, and I whip my eyes to hers. Ancient understanding swirls in her silver eyes, reflecting the feeling echoing in my mind. It leaves me in a rush, and I blink rapidly at the sudden change, a little disoriented.

She smiles and reaches for my hand, her face morphing into a serious expression, and for a second, I'm worried something is wrong with her. I lean down to inspect her to make sure she is okay, until I realize her worry is directed toward me.

"Be careful, my dear. I fear your path has only just begun, and the true scope of your actions has yet to be uncovered." She gives my hand a light squeeze and continues, "I have not told you everything you need to know, as you and your group are not ready to hear it. I apologize for this, but there are some things that need time to settle. When you believe you are nearing the end of your true journey, come back here and I will tell you everything."

My first instinct is to argue with her, but the steely expression on her face warns me to back off on this particular subject. I think of all the times I was not ready to hear unsettling news or times when my mind was so chaotic I couldn't take in new information without shattering, and fear she may be right. I am not ready to hear what she has to say. I only hope that when I do need to return, I am ready.

A New Sparring Partner

SEBASTIAN

Laira pulls herself atop her horse, and I remove my attention from her and the old woman. I still don't fully trust Em, but Laira seems relatively at ease with her, so I let go of my suspicions for now. We are departing anyway, and there's no use dwelling on the strange woman when we will likely never see her again. My eyes drift around the large open clearing and the old woman's house. It's an odd place, but I suppose with this forest, there is only one odd occurrence after another. The ever-present dim blue light is still here, but the heavy clouds from the night before are at least gone—exposing dense foliage and branches crisscrossing high above like a dome. This forest is the most disorienting place I've ever experienced, but at least this clearing has provided us with a short rest and chance to breathe. I may not be as fond of the sun as Laira is, but even I miss the wide open sky of the outside, and the high canopy at least comes close.

Faldorn approaches with his elk, his gaze also focused on Laira and the old woman. He doesn't speak, but his posture is rigid, and his mouth is turned down into a thoughtful frown, just as cautious as I am and choosing not to act on it as well. I take the chance to survey the old fae male more closely. Apart from his relentless pace driving us forward and his unwillingness to stop unnecessarily, he's rather pleasant to be around. He doesn't speak much, but when he does there is often a surprising amount of humor behind his words, and I've more than once been caught off guard by his wry demeanor. It's different from the seasoned warrior full of hard edges and unwavering discipline that I expected—though he certainly has that too. He's a calm presence amidst the chaotic appearance of this forest, and I find myself more and more glad Laira, Willow, and Thelas didn't listen to me when I said we didn't need him.

Faldorn turns to me, nodding once before mounting his elk and trotting to where Thelas stands next to his antelope, stuffing maps into his pack.

I pull myself into my saddle and pat Rei's neck, his warmth and powerful energy setting me at ease. It lessens the strain of the night before, and I finally feel as if my limbs are relaxing. The way Laira clutched her head and appeared nearly lifeless in my arms struck me with far more fear than I could've ever imagined. And today I find myself seeking her out to assure myself she is recovered and back to her normal self.

The dark veins creeping up her arms flash back to me and I mentally berate myself once more for not asking more questions back in Warille. I grip the reins tightly and yank Rei harder than is necessary. But the uncomfortable feeling in my chest itches, and the need to move grips me. The sooner we can leave this glade, the better. Rei stamps his hooves and shifts forward, anticipating my need to run, but I hold him back. It wouldn't be smart to recklessly race off into this forest, even if that is the tactic I've employed my whole life. A wicked smirk curves on my face, and I flick my gaze to Laira once again. Perhaps another form of letting go would ease the tension in my body—a sparring session with a certain wildcat is exactly what I need.

"WE WILL STOP here for the night." Faldorn's firm voice sounds from the front of the group.

I exhale loudly. "Fucking finally."

Laira rolls her eyes at my comment but doesn't respond, choosing instead to ease herself from Skip's saddle and take a few unsteady steps to stretch her legs from being under saddle for hours.

Thelas does the same, immediately settling against a tree and closing his eyes. Willow jumps down from her ornery mount, green tendrils snaking from her and encouraging nearby glowing vines to guide her horse to a safe spot to be tied as Willow digs through her bag. Din pounces on her back, and another vine gently encircles him, pulling him off her before he can get tangled in her long hair. She never stops searching in her bag and doesn't make a single movement other than a quick flick of her hand to indicate she is practicing magic at all.

I raise an eyebrow.

Her casual use of her power has been increasing as of late, and I'm often left in shock at her effortless ability to wield the plant life around her. Even the witch queen has to concentrate to perform multiple spells or manipulations at once, but Willow seems to do it without thinking. As simple for her as brushing a strand of hair from her eyes.

Chittering sounds to my left, and I whip my head in the direction of the little creatures darting in the shadows. The odd mouse-like animals steal from us constantly. Always finding us even when I'm certain we have left them far behind. I watch as they sneak under the mushrooms and ferns that litter the forest floor, attempting to get close enough to my pack in order to rifle their greedy paws through it. Rei huffs in their direction, arching his muscled neck down to snap at the nearest one and nearly missing its tail. It shrieks and clambers around the two other creatures to escape his sharp teeth.

I chuckle, patting a reassuring hand to his side. "I'm not a fan of them either, bud." I face the others as they each follow their own unpacking routines. "So!" I clap to get their attention, "Who wants to partake in a friendly sparring session?"

Laira eyes me suspiciously, her voice deadpanned. "Sparring?"

I smile, showing all my teeth and reaching for my sword and dagger. "Yes, darling, sparring. A lively activity between two or more individuals who use weapons to—"

"I know what sparring is!" she interrupts me, throwing her arms wide in exasperation. "Why would we want to do that now after a full day of travel?"

I scratch my chin and rest my sword over my shoulder, twirling the ornate dagger in my hand. "Because we need the practice, love. Don't tell me you're going to let a few sore ass muscles stop you from increasing your ability to protect yourself?"

I raise an eyebrow at her, and she grumbles but doesn't contradict me. She tosses her saddle to the ground, whipping around to point a finger at me, but Thelas interrupts her before she can berate me further.

"I wouldn't mind learning." He raises his arm as he slowly gets up from where he was hunched against the tree, but quickly lowers it when everyone stares at him.

I look him up and down. He doesn't have the bearing of a fighter, but anyone can and should learn to defend themselves.

I nod and gesture to Faldorn. "Good. I'm not the best teacher, but I'm sure Faldorn could show you a thing or two."

Faldorn watches me, his gaze ever assessing, before turning to Thelas and considering the idea for a moment. "Yes. There are things that would be useful for you to know should you find yourself in danger."

"Great!" I shift my body to face Laira who stands with her arms crossed. "What do you say, love? Want to go a few rounds?"

"I only spar with Willow, thanks," she bites out.

Willow jumps up from her position on the ground to fling an arm around Laira, grinning ear to ear. "Oh, don't be silly! I have some plants to catalogue, and you are going to get rusty if you don't practice soon."

She pats Laira on the head, who grumbles again, a colorful string of muffled curses leaving her lips. But she can't hide the slight curve to her mouth, and a thrill runs down my spine at the small admission.

It's time to find out what she can do.

I roll the sleeves of my shirt up and stretch my arms back to ease the tension from my shoulders before tying my hair back in a loose knot. A few strands fall out of it back into my eyes, and I brush them aside absentmindedly until I catch Laira staring at the small action. Her mouth parts slightly, and a hungry look flits across her eyes. I huff a laugh, and she quickly looks away, guilty at having been caught staring.

Moving away from camp to a small open patch of ground, I

grip my sword and dagger and bow to her, throwing my arms out wide and keeping my eyes on hers the entire time. Her jaw ticks at my theatrics, but otherwise her stony expression remains in place.

I grin. "Give me all you got, love. I can take it."

She grabs her own sword and stalks forward, twirling her blade a few times as she goes. The soft blue glow of the ferns illuminates her face and causes her hair to sparkle and shift in the low light. Faldorn had a significant change in appearance upon entering the forest, but I have been noticing small differences in Laira as well. Her eyes a more brilliant shade of green, the tips of her hair like flickering flames, and her actions more fluid.

She settles into a firm stance, and we circle each other, the tension building as we attempt to read each other.

I dart forward first, angling my sword to get an idea of her skill. She easily blocks my advance before easing back into a practiced stance, a feral grin on her face as she takes in my raised brows and pleased smile.

I spin my sword once, bringing it in front of me, and swipe my dagger low, which she skillfully sidesteps. "Well then, let's not hold back, shall we?"

Her eyes glitter with excitement. "No holding back."

We spin around each other in an intricate dance, the movements coming easily to both of us. Soon I'm lost in our sparring, my mind drifting as I block each strike and anticipate each of her moves. Fighting has always been a release—for my muscles as well as my mind. A perfect clarity envelopes me, and for the first time in weeks I feel as if I can finally breathe. My muscles burn, and I welcome the ache. The feeling of stretching them is the best type of medicine for a conflicted mind.

And I am conflicted. Every day I spend with each of them wears on me with the secrets I am holding back. Their openness and willingness to get to know each other was grating at first, but I've grown used to their presence and have even been enjoying the time we've all spent together. Laira slashes forward again, her breathing beginning to show signs of exertion, but she's still quick, and I have to angle my body in an awkward way to avoid her. The green ring she wears flashes in the corner of my vision, and a tender feeling winds its way into my chest despite my best efforts to keep it at bay. That was the most intimate moment we've shared thus far, and I've had to stop myself from thinking of it too often. Of the way her skin felt as it brushed against mine and the wonder in her eyes as she beheld the ring. I don't know what possessed me to buy it for her, but when I saw her face in that moment, I knew I would never regret the impulsive decision.

I'd be lying to myself if I said I haven't been chasing that feeling ever since. I can't tell her the truth about me—and perhaps it would be wiser to continue my teasing to keep her away—but I do still want to know her. Is there truly a way I can do that and still hold so much of myself back? I may be able to forget my true identity for now, but it will become a problem eventually. My frustration comes out in my movements, and I drive her back with a few well-aimed strikes. She recovers quickly though, driving the blunt end of her hilt into my chest in a swift jab. I huff out a surprised breath, reeling backward, and she laughs triumphantly. The sound is beautiful, and I can't help but chuckle along with her.

"Had enough yet, thief?"

I swing my sword up and we clash in the middle together, our swords clanging as we stare intently at each other. "Nowhere near enough, wildcat."

Her answering smile could light up the world, and I'm slow to pull away. She uses my hesitation to her advantage, knocking the sword and dagger from my hands, causing them to land with dull thuds in the dirt. Her eyes are victorious until I dart forward and grip both of her wrists, smiling wickedly down at her. I squeeze her right wrist, and she winces, dropping her sword to the ground. She stares up at me, a mix of vexation and exhilaration in her eyes, and I see the moment she knows she can still get the upper hand on me. She hooks her leg around my ankle abruptly, and my balance wavers long enough for her to shove me forward and knock me to the ground. She tries to wriggle from my grasp, but I yank her forward too, determined to take her with me. We crash to the dirt, and her weight settles atop me, a *whoosh* of air leaving both our lungs as we land. She pulls herself up, her hands on either side of my body and quickly scrambles to stand, but I wrap my arms around her waist, pulling her back atop me. Her nose is

inches from mine, and her warm breath mingles with mine. She eyes are wide with shock and confusion, but she makes no move to break from my hold. She does shift her legs, however, the movement brushing against my lower half and causing my cock to twitch.

She stills. Her eyes widen further, and red blooms in her cheeks, her mouth parting slightly in realization. She arches her neck ever so slightly away, but I pull her back until our lips are a hair's breadth apart.

Heat floods me, and the way her body feels against mine brings to mind all of the tantalizing things I've wanted to do with her but haven't let myself dwell on lest I lose my mind over wanting her these last few weeks.

"Would you like to know what I'm thinking right now?" My voice is rough, full of hungry desire as her eyes dart down to my lips.

She shivers and lowers her mouth to hover above mine. I can nearly taste her, and I have the urge to pull her face the rest of the way and devour her right here. Her eyes darken, and I know she is thinking the same thing, her lips brushing against mine as light as a feather, and her hips shifting purposefully against me.

A shrill whistle freezes us both, and Laira's eyes bulge as she breaks from my arms and shuffles away from me. Her face and neck are scarlet, and she clutches her chest, breathing heavily before darting her eyes behind me.

"Break it up, love birds! Find a bush or something to hide behind at least!" Willow shakes her head, chastising us from across the camp where she sets up the fire.

I sit up reluctantly, throwing a middle finger behind me and getting a delighted snicker in response. I focus on Laira, adjusting my pants as I pull myself to my knees. She eyes the movement like she can't help herself before quickly looking away and busying herself with sheathing her sword and walking to sit next to Willow by the fire.

I collect my own fallen sword and dagger, but instead of joining the women at the fire, I make my way to where Faldorn is showing Thelas sword basics and safety. I lean against a nearby tree, watching but not really seeing what they are doing—my mind too full of Laira and the way she fought. Her movements were fluid and graceful but powerful in a way I hadn't expected. She has more strength than I gave her credit for, and I wonder at just how many times she and Willow have trained over the years. Not to mention the way she felt against me. Soft curves but also firm muscles yielding beneath my arms, a pleasant combination that I itch to explore more of.

A heavy pat on my back startles me from my increasingly indecent thoughts.

Faldorn's smooth voice quips from behind me, "An interesting tactic—taking down an opponent via almost kiss." I angle my head toward the male, a broad smile on his face. "Does that work on the battlefield as well?"

I gape at the old fae and then burst into laughter, grabbing his shoulder and swinging my arm around him, pulling us both forward into the center of our small makeshift camp.

"Wouldn't you like to know, old man."

He chuckles, the sound light and soft, and suddenly his face looks years younger—the quiet despair constantly present disappearing for a moment and allowing what I imagine to be the real Faldorn to come through. We sit down, and he immediately begins doling out rations, the same small smile on his face the entire time.

I CAN'T BREATHE

LAIRA

I stumble away from our camp, having woken in the middle of the night, and blindly tear through branches, stomping frantically over soft mushrooms and delicate ferns. Roots pull out of my way, and soon a smooth path looms ahead of me. I race down it without questioning it. Hot tears streak down my face as my breath heaves in my chest, and I have the vague certainty that the forest is shifting to accommodate my reckless running, to aid me or to further entrap me though, I'm unsure. But in this moment I don't care. The only thought pulsing through my skull is to *get away*—to run. My nightmares chase me, a cold sweat breaking out across my skin, and I feel sick with the constant images of death and destruction.

Kel trills to my right, his feathers brushing against my cheek as he darts in front of me. I stop my mad dash, clutching my hands to my chest in an effort to keep the breath in my lungs as he hovers in my view.

"Kel. I can't do this. These things I keep seeing—I can't." I collapse in a heap, my legs suddenly too weak to hold me. I sob into my hands. "I just can't Kel."

Kel lands at my feet, rubbing his smooth beak against my calf and cooing softly. I stare at him numbly. I appreciate his presence and support, but I don't think there's anything he can do for me. This is too much for me, and I'm scared. So scared of what these visions mean, of the coiling darkness inside me, and every unknown looming over us. It doesn't help that the near constant darkness of this forest feeds into every bad memory and nightmare I've ever had—my mind taunting me with monsters hiding in the shadows. The careful control I've tried to hold onto this entire time crumbles before me, and I don't have the strength in this moment to call it back.

I have the vague awareness of approaching footsteps, and a faraway thought informs me I should be embarrassed at having raced away from camp and disappearing off alone, but I can't bring myself to care. I just want to curl up here and forget that I have no control over anything and only a slim hope of purging these shadows.

"Hey, love, hey, it's me. Look at me." Sebastian's concerned voice wraps around me, and I stiffly turn my head in his direction.

I see him as he tracks my unfocused stare, unstable breathing, and tapping fingers. My hands desperately try to do the work of calming me down. I tap so often it has become second nature, and I often don't notice it, but it's all I can think about now. I repeat the same sequence I learned over the years, hoping desperately that it will bring me back into my body and out of my churning mind. I'm convinced performing the task is the only thing holding me to the ground, and without it I fear I will be swept away. Sebastian's face hovers in front of me, blood pouring from a wound on his forehead, and an arrow stabbed through his chest. I nearly scream at the image once again flooding my mind, but stop myself when I blink rapidly and realize he is *actually* in front of me and completely unharmed.

He reaches for me but stops himself at the last second. Instead, he crouches in front of me, trying to get my focus.

"Wildcat." His voice is firm but with an undercurrent of worry that I don't have the capacity to care about right now, locked in my relentless fear as I am.

Tap, tap tap, tap. Tap.

"*Wildcat*!" He sounds more urgent, but it's like he's behind a wall and I am alone. So very alone. Willow, Faldorn, Sebastian and Thelas all perish before my eyes—each time more bloody than the last. The visions are all-consuming, deadly, and destructive—I attempt to reach for them to save them, to do anything to help, but they die one by one before me. My breathing increases, and the panic constricts my lungs. I nearly weep at the feeling, because it means I may be able to join them in death's embrace. I can't possibly go on without them, I—

"Laira!" He grabs my face between both of his hands and

forces my gaze onto his.

He – he said my name.

The words ping through my mind like a tinkling bell. He's only said my name once before, when I first told him what it was in Taslae, and it's this thought that finally snaps me out of my tumbling thoughts.

"Laira, love, how can I help you?" He glances at my still tapping hand. "Is tapping helpful?"

I stare at him dumbfounded. He wants to help me? He knows what this panic is?

I respond in shaking breaths as I am still caught in the web of my nightmare. "Tapping is good. But physical t-touch helps too…"

I trail off as I realize he is rubbing slow methodical circles on my arms. It feels… good. Too good. But I am past the point of caring, I only want this crushing weight and fear to go away.

"Can I try something?" He looks almost nervous as he asks me, his hand pausing the slow circles on my arm to roughly rake through his long hair.

I stare into his green and gold flecked eyes. He seems so earnest and sincere, like he really thinks he can help me. I speak before I have the chance to think better of it.

"Yes."

Tentatively, he pulls away, and immediately I miss his warm touch on my arms. But he doesn't move far, in fact, he places himself behind me. Cradling me against his front and tucking strong arms around either side of me as we sit together on the forest floor.

"Is this okay?" he asks quietly.

His warmth surrounds me, and though I am still breathing erratically and shaking, his body is a firm strength anchoring me to the world and holding me steady.

"Yes." The only word I can seem to speak right now.

He continues to whisper in a soothing voice in my ear. "I've got you, love."

His breath is the subtle warmth of a spring day, and it makes a cascade of shivers roll down my spine as I focus on taking a full breath.

"I've got you."

He repeats that phrase over and over, and I find myself growing more relaxed after each whispered word. My breath evens out and my racing heart slows. Time seems to continue forward again, and I can feel the dirt pressing beneath me, his steady presence pressing close to my back and the sides of my thighs. His arms are resting on my knees, but when I finally return to my senses, he seems to understand my need to move and pulls away. I slowly unbend my knees and push myself out of his embrace. I miss his warmth immediately and almost sink back into him.

Almost.

Instead, I turn around and face him with a puzzled expression. Where did he learn to do that? How was he able to spear through the chaotic cloud of my mind to pull me to the surface?

He seems to understand the question in my gaze. And this time, I am not annoyed that he knows what I'm thinking because I'm not sure I could voice the questions if I wanted to. This feels too personal. Too close to a part of myself that I don't want anyone to know.

"I had an old friend."

He trails off as if the next part of the memory of this friend is difficult to uncover—like a bone weaver painstakingly cleaning the tiny crevices of a vertebrae before it can be used to reignite the dead.

"I had an old friend. He… he did not have a good childhood, and it caused him to have breathing attacks not unlike what you just experienced. It was like the world didn't exist, and his body was fighting with his mind. I remember feeling so helpless the first time I saw it happen. After that, I swore I would help him. So I read every book I could find on illnesses, breathing practices, meditation, the bodily processes, you name it. It took a long time, but eventually we found a method that helped him."

"And that's what you did with me." It wasn't a question and instead comes out as a breathy exhale. I look away, embarrassed at the intimacy of this moment.

He's solemn as he responds, "Yes."

I stare down at my hands, unable to meet his eyes. "Your friend, does he still struggle with these attacks?"

He is silent. So silent. After many seconds pass, I assume he is done with the conversation, but then he breaks the silence.

In a heartbreakingly wry huff of air, he says, "Hah, no. No, he doesn't."

I look at him as his eyes glaze over with painful sorrow. He seems to feel my gaze and when he looks at me, there is a second where we both share in each other's fear and pain: his past grief, and my current anxiety. But before I can even process the fleeting moment, his eyes change, his mouth quirking up to the side as he says in a sardonic tone, "He got sick and there was nothing to be done. I've come to think, actually, that the people closest to me are destined to fall apart in one way or another. Maybe I'm cursed."

He's attempting to disarm the charged moment with another one of his crude jokes, but I see his pain—how the dark humor is the only thing holding him together. Because to feel the grief, pain, and unending sadness would mean facing a part of himself he doesn't want to touch. And that is something I can understand, so I play along.

"Well, I think I was cursed with these shadows before I met you, so you can't blame your curse on that at least."

He huffs a low breathe in surprise and quirks a brow at me, like he can't believe I didn't scold him for another poorly timed joke.

His smile is forced, as brittle as glass, as he responds, "You got me there I suppose, wildcat."

He takes one last look at me, scanning my body to assure himself that I really am recovered, pausing on my hands to make sure I am not tapping any longer. Once satisfied, he turns away and walks back to camp, gesturing for me to follow. The path the forest opened for me is still clear, but I don't know how long it will stay that way or how far I managed to run.

I know time is of the essence, but I don't make a move because I am still reeling from everything that just occurred. He doesn't rush me. He simply turns around and waits a few paces away, giving me the space to get to my feet without prying eyes but staying close in case I need help again. I stare at his broad back as I slowly get to my feet. All I can think about is how it felt to be in his arms and how safe it felt to be there. He brought me back from the brink of my panic—something no one but Kel has been able to do. I brush the dirt from my legs and walk to stand next to him.

I look up at his face, but he doesn't return my gaze—only staring straight ahead, a muscle ticking in his jaw and a stiffness in his shoulders that is not familiar. I place a gentle hand on his lower back, and hope the touch is reassuring. He may not be ready to talk about it now, but perhaps he will tell me one day.

A GLIMPSE OF SUN

FALDORN

"I see light ahead."

"Actual light or more of this mushroom glowing nonsense?" Sebastian says morosely from the back of the group.

I turn to survey them all, but besides Sebastian, the others don't react much to my news of light. It has been several long weeks since we entered this forest and it is showing—even the horses and Thelas' antelope are showing signs of weariness, with drooping heads and plodding steps. The near constant darkness makes it difficult to count the days, so it's possible we could have been gone far longer than a few weeks. Without the sun as an indicator, it's hard to say. Willow has been attempting to find a way to better account for our time in this forest by surveying plants and communing with the trees, but so far has had little luck. So, we travel as far as we can and rest when we can't go any further—repeating the cycle for the next 'day'.

I fear the mortals are at their limit for what they can handle physically, not to mention the mental strain the darkness of the forest can have. Laira, Thelas, and I can at least see well, but Willow and Sebastian have had to rely more heavily on the rest of us—their eyesight not as primed for the dusky light in this forest. They are also clearly suffering from lack of sleep and the constant paranoia that comes with traveling through a strange and dangerous place. Sebastian even looks a little worse for wear, though he tries to hide it with his sarcasm and bravado. Unfortunately, even he can't hide dark circles under the eyes or darting glances into the woods.

Hopefully this light ahead is something good. They could sorely use it.

"We shall be upon it soon, and then your mortal senses will catch up."

"I wait with bated breath," Sebastian replies dryly.

We come upon a large circular field set curiously in the middle of the dense forest. Unlike the clearing with the old woman's home, the sky is clearly visible here—shining a brilliant cobalt in the afternoon light. I crane my neck to see the tops of the trees and realize that I can finally see them. They are incredibly tall and reach far higher than even I thought possible. No wonder the forest is so dark with a dense upper canopy like that.

S'alorr sniffs the ground, but I pull him away before he can investigate further—we do not need a repeat of the last strange meadow we came across.

Looking at the witch, I signal her with a hand that she should use her skills and determine if this meadow is safe. Despite her exhaustion, she leaps from her mount and barrels toward the meadow and the first cluster of flowers and grass. The field is awash in many varied colors, and the way they sway in the breeze brings to mind an undulating rainbow.

I breathe in deeply. This space feels much more alive than what we have traveled through so far. Behind us is decay and slow-growing things, a fight for life and a constant quest for survival.

But this field is the opposite. Apart from ancient looking ruins set far on the other side, it teems with life and smells of fresh soil, and the sweet tang of a flower in perfect bloom. I open my senses and seek out any potential danger, but nothing piques my interest. And I know before Willow finishes her tests that this will be a refuge for us, though I wait for her approval before dismounting and setting S'alorr to roam. The others follow my lead, each of them dismounting and carefully removing their saddles before allowing their mounts to wander and nibble on the grasses.

Laira and Thelas wear similar expressions of awe, and I feel the muscles in my face contract in an involuntary smile.

Laira's voice is cautiously hopeful as she asks Willow directly, "It's safe this time, Lo?"

Willow beams, holding up flowers—roots and all—and a pair of small shears. "Yes! Nothing to worry about!"

At her friend's reassurance, Laira takes off in a run. I raise my eyebrows, watching in mild amusement as she throws her arms wide, hollering with reckless abandon, and throws her face to the sun with joy. She spins in a few circles, Kel twirling around her, before crashing to the ground on her back, giggling all the while.

The only ones who don't seem surprised by her outburst are Willow and Sebastian. At my bemused expression, Willow says offhandedly, "She likes sunlight. Thrives on it really—must've been awful these last weeks in near total darkness." She frowns before shrugging and returning to her dissection of her chosen petals. Willow gestures toward the ground in the middle of the field with her shears. "Hence the giggling."

A smile creeps onto her face at her words but is quickly replaced by a look of intense concentration as she focuses on her work. Tendrils of magic flow from her, and my own magic itches to respond—the long dormant power opening a single eye in interest. I can't control plants as she does, my abilities lie with creatures, but her joyous expression of her magic has stirred my own, and I've found myself missing that part of myself.

"Her favorite is the sun in the morning glowing through an open window. Says it feels like being bathed in honey," Sebastian says nonchalantly next to me, and I raise a curious brow. They must have gotten closer than I expected during our extended stay in Warille and our journey since then.

"And what about you? Going to follow her?" I prod.

Thelas' lopsided grin and disheveled hair pops into view as he leans around Sebastian. "It does look quite fun."

Thelas watches her for another moment before throwing off his bag and white coat, racing in Laira's direction, yelling, "Wait for me!"

Laira squeals as he gets close and kicks up loose dirt into her face, but they both dissolve into a fit of giggles and sink to the ground to stare up at the sky.

I nudge Sebastian with my shoulder, realizing for the first time that we are close to the same height, and nod toward the laughing and chatting pair.

"I'm perfectly fine right here," he says, his voice firm and confident, though his face tells a different story.

I huff out a small laugh. "Yes, I'm sure it's much better to stand on the edge with an old fae. Especially when compared with a comrade your age and might I say, a rather lovely young lass?"

A smile pulls on the corner of his face, and though he doesn't take his eyes from them, he also doesn't move to join. "It's better if I don't get involved." He frowns, looking over at me, and a pang of sympathy alights in my chest. I understand all too well the need to distance yourself from others.

Laira and Thelas peel with laughter, and the sound is so joyous that it almost brings to the surface a memory from long ago—of a warm summer night and a lazy evening spent in the company of family. I push it away, choosing to focus on the present lest I lose myself to the past once again.

"She does have a smile to rival the sun, doesn't she?" I say.

He's quiet for so long I make myself comfortable on a wide stump, retrieving my swords and beginning the lengthy process of cleaning and sharpening them.

"Yes, she does." His voice is soft and wistful, staring after them for a short beat before seemingly coming to a decision. He removes a coin from his pocket, flipping it into the air, and before it has time to return to his palm, his uncertainty is replaced by his usual cocky confidence—reminding me so much of myself at that age that I almost laugh.

Without another word, he walks out to the middle of the meadow.

RUINS & DEATH

LAIRA

After my initial bout of freedom as I basked in the lovely glow of the sun and the oddly comforting feeling of lying next to Thelas and Sebastian, we all went our separate ways to quietly explore. The ruins at the far end of the meadow caught my attention, and I heard the others not far behind me. Stepping through a crumbling doorway, I marvel at the carved lines and swirls cut into the stone. Though green moss covers most of the surface and the carvings have faded with time, I can still see the skill that went into creating them. I run a hand over a low wall, certain this place was once well-loved and cared for.

The glade grows quiet as I pull my hand away and brush against a strange clump of brown goop, and as I do, a spray of dark liquid splatters onto my face, with some going into my mouth. I swipe my hand across my face and spit out the disgusting substance on reflex, but it sticks to me like glue and I can feel it inside my mouth like a coating of paint over a wall.

A sudden dread builds deep in my stomach, warning me that something is wrong, but nothing appears out of the ordinary besides the disconcerting feeling of the strange substance on my face. On closer examination of the hand I used to wipe my face, I see that the substance is thick like oil and dark as ink.

That would explain the way it sticks to the inside of my mouth.

"I'll just need to wash it out and then get Willow to make sure it's not toxic," I say to myself, feeling more at ease with the plan spoken aloud.

Turning in the direction of our makeshift camp, I pause at an odd silence that permeates the meadow. The ruins sit like silent broken sentinels in the sunlit meadow, almost peaceful in their watchful silence, but I suppose that is to be expected of long-lost ruins. I reach out my senses to determine the reason for my growing alarm, and that's when I realize the source of my disquiet—not just the all-consuming silence, but also the fact that I am alone. How could I be alone? I stepped away from the others for just a moment to touch the broken stones, and they were well within eyesight before I did so.

My voice sounds loud and reverberates off the walls as I shout for the others. "Willow?" I strain my ears, listening for any sound, any movement at all that would indicate where she is.

"Thelas?" Nothing. Not even a twig snapping underfoot.

"Faldorn?" I call out, desperation twisting my voice each time I don't hear an answer.

I'm hesitant to call for the thief, but I do anyway, the sound of his name strange on my lips. "Sebastian?"

Silence.

I walk forward a few steps, the air heavy like I'm walking through soup, and I gape at the horrifying realization that I am the only creature making sound at all. A strange-looking bird with bright blue tufts of fur at the end of its long tail and sharp black eyes stares at me intently before flapping its wings and disappearing into the forest. Even with my limited fae heritage and abilities, I should at least be able to hear its flight from this distance.

Something very strange is going on here. Though I suppose this entire forest is one odd encounter after another. What with the towering deer-like creature Faldorn conversed with and saved, the tiny mouse-like beings constantly stealing our stuff, and the abundance of eyes that seem to follow us everywhere—this forest is feeling more and more mystical by the day. The creatures here aren't bad, just… different. Strange in a way that I've never encountered before and more intelligent than I initially believed was possible outside of the nyradonn.

The silence is unnerving, especially after the constant chatter of the last few weeks. With everyone finally feeling a little more comfortable with each other, it's felt downright jovial. I sweep my eyes back and forth, combing the meadow for traces of anyone. The others can't be far. I don't care what magic is going on here, there is no way they are just *gone*. It has to be an illusion of some sort, or they simply went back into the forest and I didn't notice.

I settle down next to a short, dilapidated section of what was once a wall and survey the surrounding ruins. "I'll just sit here and wait for them."

My voice once again sounds far too loud for the space, and the needling in my chest increases despite my best efforts to quell it and stay calm. It's then that I notice a presence next to me—not a physical one but a weight to the air that feels as if something I can't see occupies the space beside me. I feel the presence sit down against the ruins, and a slight warmth emanates from the shifting air next to my shoulder. Is some sort of ghost or spirit sitting next to me right now? Like whatever Faldorn talked to that night we first met him? I'm still unsure of what exactly that was—nor could I hear much of what was said—but I'm almost certain he was talking to someone important. Faldorn seemed surprised by its arrival, so perhaps this is a rare phenomenon?

"Hello?"

The spirit stills at the sound of my voice. *So, it can hear me.*

It doesn't reply, but I sense it get up and race away from the ruins. I make a move to follow, stumbling after it and leaving the ruins behind.

My vision goes black, and I almost fall into a panic, collapsing to the ground and ceasing my fruitless chase until my vision returns almost as quickly as it left. I open my eyes to find I'm not at the edge of the pleasant meadow full of crumbling ruins—instead a golden throne sits in front of me. It gleams brightly from the many windows in the space that shower it with warm sunlight. I gape at the throne's intricate details, and I catch a glimpse of trees, a long serpentine dragon, and a sword before my eyes snag on the rest of the room. I tilt my head back to look in fascination at the carved ceilings and arched beams shining just as brilliantly as the throne itself.

A door behind me opens with a loud *bang*, and I jump, startled at the sudden sound after the quiet of the meadow. *The meadow.*

"Where in the stars am I?" I say aloud, the sound echoing through the throne room.

Three people barge into the throne room, led by an incredibly large white bear, and make their way to the center. I freeze for a moment, expecting them to say something to me or demand I explain my presence, but they all look at something behind me. They stop just in front of me, fanning out around the bear and gripping various weapons. The bear roars, and I let out an involuntary squeak before running to the side of the throne room. I grip the wall, breathing heavily and try my best not to panic.

Nothing happens, but they rest their hands over weapons anyway and the bear sniffs the air in anticipation. A witch with a gold staff and bright red hair takes another step forward, her gait slow and controlled, but brimming with superiority. Her face is twisted in a malicious smile—disturbing what would have been a pretty face, with green eyes and freckles scattered across her rosy cheeks. I don't get much time to survey the others in the group when a gravely voice echoes from behind the gilded throne, sounding extremely annoyed.

"She's not here. Take your companions and leave. You know she does not take well to displays of aggression such as this."

A man appears from a hidden compartment, undoubtedly the source of the voice, and stomps down the stairs from the throne to meet the intruding party on the floor of the room. He appears human, his black hair disheveled as if he just woke up—his relaxed posture is in sharp contrast to his biting words. He's incredibly handsome, with thick brows, dark brown angular eyes, and just the smallest hint of stubble across his strong jaw. He has the bearing of a fighter, and the confidence of knowing he is familiar with his surroundings and these intruders.

What did I walk into?

The red-haired witch steps forward, her large overly-jeweled gold staff catching the light and ricocheting it across the throne room.

"Kairelo." She purrs the name. "Always a pleasure to see you."

Her silky-smooth voice and swaying hips give me the impression that these two have some history. Though from the sour look on the man's face, it seems like it didn't end well, whatever it was.

The man's voice is like ice as he bites out, "Dalia. I wish I could say the same." He surveys the group, pausing on each of them. "Since when do you bother to travel to our *humble* forest?"

He says "humble" like it's the start of some secret joke—and it appears that it hits home because the intruders scowl. Even the bear somehow sneers, its lips pulling back to expose wicked sharp teeth. It growls, and the witch steps forward, lightly placing a hand on the bear's haunches as she does. Her eyes glint with malicious fire—the pure murderous intent enough to make me freeze in an attempt to avoid her wrath, though it's clear no one here can see or sense me. Perhaps I fell asleep, and this is some lucid dream?

Dalia answers the man in a voice dripping with hatred. "Since your bonded created that wretched weapon and nearly all of Ilphemoura was destroyed in the process."

In a blink, Kairelo is in front of the witch—they are nose to nose and she falters a moment, backing up a step before seemingly catching herself and puffing out her chest in irritation. She may put on a good show, but this witch is afraid of this man. *Interesting*.

He smirks, clearly pleased at his ability to startle the stoic witch, before his face morphs into a darkly serious expression. "You asked her—no, begged her to make that weapon for you. For your cursed war." He waves a hand toward the entire group. "But it appears as if alliances have been made if you're all willing to stand in the same room as each other to confront her."

With no warning, Dalia thrusts out a hand and dark green tendrils of magic snake out, roots burst through the white stone floor and spear straight through Kairelo.

Dalia moves forward to whisper in Kairelo's ear as he's held aloft by the roots, "Oh, my dear, you mistake us. We are not here for *her*. We are here for *you*."

The surprise on his face appears for only a moment before his eyes scrunch together, and a groan of pain escapes his lips. The roots recede and he falls to the floor, barely managing to catch himself enough to stop his head from hitting the ground. The white bear suddenly shifts into a broad-chested man—everything about him the same shiny hue as his fur. Crystal blue eyes look on with malice under white brows and lashes, locking on Kairelo's writhing form. Sharp canine teeth glitter as a pleased smile crosses his face that is at odds with the cold look in his gaze, and a chill runs down my spine at the sight. This is the sort of man—of shifter—that I would avoid at all costs. The hard lines of his face and the satisfied way he unsheathes his claws tells me he enjoys the prospect of violence. Revels in it.

A fae with light brown antlers and shining purple and blue wings is the only one who appears apprehensive, and through Kairelo's agony he must see it too because he grits out to the fae, "And you? She trusts you with her *life*."

Dalia answers for the fae, staring daggers at Kairelo. "They saw reason and were able to accept the facts of the matter and the danger. They have no loyalty to you or her any longer."

The fae's brown deer-like eyes are filled with unshed tears and they trip over their delicate hooves as they approach, something uncharacteristic of the normal light and graceful nature of the fae. Wringing their hands together and taking another small step forward, the fae says, "Perhaps we should reconsider."

They speak to Dalia, but their eyes roam to Kairelo, a sort of sorrow and apology in their eyes that is impossible to miss.

"It is too late to reconsider." Dalia's eyes sharpen, and the fae deflates before taking their place on the other side. The witch flips her long hair behind her shoulder and smiles pleasantly as the four surround Kairelo in unison.

I realize they represent the four different races of Ilphemoura—fae, witch, shifter, and human. The human has so far been the only one to not show much emotion to the entire ordeal. He's older, perhaps in his mid-forties, and sports a light auburn beard that appears to cover a multitude of scars scattered across his face. He watches Kairelo carefully, the same way he watches his apparent comrade—a sort of strategic calculation in them that makes me think he isn't completely sold on what they're doing, but is willing to follow for now. A large cat-like nyradonn

keeps close to the man, and appears to aid the entire group by keeping watch on the windows and only doorway. It prowls in a protective circle around them, its claws and low growl echoing off the high ceiling and making my hair stand on end.

This was well thought out. A careful plan to corner this man when the throne was empty and he was alone. I'm not sure what this Kairelo did to deserve their ire, but it must be severe for these apparent warring factions to work together. They fear something, or someone, otherwise they wouldn't need the protection of a nyradonn or each other, and they wouldn't be eyeing the windows and the door even as they begin a strange ritual. They chant in a language that I don't recognize, and Kairelo bellows in agony. *What are they doing to him?*

This is likely just another awful nightmare triggered by the strange magic of the forest and the darkness slinking around in my mind, but it feels so *real.* And I have the overwhelming urge to help the man. His cries of pain crack me in two, and I feel a deep chasm of agony open in my chest. The sudden pain causes me to shudder as I continue to watch the horrid scene unfold. I'm utterly helpless in the face of what is going on. Dream or not, I doubt I could move if I wanted to. It's as if I'm frozen through some mix of fear, anxiety, and a distant echo of the pain he's experiencing.

Hundreds, if not thousands, of red strands curl and twist from his prone body. They are beautiful and delicate. Each with varying degrees of brightness and thickness. One thread stands out in particular even from where I sit in morbid fascination across the room. It's the deepest red I've ever seen, and it's braided into a thick cord. It looks utterly unbreakable. I marvel at the bond this man must share with someone to have such a strong thread.

The woven strand is suddenly yanked harshly from his body, causing another painful shudder to wrack him. The witch snatches it from the air before it can snap back into his body, and my jaw drops at her action. She can see the strands too? And she was able to grab it? I look down at my own hands as if imagining a red strand in my grasp. I shudder. It may be possible, but it feels absolutely and completely wrong. A shout of pain draws my attention back to the scene unfolding in front of me, and a new wave of dread follows.

The churning in my gut nearly makes me double over, sick to my stomach, as

I watch her wrap the woven strand around her hand to hold it firmly in place. I can feel the utter *wrongness* of it—of forcing the thread to bend to her will and keep it still. My vision becomes hazy as the group continues to chant; it feels as if the world is tilting and crumbling at the same time, like whatever is about to happen next will alter the fabric of the entire realm.

The growing cacophony grates against my ears like metal against metal. A heaviness permeates the air, and it's all I can do to intake each haggard breath. The heavy energy rolling from the scene keeps me firmly in place, and I don't try to fight it since I'm too busy trying not to pass out from the force of it all. The glow from the writhing thread becomes almost blinding—its energy bleeding onto the floor in wisps of crimson, and I nearly weep at the sight. To do this to a thread, to force it in such a way and command it as she is—it's *wrong*. A manipulation such as this goes against the bounds of nature, and I don't want to look as I realize what they intend to do.

But I can't tear my eyes away.

Hot tears slide down my face, and I cry out, unable to stop myself as I push myself roughly to my feet and try to charge forward to stop the ritual. My arms fling uselessly through the gruesome scene, as if they are simply made of smoke. I can do nothing but watch in horror as they conclude their chanting and the witch squeezes the thread clutched in her hand until it disintegrates before my very eyes. The shifter pulls a heavy sword from his back and stabs Kairelo through the chest without hesitation, and I almost vomit at the sight of the blood that pools beneath his body.

I sink to the floor. My entire body numb—the aching sorrow not unlike what I've felt after my previous nightmares. Like a soul deep grief that I will never wake up from—that the realm will never recover from.

That's when the screaming starts.

It shatters the windows of the throne room in a thundering wave. The glass scattering down on us, passing harmlessly through me, but cutting the four upright members of the group as well as the still body of Kairelo on the floor. Blood quickly spreads even further across the floor, and the shifter returns to

his white bear form, roaring and turning to run. The fae points their slender limbs toward the far wall and mutters an incantation, causing a portal to open with a view of a tranquil city street beyond. They race for the portal, but the ground shudders and cracks, causing them all to lose their footing. The shifter grabs the human by the back of his shirt and drags him through the portal while the witch and fae struggle to rise to their feet.

The human yells from the other side, "Run!"

Inky black tendrils filter through the broken windows, cascading down the walls and pooling on the floor. They yank angrily at the witch and fae, attempting to restrain them. The witch flings a hand out and roots explode next to her, giving her just enough time to race forward through the portal before the darkness can pull her under. The fae is not so lucky. The dark mist travels up their body and fastens tightly to the antlers protruding from their scalp. It binds their iridescent wings and pulls the fae down to the floor. The fae lands with a *thud* onto its knees and looks around in fear. The shifter, human, and witch disappear from view as the portal closes, and I see the hopeful light leave the fae's large eyes when it realizes their chance for escape is gone, and the screaming has stopped.

A figure appears in the mist, their hood pulled low and features indistinguishable. The figure approaches the fae slowly, like a cat enjoying a hunt, and stops just in front of where they're kneeling on the floor. The figure's back is to me as it tilts the fae's head up and says in a voice like liquid night, "That will be the last mistake you ever make, Tanene. Ilphemoura will *burn* for what you have done here today, and I will take great pleasure in hunting each of you down before I take my rage out on your people."

A brilliant sword suddenly appears in the figure's outstretched hand—like an answer to an unspoken call—and she slices it down upon the fae's sorrowful face without hesitation. Blood spatters the blade as a large cut is opened on their face. The blood obscures the warm glow emitting from the blade, making an eerie light shine instead.

The hooded figure points the sword at the fae again, shouting, "Go! Leave this place. Take this permanent reminder of what you have done to an innocent soul.

May it forever haunt you. For the friendship we once shared, I will permit you to leave here alive, but should I see you again I will not hesitate to cut you down."

The fae reaches a solemn hand to their face. Dark shimmering blood cascades down their tanned skin as they rise, bowing their head in pain and shuffling to leave the throne room.

The figure watches them leave, standing unmoving and waiting until the fae is out of sight to drop the sword, the loud clatter echoing through the large room. She falls in a heap over the still body of Kairelo, her sobs tearing into my already battered heart. I somehow make myself stand to walk over to the pair. Her pain pulls me in, and I can't help but reach out a hand to run it over the man's face, which is frozen in agony even in death.

I concentrate on him, attempting to catch even a glimpse of the red threads I expect to be there. Hoping that what I saw is not the truth, that whatever sick ritual was performed did not dissolve the threads.

But there's no trace of that bright woven strand—even in death there should still be traces of bonds left over from life, but he has nothing. As if every connection he ever made has been erased. Even that one particularly strong thread the witch held could not withstand the power of the magic performed. Something like this should be impossible. Never have I seen a bond destroyed in such a way—a slow fade because of time and a frayed relationship sure, but never truly gone.

His threads are gone. I shudder. How could this happen?

My body stills as I feel a heated gaze. I slowly glance up and catch a hint of red glowing eyes, the malice in them causing my body to run cold as ice, and I know that while no one else could see me, this person certainly can. Something deep inside me screams to be still, and I quaver at the bleeding crimson eyes ringed with gold, as if I'm caught in the gaze of a predator—my entire body preparing for flight. She reaches out a hand, and her bloody sword crashes into her waiting palm. The sword comes into my vision, too fast to stop, and I flinch in preparation of my head leaving my body when instead I'm grabbed roughly around the wrist by a large hand. The throne room dissolves before my eyes. The last thing I see

before descending into darkness is the two crimson eyes of the hooded figure and her sword slicing dully through the air.

Rough hands shake my shoulders, and a light tap on my cheek startles me from the darkness. "Laira! Come out of it!"

I blink. Faldorn kneels in front of me, a concerned and hurried expression on his face. "Are you back with me, Laira?"

I nod slowly, barely comprehending his words, before he races off. I tilt my head to follow his departure and realize the reason for his frenzied state—Sebastian, Thelas, and Willow are all sprawled across the ground. Each of them is speaking to the air, with Sebastian and Willow flailing their arms about as if they are fighting invisible adversaries. Faldorn rushes to Thelas first, his body unnaturally still as he screams over and over again. His voice must be ragged, yet he continues to cry out. I attempt to stand to offer what help I can, but whatever just happened to me has made my body weak and the best I can do is prop myself against the moss-covered stone wall and watch as Faldorn hauls Thelas upright and pours something in his mouth. I realize then that I have an awful taste in my mouth from whatever he must've poured into mine as well. Thelas flails about, but Faldorn holds him steady as he comes out of the trance he was in. I distantly hear Faldorn speaking to Thelas; I imagine he's asking him the same questions he posed to me, before jumping again to his feet and moving to Willow.

A sudden sickness overtakes me, and I throw up the contents in my stomach unceremoniously on a patch of ground next to me. The retching continues for far longer than I'd like and I know when Willow catches sight of me because she yells in despair, "No! Sto—you'll make me— ugh!"

I grimace. She likely would have thrown up just as I did because of whatever substance Faldorn poured down our throats, but she already has a weak stomach in the face of someone else evacuating theirs, so I'm sure it made it that much worse.

To block out the now very loud sound of my friends retching, I stand and search for Kel and Skip, wanting to make sure they were also not affected by whatever just happened. My eyes connect with the group of horses, Faldorn's elk, and Thelas' antelope back where we left our things before we foolishly let our guards down and assumed because the meadow was safe that these ruins would be too. Scanning the skies for Kel, I don't see him, and my heart drops, a sharp spike of fear zipping through my blood. But a light touch on my head and a brush of feathers against my skin immediately sets me at ease. Kel snags a few strands of hair as he flies just above me, the gentle touch a reminder that he is here and I shouldn't worry.

My precious Kel—always knowing when I need reassurance.

He takes to the skies again and perches on a large branch high above us with a full view of the meadow and ruins. I grin and shake my head in amusement. Always the watch dog, that funny little bird.

Turning back in the direction of the others, I see they have mostly recovered from the vomiting episode and sit in various states of misery.

What in the stars is going on right now?

By the time I'm starting to get a little more strength in my limbs, Faldorn has completed his task. Each of us stares blankly at each other as he slumps to the ground, clearly exhausted.

I sound groggy as I ask him, "What just happened?"

Faldorn runs a hand across his face and breathes out a long sigh. "*That*—was the work of magic."

"It was a spell?"

"A particular dangerous spell meant to keep others away and cause irreparable harm by making you experience nightmares and hallucinations. It's not often left on purpose; most of the time the spell is activated by accident when an extremely powerful individual experiences their own worst nightmare. The pain and horror of the event seeps into the ground and takes hold like a parasite infecting a host."

"But if that's true, how were you not affected?" I ask.

"I was. Only a bit, mind you, but enough that it took me a long time to realize what was happening and push through the madness that was attempting to sink its teeth into my mind. I've had hundreds of years to sit with my pain, so when confronted with it, it doesn't often break me."

We are all silent, carefully processing Faldorn's explanation.

My heart aches for him at the mention of him sitting alone with his suffering for so long that it no longer holds much of an effect on him.

Sebastian pipes up then. "But it broke us?"

Faldorn sighs heavily, "You are young and more susceptible to influences of strong magic than I am. But you are safe now, the concoction shocked your systems enough to pull you from the visions, and by knowing what has occurred, the spell should have no effect on you anymore." He brushes himself off, shifting to stand above us.

"That being said, we should move on. I don't like the idea of being so close to such powerful magic."

"Agreed," I say. "Let's find a new place to camp for the afternoon and evening. I think it best we rest for the remainder of the day and start fresh tomorrow."

Faldorn nods in agreement before walking away to begin packing up our supplies.

Thelas, Sebastian, Willow and I stare blankly at each other for a long moment, each of us lost in the awful visions we saw and sharing a collective understanding of what we just experienced. Willow gets up first, followed by Sebastian, but Thelas makes no move to rise, and I eye him with worry. His desperate screams echo in my mind, and I wonder again what he has experienced in his past while simultaneously being afraid of the answer.

I get to my feet and walk the few paces to stand in front of him. I don't say a word as I hold my hand out in support. Mechanically, he takes it, and I pull him to his feet, quickly letting him go but choosing to walk beside him back to where our mounts graze contentedly.

WE PACK UP swiftly and I stare a long time at the blue sky and flower covered meadow when we leave, as if committing it to memory. I'm not sure when the next time we will see the sun and sky, and despite the problem with the ruins, I am glad for the short respite. We travel for another few hours back in the darkness of the forest before finding a suitable spot for camp in a small clearing peppered with blue ferns. A stream ambles into the trees, and as the flowing water disappears into the dense trees, I find that I can follow its trajectory far in the distance because it glows with a brighter light than the ferns and mushrooms normally provide. The rest of the area is more or less the same, with small mushrooms and moss creating a blue-green glow just bright enough to see by and illuminate our immediate surroundings. It's still disconcerting not having the normal light of the sun, but I am growing more used to it the further we travel in this strange forest.

I throw my pack down and pull Skip's saddle from her back before tying her to a nearby tree branch, not giving her the opportunity to wander. A skittering sounds from the direction of my pack, and I half-heartedly roll my eyes at the quick appearance of the devious little creatures constantly following us around and stealing items from our supplies. I don't bother shooing them away as it wouldn't make a difference anyway, and since they don't usually steal things for long it's not worth the hassle. Even if they do take things permanently, they are almost always replaced by something of similar value. Such a trade was how we discovered certain plants that were safe for consumption in this forest—a fantastic discovery after only living off the dried rations we brought with us for weeks.

I settle down, using my bag as a backrest and the others follow my lead, each exhausted in their own right, and more than happy to put off creating a fire or setting up a proper camp for a while.

My mind drifts, and before I know it, my eyes are closed and I slip into a light sleep, still mostly cognizant of my surroundings, but also in that state in between sleep and full awareness. A sword flashes in my memory, and I stand upright in a rush, my eyes flying open and my breath leaving my chest in a *whoosh*, a single name falling from my lips as I recall the person from the nightmare the ruins showed me.

"Kairelo."

Faldorn is the only one to hear me. "What?"

I look to him, a sinking realization that causes my breathing to become erratic. I clutch my chest and nearly fall back when I feel a warm body and strong arms encircling me, holding me upright.

Sebastian's voice is strong and cuts through my growing anxiety as I piece together what I must've just seen—despite how impossible it is.

"What's going on, Laira?"

The others crowd around me, and I imagine I have a wild look in my eyes because they all look at me with alarm and concern. Willow reaches out a hand to squeeze my arm in reassurance. "Lair?" she prods carefully.

"Kairelo." I reach into the rectangular pack at my hip and pull the old worn brown book from it. I flip to the page containing the prophecy, pointing to the appearance of his name as I shout, "Kairelo!"

Sebastian comes to stand in front of me after assuring himself that I'm not about to fall over, joining them in giving me a puzzled look.

I sigh. I have a lot of explaining to do.

"Come on. Let's get camp going and a warm fire started, and I'll explain what I mean." I pause, my voice turning serious and faraway. "And what I saw in those ruins."

THE FLUTE

THELAS

The camp is silent as we all stare into the crackling fire in the middle of us. Its flames dance happily above the precise stacks of wood Faldorn created, providing more light than usual over the dark patch of dirt we found to rest in for the night. The trees wait in the shadows, and even though they have been easier to outsmart since leaving the witch's house, I'm certain they enjoy our game, and I'm not about to let my guard down any time soon. A root slithers in my direction, twisting back and forth above the ground before darting underground and disappearing from view as if hearing my thoughts.

The silence is heavy in the air, and for once, I find I'm actually bothered by it. Willow is usually the first to break any long bout of quiet, but instead she sits with her arms wrapped tightly around her knees, her chin propped on her hands. There's a faraway look in her eyes and a deep frown carved on her face. She's a joyful and seemingly carefree person, but I wonder sometimes what that bubbly persona could be protecting. Her magic hangs limply in the air—the strands now out in the open constantly and performing small bouts of magic with a simple flick of her wrist. Despite her despondent appearance, my eyes soften at her easy display of her magic, even if it appears as forlorn as she does.

Faldorn pokes at the fire, and a flurry of sparks floats into the air before dissipating. I catch Sebastian's stare from across the fire, but he quickly passes over me to focus on Laira at my side. Her posture is stiff next to mine, her hands absentmindedly twirling a glowing blue fern she plucked from the ground. She doesn't

seem to notice Sebastian's attention either, her eyes pinched and her face echoing an endless sorrow.

I think of the way she reached for me back in the ruins. How she didn't say a word and knew what I needed in that moment. The wretched clarity of my past had reminded me I was deluding myself into growing comfortable with everyone here, but she had offered a hand, cutting through that haze of doubt, and even if I wasn't certain, I took it anyway.

My flute weighs heavily in my pocket despite its small size. I haven't played it since before we left on this wild journey, and the loss of its beautiful sound echoes in my mind. Sometimes it was the only pleasant thing I heard all day when I was young, when my days were filled with dodging older siblings and my callous stepmother. I had found the silver flute while hiding; its metal was dented, and it was covered in so much grime I didn't know what it was at first. But I managed to fix it up and even carved designs into its surface—making it my own. I taught myself to play in the blessedly quiet hours when everyone was out of the house. Its sweet melody cascading over my aching limbs and soothing my frayed nerves.

Laira shifts next to me, and I ache to provide the same comfort she offered me earlier. I've never played my flute for anyone but myself, and a wave of fear startles me at the possibility of their rejection.

The monster deep in the back of my mind opens an eye and stretches lazily. His voice is a deep timber, and I shiver as he speaks.

"You need not hide everything, Thelas."

I scoff at him. I may not need to hide everything, but that doesn't mean I should tell them of my past or what I can do—about this monster living in my bones and speaking in my head. The fear of their rejection is enough to make me cower again inside my mind.

No, I definitely can't tell them, can't risk that they would be afraid of me. Not when I've begun to see them all as friends.

The beast huffs. ***"You can't push me away forever. We are one and the same."***

I growl at him. *"Do you not remember what happened the last time I let you out? Of the way Stepmother screamed and called for Father? How they caged us in a dark cell and beat us until I gave in and swore to never let you out again?"*

The beast shrinks in the back of my mind as I berate him—angry with him for not protecting me, but angrier with myself for being this way.

"You didn't protect me then, so why should I ever let you out? You let them do that to me – to us!" I silently scream at him.

I'm lost to the memories once again and I picture my father as he stands over me, a bloody whip in his hand. The anger in his eyes was penetrating but the fear was worse, and I know it was what ultimately drove him to his actions. My other form was hideous, and it was my fault that he was so horrifying to look upon. He wasn't some common creature, but a monster wreathed in darkness and vicious claws—a horrific nightmare made flesh.

The beast steps forward hesitantly, a heavy sorrow in his yellow eyes. ***"I know I couldn't protect you and I'm sorry. But look around at them and tell me this—do you truly believe they would forsake you as your blood did?"***

I look at Faldorn, Sebastian, Willow, and Laira sitting around the flickering fire and ponder the question, shocked with myself that I am even listening to the creature. Faldorn likely has some inkling of what I really am based on his questioning before I found the entrance to the forest and didn't seem perturbed by it—*though he never actually saw the beast,* I think to myself dryly. Willow clearly has some demons of her own, and I doubt she would bat an eye at a terrifying creature standing before her. Sebastian is sarcastic and unserious most of the time, but I've caught glimpses of his true character, and I can't picture him turning away from me either.

My eyes snag on Laira beside me. She has witnessed horrible things in her nightmares, of that I have no doubt, but she is still so kind and thoughtful.

I blink away tears and shift my attention back to the beast. *"You're right, I don't think they would."* I inhale a shaky breath, and Laira notices enough to place a gentle hand on my shoulder in support, even as she's lost to her own thoughts. *"But that doesn't mean that I'm ready."*

The beast nods, still sad but understanding. ***"I will wait for you when you are ready."***

A NEW PIECE TO THE PUZZLE

LAIRA

"Can you tell us now what you were talking about earlier?" Willow asks, glancing at Thelas and Sebastian. "The rest of us seemed to experience painful past memories. What did you see that has to do with the prophecy?"

Sebastian's voice is surprisingly sharp as he cuts a look at Willow. "She doesn't have to explain more than is necessary."

He looks at me then, a soft and equally haunted look in his eyes. "You don't have to go into detail, if it connects to the prophecy somehow then just the basics are fine. I'm sure what you saw was intense if it was anything like what I saw." He looks away at his last words, noticeable pain in his features.

A strange warmth blooms in my chest at his defense of me, though it's unnecessary. I have no problem telling them every detail of what I saw. But my heart aches for the haunted looks on each of their faces. What I witnessed was awful, but if I'm right, it was long in the past and a vital piece of Ilphemoura's history, not memories of my own.

I give them both a soft, if somewhat strained, smile.

"It's okay. We should talk about what I saw, and I don't mind sharing the details, as I believe it will be necessary information for all of us to know." Absentmindedly running a finger over the worn cover of the prophecy book, I continue, "I get the feeling it's tied to the prophecy based on the name I heard in the vision… if all of this is indeed real and not just a figment of my imagination."

Sebastian sits up, eyeing me intensely. "Do you believe it was just your imagination?"

I search through my memory of the vision, of the way I felt, what I heard, and how those intimidating eyes stared right through me before I was yanked out of it by Faldorn.

A certainty settles in my bones, and my voice sounds as sure as I've ever heard it as I tell him, "No. It wasn't."

He throws both hands behind his head and leans back on his pack, a crooked grin on his face. "Well then, that's good enough for me."

His sudden relaxed demeanor would be a shock if I didn't know him better. And I'm surprised that I do, in fact, know him better. The time spent traveling together outside this cursed forest as well as inside it have taught me one thing about Sebastian: his carefree attitude is a carefully crafted illusion. Perhaps I'll push back on it one day and see what really lies underneath that sarcastic exterior—if nothing but to annoy him at my ability to see right through him. But now is not the time for such revelations or bonding.

I start my story by telling them of the immaculate golden hall I found myself in, of the throne carved with intricate details, and the handsome human man who appeared to confront the intruders. Willow inhales sharply when I explain the threads I saw coming from him, and Thelas gapes at me in horror as I describe the way the witch snatched the strongest of the threads and somehow dissolved it before my eyes. Sebastian's eyes darken as I tell them of the awful feeling of helplessness I experienced and how I knew what was happening was irreparably *wrong*. Faldorn is thoughtful when I finish, asking only a few clarifying questions about what the fae looked like, a faint spark of recognition lighting his eyes before he looks away.

Willow sets a comforting hand on mine. "Oh Laira, I'm so sorry you experienced that. And I believe you, that doesn't sound like simply a nightmare at all, and the fact that the man's name was Kairelo... what do you think it means?"

I shrug as Kel rubs against my hand as well, offering his support and attempting to lift the heaviness from me at having to share the memory.

I reach behind me to grab the prophecy book and pass it to Willow, who shows it to the others. "His name is mentioned in the prophecy. I almost forgot because it's been weeks since I last read the words. But it's there."

Thelas' brows scrunch together. "So, he must have something to do with this then." He points to the book, "And this, 'a single death served as punishment, by the name of Kairelo'." He looks at me in shock and the others do the same as the realization hits them too. "You *saw* this part of the prophecy. It's something that actually happened."

I nod, having come to the same daunting conclusion.

"But how long ago? It must have been a very long time, indeed, for I have no recollection of the magical weapon they spoke of," asks Faldorn.

"Not quite that old, huh?" Sebastian smirks from beside Faldorn, the former scoffing softly at the joke.

"No, I am not. There are fae far older than I. In fact, there is one fae who may know something—one of the oldest among us all and a revered elder. I'm certain they must know something..." he folds his arms across his broad chest, taking a deep breath and hesitating before speaking his next words, as if he isn't certain he should share them. "Especially since your description of the fae from your vision is far too similar to that of this elder."

I perk up at that. "Really?"

He's quick to contradict himself. "It's possible I am incorrect, there are many fae with similar features such as the ones you described. Without a name, I can't be sure."

"Tanene," I say abruptly, the name the hooded figure spoke suddenly coming to mind.

Faldorn's widen in surprise, his mouth hanging slightly open. It's the most shocked I've ever seen the fae, and if it weren't such a serious moment, I might have chuckled at the sight.

"I take it that is the fae you are talking about?" I question carefully.

He nods. "Yes. It is. Tanene..." His voice drifts off and his eyes look faraway. I want to ask him more, but I also don't want to push. He comes back to himself, saying, "There are those who I could ask to help me locate Tanene. They are a traveling fae, and difficult to pin down. But it would take time and I'm unsure where I will be after we find the sword…"

He trails off and my shoulders slump at his meaning. That he is not planning to continue being with us once we have the sword and this journey is complete. My heart falls at the prospect of him leaving, but I can't force him to stay.

My head nods in understanding and he gives me a sad smile. Silence permeates the group and my mind drifts from my sadness at Faldorn leaving eventually, to the possibility of this new connection. What if this fae is truly the one from my vision? Could they help us? Or give us more information on the prophecy? I hazard a quick glance at the others and find they are as lost in thought as I am; I have no doubt they are pondering the same questions.

I don't tell them about the figure that arrived at the end that terrified the intruders so much they were stumbling past each other to flee, or of how she screamed when she held Kairelo's limp form. Something about the scene felt too familiar and vulnerable for me to voice aloud. I decide I need to sit with the odd familiarity awhile longer and what I think it means before bringing it to the group.

Willow blows out a breath, shifting strands of hair that fall into her eyes. "By the stars, was that heavy! Anyone have any liquor?"

I laugh despite myself. She knows exactly what's in each of our packs since we pooled our resources long ago, and there certainly is no alcohol.

Thelas surprises me by reaching into his pocket and retrieving two small cylindrical objects, which he slots together to create a long silver flute. It shines in the blue-tinted light from the mosses that climb high up the trees, and I can see swirls and shapes etched into the metal.

"No liquor. But what about some music?"

Sebastian slaps Thelas' shoulder, grinning. "You can play? Why didn't you say so?"

Thelas doesn't reply to Sebastian, posing a question to Faldorn instead, "This is a relatively safe spot, right?"

Faldorn nods. "I sense no immediate danger."

Thelas' smile is bright, and his eyes crinkle in the corners as his blue eyes sparkle. "Then, we should be able to relax for a few hours and enjoy a song or two?"

Faldorn nods again, and Thelas brings the instrument to his lips. The sound that follows is a bright and clear melody that sings of warm summer days and dancing under moonlight. I laugh in delight at the glorious sound and close my eyes to feel the music wrap around me in a warm embrace. My feet tap, and I play an invisible instrument with my fingers as he continues the song. A tender feeling fills my chest as I realize I'm tapping not because I need to calm myself, but because of this buoyant feeling in my body that wants to get out any way it can.

Sebastian taps Thelas on the shoulder at the end of his song, indicating that he would like to try, and Thelas hands it over. I'm intrigued to see what Sebastian means to do with it—surely he can't play as well as Thelas too?

My mouth falls open as he brings the small flute to his lips. He catches my eye and winks as he produces a jaunty tune that speaks less of innocent fun like what Thelas had played and more of a salacious dance in a tavern. I'm pretty sure the song is actually a barmaid's saucy tale, but I find that I don't care and push myself from the log I'm sitting on to dance in the open space around the fire.

Tiny creatures descend from the upper canopy and float around us. They light up the relative darkness and buzz around our heads in quick patterns. I hold out my hand to one, and it flies around me, pulsing with light and intertwining through strands of my hair before zooming into the dense canopy far above. I giggle in wonder at the little creatures. They seem to be drawn to the joyous atmosphere and bob to the song Thelas and Sebastian weave into the night. I twirl with them, Willow joining me soon after, and before we know it, we are spinning each other around and laughing. Faldorn even joins in, his movements somewhat stiff as he moves more like he would in a fight than a careless dance in the woods, but it is just so Faldorn that I only smile wider.

THE POOL

LAIRA

The evening passes, and soon we are all exhausted from our frolicking and singing. I haven't been this wonderfully tired since Sebastian and I danced back in Warille. My exhaustion these days is tied to our relentless hike through the forest and sleepless nights battling hard dirt and nightmares alike. We needed this pleasant distraction, especially after the ruins.

I collapse against a nearby downed log, it's rough surface dotted with tiny glowing mushrooms that blink at me with mismatched eyes, and sigh contentedly—maybe I'll actually get some decent sleep tonight if I'm this tired and happy.

Faldorn's voice sounds across the fire. "I've located a safe source of water nearby. We should refill our canteens and take turns bathing while we can."

Willow practically squeals as she digs through her packs, pulling out soaps and combs and hopping in place as she waits for Faldorn to show her where the water is. He shakes his head, exasperated, but smiles anyway and gestures for her to follow.

I giggle after them. "Well, then I suppose Willow goes first and the rest of us can go next."

My grin falters when my eyes land on Sebastian, his expression intense enough to make me inhale softly. His eyes are pools of mossy green, and he peers at me through strands of his dark shoulder-length hair as he leans his arms forward to rest on his thighs. I stare transfixed at his unexpected expression—a heat is in his gaze as if he wishes to devour me.

I shiver.

No devouring will be happening on this trip. I avert my

gaze from his, but the feeling of being watched does not cease.

I can hear the smile in Sebastian's voice as he asks, "Rest of us? Does that mean we all go bathe at the same time? I didn't know you had such sinful thoughts, wildcat."

My cheeks grow warm, and I have no doubt they are as red as a perfect apple right about now. "I—that's not what I—"

I trip over my words, embarrassed, but Thelas saves me. "There's no way she meant it like that you bird brain—sorry Kel." He reaches over to pat Kel's skull before continuing, "Plus—ew! Sorry Laira." He pats my head as well.

"Hey!"

He shrugs. "Sorry, it's the truth. I have no interest in bathing with either of you."

I slap a hand to my forehead. "That's not—ugh! You know what? It doesn't matter."

Sebastian's dark chuckle flits across my skin, and I grit my teeth. "Something funny?"

His teeth gleam a bright white in the soft glow of the fire. "Just a little."

Faldorn returns, and we all sit in silence as we wait for Willow to return as well. She takes her sweet time, though I suppose I can't begrudge her the opportunity to finally bathe after so many weeks traveling through this forest—I will most certainly do the same.

When she does finally show, her hair hangs wet down her back, and she wears the same dirty clothes as before, but she smiles as if she is wearing the finest gown.

"Must be a good bathing pool," I tease.

"Oh, it's fantastic! Here—" She shoves her soaps into my hands, and I grab them before they can fall into the dirt. "I'll show you where it is!"

I stand to follow her, but Sebastian does the same. "Oh no you don't! You will not be coming with me."

He holds up his hands in surrender, a smirk curving on his face. "I was only going to offer to take everyone's canteens to the connected stream Faldorn mentioned."

I narrow my eyes at him, immediately suspicious but have an unwelcome thrill run down my spine at the challenge he is throwing down: just how close will I allow him to get to me while I'm in the water and completely naked?

The right answer, of course, is absolutely nowhere close, but my traitorous heart thunders at the prospect of his dark eyes watching me. The possibility of having an audience sends a shiver down my arms, and I clutch the soaps closer to my chest.

I eye him up and down, my internal debate raging between what I should do and what my body is screaming at me to do.

"Fine. Mine's in my pack. I'm sure Faldorn can show you the stream."

His eyes are triumphant, and I nearly gasp at the heat that simmers in them. A heavy anticipation falls between us that dissolves only when I turn to continue following Willow to the pool.

She raises an eyebrow at me, a knowing smile on her lips.

"Don't. You. Dare." I say before she can release the teasing remark I know she has building.

She lets out a snort of laughter. "I wasn't going to say a damn thing."

I huff a disbelieving breath. "Let's just get moving."

Her eyes shine as she gestures me forward. "But of course."

We come upon the small pool after a short walk through the trees, familiar mushrooms and tiny curled ferns illuminating the way, and I nearly drop everything I'm holding when I get a good look at it. Large boulders curve around the pool, blocking it partially from view, and a slow stream trickles from it and disappears off into the trees. The water is clear and perfectly still with a blue tint that is so vibrant I almost imagine it as one of the magical potions in Willow's pack. I can see to the bottom of the pool and spot small fish and smooth stone.

"It's not very deep, but there is a section toward the back where I had to swim because I couldn't reach the bottom," Willow advises beside me.

"Yeah, well, you are pretty short."

She snorts. "Yes, yes. I think even you will not be able to touch the bottom though."

She turns to leave, throwing a hand over her head and calling out, "Have fun!"

Alone, I set down the soaps and combs in a careful line as I keep my senses open. I may not have openly refused Sebastian's secret offer, but that doesn't mean I want him to suddenly appear before I have a chance to get in the water. I eye the pool. It's considerably clearer than I expected it to be, so my plan to hide most of my body in the water is not going to work.

Maybe this was a bad idea… I groan internally.

No.

I have nothing to hide. And what is so wrong with feeling desired?

I strip down, peeling off my various travel layers until my skin is bared to the dim light. I shiver as a cool breeze drifts across my skin, and I use the time alone to survey my body, checking for scrapes, bruises, and to see just how filthy I've become from spending constant nights in the dirt and trekking through the forest.

Satisfied nothing is going to sting or ache when I step into the water, I test the pool's temperature with a toe and release a moan of pleasure as I notice it's not cold like I expected, but blessedly warm like a normal bath. I slide into the water, bracing my arms on one of the boulders until I get accustomed to the smooth stone on the bottom. Grabbing a random soap bar from the edge, I start lathering the smooth bubbles over my skin. The purple and black veins under the skin of my hand have crept up my arm over the last couple of days, and they seem to inch closer to my shoulder every day. I frown at their presence, an icy feeling slicing through my gut at their twisted appearance while a hidden shadow curls in my mind as if enjoying my discomfort. It peers out of my eyes, observing where I am, and I have the sudden fear that it is going to spear out of me again, so I picture a rope connecting to it and tug as hard as I can. It seethes in anger but doesn't fight me, and curls back up in the far reaches of my mind. Dormant once again. Though I get the feeling it is still aware of my movements.

I angrily scrub the soap over my hands, cursing the darkness but it doesn't make me feel any better, nor does it leave. I blow out a breath, knowing there's nothing I can do about it right now and I should put my energy elsewhere. I look around the glittering pool of water and the dark trees surrounding it. It's all incredibly beautiful and I don't want this otherwise pleasant memory to be disturbed by the malicious darkness in my mind. Determined not to let it win this time, I push the shadows far away and continue washing myself in the water, my hands gliding over my plush hips and ass, my strong thighs and arms, before finishing with my soft middle. The muscles on my arms flex as I twist them, thoroughly scrubbing every inch of skin. I flex my thighs too, feeling pleased at the muscle I've built over the years training with Willow.

I've washed myself a thousand times before, but this feels different. It could be the fact that I am washing myself in the single most beautiful pool of water I've ever seen, in a magical forest no less, or it could be my ever-present awareness that Sebastian could show at any time and find me naked in the water. Even when we stayed in the same room in Warille, he never got close to seeing me without clothes. My thoughts drift, and I find myself imagining what his hands would feel like on me instead of my own. A silent thrill runs through me, and a secret smile plays at the edge of my mouth.

"Oh how I would love to know what thought is causing that particular smile." A silky smooth voice sounds from behind a boulder to my left, and I shriek as I cover my chest and turn to face Sebastian.

"Like I'd ever tell you." My face flushes, and my eyes drift down his body of their own accord, effectively giving me away.

His answering smirk makes my stomach flip as he says, "Oh, I think you just did."

I stare at him, determined to not be the first to look away. We blink at each other as this new pointless game ensues until I realize I have an advantage. My smile turns devilish as I remove my arms from my chest. By the way his eyes widen and his confident smile falters for just a second, I know I was correct in assuming the water was clear enough to show *everything*.

He breaks eye contact with me, shifting his body until his back is facing me, and I delight in the fact that I won this game.

"Wash up, wildcat. I'm next."

I roll my eyes, not bothering to answer him. I dunk my head under the water and continue to take my time relishing the feeling of being clean and the warm water as it cascades over my skin. My eyes flick to him every so often, but I'm determined to

not let his presence cause me to rush—after all, when will I be able to swim in a pool like this again?

Finally fully clean and hands pruny, I reluctantly leave the water and change into my clothes. I peek at Sebastian and find him still diligently facing away from me. A part of me is disappointed at his refusal to look at me, but another part is shy enough to hope he never turns around. I'm nearly finished pulling my loose shirt around my head and buttoning my brown pants when I feel a heavy warmth at my back. I inhale sharply as Sebastian reaches a hand to graze my shoulder. Even through the fabric I can feel his touch like a searing brand. A flood of want races through my system, and I have to use every rational thought in my head to stop myself from leaning into his touch.

"Did you enjoy winning our standoff earlier? I have to say, you caught me off guard when you dropped your arms and gave me a full view of yourself."

I flip around to face him, backing up a few steps until my back is flush with a nearby trunk. He follows after me, a deliciously dark glint in his eyes, and my blood heats in response, the feeling traveling down until it pools at my core.

"And what if I did?"

He stops in front of me, gazing down as he trails a lazy hand along my hip and onto my thigh, slowly caressing me while he pins me with a heated look. I nearly buckle when he drifts to the sensitive area on my inner thigh, and I have a momentary thought of, *higher*, before I banish it into the deep depths of my mind.

His mouth quirks up at the side. "Then I'd say that you are a wicked creature that enjoys driving me wild."

My voice sounds more seductive than I mean it to, the sound velvety smooth even to my own ears as I say, "I'm not trying to do anything. Perhaps it is your poor self-control that is the problem."

He digs a hand into the bark of the tree causing small pieces to fall on my shoulder as he grits out, "Oh, trust me. My self-control is well in hand, seeing as it's the one thing holding me back from devouring you now."

I shiver at his words, desperately fighting to maintain my own control and prove to myself, and to him, that he doesn't have the same effect on me.

But it's not working, and I feel myself slip as I push my body into his, inhaling deeply as I take in his scent. Moss and a musky spice invades my nostrils, and the scent is so pleasant that I almost decide to take up his offer and let him have me.

I steel my spine. *But he doesn't need to know that.*

I'm about to fire off a response when I inhale sharply instead, a delicious heat pooling in my belly and lower as he gets to his knees before me. He cups the back of my legs, staring up at me with such intense desire that it renders me speechless.

No one has ever looked at me with such fathomless *longing*.

He is so achingly beautiful in this moment. His black hair falling away from his face as he looks up at me to reveal darkly playful green eyes, sensuous lips tilted in a smirk, and piercings that bring a wildness to his features that is just so *Sebastian*.

I ache to touch him and run my hands through his long hair, but I hold myself back, pinning him with a heated look instead and waiting for what he'll do next.

MOTH TO A FLAME

SEBASTIAN

I hold eye contact with her as I get down on my knees before her, sliding my hands down from where they rest on her waist to her ample hips. I feel her shudder under my touch, and the liquid fire in her gaze ignites my own desire into a blazing inferno. I want to do so many things with her—show her every way that I can satisfy her. I want to put my wicked mouth to use and pull that raging wildcat inside her to the surface.

"You're not at all affected by me?" I smirk, certain of my obvious effect on her, but crave the admission from her perfect lips.

She's breathless as she responds, "Nothing. I feel nothing."

I hum. "Not the answer I was hoping for, darling, but I suppose I can try a little harder."

She rolls her eyes. "How many nicknames do you plan on giving me?" she asks, a sly grin curving on her beautiful face.

I match her smile with one of my own. "As many as it takes."

She raises an inquisitive brow. "As many as it takes for what?"

"For you to admit you like them."

She scowls at me, her bottom lip puckering out and making me want to rise to my feet and capture it with my mouth. My eyes dart from her lips back to my hand on her hip; the fabric of her shirt lifting just enough that I can slip a thumb under it. I swipe my thumb across her side and the soft gasp that leaves her lips at the contact has me standing to my feet and pushing her against the tree before I can think.

I want to devour that sound. Taste it on her breath and caress her silky skin until she does it again. She places her hands on my arms, but doesn't push me away—instead, she grips me closer, the hungry look in her eyes nearly bringing me to my knees before her once more. Dropping my head to her neck, I breathe in deeply, lost in the way her scent envelops me and the way her body feels flush against mine. I hadn't been able to stop thinking of the last time we were this close when we were sparring and how I could feel every curve of her against me. It's haunted me ever since and I'm sure this encounter will be no different. Like a moth to a flame, I can't seem to stop reaching for her.

"Sebastian."

Her voice is breathy as I press a kiss to her neck, just above her collarbone and I hum at the sound—my name sounds so tantalizing on her lips.

I angle my head back slightly to look at her, swiping my thumb against her skin once more. My voice is teasing, seductive, as I ask, "Yes, Laira?"

She doesn't answer, but she does shiver as my entire hand finds its way under the fabric of her shirt and grips her waist tightly.

I smile. "Do you want me to stop?"

Indecision wars on her face, and I immediately still, readying myself to pull away when she stands a little straighter, a clear decision in her bright eyes, and gives me a hungry look.

"No. I don't."

A slow smile spreads across her face, and she leans closer, shifting her hands from my arms to my chest and it's my turn to inhale sharply at the contact. Her lips stop a hair's breadth from mine and the forest falls silent as she whispers, "Kiss me, Sebastian."

We crash together, a tangle of lips and breath, a roiling tempest of desire that devours us both. The entire world could be falling apart, and I wouldn't know—I'm lost in her and the heavenly way she tastes, even better than what I thought possible. The kiss is passionate and frenzied; born from withholding desire and finally giving in—a product of the dance we've played this whole time. My hands drift from her sides to caress her face and the hum of pleasure that she

emits makes me smile into her kiss. She is the brightest star in a dark sky, a sip of water after a long drought, and the answer to a song I heard long ago but had forgotten. An intoxicating sensation that I fear I will never get enough of.

Our kiss slows and she pulls away. I swipe a thumb across her jaw, the gesture tender and find my own emotions feel the same. She's opened something inside me—broken through a wall and claimed the ragged interior as her own. Every stolen look, familiar conversation, and brief touch have captivated me, and I've found it harder and harder to pretend I don't feel more than simple attraction. Her eyes widen with something like alarm as she takes in the vulnerable change in my expression, and I drop my arms to give her the space she needs.

She quickly averts her gaze and adjusts her shirt to pull it back into place. There's a strange ache in my chest when she continues to avoid my eyes, but I'm not about to push her on what just happened. It's not something we need to get into now, and I'm not sure I'm ready to share my own turbulent emotions on the subject.

I clear my throat and back up another few steps, opening my mouth to speak, but she beats me to breaking the awkward silence. "I'm going to head back to camp," she gestures to the pool. "Feel free to use the soaps at the water's edge, but make sure to leave plenty for Thelas and Faldorn when it's their turn."

"Not going to stay and watch me?" I tease, attempting to ease the tension with our normal back and forth.

She stands straight, a small smile on her face as she takes the offered escape. "I think I've had enough voyeurism for one night," she quips.

I chuckle. "Fair enough."

She gathers her cloak and pulls on her boots before quickly exiting the glade back to camp. I watch her go, tension knotting in my shoulders and wishing I could call her back to continue what we started.

When she's completely out of sight, I turn to survey the small pool properly for the first time. I'll admit it does look pleasant, and if Laira's moan when she entered the water is anything to go by, I'd say the water is quite warm. I strip quickly, not wanting to waste any time, and sink into the water without bothering to check its depth. I scrub myself thoroughly as I stare out into the darkness surrounding the pool. It's not ever entirely dark in this fucking forest, what with all the little strange mushrooms that grow everywhere, but it definitely doesn't make it much easier to see. Not for the first time, I curse my human eyes, wishing instead for fae or shifter vision, or even Willow's ability to sense roots. Would make not tripping over them a hell of a lot easier.

I start scrubbing my arms and shoulders when I catch a glimpse of the tattoos I've so carefully hidden over the last weeks. I'd almost forgotten they existed. They start above my elbow on my right arm, curling and twisting up in smoke-like patterns up my bicep and onto my chest—the tips just barely scratching at my collarbone. Laira caught a peek of them that first week when she was pretending to flirt with me. I nearly lost my composure when she mentioned them, afraid she would know their meaning, but she didn't seem to have any idea as to what they were. I smirk at the memory of that day. I'll admit, she did have me going there for a minute, and I have tried every single day since to get the same fire from her.

My thoughts wander and drift once again to what might be happening back home. I left in a hurry in the middle of the night, not wanting to chance being stopped on my way out and not bothering to leave more than a simple note about my departure.

I'm sure my father is furious, but I have no reservations about leaving the way I did. With the increasingly alarming reports coming in from the guards, it was clear that something drastic was needed. After too many long hours arguing with my father about what should be done regarding the concerning reports, I decided that I needed to leave to find information on my own and to seek out a solution that was not going to be found in the perfect halls of Ferrill's Imperial Castle.

Laira's face flashes into my mind, breaking up the vision of the simple note resting on my father's large wooden desk. She hasn't exactly been trusting toward me since I joined them, but she also hasn't been as outwardly hostile as I expected—I did steal her bag upon first meeting her after all.

I grumble. She really is nicer to me than I deserve. The pit in my stomach that began filling with stones as soon as I made the choice to conceal the truth from them grows heavier with each passing day. I drag a hand through my wet hair and stare into the crystal clear water, feeling as if the weight of my past is trying to drag me down. The closer I get to her—the closer I get to them all—only makes it worse.

"I'll tell them when they need to know," I say the words aloud, hoping that will make them more reassuring. But the forest is silent as it swallows my promise whole, and I feel no more confident about withholding my secrets than I did before.

I fear by that point, it may be too late to voice my secret, and I will lose all I have built with Laira and the others. The ominous thought settles over me, and I no longer feel the warmth of the water. I quickly pull myself from its depths and yank on my clothes before slowly making my way back to camp.

PAST & PRESENT

WILLOW

Roots wrap loosely around my wrists as I wake, and I blink rapidly into the soft blue light of the ferns glowing beside me. The absence of normal light had been strange at first, but as I grew accustomed to the different life present in this forest, I found I enjoy the darkness. It's been over a month of hard travel since we entered, and I'm not sure why, but I feel as if we are finally reaching the end of the forest. The roots surrounding me hum in agreement and cradle me in a soft embrace. I smile warmly at their steady presence. They've done this every morning for over a week now, and each time I feel as if I get to understand them a little more. Like us, they have a job to do—a task they feel compelled to follow, but since we met Em, they have ceased their persistent maneuvering and only halfheartedly try to stop us. I've tried in vain to discover who made them guardians, but they keep that knowledge deep in their ancient trunks.

I ease from the roots and Din swats halfheartedly as most of them gently recede into the soil. My blanket falls down as they depart and I shiver slightly at the cool temperature of the forest before reaching to pull on my cloak. It's been difficult to tell day from night here, but there is a temperature difference that generally seems to signal morning, afternoon, or evening. And there are more than a few plants that follow a clear pattern of opening and closing. Still, our 'days' are only an estimate, and it likely won't be until we get back to a town that we realize truly just how long we've been gone. Not to mention, it's entirely possible that time flows differently here.

I glance at Laira who lies on her bedroll in a restless sleep, her eyes darting under her lids and her hands twitching at her sides. Tendrils of my magic reach for her but quickly recoil when met with the suffocating darkness coiling inside her. I haven't been able to reach her with my magic for a few days now to mitigate the shadow's effects on her, and it shows. Her skin has developed a sickly pallor and the black veins that were once confined to her hands and wrists have spread to her shoulders and inch closer to her neck and chest with each passing day. My magic whispers to me that she is slipping away—using the last dregs of her strength to push through the day and lock down the shadows to prevent them from spearing out of her again.

I'm not certain if the others can sense when her shadows test her boundaries and drive out of her in reckless abandon, grasping for a new hold like vines winding up an old stone house. I've been able to intercept them for the most part, but they escape with no warning, and even my magic isn't fast enough to catch them all the time. The strain on Laira's body only grows as she's forced to wind them back inside her. I think of the queen's army back home and how her spirit-cracking tests would pale in comparison to Laira's suffering now.

I grimace as I picture the queen's face. Knowing exactly what she would want me to do in this situation as her perfect obedient weapon. How her eyes would alight with poorly contained glee at the possibility of using the darkness inside Laira for her own selfish desires. I sink into the earth and Din bumps his head affectionately against my chest. I sigh and smile gently, grateful for my little shadow and the comfort of the plant life around me at least. I remind myself once again that I left that vicious woman far behind, and I will never be her weapon to wield again.

Thelas grunts from my right as he nearly trips over the roots still loosely surrounding me, but otherwise isn't perturbed by the sight and goes about his business of scribbling in his notebook. I watch Laira again but decide to let her rest for a little longer before giving her another tonic to bolster her strength. Faldorn sits across the dwindling fire as I approach and hands me a warm cup of tea. I inhale the lovely scent, adoring the floral notes, and feel my shoulders relax.

He gestures beside him to another cup that sits on the ground full to the brim with coffee and spices for Laira when she wakes. He nods in her direction as I take a sip of my tea. "How is she?"

The soothing liquid warms my belly, but it's not enough to stop the ache behind my ribs. The darkness inside Laira hasn't physically cut me like it did before, but constantly stopping the attacks with my magic has created a different pain. A fatigue that pulls at my strength and challenges the magic inside me with every strike. It's enough that I now have a constant pressure in my chest, like a sharp thorn that I can't remove.

I rub the spot on my chest, hoping to ease some of the strain. "She's getting worse. It's only a matter of days until she won't be able to stand any longer and perhaps only a day or two after that before they explode out of her completely. And I'm not sure there will be anything any of us can do if that happens."

The corners of his mouth turn down ever so slightly as his eyes shift to her, showing a softness in them that speaks volumes to his true concern, even as his face remains passive.

Sebastian plops down beside me, his hand settling on his upright knee as he pokes at the fire with a thin stick. "What happens if this sword doesn't work?" he asks, stabbing at the dying embers, his brow furrowed.

I sigh. "It will work. It has to."

He looks at me then, a haunted hopelessness in his normally bright eyes. I reach out a hand, giving his forearm a gentle squeeze.

"I know. But for now, I will put my faith in this prophecy and the magic that brought us together." I pull my hand away, glancing at Laira's sleeping form. "She's not done yet. And neither are we."

JOURNEY'S END

THELAS

It was relatively simple to navigate the rest of the way out of the forest. I had already figured out how to maneuver around the trees—predicting their movements and adjusting throughout the day whenever we got blocked. I had theorized that they could only move a certain amount in a day and likely needed to rest for long periods in between to be able to cut us off effectively. Willow was able to have a vague sense of when and where they were congregating nearby, and from there it was a game of strategy that I was well suited to play. But whatever the old witch said to them made my task that much easier, and I was no longer having to plan my next move against them. It was a good thing too, because it meant our pace had increased significantly, and we could get Laira to the cave and the sword hopefully hidden in its depths that much sooner. She had gotten worse over the past few days after the brief reprieve we had at the pool, slumping in her saddle and appearing listless in the evenings. The stark change so at odds with her normal self that we all felt the loss. Willow was especially worried about her, as I'm certain she understood the direness of Laira's condition more than the rest of us—and being a healer with nothing to do must be agonizing.

And poor Kel. Everyone could tell his repeated check-ins with Laira were born of immense concern, and he was more often sitting beside her or resting on her shoulder than flying in the air. A telling difference from the diligent guarding he'd done the past weeks.

I glance behind me to see how she's faring, my stomach tumbling as I pinpoint dark pulsing veins under her skin, not just on her hands and arms as before, but crawling up her neck and even spreading to her jaw. Her skin is sickly and pale, and I note with alarm just how tightly she holds onto her horse to keep from falling, a sheen of sweat on her brow from the effort.

We need to get to that cave *now*.

A wiry voice rumbles in the back of my mind, and despite it being muffled by the thick door I shut it behind, I can still hear the beast perfectly.

"She is strong. She will make it."

My shoulders fall and I stare at my hands, my head suddenly too heavy to hold up. I despise this creature inhabiting my mind, but I don't have the heart to shut it away again after those words. I want so badly for Laira to be okay, and even if it's from the monster crawling in the darkness, I will take whatever words of encouragement I can get.

Even if we do find the cave and the sword, there's no telling if it will actually help her. That is a possibility that I know none of us wants to entertain, and it's certainly one that I banish as soon as it crosses my mind. The sword *has* to work, there is no other alternative.

We need her.

I rub my chest, feeling an ache there that I've never felt before. My family never gave a damn about me, casting me aside and ignoring me at best, locking me away at worst. The only comfort I ever found was when I was wrapped in the pages of a book and in the deep bowels of a library or through the soft notes of my flute—the solitude my only ally. The pang in my chest grows as I recall all the times this group has felt something like family over the last months. Jokes and laughter that ran long into the night, stories and ideas passed between us all, not to mention the fact that they believed in me enough to follow me into a dark and forbidden forest, trusting that I would lead them through solely based on my word. I think of the quiet moment in the witch's cabin where Laira offered a listening ear and a comforting touch as she began to suspect all the horrors I experienced as a child.

She had begun to feel like a sister, Willow too. Both being sounding boards for my theories and never once insisting that

I was too much or that I got too excited when I would talk about my map-making trade. Faldorn is like the father I never truly had, offering advice and teaching me how to defend myself. He is a figure for me to look up to, someone who is calm under pressure and resilient. My eyes land on Sebastian's back in front of me. He's a teasing and sarcastic man, but he means well and has lit a fire under us all. I imagine that is what a big brother is for, and I'm more than happy to replace the image of my cruel blood-related brothers with Sebastian's boisterous presence.

The beast in my mind hums a pleasant sound, and I almost mimic it before pulling away from him and distancing myself once more. I may have found myself in a new sort of family, but that doesn't mean they would necessarily accept me if they knew the entire truth. My heart thumps a stubborn rhythm, knowing deep down that they wouldn't judge me, but that long-standing kernel of fear is enough to keep me doubting and continuing to hide.

Whatever their reactions would be, it is not something they need to know now. I like being just Thelas the Cartographer and don't want to muddy that image with a dark monster and claws.

Faldorn slows ahead, and I realize with belated interest that we have come up on the edge of the tree line, a blazing light shines through the trees and illuminates our group. We haven't seen true light since that day with the meadow and the ruins, and I look behind me with interest to see Laira's reaction. Even in her worsening condition, she still turns her face to the sun, basking in it like it's the only thing she's ever wanted in the world. Her grip on her reins loosens, and her chest rises and falls in a steady rhythm.

I smile, grateful the sunlight seems to have lifted her spirit enough to keep pushing on. I'm not sure how much more she could have survived in such darkness. We push on and quickly pass the tip of a small river, its waters lazy and dull compared to the often vibrant blue glow of the streams in the Forbidden Forest. A few trees are scattered about, but most of the landscape past the river is awash in golden swaths of tall grass and rolling hills. It undulates like waves in the brisk afternoon winds, bringing forth the slight tang of salt and sea—we must be closer to the ocean than I thought. I call to the others to stop so that I can pull out the map

I've been working on for weeks. The one that will hopefully lead us from the edge of the forest to the cave system that houses the sword. From what I could gather from a few clipped sentences in my book, the caves are located on the coast—hidden above rocky cliffs and overlooking the ocean. My map is somewhat crude, but it's enough to give us a good direction to follow and from there my plan is to travel along the cliffs and search for the caves. I relay the information to the others, and Faldorn nods approvingly. I beam at the praise, feeling an immense sense of pride at having come this far.

Hours pass of the same golden hills until the ocean begins to come into view. It sparkles in the light but is abruptly cut off in the distance by dense mist. I retrieve my map and take notes as we amble along the coastline, drawing new features as they appear and correcting my previous lines. It takes the rest of the day, but the terrain shifts and soon we are trekking up a steep hill, the glittering ocean still on our left. When we reach the top, the landscape flattens, revealing large hills to our right and massive cave openings embedded in their rocky surfaces.

The cave openings are littered with scattered rocks and boulders, but Hael's nimble hooves make quick work as we approach the largest of the caves, the others following more slowly, until we are all standing in front of the massive opening. It's wide enough for all of us to stand with our arms out side-by-side and then some. It yawns far above my head and appears to be made of carved grey stone instead of being naturally eroded. I can't see far into the cave, but I feel a foreboding energy emanating from it and know that this is Sela a' Core, The Cave of Swords. We investigate the outside for a bit, but with the rapidly waning light and our fatigued state from riding all day, it's not in our best interest to enter now. So, we pick a spot nearby for the evening instead.

The cliffs are open in front of us and covered in a thick seagrass that waves in the wind off the coast. The sky so far is clear, but I know that can change quickly when the ocean is involved. I survey the air carefully, giving it a long sniff, and hope we won't have rain in such an exposed place. I study the coastline, but don't see anywhere that could offer us shelter beyond the cave, and we certainly don't want to shelter in there. The ocean spreads before us, its color dark blue and full of white frothing tops from the crashing waves. The view cuts off quickly as a heavy grey fog engulfs the rest of the horizon. I flip through my catalogue of mental maps, gauging how far we've gone, and realize this must be what the *inside* of the Mists of Sela looks like. The mists are too dense to travel through, and so this coastline is nearly impossible to travel to. It's likely the reason for needing to travel through the Forbidden Forest, though I also wonder if there is some magic involved that only reveals the caves once you've traveled through the forest. We found these caves a little too easily, and that's the only way I can think of to account for our quick discovery.

"I'll need to write all this down," I mutter to myself, already planning a new set of maps when I hear a shout and Kel squawk in alarm behind me. I whip around, my hand reaching for the dagger Faldorn gave me at my belt until I realize we aren't being attacked. Laira is cradled in Sebastian's arms, seemingly unconscious. Her arms hang limp at her sides, and her face is utterly devoid of color. Skip throws her head, and I grab her reins to calm her.

"What happened?" I ask, my eyes fixed on Laira's pale face.

"She fell from her horse, but I managed to catch her." Sebastian brushes a strand of hair from her eyes, his voice growing soft. "I've got you, I've got you." He repeats the phrase over and over to her as he settles her on the ground, Willow already appearing with a small bottle to pour down Laira's throat.

"This will ease her into a hopefully restful sleep." Her face falls, and I ache for her as she looks into Sebastian's stricken face. "It's all I can do for her."

She gives the mixture to Laira, and while I don't notice a difference, Willow's shoulders relax. Faldorn and I stand above them, exchanging equally helpless looks. There's nothing any of us can do for her besides get that sword and pray to the Goddess it does what the legends claim it can.

I glance in the direction of the dark cave looming behind us. "Are you sure we shouldn't try to enter tonight? What if she gets worse?"

Willow sighs. "She likely will get worse by morning, but it won't do us any good to not be at full strength."

Faldorn approaches me and I settle slightly when he places a firm hand on my shoulder. "She's right. We need rest, and a chance to come up with some sort of plan for what we will face in there. We do her no good by denying our own well-being, and you know she would say the same."

I nod glumly. "You're right."

Sebastian keeps Laira's body against him, stroking a hand over her hair and smoothing out the sweaty strands that stick to her skin despite the cool evening. Kel joins them and hops around a few times before settling his head in her limp hand. The simple action brings a sharp prick of emotion to my eyes that I blink quickly away.

The rest of us set about preparing camp. We have it down to an art at this point, so it isn't long before we all sit around a crackling fire. The heavy silence is like a boulder weighing on us all, and concerned eyes dart to Laira every time she moves or makes a sound. She appears to sleep soundly, and I can only hope she is getting some actual sleep. She'd been having nightmares lately that would wake us all up, but I know she's been having them far longer on this trip than just the last few nights. I know the signs of a person covering up such things since I employ similar tactics myself.

The worry in my chest threatens to crush me, and I know the others must feel the same, so I decide to break this awful silence myself. "So… about that plan for what we might face when we get in the cave?" I shift my eyes to Faldorn. "You said there's another beast in the cave guarding the sword?"

He blows out a breath, nodding. "From what I've heard. But these are folktales and stories. It's impossible to know what is true and what is false. But I think it wise to prepare for a fight."

Willow straightens her spine next to me. "I can help Laira through."

"Are you sure? It could be a long trek through the caves." Sebastian challenges, not in an unfriendly way but wanting to be certain.

"Yes. I can do it. Plus, with my magic and healing it's best if I stay close to monitor her in case she gets worse."

He nods, conceding, though I can tell he wishes he could be the one to help Laira.

"Alright, then since we have that settled, I suppose it's just a matter of making sure the animals are safe while we'll be in the cave and preparing for a fight," I say.

They nod in agreement, and we fall into another bout of silence. The question that has been on my mind since we started rushes from me before I can stop it, and I wince at the blunt delivery. "So what happens after this?"

"What do you mean?" Sebastian asks.

"Well... Laira is healed, and we have the sword and defeat whatever monster lies in the cave. But what about after that? The prophecy was torn at the bottom, but I'm sure there was more to it. Not to mention the disturbing rumors you talked about." I look at each of them in turn, hoping they can give me some sort of answer. "There must be more to what we need to do. There's something big brewing here, something thousands of years in the making, and we are at the very center of it."

Sebastian broaches the silence, offering information though he seems hesitant to give it. "It's being theorized that there is a figure who is controlling dark, mindless nyradonn and forcing them to maim and destroy towns along the coast of Eislekest and Kerimaea."

I gape at him, not expecting that response.

Willow also appears shocked at this information, asking him, "That's what's been causing the destruction and disappearances you mentioned? But how is that possible? And how is this mysterious figure able to even control them? Humans, shifters, and witches can only bond to one or two nyradonn, and even the most ancient of fae can only bond to a handful of nyradonn at a time, according to what Faldorn said."

Sebastian shakes his head. "That I do not know. Somehow they are able to control hundreds, if not thousands of bone creatures over great distances. And these nyradonn in particular obey without question and cannot be reasoned with, unlike most of their kind. They are dark, malicious, and dangerously violent. They have caused horrible losses and destruction up and down the coastline, decimating small villages, but for some reason avoiding the larger towns and never venturing farther than a few miles inland."

We stare at Sebastian as he continues speaking, and it's as if a dam has broken loose as he spills more and more information.

"It's thought that the beasts originate from V'oloth and that they swim to their destinations, though there have been reports of some flying. All of this started almost a year ago, but until recently has been kept under wraps by both Eislekest and Kerimaea. It appears as if they are searching for something, though no one knows what. If we do manage to get this sword…" His eyes dart to Laira's sleeping form. "Then I think we should take it to Ferrill to see what the king's plans are."

"How do you know all of this?" Faldorn leans forward, eyeing Sebastian with a penetrating gaze, his brows furrowed ever so slightly.

A HIDDEN IDENTITY

SEBASTIAN

Because I'm the crown prince of Eislekest.

"I've picked up a lot," I reply, hoping I sound nonchalant.

Laira stirs from her induced sleep, and Kel perks up immediately, creaking softly as he jumps back to give her room to shift. Her voice is thick, but she still manages a light sarcastic tone as she chimes in, "Ah yes, thieving not just pretty objects and maidenhoods, but also secrets."

I whip my head to look at her, seeing that she has pulled herself upright and leans against her pack, her appearance slightly more encouraging than it had looked earlier.

I smirk, giving in to the familiar teasing between us. "Maidenhoods? Give me a little credit. I prefer a more experienced partner."

Laira rolls her eyes, but I see the slight flush to her cheeks at my response, made more noticeable by the increasingly ashen color of her face.

Willow smiles at her friend's slightly increased energy, checking over her briefly with her eyes before asking me, "So, this figure controlling the nyradonn... what are the chances this is the dark foe mentioned in the Prophecy of Souls? The Lady in Blue?"

Thelas sounds doubtful as he says, "I know the prophecy has had a few moments of truth so far, and it is the reason why we are here. But is it really *all* true? What if it's a series of coincidences? We don't even know the full thing. What if we're missing something huge?"

"But what are the chances that now there is this mysterious powerful figure corrupting and controlling nyradonn, *and* there is a dark and mysterious person mentioned in this prophecy we have been following?" she fires back.

I huff, tired of this prophecy and how it controls our lives, and rebelling at the thought of a folktale coming to life.

"The Lady in Blue is just a children's story to frighten kids into washing up before dinner. The sword and the Forbidden Forest may be real, but really, The Lady in Blue? There's no way that's even her real name," I interject between Thelas and Willow and they both fall silent.

Laira lets out a loud exhausted sigh. "This is getting us nowhere. Whether this person is or isn't the one referenced in the prophecy, the fact of the matter is that it doesn't matter right now. We need to focus first on getting that sword, and then we can attempt to unravel the prophecy and deal with this threat."

She looks at each of us, making sure we are all on the same page. "That's what this sword should be good for, right? If it's as powerful as the prophecy says?"

Willow smiles deviously. "That, and knocking those shadows inside you senseless. With that sword, there's no way a handful of corrupted nyradonn and their puppet master can continue their reign of terror!"

"Reign of terror?" Thelas deadpans.

"Did I stutter?" Willow bites back.

"What else have you picked up through your… thieving?"

Faldorn's voice cuts through Thelas and Willow's banter, and I can't help but pause at his tone. He didn't at all sound convinced of the "thieving" excuse I used to explain my knowledge, and the carefully passive look on his face only proves that. He may not know exactly what I am hiding, but he knows there is something I'm not saying. I only hope he keeps his suspicions to himself for now.

I quickly glance in Laira's direction. I should tell her—I should tell all of them—but now is not the time. We do not need to be divided right before entering possibly the most dangerous cave in all of Ilphemoura and certainly not until Laira is cured of the darkness that swirls around her now. She's gotten exceedingly worse over the last few days, requiring more help from each of us to walk and waking from more frequent nightmares. We picked up our pace considerably to reach the cave once we exited the forest, but I wonder how much time she actually has left before the darkness swallows her whole. Consuming her and then coming for the rest of us.

My chest constricts at the thought of losing her like that.

I'll tell her after.

I focus back on Faldorn and reply in a smooth tone, "I can't trade all my secrets for free, old man. I need to keep some things for myself."

Laira grumbles, and I slide my gaze to her. "Don't approve of my answer, wildcat?"

"If there is something you aren't saying that could help us, then you should say it."

I drop my charming act for a moment to really look at her, studying the dark circles under her eyes and the crawling dark purple veins that pulse beneath her skin. Her cloak and shirt slips to the side as she shifts, and for a brief moment I am able to see that the veins have found their way onto her chest, edging closer and closer to her heart.

My smile drops at the sight, and I sound more somber than I mean to as I say, "I have told you all I know of the destruction occurring in Eislekest. I swear on my future bonded that I would never place you or this group in danger."

She holds my eye contact for a long moment before seemingly finding my answer, and whatever she finds in my gaze, adequate and nods.

"Well," Willow says, "since we have that out of the way, shall we rest for the night and enter the cave at first light? The sun is close to setting, and it's probably best we are well rested for whatever we may face in there."

Faldorn nods and adds, "Yes. We may have passed through the forest relatively unscathed, but that doesn't mean there isn't a last test before we can get to the sword."

"Wait—just one more thing." I point to Din, who is sitting contentedly in Willow's lap. "I've been wondering since before we entered the damn forest…what is his real name? It can't possibly just be Din. And what kind of name is Kel anyway? Is that short for something?"

"What's wrong with the name Kel? And no, it's just Kel," Laira huffs.

"And what about yours? Din?" I ask Willow. "That has to be short for something."

She gives me a sly grin. "Oh, it's short for something."

Laira barks a laugh, and I whip around to face her. "You know his full name?"

She rolls her eyes. "Of course I do, I'm her best friend."

"Hmph." Turning back to Willow, I point an accusing finger at the cat, as if it's his fault that I don't get to know his actual name. "You won't tell me?"

She grins. "Nope!" Her voice sounds in a sing-song as she adds, "But I will tell you if you guess it correctly." She holds out a hand to shake on this new ridiculous deal.

I grip her hand firmly and agree, immediately sounding off names, each one more and more ridiculous. I know this is the least important thing to be doing right now, guessing absurd names for an undead cat, but it's the only thing I can think of to brighten everyone's mood.

Dinly.

Dina.

Dinlo.

Din perks up from Willow's side, and I almost think he is responding to my last name suggestion, when he hisses instead.

"Oh—didn't like that one, did we?" I chuckle.

Willow and Laira laugh as Din swipes at me, and I'm forced to lean back to avoid his claws. I smile at their secret looks, my eyes snagging on Laira's bright smile, and a warmth floods my system at having been the one to bring that look to her face.

Willow pauses her laughing to tease, "That's the best you can come up with?"

I put a dramatic hand to my chest, pretending to be affronted. "Hey! Din is a very strange nickname, okay?"

Laira dissolves into giggles alongside Willow and they fall into each other as they cackle at their newfound informational high ground.

Thelas joins in on the pointless game, calling out, "Dinaria?"

Faldorn pipes up from his place by the fire. "Paladin."

"Oh, not you too! This is going to be a whole thing isn't it?" Willow groans half-heartedly.

"Hey, you threw down the gauntlet," I say as I throw my arms around Faldorn and Thelas. "And we are simply answering the call."

"Fine! But I really am giving you nothing unless you actually guess correctly."

I chuckle and release Faldorn and Thelas. "Deal."

A SILENT PROMISE

LAIRA

The morning is cold and grey when I wake from my restless sleep. The fog hangs low, clinging to my clothes and causing a shiver to run over my body. Though that could also be because of the pulsing waves of darkness cascading from my skin. My necklace hangs dully against my chest, and I wonder how it got put around my neck. I purposely hadn't worn it for our entire trip, equally uncertain and unnerved by its potential meaning regarding the prophecy and that I had it for so long and never knew—like a once comforting friend suddenly revealing they had ulterior motives the entire time.

I decide taking it off isn't worth my energy, and instead I attempt to recall the nightmares I experienced last night. I have a vague recollection of being surrounded by the others and each deciding to sit with me throughout the night. I don't have the energy to feel guilty at being such a burden, and I know they wouldn't want me to feel that way either. I stare blankly at my hand as it appears and disappears whenever the shadows coalesce over it, like when the moon passes across the sun and completely obscures it from view. It's disconcerting to watch, but I only feel a prick of the emotion before it's flooded away by a surge of numb emptiness. Kel jumps into my lap, dispelling some of the darkness, and his comforting presence lifts my mood. I cradle his head gently in both hands, whispering, "Thank you, dear friend. I can always count on you."

He chirps softly, the sound reassuring but tinged with sadness. As if he knows I am one step away from drifting off completely.

Willow's concerned voice and soft touch alert me to her presence, though I don't pull my eyes from Kel, unsure if that is because I don't want to see the look in her eyes or if I just don't have the energy to turn my head.

"Hey—want me to help you up? We secured the animals, and we're getting ready to head in."

I eye her empty hands and spy her staff sitting securely with the rest of our items. I lift an eyebrow before meeting her gaze. "No staff today?"

She crosses her arms, darting a glance at her weapon, and shakes her head before walking closer to help me up.

I reach out my awareness to my limbs, wanting to stand on my own, but they feel as distant as my emotions, so I let her help me. She may be shorter than I am, but her body is strong. She pulls me to my feet without much trouble, my arm slung around her shoulders and hers wrapped firmly around my waist, supporting my weight. I hang almost limply around her, and a deep sorrow wells in my chest at how I am so utterly useless in this moment—my body not listening to me and my normal desire to keep moving forward absent.

My voice sounds weak in my head as I tell myself mournfully, *I used to be strong*.

"The others are gathering at the mouth of the cave. Can you move your legs, or should I get Sebastian to help me carry you?" Willow asks, her voice gentle but full of the pragmatic authority that comes from being a healer and dealing with difficult patients.

I grit my teeth and force my feet forward. Din brushes against my legs, as if trying to give me some of his strength. I'm not sure it helps, but I give him a soft smile to thank him anyway and lift my head to look straight ahead. "I can walk."

Willow nods, still keeping a firm grip on me, as we make our way to the others. I try not to look too closely at their faces, expecting pity or perhaps even annoyance at being made to wait so long, but they give me no such looks. Only genuine concern and even a hint of pride shine on their faces. It bolsters my determination, and I walk with a little more strength to my steps.

Of course they would never think so poorly of me, I remind myself.

I've seen just how much they care for me since this journey started, and I hope they know how much they mean to me as well. As we stand in a line at the cave's opening, I welcome their warmth and their strength and feel—not for the first time—that we are a family.

Inscribed above the entrance are the words, 'Sela a' Core' in flowing script. I would normally be able to appreciate the artistry of the intricately carved words or even feel excited at the prospect of finally reaching our destination, like how I felt when we entered the Forbidden Forest, but I'm already so exhausted and only feel a numb awareness of my surroundings.

Faldorn breathes, "The Cave of Swords." Breaking the silence and peering into the darkness beyond.

Sebastian's voice is light but edged with something sharper, as if he is attempting to dispel the tension among the group but can't quite rid it from himself. "I just realized it says 'swords?' As in multiple? This is going to take forever if we have to find one among many."

Thelas' logical mind pounces on Sebastian's attempt at a joke, snuffing it out in the process. "I think it's more of a metaphorical swords, on account of the giant pointed pillars of smooth stone I can see just past the entrance. Very swordlike."

Sebastian gives him a look that says "you just had to get practical" but Thelas ignores him and looks to Faldorn, who steps into the cave first. Thelas goes next, followed by Willow and me shuffling behind him, and Sebastian taking the rear.

It takes a moment for my eyes to adjust to the all-encompassing darkness, but once they do I realize it's not entirely pitch black. Once the light from the entrance fully recedes, massive pillars of white translucent stone jut from the ceiling, walls, and floor and cast an odd hue to the cavern. I attempt to put a name to the light but am unable to think of anything that comes close to it. It's almost as if light is somehow being produced inside the stones and reflected off the surface, like the steady light of the moon, though dimmer. It provides enough light for my fae eyes to see just fine, but I notice Willow and Sebastian stumble a few times—though Thelas seems surprisingly fine, seeing just as well as Faldorn and I.

Water drips from somewhere around us, and there is a dampness to the air which further pushes me to my limits, making me even colder than I was before entering the cave. Kel flies just above Willow and me, but his jangling bones echo loudly off the cave walls, and I soon call to him to perch on my shoulder instead, not wanting to alert whatever monster may be lurking here of our approach.

My skin crawls as the shadows pulse and twist beneath, and I realize with a sickening certainty that they are excited, gleeful even, at being in the cave and surrounded by near darkness. Startling clarity pushes the shadows from my mind long enough for me to regain control of my thoughts, and I realize where the dread I'd felt earlier was coming from. The shadows had been pushing me to this destination all along. They wanted me to find this cave—and the sword—and are not fearful like I'd expect them to be if we truly were approaching a weapon that could dispel them from my body. They are certain of their success and dig their claws into my muscles to force my legs faster and reach our destination that much sooner. My heart feels close to breaking, and tears threaten to fall from my eyes as the certainty that I will fail and not leave this cave stabs into me.

I push the tears away. It doesn't matter that these shadows will consume me. What matters is that my family is safe. I make a silent promise to myself as we shuffle through the dark cave. I will rage against the Goddess herself to keep them safe—fight any foe and pull them all from the depths of death if I must. The promise sits in my chest. A steady flame in an otherwise dismal atmosphere. I lock the knowledge of what I plan to do if we don't find the sword or its power is exaggerated, not risking the chance of anyone seeing the resigned decision on my face and guessing at my thoughts.

These shadows won't touch them if it's the last thing I do.

THE GUARD & THE SWORD

LAIRA

The light from the crystals protruding from the walls dims suddenly, and my eyes strain to see as we enter an enormous cavernous space. I can't see the ceiling, but I can feel the openness of the space yawning before us. It almost makes me dizzy at the sudden difference from the smaller tunnels, especially as a blast of air *whooshes* over us. Instinctively, I duck my head, but the wind stops as quickly as it appeared, and I'm about to ask if everyone is okay when I feel a heavy presence settle in front of us. My body freezes in fear, and the only thought that pulses through my mind is *prey*—some long buried animalistic part of myself knows something waits in this cave far stronger than I, and despite my tired muscles and limp frame being supported by Willow, I itch to run back the way we came.

"Laira."

A booming voice sounds, echoing off the walls, and it takes me a moment to realize that whatever it was said my name. Unseen sconces flicker to life along the walls and ceiling, providing a clear view of what spoke my name and what has my self-preservation instincts firing.

Faldorn, Sebastian, and even Din & Kel form a protective half-circle around Willow and me, covering us as Willow reaches her free hand into the pouch at her hip to grab a bottle and widens her stance in anticipation of a fight. A dozen green tendrils snake from her body and point in the direction of the beast. I marvel at how much we've changed and how far we've come. Apart from Willow and me, we were all complete strangers before this, and now they defend me and each other without hesitation. A warm tingling pools in my chest at their protection and courage.

The dragon roars when we don't answer and glistening fangs shine in the torchlight. It tucks its wings in close to avoid scraping on the rough wall, its dark green scaled body rippling with muscle as it swings a wide set of shimmery gold antlers into a nearby crystal, crumbling it to pieces. The shards bounce harmlessly off its hide, and I flinch as some pieces soar in our direction, though they skitter off to the side before they can reach us. The noise is deafening, and I have to consciously stop myself from covering my ears to block it out, not wanting to move suddenly and provoke the creature further. Despite the aggressive display, I feel only a surge of love for my fellow comrades, which is perhaps why I have the strength to stand taller and speak to the dragon in a confident tone.

"I am here."

The others whip around to stare at me, each with a bewildered and uncertain expression. I push forward, gently pulling Willow's arm from my waist and walking stiffly toward the front of the group. The dragon calms as I do, dropping its head slightly and pausing its destruction of the area. It sits on a large stone platform on the other side of the cavern, its massive body nearly as wide as the cave itself, though even it doesn't seem to reach the top. It must be two or three times the size of the giant deer-like beast we encountered in the forest, and I feel as small as an insect in its presence.

Sebastian thrusts out an arm to stop me from continuing past him, the pleading look in his eyes begging me not to engage in whatever trap the dragon has set. I place a gentle hand on his and give him a reassuring look. At this point, with the shadows consuming me, I am the most expendable. Not only that, but the dragon called me out by name. If I have to make some deal to save them and get the sword, then I will, even if I must face off with a beast who could swallow me whole.

Reluctantly, Sebastian lets me go, though I can see it pains him to do so, and I stumble forward slowly before bracing my legs to center myself and stand upright. Kel is the only one I allow to follow me, and his talons scrape against the stone as he jumps into the air and lands on my shoulder. My body is growing weaker by the minute, and I can feel the shadows as they sap the strength from my limbs, but I throw the last dregs of my spirit into standing firm before the dragon.

I stare into its bright orange and yellow eyes, unflinching even as it opens its mouth, exposing rows of wickedly sharp teeth and rumbles out a deep growl that I feel straight through my bones.

"I am Laira. We are in search of a great sword of legend and have journeyed through Daer e' Mista to find it." My voice is strong as I speak and hope using the forest's original name will appeal to the dragon.

The statement hangs in the air, and the dragon blinks once, it's body utterly still before it prowls down from its perch on the rock ledge. It slinks toward us, its head low as it walks nearly silently across the floor. The only sounds are our intake of fearful breaths and the scraping of its claws.

Kel hisses and throws his wings wide behind my head when it stops in front of us. I have to crane my neck uncomfortably to keep its head in my sight despite it still being twenty or so paces away. The dragon drops down to rest lightly on its legs, but I'm not put at ease by the motion—it reminds me too much of when Din pretends to lie down but is actually keeping his legs poised to jump and attack. I force myself not to move an inch as the dragon moves its giant head parallel with my body, its antlers arcing above our group and its eyes glowing like fire. With this new position, I can't see the entire head, or even most of the dragon's body as only one eye is in my view.

"You've come for the sword," the dragon rumbles.

It's not a question, but I nod anyway.

The dragon challenges, "And why should I allow you to take it?"

Sebastian asks from behind me, "So it is here?"

The dragon flicks its eyes to him, a growl building in its throat, and a flood of words leaves my mouth as I desperately try to keep the dragon's attention on me.

"I found a prophecy that spoke of it, and I've been plagued by dark magic. I fear it's the only thing that can save me from the shadows swallowing my mind. Even now they taunt me and steal everything from me, forcing me to succumb and striking out at my friends."

I'm once again struck by the odd sensation of voices and emotions other than my own echoing in my head. The words are incomprehensible, but the feelings of sorrow and concern are there. I don't know how, but they feel like the internal reactions of the others behind me, who still wait with swords drawn.

The dragon flicks its attention back to me and I sigh in relief. "Dark magic…Yes, the sword is capable of what you say. But why should you be the one to wield it?"

Tears roll down my face, and even though my legs hold me upright still, I crumple inside. "I should not be the one to wield it. I am weak, but I have no choice if I want to save them. I am a shade of the person I was, but even before that, I would not have been truly fit for the task." I ball my fists at my sides, forcing the words from my mouth as I stare into the eye of the dragon. They feel like acid falling from my lips, but the darkness inside me affirms they are true.

"I am not brave. I am not selfless. I am not perfect nor admirable. I am not a leader and have very few useful skills. Without my friends, I never would have made it out of Taslae." My head drops, and I watch numbly as the shadows curl further up my arms, digging a path up my forearms and onto my shoulders. My hair falls in front of my face, shielding my pathetic display from view and further creating a feeling of isolation, which draws me deeper into myself until my body feels distant.

"I am not worthy," I say finally, unable to lift my head.

Sorrow and sympathy pour into me from behind, but my mind is too far out of my control to feel it fully.

The dragon's voice rasps, otherworldly and ancient as it says, "If that were true, why do your friends believe otherwise?"

"I—"

"Why is their energy drawn to yours? Why do you act as a conduit, their threads connected first to yours?"

My mouth parts, and I slowly look into the eye of the dragon, my mind snagging on the word it just said. "Threads?"

"I did not ask if you were worthy, I asked why you should be the one to wield it. I smell in your blood the power and ability to command a legendary sword such as Guensylhir. What I want to know is why it is *you*."

"I don't know."

"Then I have no use for you or your comrades."

The dragon opens its mouth wide, and I gape in horror at the orange light emanating from within. I throw myself onto its snout, desperately hoping it will stop the ball of fire that is about to incinerate the others.

"Wait!"

I see them move from the corner of my eye, reaching for me to help and pull me from the dragon, but I hold up a hand to stop them. "Let me handle this."

The dragon hisses but inhales, pulling back the threat of fire. I slump to the floor in relief, the last of my physical strength leaving me. The dragon stares intently at me, waiting for my answer, and I rack my brain for what it could want from me. Our lives depend on it. A surge of panic leaves me gasping for air until I feel warm hands at my waist and a calm voice in my ear.

"We believe in you. We've got your back."

I settle back into the solid body behind me, borrowing strength as Sebastian's words stir the hair at the nape of my neck. The shadows briefly recede at his touch, and I inhale deeply to calm myself, using Sebastian's chest as a base to prop my limp body up so I can stare straight into the dragon's eye.

My voice is surprisingly even as I tell it, "I will wield the sword to save my family from the darkness infesting me, to protect them from further harm and dispel the shadow's claws. After that, I do not know, but I will put my trust in the threads, as they have not steered me wrong yet."

The dragon studies me, weighing my words, and I send up a prayer to the Goddess that it is enough.

"That is acceptable. For now."

A quiet hope blooms in my chest at the dragon's words, which grows into a full-blown wave as the dragon lifts a clawed foot and a shining sword descends from the ceiling and floats in front of us. Its hilt is wrapped in supple brown leather with a glowing rounded stone at the pommel and another larger one at the top of the hilt. The entire thing radiates a striking orange color, a red aura emanating from it like the sun itself. Intricate curved metal pieces of the same color hold the blade up, which gleams in the torchlight a dark silver.

The dragon's voice booms again. "My name is Luvarn: 'He Who Awoke With

The World.' I am the sworn guardian of Guensylhir, charged long ago by the Goddess herself to its protection. I give this sword to you willingly, recognizing your strength and the promise that you follow the path to your true destiny."

The sword hovers in front of me, and I reach carefully for its hilt. A buzz of power skips through my blood when I make contact, the shadows hissing in agitation under my skin. A cascade of emotions floods me, and I nearly double over at the nauseous feeling that causes the room to spin. Awe, pride, disbelief, and resignation mix together. A prickling on the back of my neck makes me turn to face the others, Guensylhir firm in my grasp. I scan each of their features, searching, but the emotions leave almost as soon as they arrive, and soon I'm left with my own thoughts.

Luvarn scrapes a claw across the stone floor, carving a symbol in front of us. "Guensylhir goes by another name as well: Light Bringer. Your group also has a name, one whispered about since the dawn of time—a group that appears when the realm is at the brink of chaos." He pauses for a moment, allowing his words to sink in before continuing, "You are *Ilekiir*, and your strength radiates from your shared bonds."

He finishes the last of his markings, and I study the symbol, recognizing a curling braided thread encompassed in a circle. A tug in my chest makes the breath leave my lungs in a soft *whoosh*, and I distantly notice the others experiencing the sensation as well, as I stare intently at the carving on the floor.

DARKNESS & LIGHT

LAIRA

"Are you ready to face the darkness? It will be difficult," Luvarn warns.

I wrench my gaze from the carving and grip the still glowing sword, replying solemnly, "What choice do I have?"

He dips his massive head, and I take that as my signal to study the sword, Guensylhir, more closely. It's lighter than I thought it would be, and it emits a warm energy that radiates down my arm, filling my body with soft ripples, like I'm bathing in a pool of warm water. The shadows constrict again under my skin, and I hiss in pain. They writhe beneath me, clawing and scraping as they clamor down my arm that is holding the sword, reaching for it and buzzing with excitement.

"What do I need to do? Recite a spell to make it work?"

"No. A true bearer of this sword requires no such knowledge. Look within yourself and you will find the answer you seek."

Luvarn turns without another word, making his way back to his perch and watching us with ancient eyes.

"Right."

I'm uncertain of what to do next, and the intense feeling from the others' worried eyes doesn't help. I tear my awareness from them, needing for once absolute focus and distance. Luvarn is right—this is something I must do on my own.

Kel squawks unhappily as I place him from my shoulder onto the ground. "I'm sorry, bud." I brush my hand across his smooth skull, and he leans into the touch. "You know this is something I have to do alone."

He wilts, his wings drooping, but he doesn't stop me as I move to a section of the large cavern away from everyone.

Taking a deep breath, I stare at the sword, looking for anything that could give me a clue as to what to do next. When that doesn't work, I sit cross-legged on the floor, the gleaming sword in my lap, and place both hands on the blade. I close my eyes, feeling the heat from the sword through my palms, and with nothing else to try, I start speaking in my mind.

Nonsense at first and doubt at my sanity for talking to a literal sword, but soon the scene in my mind changes from darkness to a small room, and I am swept away—my body no longer sitting in the cavern. The room I find myself in is devoid of furniture aside from a single white podium on which Guensylhir sits. My voice echoes in the space as I continue muttering to myself, and I glance around uncertainly before deciding to approach the sword.

"Hello?"

Silence.

"I need your help. I don't have much time before the shadows infecting me spill out completely and kill everyone in my vicinity or possibly further."

More silence follows, and I feel utterly stupid talking to an inanimate object, even if it's a supposed magic sword.

I sigh. "Look. I don't care if I'm actually cured or not. What I need are these shadows destroyed, and if I have to go along with them, then I will do that. But what I will *not* do is leave my friends in danger because of me."

The words twist in my gut. I don't want to die, but if it's the only way to protect them…

I steel my spine, pacing in circles around the sword and try to find a new angle to look at it while simultaneously willing it to do something. I cast out my senses, hoping to find anything to hold on to and follow as a potential solution, but I find nothing but silence and still air. I open my mouth to try speaking to it again, not knowing what else to try, when the walls start seeping thick dark blood. It coats the entire room in a matter of seconds, and I yelp as it pools beneath my feet, my apprehension turning to full blown panic as I'm yanked under and swallowed whole.

The feeling of falling stops, only for me to find myself in a small, enclosed space nearly devoid of all light. It feels as if I am drowning despite not being in water, my chest heaving with the burden of forcing each breath out. I have only the vaguest sense of what is in front of me and can't make out much more than outlines in the gloom.

Voices taunt me, telling me of my worst fears and saying every reason as to why I am useless to them. I'm about to tell the voices to shove it when I realize who is saying the destructive words. Thelas, Sebastian, Willow and Faldorn stand in a row, obvious disappointment on their faces as they speak over each other, each with a new and more awful thing falling from their lips. Behind them, my parents stand tall—my sister between them—as they shout similar taunts at me. Rows and rows of people gather behind them: the surly mapmaker Hannon, slimy High Elder Torghul, past lovers, and taunting townsfolk alike. It seems as if every person I've ever known files neatly into the dark space to hurl accusations and horrible words. They land like knives on my skin, lacerating me with tiny cuts until I fall to my knees before them all, repeating back their words and believing each one. This seems to satisfy them, and the unrelenting torrent slows as I recite the phrases back to them.

"I am not enough."

"I am a burden."

"My sister does not love me."

"I am difficult. I take up too much space and don't know my place."

"I am too loud. I am unlovable."

They greedily consume the words, growing larger until they tower above me and push each other excitedly. The words fall mechanically from my mouth, and I feel myself slip away with each uttered sentence.

Soon, I'm lost in my memories, and the dark scene suddenly changes to a brightly lit day—the sun shines cheerily and my feet shift nervously over cobblestones as I stand before a heavy wooden door, my arm raised to knock.

Panic wells in my chest. *No. Not this memory, please*. I beg the shadows, I beg myself, and I scream as I watch the scene unfold like I'm trapped in my own body, unable to escape. The door swings open and my sister stands on the other side, a surprised look on her face. Her bright copper hair is the same as it's always been, the shade slightly too luminous for a normal human. She quickly schools her expression, crossing her arms across her chest and eyeing me with something close to contempt.

My voice is rushed, and I stammer as I try to speak. "I—I was in town and I thought I'd find your shop and—"

She holds up a firm hand. "Stop. Just stop. We haven't spoken in years, and you show up now," she raises a brow and looks me up and down, her voice turning hard and unyielding. "Why?"

My hands are useless as they hang limp at my sides and my head swims with sorrow at how we got to this point, and I nearly collapse at her feet from the weight of it all.

A tear streaks down my face. "Because I miss you."

I turn away from the memory. Forcing my eyes shut and screaming until I can no longer hear her words. But I don't need to hear them to know exactly what happens next. Don't need to see the scene in front of me to know how she looked when she said she didn't miss me, or the steely look in her eyes as she said it. I can remember just fine how my heart broke into a thousand pieces at her feet as she told me she had no interest in having a sister ever again. How she never forgave me for leaving her after our parents died and how she had to learn to survive on her own. I cave beneath her harsh words once more, shaking as every single one slices me to my core and knowing it was all my fault.

I look up blankly and clutch my arms around my chest desperately, as if that will save the bleeding heart within. My sister no longer stands before me, but a new wretched scene unfolds, and it's all I can do not to weep as I recognize my surroundings once more. A soft bed, plush pillows, and a warm body beside me. The smell of his cinnamon scent so familiar, I nearly rise to my feet to capture it once more.

But I know how this scene ends too.

Thrown off blankets, raised voices, and an argument in the night that ends with him leaving, and me on the floor reaching after him as he goes. His words reverberate through my head once more, "*What is wrong with you? They were right you know, there is something missing within you.*"

He stands in the doorway, his clothes haphazardly thrown into a bag as he stills in surprise, as if shocked the words actually left his mouth. But it doesn't negate them, nor does he take them back.

He straightens, his grip on the door handle firm as he turns to leave, and a pitiful plea for him to stay climbs up my throat. His brown hair falls into his eyes, obscuring them from view and his voice is quiet, lacking the warmth I'm used to hearing from him. "I'm not certain you could ever love someone. Never open yourself up enough to do so. And I can't wait around any longer, hoping it will happen."

I slump to the floor as he leaves, tears streaming down my face as something withers and dies in my chest and I'm brought back to the blood-red room as before. I look upon the faces of those I hold dear, but they no longer appear as I remember. Horns sprout from their heads, and their mouths split into unnaturally wide smiles, exposing rows of sharp teeth and crimson gums. Some narrow multiple eyes at me, while others use wickedly sharp claws to remove the skins they had been wearing—exposing oddly bent limbs and bodies that are vaguely humanoid but ultimately the type of monsters that I'd always feared lurked in dark corners.

Darkness coats my vision and I'm suddenly dizzy, as if I'm standing on the edge of a precipice and looking down. The monstrous creatures swirl around me, each clawing at me and howling in anticipation.

"Just one step," they say. "One step and it will all be over."

I'm numb. My heart empty and broken, and I'm certain it will never come alive again. I lift my foot and hover it over the darkness in front of me, and the monsters cackle with glee.

A tingling starts on my left hand, but I swat it away, annoyed by its presence and angry at being distracted from stepping forward. But it returns, and I finally glance down to see a golden ring, its center stone an odd shade of green. I ignore the figures around me just long enough to halt my step and hold my hand up to my face. I scrunch my brows in confusion, feeling an indescribable sense that I've forgotten something. The shadowy creatures in front of me let out agitated noises, and I nearly drop my hand to focus back on them when a vision flashes through my mind of a rough hand bathed in golden light as it places a ring on my finger. I reach out my hand as if to touch it, and am puzzled when I don't feel the warmth of the golden light, but frigid muck. I'm vaguely aware of the fact that I love sunlight, but the thought is fleeting and faraway.

I pull my foot back from the precipice when dozens of new scenes rush through my head like a tidal wave. I feel once more the cool water of a brightly glowing blue stream, and a fae with sadness in his eyes telling me of his ability to connect with creatures. I see the slow smile on his face that grows as he speaks and the spark of energy that lights his eyes when I ask yet another question.

I see a set of maps spread out on the forest floor, a blonde young man sitting beside them. He smiles broadly when I approach, and I knock an affectionate shoulder against him as I sit. A nyradonn bird hops into my lap and snags a golden compass from the man, making us both laugh.

I lean into a young witch with warm brown eyes as we cackle into the night, and groans from half-sleeping forms echo, which makes us only laugh harder. Two bone creatures chitter along with us as we light up our surroundings with the bright sound.

I see kind eyes and feel soft lips, and a passion that could light a forest aflame. A man with dark green eyes stares at me, holding me like it's all he's ever wanted, and I feel *seen*. I hear a teasing joke and see a welcoming smile; feel the rush of freedom as I race through a field and understand the quiet comfort of being surrounded by those who truly know you.

My voice is quiet, almost a whisper, as two words falls from my lips. "My family."

The monsters dive for me, anchoring themselves to me and biting into my flesh, but I hardly notice as more memories flood my mind like a river rushing over dry ground. Emotions well in my chest, choking me with their intensity, but they don't feel overbearing like what I felt before. Love, acceptance, pride, familiarity, joy, and hope swirl together and I laugh in relief as I remember everything. As I remember *them*.

Willow, Thelas, Sebastian, Faldorn, Kel and even Din.

Red threads coalesce before me, and I feel them more than I see them—the strands weaving tighter until they are each a thin rope. It pulls taught in my chest and I reach for it like a lifeline. The monsters thrash around me and I know I don't have long until they will truly tear me apart, even without falling into the abyss. I dart my gaze around the room, hoping to find something to help me, but there is nothing but darkness.

The ring pulses again, and I clutch it to my chest, willing it to help me. A pinprick of yellow light opens in the dark wall to my right, and I dive for it without hesitation, desperate to escape the monsters and the darkness of the room. I dig at the opening, hoping to widen it further so I can escape.

Pain slices through my calf and thigh as the shadows shred my skin and clothes like paper. My panic threatens to pull me under again, as I cry out in agony, but I find that my voice is also laced with determined rage, and an absolute all-consuming wrath at my current situation.

How dare these demons dig at me, pretend to be those closest to me and show me some of my worst memories? I have done *nothing*, yet they attack me as if they have a personal vendetta against me. The unfairness of it all drops heavily in my stomach like a boulder tossed into water, rippling through my body until every part of me is primed into action.

They claw at me again, trying to yank me back, but I keep my focus on my rage and scream my defiance at their cruelty, kicking back at their monstrous forms with all my strength and angling away from the small hole of light to swipe at their faces with my bare hands. Their grotesque features roar in surprise and fury, spraying chunks of dark spittle the consistency of mud. It splatters on my face, and a horrid decaying smell invades my nostrils, but I don't flinch or stop my vicious attack on their constantly morphing forms. The opening widens bit by bit out of the corner of my eye, and I take that as a sign that the way to escape is to *fight*.

I tear at the demons with newfound strength, keeping the light's opening at my back. They fall back momentarily, their forms reshaping into more solid figures, and I know this is my chance. I whip around to the light and scrape at the edges, clawing furiously and lacerating my hands in the process. Blood flows, mixing with the reddish black sludge around me, but I do not slow my attempts to widen the hole enough for me to slip through.

I tumble through the opening, landing hard on my back and am blinded by the sudden light that surrounds me. My body acts on its own, racing toward the sword that once again sits on a perfect pedestal in the center of the room.

This time, I don't hesitate. I grip the sword with firm hands, brandishing it against the monsters that followed me, bellowing in anger and defiance. I'm nearly knocked off my feet as slicing heat floods my body, but I manage to stay upright through the onslaught of power emanating from the sword. I stare at the blade as it lights with brilliant intensity, shining as bright as the sun, and I know to the very core of my being that I can't hold onto this sword for long and that it will soon burn me up from the inside out.

"I'll have to make this quick then."

I dart forward before I even finish uttering the words, slicing through each vicious creature, cutting off their heads one after the other. They hiss and bubble as they hit the floor, melting into useless puddles before dissolving completely. One strike from the sword is all it takes for them to fall, and soon they are all nothing but dust. A surge of energy bolsters my limbs, and I smile broadly at the power—this sword could defeat any enemy, and I could do so much more than just heal myself.

I blink twice, taking a step back and clutching my chest, uncomfortable with the sudden thought of using the sword for anything but self-defense. I drop the sword to the ground, watching as it clatters to the polished floor with a loud crash. I collapse in an exhausted heap next to it, falling to my hands and knees and gasping for breath. The weight of what I've just done and the violence I took part in pulls me down. My muscles ache and my bones feel made of stone. My body shakes as I recall the horrific visions and taunts the beasts forced upon me and how easy they were to rip apart. Darkness invades my vision again, and I almost panic at the thought that the monsters have returned, but I realize instead that I am on the verge of passing out. I struggle to lift my head, trying to focus on a way out of the room when I sense a drifting energy like a soft breeze flowing toward me. I feel it more than I can actually hear it, but words do coalesce in my mind anyway.

"You have a kind soul and a loving heart. Your spirit sings of a life full of curiosity and acceptance—your loyalty nearly endless. A previous sword-bearer once had the traits you do, but she was lost long ago, having succumbed to despair and chose to act on her hidden wrath. Do not succumb to the same darkness your Twin Flame did, or you will lose far more than she."

"Twin Flame?"

"Cycles repeat as Ilphemoura works to right the wrongs of history. You must not fail the way she did."

The voice leaves as quickly as it appeared and I'm left alone in the brightly lit room, the sword by my side. Exhausted, I lean back against one wall and prop my head against it. What I just did comes rushing back to me and new tears spring to my eyes before I can stop them. The shadows are gone, and my body and mind are once again my own. A sob threatens to tear up my throat and I don't stop it this time as it comes tumbling out. I double over, clutching my body as I cry. Those wretched shadows almost had me. I was going to step over that ledge, and I have no doubt I would have been lost at that point. But I didn't.

The ring saved me.

"No," I say aloud, correcting myself. "*They* did."

I get to my feet and move to pick up the sword. A new realization sparks and more words tumble softly from my mouth, as if I can't quite believe them and must speak them aloud for it to be true. "And that gave me the strength to save myself."

I lean forward suddenly, losing my balance, and try to get my bearings as the ground beneath me shifts and is no longer polished marble but dusty dark stone, and the blinding light that once surrounded me has dulled to a warm glow. I pull the sword from my lap, and feel its warmth leave me in a rush. I almost have the urge to pick it up again when I realize I'm being watched. I lift my face, finding lit sconces in a wide cavern and Sebastian, Willow, Thelas and Faldorn surrounding me.

They're here.

The sword is no longer my priority as I scramble to my feet and charge toward them, colliding with Willow first and blindly reaching for the others. They are shocked at first, but quickly recover and soon I'm held in a tight embrace. My breath evens out and I feel so at peace in this moment that I could stay here forever. Willow pulls away first after several long moments. Relieved tears roll down her face as she squeezes my shoulders, a choking half-sob, half-laugh escaping her. Kel brushes a wing against my cheek, and I reach for him, pulling him into my arms.

"You had us scared to death, Laira! Don't ever do that again!" she sputters.

I hug her again with surprising strength, and marvel at the fact that my body is my own once more, and I don't have to fear hurting any of them again.

Thelas, Faldorn, and Sebastian stand just behind Willow and I give them a watery smile as I notice their own eyes shining with unshed tears. "And what about you three? Did I scare you too?"

The question surprises them enough that they choke out a laugh, their eyes still shining. Thelas and Faldorn don't have a chance to respond to my poorly timed joke when Sebastian rushes forward and crushes me in his arms. A squeak of shock leaves me, and the desperate way he clutches me to his chest has me wrapping my arms around him just as fiercely.

"I thought you were gone," he whispers against my neck.

"I'm sorry," I whisper back and bury my face in his chest.

He relaxes and I settle more deeply into his embrace. A warm hand brushes against the back of my head and I feel the barest kiss against the top of my hair as he pulls away. He wipes the tears from my cheeks with a thumb, his eyes soft as he takes me in.

"Don't be sorry, wildcat. I'm glad you fought and came back to me."

I grin and raise a brow. "Back to you, huh?"

His mouth quirks up at the side and his eyes turn teasing. "Always."

SECRETS

SEBASTIAN

Luvarn lifts his head as I approach alone to the stone ledge he rests on—the others having decided to leave the cave and check on the horses. His wickedly sharp teeth glimmer in the flickering light, and I stop far away from him and out of his immediate reach. Just because he helped us doesn't mean he isn't still a massive beast capable of killing me in a single blow.

"Something on your mind, human?"

I cross my arms, making sure to maintain eye contact with him but staying aware of my surroundings. "Yes. The sword... is it as powerful as Willow and Faldorn's legends claim? Is it actually capable of winning the war?"

Luvarn's tail swishes, and the hair on my arms stand on end as pebbles tumble off the ledge and into the darkness. "What do you think it can do?"

Frustration bubbles under my skin, and I pace back and forth, brushing rough hands through my hair. Can't this dragon give us a straight fucking answer for once?

"That's what I'm asking you. The supposed protector of the sword." My voice comes out more sarcastic than I mean it to, but I don't care. I'm exhausted and still on edge from watching Laira purge the darkness from her body. "I need to know or else I can't do anything about it."

"Oh? And if I told you that the sword, along with your group, is all you needed to win this impending war you speak of, what then?"

I stop, the answer on the tip of my tongue, but I still can't voice it.

"Would you bring the information to Eislekest's king? Present the sword and the five of you and paint yourself as a savior? Or would you steal the sword, leaving the others behind to protect yourself and them from the truth?"

I nearly choke at his words, the heavy weight of my identity crushing my chest. To expose it would mean facing the lies I've told each of them thus far and accepting my place back home.

"I wouldn't leave them, nor would I take the sword. It's hers." My head falls back, and I stare into the endless darkness above, aching for a way to make this decision easier. The noose of lies constricts around my neck, and the pressure is unbearable. "I wouldn't do that, but…I can't…"

Luvarn hums, his tail whipping once again, and he shifts his claws underneath his large frame. The grating sound echoes through the cavern as he sits up, his serpentine body coming into view in the dim light.

"Tell me, how long will it take before you confess to being the crown prince of Eislekest?"

Luvarn's gruff voice drops the one piece of information I have struggled to keep hidden our entire journey, and I wince at the shame that floods my system at not yet having told them. At not having told *her*.

A skittering of rocks behind me and a sharp intake of breath freezes my heart to ice. I turn my head to see what caused the noise but already know the answer—I could recognize that voice in my sleep.

Laira stands agape, a hand pressed to her mouth in shock and her eyes wide as she processes what the dragon said.

I step forward, hands outstretched, excuses already flowing from my lips and I damn them the second they escape me. She doesn't need more lies and deception. She needs the truth. But as I stare into her crestfallen face, I can't force myself to speak the words, and I watch as she shifts from surprise to betrayal, a cold look steeling her eyes before she turns away from me and walks purposely from the cavern. Her cloak billows around her form, and my heart breaks for the first time in ages at her retreating back. I squeeze my eyes shut, pressing a rough hand to my face as I feel the utter disappointment and shame at what I've hidden from her, after she shared so much with me.

She knows.

And I don't know if there is any hope of returning from that.

THE PAST HAUNTS US ALL

LUVARN

The young prince leaves quickly, his aura radiating quiet despair and resignation. He knew this moment would come, and though it perhaps wasn't my place to voice it aloud, knowing the young thread reader was in our presence, it was something that needed to be done.

Soft footfalls echo into the wide space, and I sense the return of Laira, her nyradonn following closely behind her. She has wiped any remaining tears from her eyes, but redness still lines the rims, and her voice is thick as she points an accusing finger at me.

"You knew I was there."

I smile at her boldness, pleased to see fire under her skin once again. "Yes."

She narrows her eyes. "And you revealed his secret anyway. Why?"

"We do not always get to reveal our secrets in our own time."

She huffs and paces the space in front of me, her bird doing the same. I watch the nyradonn, wondering when he will admit his true purpose to Laira and who his bonded is. I've known him a long time, and it's unlike him to withhold so much, but I am not one to question the Goddess's machinations. And unlike with the young prince, I will not be the one to divulge the nyradonn's secrets.

Laira grumbles again, and I turn my attention back to her. She watches me with careful eyes as she paces, before finally coming to a stop and taking a step toward me—something even the prince did not do. It seems dispelling the shadows has made her bold.

"What am I going to do? He's a fucking prince! And why would he not tell us?"

"Do you think you would have trusted him to join you if he had?" I ask.

She lets out a resigned sigh. "No. I had a run-in with some of the king's guards, and let's just say they were not the least bit helpful as well as being entirely corrupt."

"So he chose well then."

"No! Ugh." She arches forward, covering her face in her hands. I watch her with mild fascination—human emotions are such volatile things, affecting both the mind and the body. It is a wonder mortals can exist at all with so much pent up inside of them.

"He didn't need to tell us at the start, but he should have told us somewhere along the way as we all became closer." She gestures to the cave exit, glancing forlornly behind her before returning her gaze to me. "But I suppose I understand his reasons."

I do not answer, but she doesn't seem to need one.

Silence follows, but she surprises me by not leaving and posing a new question. "The shadows inside me were excited to reach the sword, but if the sword is what could kill them, then why did they want it?"

I tap a long claw, considering what to reveal. "The shadows were overconfident of their hold on you. You see, you were just as likely to wield the sword's light as you were to allow it to be corrupted. Had that happened, the shadows would have infected the sword again and nothing but the Goddess's power can reverse it. Even then, it's a nearly impossible feat—something I'm not certain could be done a second time. The sword was crafted by a powerful magic user for the benefit of the world, but its innate power can be used for healing as much as it can be used for destruction."

Her head tilts to the side and her eyes narrow as she asks, "Infected again?"

I stare at her, my gaze unyielding—that is not an answer I will provide today.

She grumbles and turns around when it's clear I don't plan to explain. She exhales loudly, pinching the bridge of her nose in exasperation, and leaves without another word.

As she reaches the tunnel's opening, I say, "I failed to stop a great evil when

I had the chance. I thought to leave this realm to its own problems and not get involved, and in doing so, I played a part in the destruction that followed. I will not make the same mistake now."

She stops walking but does not turn around to face me as I continue. "The necklace you bear is a piece of the crystal that resides in this cave. Speak my name to the crystal and I shall come to aid you. But I warn you, this spell to call me works only once. Use it wisely."

She tilts her head to the side, nodding once in acknowledgment before leaving the cavern behind.

TRUE FAMILY

LAIRA

A *hidden identity.*

The single line from the prophecy crashes through my mind as I walk along the cliff's edge outside the cave. The water below churns, and the cold wind whips through my hair, echoing my own restless thoughts. How many times have I agonized over the meaning of the words? I should have known. I should have seen it. Should have built my walls higher, instead of slowly removing the bricks and letting him in.

I let him in, Goddess damn it. And I'm not sure I can ever undo that. I let him kiss me—*asked* him to kiss me, actually.

"Kiss me, Sebastian."

My words slice through my head, and I shiver at the memory, of how I wanted him. I kissed the Goddess-damned crown prince of Eislekest and I enjoyed it. Oh, how I enjoyed it.

I bring a hesitant finger up to my lips, tracing them and recalling the way his soft lips felt against mine. The heat of the moment was so intense I was certain I would be carried away on it forever. And the way he looked at me after—his eyes had changed. They were gentle and full of an emotion I was afraid to name. How could I have let it go so far? How could I have been so stupid? *He's a fucking prince.*

Kel coos softly from the ground beside me, and I drop down to him, sighing heavily.

"It's not that I don't get it, Kel, I do. We all have secrets." Kel hops up into my arms, and I stand, staring back in the direction of the cave as he brushes a gentle wing against me. "It's just that at some point, we all became something more, and he should have said something, that's all."

Kel coos again and curls deeper into my arms. I watch passively as Sebastian walks to where Faldorn, Thelas, and Willow stand off to the side of the cave's entrance. His shoulders are slumped, and he rubs the back of his neck as he approaches the trio, dropping his head as he speaks. Willow and Thelas appear surprised, but Faldorn only crosses his arms and nods like he saw this information coming. I think back to the fae's extra prodding and investigative looks and wonder how long ago he started to put the pieces together.

Thelas is the first to react, offering Sebastian a simple handshake and saying something that I can't make out from this far away. But whatever it is, it's enough for Sebastian to forego the handshake and pull Thelas in for a quick hug—surprise written across Thelas' features at the contact. Faldorn pats Sebastian's shoulder as he walks away to tend to his elk, and Willow says something to Sebastian before darting her eyes to where I stand in the distance. He nods to her, and she gives him a pitying smile as he turns away. His shoulders heave once before he makes his way toward me.

I put up a hand once he gets close, needing to get my words out first. "Give me one day. One day alone for me to figure out my anger, frustration, and confusion. I need time to come to terms with this new reality and this new version of you."

He runs a hand through his hair and nods once before shoving his hands in his pockets and opening his mouth like he wants to say something. He closes it quickly, giving me a long, pleading look before nodding again and walking away.

I hold up a hand to stop him before he goes, and he gives me a slightly hopeful, but confused expression. "I do need to know one thing though. Was this all some ploy by the king, by your father? Do you agree with how he's hidden everything from his people?"

His shoulders slump, but he lifts his head anyway to look directly at me. "I was not sent by him. I left on my own because I did not agree with him and wanted to do more. I was desperate to find some sort of solution, and somehow, I wound up in Taslae and found you."

I nod, his words ringing with so much truth that even in my current state of distrust, I can't deny them. "So, what will you do when you confront him?"

"I don't know yet."

I sigh, a little frustrated with his answer, but I'm not mad at him. There are so many things we don't know, and I can't blame him for not having an answer to my question yet. I just need some time to readjust to how I should act around him. Things are different now, after all. He's no longer just a simple thief—now he's the future leader of an entire kingdom, and I know that fact will cause trouble in the future if we were ever to continue whatever ridiculous game we've been playing the past couple of months. *And that kiss.* I need to find a way to put it behind me because it cannot happen again.

He watches me for a moment, as if hoping I will continue the conversation. But when it's clear I don't plan to speak further, he turns to finally leave. I watch him go, feeling strangely like a part of me went with him. I shake my head to clear the odd sensation, catching Faldorn out of the corner of my eye. He leaves his elk to stand on the cliff's edge close by, still as a statue, and I decide to approach him, wishing to get a different difficult conversation out of the way.

"So, are you going to the Eternal Realm?"

He looks at me, eyebrows raised. "What?"

"That's what you said back on that first night, right? You would join us until the task was completed, and then you would pass on?"

He's silent for a long moment. "So you did see that night."

"I did. But I don't know exactly *what* it was that I saw..." I trail off, hoping that my unspoken question will be heard.

He gives me his full attention and does the last thing I expect him to do—he smiles. A sad, but warm smile nonetheless. The deep emotion on his face is apparent as his eyes soften at whatever memory is playing in his mind.

"She was my mate." He turns back to the ocean, surveying it for another long beat before continuing.

"She came to me that night. She should not have had enough power to appear in the mortal lands, but somehow, she did. Despite being far from our ancestral lands and our well of magic, she found me anyway." His head drops in shame. "I ran from her for a long time. It's why I came to the mortal lands to begin with. I simply could not be reminded of her loss any longer, and I knew, in coming here, that she could not follow, and that the rest of the family haunting me couldn't either. She encouraged me to join you, and I convinced myself it would be the final step I needed for my soul to finally feel ready to pass on. You see, fae have some ability to control when they pass on. With our immortal lives, it often happens when our souls are at peace and we instinctually feel the call to leave," his voice darkens slightly, his eyes growing distant. "Unless, of course, you are taken by force through external means. We may be immortal, but other beings can still kill us."

"So, you were hoping that you would feel the call to the other side once you helped us?" I ask.

"Yes," He smiles wistfully and glances back over at me, eyes shining with unshed tears. "But I was wrong. I was wrong about so many things."

I curl an arm around his middle and squeeze, hoping to offer some physical assurance along with my next words. "Being wrong is not a bad thing. Sometimes it leads to the best things. Like being with the four of us—you thought we wouldn't mean much to you. But that's changed, hasn't it?"

He nods solemnly. "Indeed it has."

I tilt my head against his shoulder and stare out at the sea along with him. The sun sets in beautiful swirling colors, and the ocean sparkles in the waning light before giving way to dense fog far in the distance.

"You're not going to leave us, are you?" I ask, breaking the silence and tilting my head to look up at him, though I already know his answer.

He looks down at me, leaning into my touch and wrapping a strong arm around my shoulders. He even scratches the top of Kel's head, who still rests comfortably in my arms and smiles so wide his canine teeth peek from under his lips.

"No, I am not."

The words are a grand reassurance and my shoulders relax. For better or for worse—my mind flits to Sebastian's confession before I shove it away—we are now a family.

We stand in companionable silence for a long time until I hear commotion behind us and Willow shouting, "Aww! Are we doing a big group cuddle?"

She races to us, throwing her arms around the two of us and squeezing as hard as she can. I can't help the laugh that escapes me, as well as the large puff of air that leaves my body at her vice grip.

She doesn't let go though. Instead, she pulls us in even tighter and yells over her shoulder, "You two lazy lumps! Get over here! We just got a freaking magic sword and met a dragon and now we need family bonding time!"

Twin groans sound from my right, but before I know it, another warm body encircles mine. The shiver that runs through me at the scent of moss and pine informs me Sebastian joined my side of this group hug.

Figures.

Though I can't bring myself to be truly upset—secretly pleased with the thought he wants to be close to me.

Willow squeals with delight once we are all squished together in a choking embrace of flailing limbs and wild laughter. Kel crows loudly, and Din answers from Willow's feet, upset that he isn't in her arms as well. Thelas grins and snatches him, returning to the tangle of limbs and passing him to Willow, who squishes him right in the middle of us all.

I close my eyes for a moment, reveling in the feeling of this joy and camaraderie.

Willow is right—we did it. We actually retrieved the mystical sword of legend, and not only that, but we survived a fire-breathing dragon and traveling for many long weeks in the Forbidden Forest. I soak in this moment as much as I can, because I know very soon we will be back to facing dangerous adversaries and insurmountable odds. Because there is a war coming, and it's clear that we will undoubtedly play a part in ending it.

But for now, I lean into my family and laugh alongside them until we pull away and stare off into the brilliant light shining off the ocean. Willow leans her head against my shoulder, and I notice Faldorn and Thelas standing comfortably shoulder to shoulder—neither of them much of the touchy-feely type—and Sebastian surprises me by placing a hesitant hand at my back.

I'm still confused and upset with him for lying to us, but with how happy I am right now watching as the sun peeks through the clouds, I can't find it in myself to push him away.

The dragon's words as he carved the symbol into the stone floor echo in my mind and tears well in my eyes from the love and reassurance I feel as the note from the prophecy falls into place. I know with grim certainty that this family will ride together until the breath has left each of our lungs.

The bonds of Ilekiir offer strength in the end.

Luvarn approaches, his massive body shining a brilliant emerald green and his wings sparkling gold, as he leaves the dark cave and steps into the waning light. His antlers glow with the sun and arc on either side of his head in elegant curves. He's focused on us, his head low, but his steps sure as his claws carve into the soft dirt. A prickling sensation crawls over my arms and up to the back of my neck, and I shiver. The exhilaration I felt moments ago is replaced by heavy anticipation.

"I can get you as far as the opposite coast, and then you are on your own. Do you have a plan?" He speaks bluntly, almost cordially, as if we are guests who have overstayed our welcome and it's obvious we should be on our way.

I speak first, my voice wary. "A plan?"

His penetrating stare lands on me, and the weight of it douses me in dread.

"Yes. You did not think this was over, did you? You obtained the sword, but there is a long road ahead." He looks out to the mist creating a wall on the horizon, his voice turning solemn. "Something crouches in the shadows, waiting until the moment to strike and the Prophecy of Souls has yet to be fulfilled."

I look to the others beside me to gauge their reactions. Faldorn wears a tired look, his hand resting on the sword at his hip. But it quickly changes to grim determination as he makes eye contact with me.

Thelas drifts closer to Willow but stands tall as his hand pauses on the dagger at his belt. Willow gives him a comforting smile before twirling a green strand of her magic from her fingers and widening her stance beside him—as if preparing to fight here and now.

Sebastian crosses his arms. His demeanor is different than I've seen before, with a new purposefulness straightening his spine and an immovable expression that I can't read. Perhaps it's because of the truths I now know, but he almost has the bearing of a king. The thought doesn't shock me like I thought it would; in fact, he seems more natural this way. He nods to me and I return the gesture. There may be an ocean of secrets between us, but we have bigger problems now.

Luvarn breaks the tense silence. "It is best you depart swiftly. I can hear the drumbeats of war even now, and there is no time to waste."

Acknowledgements

The idea for this story began in June of 2024 after I visited the Natural History Museum in Washington DC. I was captivated by the fossils and bones and when I saw an inquisitive looking bird skeleton, I immediately created Kel. In the weeks that followed, I created the magic system of this new world and even started naming some of the characters! One of the first scenes I wrote was a silly interaction between Willow and Laira, which didn't make it into the book but was fun to write anyway. Truly, this adventure has been so much fun and it's something I never thought myself capable of. I spent months utterly engrossed in my new world, but it wasn't until I joined a couple of writing groups that I really started putting everything together.

And so, I'd like to first start off by giving a huge thank you to the gals in the Accountability Coven—an extraordinary group of ladies that have pushed me and encouraged me to keep going! Lilybeth Schultz, Stevi Lynn, Jade Nioma, Anastasia Arellano, C.A. Fray, Rachel Hanks, and Sareya, you are a beacon in the dark and I appreciate you all endlessly.

Thank you to another fantastic writing group, 2025 Authors! This group is the most encouraging and joyful group of individuals, and I adore them all. I'm so excited to have all of their books on my shelf, and I would like to give them all a shoutout: Charlene Antrobus, Alaina Hope, Bree Wilde, Emily Eve, Elle Reid, Jadis Moon, Jess McFarlane, Jordan Lynde, Kathryn Breaux, Marie Violet, Megan Gilbert, Rutendo Samantha, and Taryn Knightly.

Thank you to my amazing husband for his support and excitement as I started this new author journey. He always encouraged me when the imposter syndrome would hit, and I could always count on him to work through new ideas and scenes! He also is one hell of a beta reader and helped me work out so many of the kinks of this story. I love you to the moon and back. I also want to give a special kiss and head scratch to my favorite writing buddy, Bella—I love you so much my precious girl.

Thank you to my incredible friends and family who have constantly asked when this book will be done and insisted on getting a copy of their own. Kaitlyn Keilty, Jocelyn Sten, Ezra Rapaport, Elizabeth Schultz, Sarah Cramer, Paige Harns, Kooper

Lust, Mike Hagen, and Chelsea Heisler—you guys are the best!

I would also love to shout out some very special people in the book community who have shown me so much support and love! Truly, their posts, reactions, DMs, and comments never failed to make my day and they often gave me the push to keep going! Thank you to Rach at @Rachs_bookshelf_, Emmaline at @emmaline.edits, Meg at @bookish.apothecary, Brandon at @btlitellauthor, Meghan at @megreadslotsofbooks, and Amanda at @amandareadsmore.

And lastly, I'd like to thank YOU, the reader. The Cave of Swords is a story of family, love, grief, and adventure. But even more than that, it's a story of the way other people's doubts can become our own and how we begin to lose hope in ourselves. Laira, Willow, Thelas, Sebastian, and Faldorn each have a different demon that keeps them awake at night and tears at their self-confidence, instills fear, holds them back, or doesn't allow them to move on. And while some of them get closer to unraveling this inner turmoil than others, they all still have a long way to go.

But that's the joy of family that you choose—they will always be there to help you to the finish line.

I hope you laughed at the group's antics, felt warm and cuddly inside at the friendly banter, swooned at the romantic tension, and enjoyed the cozy adventure of it all! But I also hope that if you saw yourself in one of the characters, especially Laira, you felt seen.

ABOUT THE AUTHOR

When not writing, Taylor Lust can be found collecting books, watching trash tv with her husband and pets, thrifting, hiking, and line dancing with the girls or playing Stardew Valley on the weekends! Her debut, The Cave of Swords, is a passion project born from a love of writing from a young age and the desire to create a cozy found family that rivals her own. She's an advocate for mental health, and made it a priority to not shy from the difficulties of anxiety with her main character, Laira. Diagnosed with generalized anxiety in 2022, she knows just how much our minds can play tricks on us and wanted to show that on paper. Taylor has many new stories to come, along with finishing The Cave of Swords trilogy!

You can follow along with her writing progress through her website, www.authortaylorlust.com or on her Instagram @itbeganwiththestars.

www.ingramcontent.com/pod-product-compliance
Lightning Source LLC
Chambersburg PA
CBHW020915310726
48980CB00011B/903/J

* 9 7 9 8 9 9 2 6 9 8 8 2 4 *